D0282799

Scarlet and Gold

Scarlet and Gold

Ellen Tanner Marsh

BERKLEY BOOKS, NEW YORK

SCARLET AND GOLD

A Berkley Book/published by arrangement with
the author

PRINTED IN THE UNITED STATES OF AMERICA

To my editor Meg Blackstone
with affection

One

Athena Courtland swept off her tricorn hat and urged her stallion into a whirlwind gallop. The brisk autumn wind tugged at her chignon as though urging the long, golden curls to stream free. She had deliberately waited until the house had dropped from view behind the hill before indulging in such wanton behavior in order to avoid a tiresome lecture from her aunt upon her return. Because Aunt Amelia was terrified of Ballycor, she had expressly forbidden Athena to ride him, convinced that the enormous animal would someday be the death of his young mistress.

Though Aunt Amelia meant well, Athena chafed at the numerous restrictions that had been imposed upon her since her aunt had come to Courtland Grace to live. No one had ever forbidden her to ride Ballycor before, and Athena had found her loss of freedom almost as painful to endure as the death of her father eleven months before.

There had been no funeral for the master of Courtland Grace, whose ship had been sunk by the French and whose body had never been recovered. Instead, a simple memorial service had been held, attended only by his four children and several close family friends. No one had thought to inform Aunt Amelia until long after the stone marker bearing his name had been placed beside the grave of his wife, Fiona, in the small churchyard in the village.

Even then Athena had scoffed at her oldest brother Fletcher's insistence that Amelia be notified. Everyone knew that she had never seen eye to eye with her brother-in-law, and in fact Amelia hadn't come to visit them at Courtland Grace since Athena was seven years old.

Yet despite her estrangement from the family, Aunt Amelia had astonished everyone by announcing her intention to give up her comfortable home in Boston and come to Courtland Grace to live. Appalled to learn that Athena was living there alone now that her brothers Jeremy, Colm, and Fletcher had joined the Provincial Militia, she had taken it upon herself to become the girl's new chaperone.

Aunt Amelia's reason for this unpopular decision was simple. Not only was the colony a battleground for French and English troops, which placed any young woman in extreme danger, but it was altogether improper to permit Athena to live alone in a house the size of Courtland Grace with only a handful of servants to look after her. Furthermore, Amelia had been shocked when she arrived to find herself confronted by a wild creature not at all resembling the sweet-natured little girl she remembered.

In her opinion Athena Courtland had grown into a thoroughly rebellious young woman who spoke to her servants as though they were equals and shunned every aspect of social convention. Not only did Athena refuse to don gloves and a bonnet when she went outdoors, but she could not be persuaded to abandon her colorful wardrobe for the mourning black that convention decreed she must wear for the next twelve months. Amelia could scarcely believe the negligence with which Foster Courtland had raised his only daughter and declared that she would stay here at Courtland Grace until Athena's careless upbringing had been corrected.

Naturally Athena would have preferred living alone at Courtland Grace. No matter what Aunt Amelia kept insisting, she wasn't afraid of the French or the marauding Indians who aided them in their fight against the English. She had Tykie to look after her and servants who would fight tooth and claw, if need be, to protect their beloved home. Furthermore, she resented the restrictions placed upon her by her aunt, for she had always felt quite at home riding alone through the forests that bordered Courtland Grace's grazing land.

In a show of defiance Athena leaned low in the saddle and urged the magnificent white stallion to increase his stride. Her dark blue eyes sparkled as the ground began to blur beneath his drumming hooves. A low stone wall that served as one of Courtland Grace's numerous boundary markers appeared on the crest of the hill before them. Ballycor cleared it without hesitation, Athena leaning gracefully over his muscular neck.

She was an accomplished horsewoman, and the picture she made astride the big stallion was breathtaking to behold. Her habit was of dark blue velvet, the slim shoulders tufted and the full skirts piped with lemon satin. Her small tricorn hat was adorned with a rosette of the same bright yellow ribbon. Holding it in her gloved hand, she turned into the wind, her lips parted as she savored her freedom.

Athena's face, raised to the warmth of the pale autumn sun, would never have been judged beautiful by current standards. Her jaw was too square and her nose too haughtily straight to be considered desirable attributes, and yet no hot-blooded New York male would have championed the charge that Athena Courtland was not beautiful. Hers was the sort of beauty that was too wild and alluring for the genteel environment of a candle-lit drawing room. Her hair, the color of ripened wheat, glowed with a radiance of its own, while silver fire seemed to burn in the depths of her sapphire eyes. Her dramatic looks were further enhanced by her stature, for she was taller than most young women and carried herself with enviable grace.

There was a restless energy about her that was difficult to ignore, and Fletcher had often likened her to a young spring filly, all legs and skittish temperament. It was exactly this blend of youthful exuberance and haughty indifference that her numerous suitors found so appealing and that every female, young or old, dismissed as thoroughly unladylike. Athena would have laughed at their sentiments, for she cared not a whit for foolish convention or what others might think of her, nor did she have any intention of changing her ways for anyone.

"Especially not for that arrogant boor Stephen Kensington," Athena muttered to herself, scowling fiercely as she suddenly recalled her aunt's suggestion that they pay a social call on the Kensingtons tomorrow afternoon. Stephen had just gotten back from England, and though his parents were planning a ball in honor of his return, Aunt Amelia was too impatient to wait. No telling how many eager mamas intended to parade their marriageable daughters in and out of the Kensingtons' parlor before then, she had told an indifferent Athena at the breakfast table that morning.

Athena's eyes began to glitter with annoyance as she recalled the scheming expression on her aunt's sallow face. 'Twas obvious that Aunt Amelia was hoping to make a match between her niece and the wealthy Kensington heir, yet Athena had no intention of encouraging Stephen, especially not after what had happened the last time she had seen him.

There had been a small gathering at Kensington Manor the evening of his departure, yet the mood had hardly been festive, for everyone had been aware of how dangerous the crossing might prove now that the Atlantic was filled with roving French frigates. Under cover of the avid discussions of the war that had flourished that evening, Stephen had lured her out onto the balcony. Athena was still furious with herself for having agreed. What an ignorant little fool she had been!

Stephen hadn't wasted any time in taking liberties with her. He had kissed her fiercely and his hot breath on her neck had made her skin crawl. Athena had slapped him, and when that proved ineffective, she resorted to kicking and biting. Stephen, disheveled but otherwise unharmed, had easily fended her off and laughingly referred to her as a little wildcat. Athena could have sworn he had actually derived enjoyment from her struggles, and only by vowing to scream at the top of her lungs did she manage to convince him to release her. She could well remember even now the lascivious grin on his face when he let her go, promising to pursue her even more ardently once he returned.

"Let him try!" Athena muttered to herself. Even though her brothers weren't here to look after her, she was no longer a helpless young girl in need of their protection. Stephen Kensington might have managed to fool her once, but he was in for an unpleasant surprise if he planned to renew his attentions toward her again. The same held true for Aunt Amelia if she expected Athena to meekly accept his repugnant advances.

With a toss of her golden head, Athena dismissed Stephen Kensington from her thoughts. The day was far too lovely to waste on the likes of him! The mountains that surrounded her were covered with a carpet of dark green pine and dotted with maples and oaks that were beginning to change color. Soon the forests would be ablaze with crimson and gold, Athena knew, and the crisp promise of winter would hang in the air.

She felt no sadness at the passage of the season. The summer had been long, the harvest good, and perhaps autumn might bring an end to the war. It seemed inconceivable to her that the territorial rivalries being waged between England and France could go on much longer. Why couldn't either country concede the boundaries of Acadia and the vast region lying between the Allegheny Mountains and the Mississippi River —territory that included her beloved home as well? Athena would have thought that the New World was large enough to offer unlimited room for everyone, but apparently the enmity between England and France was too old and deep-rooted to allow either to compromise.

The conflict itself had been sparked five years ago by a chain of forts the French had built along the Allegheny River in Pennsylvania, their presence halting the northward expansion of the English colonies. When the French had ignored an official request to abandon them, Lieutenant Governor Dinwiddie of Virginia had sent a small force of colonial troops to drive them out, and the ensuing confrontation had become the first battle of the war. Nothing at all had been resolved in the month-long skirmish, and British troops had been dispatched from overseas to help the colonials, again without results.

Two years ago William Pitt, England's highly capable prime minister, had decided to end the conflict once and for all by sending thousands of troops to the colonies in order to drive the French back into Canada. It was at this point that Athena's oldest brother, Fletcher, had joined the militia, solemnly informing his father that he could not allow himself to stand by while foreign soldiers defended the country he loved. Athena had known how hard her father had struggled to accept Fletcher's decision, yet in the end he had marched off with all of their blessings. She had seen Fletcher only once since then, at their father's memorial service, though in the interim he had written as often as he could.

Jeremy and Colm, who had enlisted shortly after their father's death, were nowhere near as thoughtful, yet Athena had expected as much and couldn't find it in her heart to be annoyed with them. She could well imagine their impatience at being forced to write letters, for they hated anything that smacked of schoolwork, preferring instead to be hunting in the forests, cleaning game in the woodshed, or helping Tykie in the fields.

Unlike the twins, Fletcher was well versed in the classics and fluent in four languages, including Latin. He was by no means a bookish recluse, however, and Athena had often teased him for the yearning female eyes that were turned his way. Being nine years older than she, he had always seemed so remote and awesome to her despite the fact that he had always made time for her whenever she had asked. The mischievous twins, Jeremy and Colm, on the other hand, were barely three years older than their sister and had always been the ones to take Athena under their wing whenever Foster or Fletcher was too busy to care for her. She couldn't count the number of scrapes they had gotten her into or the tricks they had played on her when she was young, yet they had taught her to hunt and shoot, to ride astride, and to appreciate the virgin beauty of the forests and the mountains.

Athena's expression was suddenly sad. She didn't know whom she missed more at the moment, the twins, Fletcher, or her father, and she found herself unexpectedly tired of her forbidden freedom. Even Aunt Amelia's company seemed more appealing at the moment than the solitude of the sun-dappled meadow across which she rode. Placing her tricorn firmly upon her head, she turned Ballycor in the direction of home. The big animal snorted his displeasure at having his exercise interrupted, and Athena relented by allowing him to gallop back.

Not until they cleared the last rise did she slow him to a trot. The split-rail fence that separated Courtland Grace's gardens from the pastures was visible from here, stretching across the emerald grass that was dotted with the bright yellow stalks of goldenrod. The house and outbuildings sprawled behind it, the dark slate roofs gleaming in the sun. Athena's great-grandfather Nicholas Courtland had laid the first stone himself, and his initials could still be seen carved proudly into the enormous oak mantel above the fireplace in the study.

The manor house itself stood three stories high, well sashed and elegant with its numerous gables and whitewashed facade. The wings, which ran east and west of the main block, were built of brick, the harsh lines softened by towering maple trees and lilacs, which in the spring blazed with fragrant white and lavender blossoms. Behind the house stood the enormous stone barn, and on the wide patch of earth between them lay the kitchen gardens, still green with late-ripening corn, beans, and cabbage and scrupulously maintained by Prudence, the family cook.

Athena turned Ballycor down the wagon trail that led from the fields to the barn. A smile curved her lips when she spotted the dark-headed man leaning against the gate watching her. Lifting her hand in greeting, she rode toward him.

"Did Aunt Amelia send you after me?" she asked, knowing full well that if she had, Tykie had made no great effort to find her.

"Ye be in luck this time, Miss Athena," the towering Scotsman replied, grinning back at her. "Mistress Bower hasna retairned frae her visitin' yet."

The dark blue eyes sparkled mischievously. "Well, then, I suppose there's no need to tell her I went riding, is there?"

"I'll no be carryin' tales to yer aunt, Miss Athena," Tykie responded firmly. Taking the stallion by the bridle, he waited while Athena slid from his back. His grin widened, revealing the strong white teeth in his bearded face. "Mistress Bower doesna like it when I speak tae her anyway."

This was true, Athena reflected, following him into the barn. Tykie terrified Aunt Amelia, for he was an enormous man with a bristling black beard and piercing black eyes. He wore a small gold earring in one ear and always carried a silver-bladed dirk in his boot. He was a well-respected presence about the town of West York, and there were few men who dared cross him. It was rumored that he had been a privateer or perhaps even a pirate before being hired by Foster Courtland to run the vast farmlands belonging to Courtland Grace.

Fearsome he might be, yet Athena loved him dearly and trusted him with her life. She knew that beneath that gruff exterior lay a truly gentle soul and that Tykie only pretended to be horrible because it amused him to frighten others, her aunt in particular. To tell him as much, however, was to risk incurring his wrath, which in Tykie Downs was a terrible thing to behold. Like everyone else, Athena preferred to tread softly where he was concerned, although she could take liberties with him that no one else dared to take.

Leading Ballycor back to his stall, Tykie stood leaning against the door, Athena at his side. For a moment they were silent as they watched the big animal lip at his hay. Tilting back her head, Athena glanced up at Tykie, her young face glowing beneath the point of her tricorn hat.

"Ballycor seems to be getting faster every day. I vow he'll have no trouble beating Master de Vries's colt next week."

Tykie rubbed his palms together. "There's many layin' their money on that colt o' his, Miss Athena."

"Master de Vries's colt might be fast, but Ballycor is going to win," Athena stated confidently. She reached out a gloved hand to pat the white stallion's sleek neck. Unlike Tykie and the others who attended West

York's monthly races, Athena cared little for the stakes or the amount of money one could win by betting on the right horse. For her the excitement came from the race itself, from watching Ballycor, nostrils flaring and tail streaming like a white banner, pounding across the turf to finish lengths ahead of his adversary.

Only once had the huge animal been beaten, and that after slipping on a soggy track last spring. In a few days' time he would be pitted against a mysterious colt Egon de Vries had had imported from England—a colt he'd let no one see but that was rumored to be the fastest in all the colonies. It was an event that was being discussed in every drawing room, workshop, and taproom from West York to Albany, and one that Athena anticipated with feverish excitement.

Tykie chuckled as he studied Ballycor's muscular hindquarters. "They've a' been askin' me when we intend tae start trainin' the lad properly. They willna believe he needs na further work than a ride wi' his mistress tae the forest an' back."

"Let them think what they will," Athena responded with a toss of her golden head. "It only improves his chances and betters the odds."

"And ye wouldna forfeit them rides for any serious trainin', would ye, Miss Athena?" Tykie asked knowingly. The fondness in her eyes as she patted Ballycor in farewell was answer enough for him.

"I imagine I'd better go in," Athena said reluctantly, stripping off her gloves. "Aunt Amelia will be home soon, and I did promise her I'd have my darning done before noon."

"Ye'll be waitin' a moment afore ye gae, Miss Athena?"

She turned in the wide doorway, her velvet skirts rustling softly. "What is it?"

Tykie's black eyes danced. " 'Tis a letter came for ye while ye were oot. The tinker brought it by."

Athena caught her breath as he withdrew a faded piece of parchment from his leather vest. "Did he say who it was from?" Her voice trembled, though she was trying hard to hide her excitement. Over a month had gone by since she'd last heard anything from Fletcher. Dared she hope?

The bearded face split in a flashing white grin. "Nay, Miss Athena, but 'twould seem tae me no ane but Master Jem has sich a terrible scrawl."

Athena's eyes widened. "Jeremy? The letter's from Jeremy?"

He extended the parchment to her. "Ye'll have tae look yerself, lass."

She took it with trembling fingers and hurriedly broke the seal. "Oh, it is, Tykie!" she exclaimed, running her eyes along the nearly illegible script to the name scrawled across the bottom.

"I hope the young master's well," Tykie said with a meaningful glance at the parchment in her hands.

"I'll tell you in a moment," Athena promised. She settled herself on a fragrant bale of hay while Tykie discreetly withdrew to allow her some privacy. Her eager cry brought him hurrying from the tackroom a moment later.

"Oh, Tykie, 'tis wonderful news!"

He had to smile as he gazed down into her face, her soft cheeks flushed with excitement, her blue eyes sparkling like the deep, sun-touched lakes of his beloved Highlands. Wisps of straw clung to her skirts, but she scarcely noticed.

"Master Jem's well, is he?" Tykie guessed. This was naught but the third letter the twins had written since joining the militia over ten months ago.

"He's fine, and Colm is, too," Athena informed him happily, "though their regiment was divided in March."

Tykie frowned. "The lads ain't servin' together na more?"

Athena perused the scrawled missive again, knowing that Tykie would want to hear everything. Since he couldn't read himself, it was up to her to inform him of the letter's contents. "He says Colm is currently in New Haven, but he's not sure when they'll be reunited." Her eyes were shining despite the fact that the letter was so vexingly short and uninformative. "That's all I can tell you for now, Tykie, but if you want to know more, you'll just have to ask him yourself. His regiment is on the way to Albany, and he's fairly certain he'll have enough time to come visit us here at Courtland Grace!"

A glad cry burst from the enormous Scotsman's lips. Swinging Athena into his arms, he gave her a hug that threatened to crush every bone in her body. Laughing, she returned his embrace until he set her gently back onto the stone floor. His eyes were misted as he looked at her.

"The good Lord be thanked for this, lass!"

"Athena!"

The faint but unmistakably shrill cry came from the direction of the house. Athena's hand flew to her lips.

" 'Tis Aunt Amelia!" She glanced down in dismay at her riding habit, knowing full well that if her attire didn't incriminate her, the smell of the barn that clung to her most certainly would. She groaned, not relishing the thought of a tongue-lashing.

"Go round the back through the byre, lass," Tykie suggested, taking pity on her. "I'll keep Mistress Bower busy till ye get tae yer rooms."

Her soft red lips curved into a wicked smile. "You've certainly become a proper accomplice in crime where I'm concerned, haven't you?"

Tykie shrugged. "I maun look out fer ye, lass. 'Tis what yer faither would hae wanted."

She peered back over her shoulder at him as she prepared to slip through the small door that separated the stable from the dairy. "Please don't tell her about Jeremy's letter. 'Tis best she doesn't know anything until we find out exactly what his plans are."

Tykie gave her a conspiratorial wink. "Ye'll no hear a single word pass my lips, Miss Athena."

Athena's heart was singing as she made her way through the cool interior of the barn. She could scarcely believe Jeremy was in Albany and that he might find the time to slip away to see them. Crouching by the doorway, she waited until Tykie managed to capture her aunt's attention before scampering across the lawn and into the house.

Hurrying up the stairs, she slammed her bedroom door shut and pulled open the carved oak clothespress. In a flash her riding habit had been replaced by a worn but serviceable gown of black mourning satin, the sleeves and high collar trimmed in black silk lace. Burying her gloves, whip, and tricorn in the bottom of the clothespress, Athena unpinned her hair before the mirror and did her best to rearrange it in a fashion her aunt would find acceptable.

The unruly gold curls refused to be tamed, and Athena gave an impatient exclamation as she hurled the tortoiseshell brush onto the bed. Picking up Jeremy's letter, she read it through a second time before hiding it under her pillow. Hearing her aunt's voice from the hall below, she stepped out onto the landing.

"Where have you been, child?" Amelia Bower asked, her sallow cheeks flushed with frustration as she peered nearsightedly up at her niece.

"Here in my room," Athena responded demurely.

"Didn't you hear me call you?" Amelia asked peevishly.

"I'm sorry, aunt, I didn't."

"Did you finish your darning?" Athena was behaving far too innocently, and Amelia was growing suspicious.

Athena hesitated, not wishing to lie a second time. Movement at the far end of the corridor caught her eye. It was Mercy, Prudence's daughter, who served as Athena's personal maid, gesturing to her from one of the doorways. She was carrying a woven basket under her arm, and when Athena turned to look at her, she held up a stocking for her inspection, the worn heel perfectly mended.

"I just this moment finished, aunt," Athena called down, giving Mercy a grateful smile.

"Were you out riding again, Miss Athena?" Mercy inquired in a whisper as she followed her mistress back into the room. She clucked disapprovingly as she saw the riding habit lying in a heap in the corner. "You'll be caught one day, you will!"

Athena tossed her head. "I don't care! I'm not going to stop riding just because Aunt Amelia is afraid Ballycor will hurt me."

Mercy giggled, brown eyes dancing and red curls bobbing beneath her starched mobcap. "He's thrown you often enough, that wild beast."

"He's temperamental, not dangerous," Athena replied practically. Taking the basket from the younger girl, she added sincerely, "I can't thank you enough for this, Mercy! I vow Aunt Amelia orders me to darn my stockings simply because she knows how much I hate it!"

"It didn't take me long, miss, and I was happy to do it."

The young maid's eyes narrowed as she looked about Athena's bedroom. She had cleaned it herself only a half-hour before, and now it looked as if a whirlwind had blown through it. Discarded stockings were flung over the back of the pier glass, and a pair of muddy leather boots had been left on the bedside rug. The coverlet of the four-poster was hopelessly rumpled, and the chintz-bordered woolen blanket had fallen onto the floor. Her pert nose wrinkled at the essence of horse that emanated from the clothespress, and she quickly retrieved the offending articles.

"I'll hang this from the rafters to air it out a bit," she offered, holding the blue velvet habit aloft. "Otherwise Mistress Bower will know you were out riding this morning. Are you unwell, miss?" she added, aware that Athena was scarcely listening.

"Oh, Mercy, you'll never believe it," Athena exclaimed, "but I received a letter from Jeremy today!"

Mercy's eyes widened. "No, miss, truly? Is he well? And how is Master Colm?"

"Jeremy's in Albany, Mercy," Athena informed her excitedly, "and he's hoping to get leave so that he can come to see us!"

Mercy's freckled cheeks flamed crimson, confirming Athena's suspicions that she had always cared a great deal more for Jeremy Courtland than she pretended to. Laughter bubbled inside her, and she threw her arms around the startled little maid. "Oh, Mercy, I can't wait to see him!"

The younger girl's arms went shyly about her mistress as she returned her enthusiastic hug. " 'Twill be grand, Miss Athena," she agreed in a dreamy tone of voice. "When do you suppose he'll be here?"

"I expect he'll write and tell us when he intends to arrive. Just don't breathe a word to my aunt until he does."

"Mayhap he'll simply show up on the doorstep unannounced," Mercy suggested. She took an anxious look at her reflection in the pierglass and was dismayed to see that her red curls had again worked themselves loose from beneath her cap. Mistress Bower was forever criticizing her appearance. Suppose Master Jeremy were to come home right now and find her looking like this?

"Never fear, Mercy," Athena said with a laugh as the younger girl glanced nervously out of the window as though expecting to see Jeremy standing on the doorstep. "If I know my brother, he'll give us ample warning before he arrives." Taking up the basket of darning, she added, "I suppose I ought to bring this down to Aunt Amelia before she thinks to ask for it."

She found herself humming as she swept down the landing, the prospect of a sewing inspection not daunting her in the least. Jeremy was coming home and she could barely contain her excitement. Oh, how was she going to bide the time until then?

Athena yawned widely as she waited for Mercy to finish arranging her hair. Her slippered foot tapped an impatient rhythm on the pine floor of her bedroom, causing Mercy to shake her head in frustration.

"I'll never get these braids finished if you don't hold still, Miss Athena," she chided. It was difficult enough to try to tame those unruly curls every morning without having her mistress fidget restlessly throughout the session.

"I'm sorry, Mercy," Athena said, trying to hold still. "I'm so tired I vow I could crawl right back into bed. I didn't sleep a wink last night trying to find a way to convince Aunt Amelia to let me go to Albany."

"She's already told you once you can't go," Mercy reminded her, trying not to sound disappointed herself. For two days they had waited impatiently for word from Jeremy, only to receive the discouraging news that he hadn't been able to obtain leave.

Athena had promptly decided to travel down to Albany herself to see him, but when she had approached her aunt on the matter, the older woman had been adamant in her refusal. Athena had toyed with the idea of defying her, but a horrified Mercy had managed to talk her out of it. It simply wasn't safe for a young woman to travel alone, especially not at night as Athena had planned!

"Perhaps if you told her the truth she might let you go," she suggested, but Athena shook her head.

" 'Twould be even more reason for her to keep me here. Aunt Amelia has expressly forbidden me to have anything to do with soldiers, even those belonging to Jeremy's regiment."

"You could explain to her that you didn't plan to meet him in his barracks and that you wouldn't be anywhere near the other soldiers," Mercy persisted. "Surely then she'd agree to take you!"

Athena's face was filled with helpless anger. "I'm quite certain she'd deny me a visit with him purely out of spite. I tore the hem of my best gown yesterday helping Tykie mend the fence, and Aunt Amelia was beside herself. Denying me the chance to see Jeremy would offer her the perfect opportunity to punish me."

Mercy deftly wound the thick braids into a coronet and pinned it carefully to Athena's head. The pale gold strands shimmered in the sunlight that streamed through the opened casement window. Stepping back to admire her work, she had to admit to herself that no one but Miss Athena could look so breathtaking in black. Affixing a strand of simple ivory beads around the smooth throat to soften the gown's severity, she said firmly, "I won't believe Mistress Bower would do such a thing!"

Athena bit back an unladylike snort. How like Mercy to see only the good in everyone, even someone like Aunt Amelia, whose excessive demands and constant criticism had made life miserable for the servants at Courtland Grace. No, she knew for certain that Aunt Amelia would forbid her to see Jeremy and that she must resort to other means than the truth to get to Albany. If all else failed, Athena decided with a determined scowl, she'd go alone despite Mercy's objections.

The fragrant smell of tea and freshly baked cinnamon buns greeted Athena as she stepped into the breakfast room. Like every other room in the house, it was painstakingly plastered and hung with bright painted paper that Fiona had imported from England several years before her death. The furniture was pine and apple, built by Foster himself, and a colorful carpet covered the polished floor. Sunlight poured through the numerous windows, giving the entire room a pleasant golden warmth.

Amelia Bower sat in her customary place at the head of the oval table. Like Athena, she wore mourning black, the stiff collar of her gown covering her long neck and reaching to her chin. Her nondescript brown hair was pulled into a severe chignon, and the disapproval on her face as her niece entered only served to deepen the lines etched about her wide, thin mouth.

She was not at all beautiful, and Athena had always wondered how this plain and cold-hearted woman could possibly be related to the graceful, soft-voiced creature who had been her mother. Though she remembered little of Fiona Courtland, none of her cherished memories resembled in any way the tyrannical severity of her Aunt Amelia. Small wonder her father had never cared much for his sister-in-law!

"Good morning, aunt," Athena said politely, sliding into her chair. From her aunt's sour expression she guessed that some form of criticism concerning her appearance was forthcoming, and she was not at all surprised when Amelia set down her delicate teacup with a decisive rattle.

"That gown of yours simply won't do any longer, Athena! I must make arrangements to have another made for you."

Athena blinked in surprise. It was true that this particular silk gown had grown rather threadbare and that her wrists showed because the sleeves were too short, but to have Aunt Amelia suggest that another one be made? Usually her aunt abhorred any form of extravagance and took pleasure in reminding her niece that many of her own gowns were well over ten years old and still in excellent condition.

"I think 'tis time," Amelia continued briskly, "that we make arrangements to have a far more suitable wardrobe prepared for you. I had originally intended to wait until you were out of mourning, but since you ruined your best gown yesterday and that one makes you look little better than a ragamuffin, I suppose there's no sense in waiting."

Athena's expression was one of wary disbelief. Was Aunt Amelia truly suggesting that she might soon be permitted to abandon her mourning attire?

"I expect the social season will be starting now that the harvest is over," Aunt Amelia added in her flat, nasal voice. "Though I'm doubtful that West York will be able to offer us anything as entertaining as a season in Boston, there should be at least one or two formal parties, don't you think? And you certainly cannot attend in such shabby attire," she went on briskly without giving her niece time to reply. "I suggest that we leave for Albany first thing tomorrow morning. After looking through your wardrobe and seeing what sort of things you wore before your father died, I cannot allow you to make use of them again." The memory of what she'd found in Athena's clothespress haunted her, and she shuddered.

"You'll have the services of naught but a proper couturier," she added firmly, "and I've been told that the best in the colony is a Dutchman named van Ties who happens to live in Albany. You'll have a fitting with him tomorrow and that's the end of it."

"Yes, aunt," Athena murmured with demurely lowered eyes. Actually she cared not a whit that her serviceable old gowns hadn't met with her aunt's approval, and yet she could scarcely believe that her problems had been resolved so unexpectedly. A trip to Albany. Her eyes began to sparkle. What did she care that hours of dull fittings lay ahead of her? She was going to get to see Jeremy after all, and that was all that mattered.

Two

The pale September sun had begun its downward descent when the carriage bearing Athena, her aunt, and Mercy drew to a halt before a tall house with a peaked roof on Handalaer Street. Athena, who had handled the reins herself all the way from West York, wound them around the brake pole and lifted her skirts to descend to the street.

"Wait a moment, Athena," her aunt commanded in a clipped tone as she stared up at the house, her expression one of utter distaste. "I'm not certain this will do at all. It seems quite neglected and not very clean. No telling how we'll find the rooms."

Athena forced herself not to grow impatient. It was true that Albany wasn't much to look at, with its narrow, crooked streets and small, ill-kept houses. Yet she felt certain that this particular rooming house would be no better or worse than any of the others, and she hated the thought of wasting time trying to find a more suitable one. She and Mercy had exchanged excited glances upon crossing the river when the imposing fort that sat on the hill above town had come into view. Certain that Jeremy would be there, Athena was anxious to seek him out, and she didn't care to spend the rest of the afternoon searching for better accommodations.

"I'm certain 'twill be fine," she assured her aunt as she got out of the carriage. Without giving Amelia time to protest, she crossed the small front porch, the feather in her little black hat bobbing jauntily, and boldly rang the bell.

Aunt Amelia was mollified to find the Dutch proprietor dressed in a clean apron and shirt, his deferential manner further calming her misgivings. Their bags were promptly carried up the creaking staircase by an eager young lad, while the proprietor himself saw to the horse and carriage. In order to save money Aunt Amelia had rented a single room with two narrow beds standing beneath the mullioned window. Mercy was expected to sleep on a cot in a small alcove, but neither she nor Athena minded the arrangement. They were happy enough simply to be here, and already Athena was plotting how she might best slip away to find Jeremy.

"Shall we have something to eat before we visit Mynheer van Ties?"

she suggested, seating herself on the bed and trying hard to hide her impatience.

"I'm far too fatigued to see anyone today," Aunt Amelia responded tartly. Her gaze was cold as she indicated that the serving boy was to set her valise on her bed. The young devil hadn't taken his eyes off Athena once, she was thinking to herself, and to make matters worse, Athena was hardly discouraging him by sprawling on the mattress in an unladylike fashion. Why, not only her shoes were visible, but her skirts were precariously hiked to reveal a shocking portion of her stockings and shapely ankles.

" 'Twill be all, thank you," Aunt Amelia added grimly, all but thrusting the blushing young man from the room. "I intend to rest," she told her niece, her ill temper growing worse at the sight of Athena's eager expression. How could the girl look so fresh after such a long, dusty drive? she asked herself enviously. There was a rosy blush on her niece's high cheeks that hadn't been there for quite some time. It occurred to her that perhaps Athena was excited at the prospect of receiving new gowns. Was it possible that the wretched girl was beginning to take an interest in her appearance?

"Mynheer van Ties isn't expecting us until tomorrow," Aunt Amelia added, her tone suddenly far less cross, "but perhaps you might like to visit him now and make your preliminary choice of fabrics. I can look them over in the morning."

Athena exchanged a sharp glance with Mercy, who was busily unpacking her mistress's toiletries. "Are you certain you wouldn't like to come with us?" she asked, holding her breath.

Amelia massaged her temples with long, white fingers. "I wish to rest first, child. I've got quite a headache thanks to that jolting carriage ride."

Athena made an appropriately sympathetic comment, inwardly thinking that with Aunt Amelia abed there would be ample time to visit the fort.

"Surely you don't expect us to go on foot, Miss Athena!" Mercy protested as she followed her mistress out onto the front porch of the rooming house.

Gazing up the length of Yonkheer Street, which followed a steep path to the fort, Athena gave a low laugh. "Why, 'tis half the distance and certainly far less rocky than the walk to the springhouse back home, Mercy!"

" 'Tisn't the distance, Miss Athena," Mercy confessed in a low voice. " 'Tis the neighborhood. Surely 'twould be inappropriate for you to travel without a carriage!"

Athena glanced about her. Because the afternoon was uncommonly warm, residents of the houses lining the street had come out onto their porches to sit. Most of them were Dutchmen with pipes in their mouths or women clad in homespun holding squalling infants on their laps. Their expressions were neither friendly nor hostile as they peered curiously at the two young women standing together in the street.

"Oh, don't let them bother you," Athena responded lightly. "We're here to find Jeremy, not to worry about what people might think of us."

With Mercy following reluctantly behind, she started up the street. At home in West York Athena had rarely seen soldiers, and then only when they marched through town on their way north to engage the French in places like Fort Duquesne and Fort William Henry. Yet in Albany there were soldiers everywhere. Red-coated British Regulars paraded through the streets, their bayonets flashing, while Provincial Militiamen in blue cloth coats and coarse red breeches drilled in precision lines on the fields along the riverfront. They encountered a Highland regiment just below the fort, and Mercy stared open-mouthed at their swinging kilts until the lot of them had marched out of sight.

"Did you see that, Miss Athena?" she whispered disbelievingly. "They were wearing skirts!"

"The kilt is part of the traditional Highland uniform," Athena responded with considerable amusement. "Don't you remember Tykie telling us he used to wear one, too, before King George ordered them outlawed after the Stuart uprising?"

Mercy's cheeks were red. "Of course I remember, but 'tis something entirely different to actually see them on a man. Why, 'tis . . . 'tis scandalous!"

Privately Athena had thought the tall Highlanders quite impressive. With their kilts and sporrans swinging, their broad shoulders proudly thrown back, they had seemed a far more disciplined group of men than the ramrod-stiff British Regulars parading in their finery on the streets below.

"Afternoon, ladies. You got business at the fort?"

Athena looked up quickly at the sound of the rough voice that addressed them. A soldier in Provincial uniform had come down from the entrance of the imposing stockade to confront them, a colony-issued musket slung carelessly over one shoulder. He was older than the soldiers Athena was accustomed to seeing, and his uniform was none too clean. Dark stubble covered his chin, and she didn't care too much for the way he was studying her.

She lifted her chin and returned his gaze as steadily as she could. "My brother is currently quartered here in Albany, sir. I've come to see him."

The soldier's eyes narrowed suspiciously. Athena knew she didn't look her best in her threadbare black gown with the ostrich feather in her hat drooping in the heat. She had tried to tidy her hair before leaving her room, but as usual the thick curls had had a mind of their own and refused to lie still. Yet she wasn't about to let this ill-kempt soldier intimidate her just because he didn't care for her appearance.

"My brother's name is Jer—" she began, but the soldier interrupted her with an impatient shake of his head.

"Wouldn't matter to me if he were General Abercromby himself, miss. Ain't no civilians allowed inside the fort."

Athena's heart sank. Of all the difficulties she'd anticipated, she hadn't expected to encounter a silly regulation like this.

"We'd better go, Miss Athena," Mercy suggested, tugging gently on her mistress's arm. She didn't like the fact that several other soldiers had come out of the wide front gate of the fort and were watching them with interest. She was hot and tired, too, and she prayed that Athena wouldn't turn stubborn and try to change the guard's mind.

Yet Athena was not about to let such a foolish hindrance prevent her from seeing her brother. She'd come too far to allow anyone to simply turn her away. "I don't believe you understand, sir," she said with a haughty toss of her head. "I haven't seen him in nearly a year, and I won't go home until I have."

A wide grin split the soldier's unshaven face. Pretty she was, in a wild sort of way, and when she looked at him with her golden brows arching and her little nose raised disdainfully in the air, she reminded him of an affronted kitten. Her brother was a fortunate fellow—if that's who she really wanted to see—and he felt sorry that he couldn't grant her request.

"Sorry, miss," he said abruptly, the smile vanishing from his face to be replaced by soldierly determination. "No civilians allowed in the fort. Them's the rules and I won't break 'em, not even for the likes of you."

Athena, who had thought the battle won, struggled with her temper. "May I at least get the message through to him that I'm here?" she asked irritably. "Perhaps he'll be able to meet me in town somewhere."

He was shaking his head before she even finished speaking. "Sorry, miss. Security's been tightened. No leave for any of us until . . . well—" he broke off hastily, aware that he had no business discussing military matters with a civilian, even one as pretty as the young woman in black who stood so proudly before him. "Nobody can leave the fort unless it's on official business," he explained, "and nobody can send messages in or out. At least not this week."

"Miss Athena, we'd better go," Mercy said again, aware that it would only be a matter of time before her mistress lost control of her tongue. No telling what this fearsome man with his musket would do if Miss Athena began insulting him! She shivered. The army didn't arrest civilians, did they, especially not women?

"Perhaps you're right, Mercy," Athena agreed, her sweet tone causing her maid to blink in surprise. "If the fort's sealed up tight, I imagine there's no hope of our getting in. That is, if you're telling the truth, sir."

Stung by the scorn in those vivid blue eyes, the soldier reacted defensively. "I'm a man of honor, miss, and I wouldn't be denying you the right to see your brother if the orders hadn't come from General Abercromby himself! All troops be confined to the fort during the day and to their barracks after curfew, and that's all I can tell you."

It was enough for Athena. Smiling at him sweetly, which brought a rush of answering color to his face, she took Mercy by the arm and marched down the hill. Neither of them exchanged a single word until they were back again among the bustling shops and neat rows of houses with their gabled roofs and gilded weathervanes.

"Oh, Miss Athena, what shall we do now?" Mercy asked tearfully. She was hot and thirsty, and there was gravel in her shoes, which made her feet hurt dreadfully.

"Do?" Athena repeated innocently. A wicked smile curved her lips. "Why, exactly what we came here to do. See Jeremy."

Mercy's tone revealed her confusion. "Didn't you hear what the soldier said? Master Jeremy won't be permitted to leave the fort. How do you expect to see him?"

"By going to his barracks."

This simple statement bewildered Mercy even more. "His barracks? But civilians aren't allowed in the fort. Didn't you hear him say that either?"

"Of course I did, but I intend to sneak in after dark," Athena responded as if that were the most obvious solution in the world.

"Oh, Miss Athena, no!" A sickly pallor replaced the rosy blush on Mercy's cheeks. She was familiar with her mistress's hair-raising antics, but this—this was far too dangerous! "They'll arrest you when they catch you!" she cried, hurrying after Athena, who hadn't slacked her pace.

"They won't catch me," Athena responded airily. "Not if they don't even see me." She had learned the art of stealth from Jeremy and Colm, who had been tutored in turn by a young Seneca brave. "And to make certain they won't, I shall wear a dark-colored shirt and breeches."

"And where do you propose to find them, Miss Athena?" Mercy demanded, promptly seizing on this particular detail rather than trying to talk her mistress out of the entire madcap scheme. "Do you expect Mynheer van Ties to sew them for you?"

Athena's eyes sparkled as she slanted her indignant maid an amused look. "Are you being sarcastic with me, Mercy? I fear I've driven you too far this time. Mayhap I shouldn't have told you my plans."

"They'll come to naught, Miss Athena!" Mercy cried, not caring that passersby were turning to stare at her curiously. "Even if you did have the proper attire, how do you propose to steal out of your room when you're sharing it with your aunt? You know she's a very light sleeper!"

"If her headache hasn't gone away by bedtime, she'll take a powder," Athena reminded her, "and nothing short of an invasion by the French will awaken her."

Mercy groaned, aware that this was true. Wringing her hands, she tried to think of something to say that might change her mistress's mind. Perhaps Miss Athena would be unable to find the clothes she required, she thought hopefully. After all, they didn't know anyone in Albany, and Miss Athena couldn't simply purchase a pair of breeches from some stranger on the street!

As usual Mercy had underestimated her mistress's tenacity. After spending a half-hour at Mynheer van Ties's elegant little shop and selecting several bolts of material, Athena bid the beaming Dutchman farewell and hurried Mercy back to their rooming house.

"Go on upstairs and see if my aunt needs anything," she instructed, pushing her toward the stairs. Mercy lingered in the hallway long enough to see Athena vanish into the front room, where the proprietor's son was busily waxing furniture. She groaned to herself, recalling the admiring looks he had given to Miss Athena when he'd carried their luggage upstairs. It probably wouldn't cost her mistress more than a coy smile to obtain what she needed.

When Athena appeared upstairs a few minutes later, she was the triumphant owner of a pair of brick-colored breeches, a blue cotton shirt, and a deerskin jacket. It appeared that her admirer had been so eager to satisfy her request that he hadn't even thought to wonder what she intended to do with them.

"Not only that," Athena told Mercy in a whisper so as not to disturb her aunt, who lay snoring softly on her bed, "but he took the time to tell me how to get into the fort. He says they only post a small guard on the east side, and half the time the west entrance, from the river, is left completely unguarded. I shouldn't have any trouble getting inside."

"How can you be sure he's telling the truth?" Mercy asked worriedly. Already she had visions of Athena being arrested and hauled before the commander in chief.

"He isn't old enough to enlist yet," Athena explained, "but that hasn't stopped him from visiting the fort often. He knew the exact location of all the gates and even the names of the guards who'll be on watch tonight."

Seeing the frightened look on Mercy's face, Athena's jaw tightened with determination. "I'm going to see Jeremy, Mercy, no matter what I have to do to get into the fort, but I can't succeed without your help."

"My help?" Mercy gulped.

"Yes. You could ruin everything by giving me away to my aunt, or you can help me by acting as though naught were amiss."

"I'll do my best, Miss Athena," Mercy mumbled reluctantly. She knew from long experience that it would be useless to try to change her mistress's mind, yet she would never betray her by carrying tales to her aunt.

It proved to be a nerve-racking evening for Athena. Aunt Amelia awoke in time for supper, professing herself completely recovered from their tiring journey. She was eager to hear about the material her niece had seen at the couturier's shop, and Athena was forced to oblige her with a thorough description, although she was hard put to hide her restlessness. Aunt Amelia ate heartily of the soup, baked fowl, and fresh bread that was set out before them, and Athena, seeing that she didn't appear the least bit tired, resigned herself to the possibility that her plans might come to naught.

Not until eleven o'clock did Aunt Amelia yawningly announce that she intended to retire. "Bring me a powder from my reticule," she instructed Mercy as the little maid began turning down their beds.

"Oh, are you ill, aunt?" Athena blurted, only to feel ashamed that she should sound so eager.

Aunt Amelia appeared not to notice. " 'Tis simply a precaution, child. Unless I take a dose now I know I shall wake up later with a pounding headache."

" 'Tis always best to be prepared," Athena agreed, giving Mercy a triumphant glance.

A half-hour later Amelia's sonorous snoring echoed through the darkened room. Athena, who had been lying motionless in her bed, cautiously pulled the nightshift from her body and slipped into her breeches. The sleeves of the cotton shirt ended at the tips of her tapering fingers and impatiently she rolled them back, then stuffed the baggy ends of her breeches into the tops of her sturdy walking shoes.

She hadn't unpinned her hair upon retiring, and there remained naught to do except pull the knitted cap she had made for Jeremy over her head and slip into the deerskin jacket. She suspected she looked rather odd, yet the important thing was that she wouldn't be hampered by confining skirts and petticoats while trying to make her way into the fort.

"Are you leaving, Miss Athena?" Mercy's whisper sounded loud and afraid in the darkness.

"Yes, I am. I shouldn't be gone too long. Try not to worry."

"What should I do if your aunt awakens and finds you gone?" Mercy's voice quivered fearfully at the thought.

"Pretend you've been sleeping and that you haven't noticed a thing. Don't worry," Athena repeated reassuringly. "Aunt Amelia won't wake up, and I'll be back sooner than you think. I'll give Jeremy your regards if you like."

"Oh, would you, miss?" Mercy asked eagerly.

Athena smiled in the darkness. "Of course."

Quietly she let herself out of the room, relieved that Aunt Amelia's rhythmic snoring continued uninterrupted. The stairs creaked alarmingly as she made her way down to the pitch-black hall, but nothing stirred in response. Sliding back the bolt of the heavy front door, she stepped outside. The houses along the street were tightly shuttered, and only a green-eyed alleycat witnessed her disappearance into the night. Stars shone faintly overhead and crickets chirped softly in the tall grass along the roadside. Pulling her cap even tighter over her telltale curls, Athena began to walk briskly in the direction of the fort.

Major Lochiel Blackmoor glanced irritably at the thick stack of papers that were being extended to him across his cluttered oak desk. Not another set of useless reports to be read and corrected by morning, he thought wearily to himself. His annoyance was replaced by surprise as he glanced up to see that they had been brought to him by a portly gentleman with a ruddy complexion and heavy, bewhiskered jowls. A faint light of amusement entered his slate-gray eyes.

"Been demoted to messenger, sergeant-major?" he inquired with a grin. "Since when do you deliver the reports?"

"Since I sent Barrett to bed an hour ago," the sergeant-major growled in a voice as rough as gravel. "The poor lad was fair reeling with exhaustion."

The tall, dark-headed man seated at the pockmarked desk rubbed his tired eyes with long, sun-browned fingers. "As all of us are," he agreed. " 'Tis this blasted paperwork. I can't think of a faster way to undermine a man's morale than by forcing him to fill out endless reports."

"Aye, laddie. I keep asking myself who's running this war, the bloody bureaucrats or the soldiers."

Lochiel made no response. It didn't take much to whip Regimental Sergeant-Major Andrew Durning into a froth over the ineptitude of the generals who were supposedly in charge of the combined continental armies. Since early spring the French had won every major assault, including the disastrous march on Fort Ticonderoga in June, which had cost General Abercromby the lives of over six hundred loyal Highlanders.

Lochiel Blackmoor's handsome face was bleak as he recalled the terrible slaughter. He had lost many men close to him during the campaign, and though he had long since taught himself to live with pain, the wound didn't seem to want to heal. He would have to give it more time, he told himself. Three months was obviously not enough.

"I can help if ye like," the sergeant-major offered, indicating with a blunt finger the stack of papers he had laid on the major's desk.

Lochiel glanced at the clock ticking in a small oak cabinet near the door. " 'Tis almost midnight, Andy. Why don't we leave it until tomorrow?"

A grin split the ruddy face. " 'Twould please me well enough, lad." Yawning widely, he scratched himself and added complacently, "I'm off to bed."

Left alone in his office, Lochiel found himself unwilling to tackle the enormous stack of papers. They would contain, he knew from long experience, little more than statistics and useless figures that no one would end up reading anyway. Better to let his adjunct start on them in the morning, he decided.

Rising to his feet, Major Blackmoor wandered to the window, moving gracefully for a man of his height. Pale mooonlight fell on his angular features as he stared restlessly through the grimy glass, his hands clasped behind his broad back. Tomorrow would be a busy day, he knew, what with the troops preparing to march north, and yet he wasn't ready to retire. If only . . .

Lochiel's dark head came up attentively, and without turning around he extinguished the single lamp burning on the desk behind him. With the tiny office plunged into darkness he was better able to see outside and determine exactly what it was he thought he had seen out on the deserted parade grounds. Aye, there it was again: the furtive movement from shadow to shadow of someone trying to escape detection as he hurried toward the barracks.

Lochiel's brow furrowed. Who the devil could it be? McCutcheon? The lad had threatened desertion on several occasions since the disastrous march on Ticonderoga. Or was it Skelley, out for a midnight jaunt despite the newly imposed curfew? Albany was rumored to be favored with attractive whores, and Skelley was the sort of skirt-chasing fool who'd defy the rules to find out for himself. Lochiel frowned. Hadn't he made it clear to his men often enough that rules, however objectionable, were to be respected and obeyed?

Weariness caused his temper to flare. Whoever was sneaking back into those barracks was blatantly defying the curfew, and Major Blackmoor intended to see that he paid for his transgressions. With the new push toward Quebec about to begin, discipline could not be allowed to waver, even here in the relatively dull surroundings of Fort Albany.

Unaware of the narrowed, angry gaze following her every movement across the grounds, Athena Courtland paused amid the shadows to catch her breath. She had run most of the way up the hill, knowing there was little time to waste, and hadn't stopped to rest until she slipped through the small gate at the west end of the fort. As expected, it hadn't been guarded, and Athena had simply worked at the wooden bolt until she managed to force it open.

The fort was eerily deserted. In the pale moonlight Athena had quickly been able to distinguish the outer walls and buttresses as well as the few roughly finished offices. Across the parade grounds she had seen the barracks, a small group of buildings she recognized from Fletcher's description of typical military quarters. Though most of them were dark, a few of the windows glowed with soft light, and Athena told herself she mustn't lose courage now. She trusted that none of the enlisted men would give her away and that she'd be able to find her brother without too much trouble.

Yet she was feeling decidedly less optimistic than when she'd first set out on her adventure. Confronted now with a cluster of buildings and having no clue where to begin her search for Jeremy, she found herself wondering if perhaps she wouldn't have been better off to simply smuggle a message in to him. Surely with the right amount of persuasion that gruff-spoken guard might have agreed to help her earlier this afternoon!

" 'Tis too late now, you impulsive creature," she muttered to herself. Taking a deep breath, she stepped out of the shadows, preparing to make a mad dash across the moon-drenched length of the parade ground.

"Just a minute there, lad!"

Athena uttered a terrified squeak as she felt her collar being packed from behind. What felt suspiciously like an iron band wrapped itself about her slender neck. When she tried to jerk away, it tightened painfully.

"Let me go!" she commanded fiercely.

"Stand to, lad! That's an order!"

But Athena was not about to obey. Belatedly she realized that what held her so firmly about the neck was a long-fingered hand of awesome strength and that another hand had encircled her waist, tightening about her ribcage and threatening to cut off her air. She began to struggle in earnest, aware that if that big hand moved up so much as an inch it would encounter the soft, telltale curves of her breasts.

"Let me go!" she repeated, a thread of panic in her voice. If she were to be taken before the commanding officer and he found out who she was, poor Jeremy might end up being held responsible for her behavior!

"I've no intention of letting you go, my friend, and unless you come to attention this moment you'll spend the next few nights in the stocks. Is that understood?" The deep voice held the soft burr of a native from the Northwest Scottish Highlands, and the steely edge of authority that fell softly in Athena's ear sent a shiver fleeing down her spine.

Reluctantly her struggles ceased and her captor let her go. Rubbing her aching neck, Athena stared up at him accusingly, tilting her head in order to look into his face. She felt her throat grow dry as their eyes met and held.

Perhaps it was the dim light or her imagination playing tricks on her, yet Athena could swear his eyes were silver, as silver as the sea on a moonlit night. His hair was silver, too, she saw, only to realize in the next moment that it was as black as a raven's wing and she was merely seeing the reflection of the moonlight upon it. His features were angular, sharp planes that defied description, and afterward she couldn't remember if he was young or old or whether he had been hideously ugly—or as handsome as the devil himself.

Athena could only stare up at him, her indignant expression changing to one of bewildered surprise. Never in her life had she encountered a more disturbing man, yet she could not explain exactly what it was about him that caused her breath to catch in her throat and her heart to begin a fearful pounding.

"What the devil?"

Athena heard him inhale sharply as the soft oath burst from his lips. She was unaware that his steely gaze had been roving her face and that, failing to recognize her as one of his men, he had taken a long look at her and had seen her for the first time.

Lochiel Blackmoor was shaken to the depths of his being. Never in his life had he found himself confronted by a more haunting pair of eyes. In the moonlight they seemed to change hue, from deepest onyx to sapphire, to silver. The square-jawed little face that peered up at him from beneath a dark knitted cap was far too delicate and young to be that of a soldier—or even a man.

Without warning, his hand came up to snatch the cap off her head and Athena cried out, thinking he intended to strike her. She gasped as she felt her heavy braids cascade down her shoulders where the moonlight caught them, revealing golden highlights as pale and ethereal as spun silk.

"What's your name, lass?" Lochiel Blackmoor demanded hoarsely, unable to believe that he had captured not a wayward soldier but a woman of mystical beauty, an enchanted sylph despite her ill-fitting rags.

He had caught her by the arms as he spoke, and Athena was terrified by the heat that enveloped her at his nearness. She felt as if she were smothering, this broad-chested, silver-eyed man drowning her with the sheer force of his being.

"Let me go!" she cried again, her high, frightened voice loud enough to awaken every last man in the barracks. Her foot lashed out, the toe of her shoe catching him a swift, painful blow to the shin.

With a muffled oath Lochiel loosened his grip and felt her tear herself free. He cursed again and lunged for her, but the pliant leather of her deerskin jacket merely slipped through his fingers. A moment later she was gone, swallowed up by the darkness, leaving him with nothing but her knitted cap and the memory of her dark blue eyes blazing into his.

"What's the fuss about, eh?"

"I thought I heard a woman scream!"

Several lights had sprung on in the barracks, and a small group of men were spilling out of the doorway, shrugging into their uniforms as they went.

"Why, 'tis Major Blackmoor!" a young enlisted man exclaimed, catching sight of the grim-featured officer standing alone on the moon-drenched parade grounds.

"What's to do, major?" another man asked, buttoning his shirt over his hair-roughened chest.

"What's to do?" Lochiel Blackmoor repeated in an ominous tone that caused his men to exchange uneasy glances. "I'll tell you what's to do, Corporal Martin. Someone in your company just tried to smuggle a prostitute into the barracks." His steely gaze swept the small group with deliberate intent. "I order the guilty party to speak up immediately."

The men shuffled their feet and stared askance at one another. Normally they didn't mind turning their backs while a mate broke the rules, but this was Major Blackmoor giving the orders, and right now he seemed in a dangerous frame of mind.

"Beggin' your pardon, sir," Corporal Martin said hesitantly as the uncomfortable silence lengthened, "we were all of us sleepin'. I dinna think she came here to join any of us."

The others nodded their heads and mumbled agreement.

One dark brow arched in mock surprise as Lochiel Blackmoor surveyed the uneasy group of men. "Am I to assume that she crept into the fort on her own initiative? That failing to find business in town she came here to see if any of you were willing?"

His question and the grating anger in his voice brought continued silence, and Major Blackmoor was forced to admit to himself that none of them was responsible. Rough and violent they might be, yet they were men of honor who would speak up when confronted. Still, he was determined to learn the identity of the young woman in the deerskin jacket, and his throbbing leg reminded him that he would greatly enjoy twisting her slender neck the next time they met.

"Very well," he said gruffly. "There's no sense in spending the night out here. Corporal Martin, I'll expect you in my office after reveille, and I hope you'll have the man responsible with you when you come."

"Aye, sir," the lanky Scotsman responded glumly. Damn the sod who'd been stupid enough to try to sneak a whore into the barracks! There'd be hell to pay for this one, for the major looked ready to have all of them for bloody breakfast!

Scowling ill-temperedly, Lochiel Blackmoor tossed the knitted cap onto his desk. Watching the lights go out one by one in the barracks, he admitted to himself that he had been unduly hard on his men. Whores were an accepted facet of a soldier's life and even helped maintain a certain degree of morale. Why, then, should this one's presence have angered him so?

Lochiel didn't know. He was sure it had nothing to do with her haunting beauty, though God knows she'd looked too young and bloody innocent to make a living selling her body to rutting army men. He shifted restlessly in his chair, seeing before him those wide, silver-flecked eyes and not understanding why their blue-black depths had stirred something so deep within him.

What had touched him in that moment when they had stared, disbelieving, at one another? Certainly not her striking looks, though he had to admit reluctantly to himself that he had never been confronted by a more breathtaking vision in his life. Perhaps she had brought to mind a memory so elusive that it had long since been forgotten?

Again, Lochiel didn't know. Picking up the dark blue cap, he twirled it absently in his hand. A predatory smile curved his lips. Tomorrow he would see that its owner and the man responsible for bringing her here were brought before him. He relished the thought of teaching both of them what it meant to cross an officer of His Majesty's Seventh Highlanders.

Three

"Athena, will you please stop that fidgeting? I vow you're making me positively nervous! Whatever is wrong, child?"

Athena laid down the pewter knife she had been toying with and tried to look suitably innocent. Inwardly she was churning with impatience, wishing her aunt would hurry and take herself off to town as she'd promised. Over a week had passed since she'd last ridden Ballycor, and she couldn't wait to be galloping across the fields with him.

"I'm sorry, aunt," she apologized, searching for a suitable reason for her ill manners at the breakfast table. "I suppose I just can't wait for my new gowns to arrive. When do you suppose they'll be delivered?"

Amelia Bower's stern features softened. "Mynheer van Ties promised to send them as soon as they were ready, and I did pay him well to see that he wasted no time. Perhaps tomorrow or the day after and I hope—oh, gracious!"

"What is it, aunt?" Athena asked worriedly, trying to read what was written on the gold-embossed parchment her aunt had been unfolding as she spoke. It had arrived by messenger earlier that morning, and Athena, recognizing Egon de Vries's ostentatious seal, hadn't been too interested.

Yet Aunt Amelia's reaction made her curious, and her guilty conscience caused her imagination to run wild. Suppose Master de Vries had somehow learned of her attempts to see Jeremy? They had returned to West York five days ago—ample time for the wealthy Dutchman to have heard about her misadventures from any one of his numerous acquaintances in Albany.

What nonsense! Athena chided herself sharply. She hadn't been recognized by anyone at the fort, especially not that silver-eyed Highlander who had caught her and nearly snapped her neck in two. Only Mercy knew what she had tried to do, and the poor thing had been so disappointed by the outcome that she hadn't even thought to press her mistress for details. No one on earth should have any reason to suspect that Athena Courtland had been caught trying to sneak into the Fort Albany barracks disguised as a boy.

And no one ever would, Athena decided firmly. She had been more than lucky to get away from that iron-fingered officer, and God be thanked that she would never lay eyes on him again! The irony of it all was that a letter from Jeremy had been waiting for her when she returned home informing her that he would be traveling north in a few days' time and that he would make every effort to come see her. It annoyed Athena that she had risked so much in vain, but she had decided with customary cheerfulness to shrug the entire matter off.

"Is it news from Bountiful?" Athena asked now, referring to the de Vries estate, which lay on the far side of West York.

" 'Tis an invitation," Aunt Amelia responded happily, taking a delicate nibble of buttery pastry. Her eyes glowed with anticipation. "There's to be a ball at the de Vries's to honor the appointment of General Jeffrey Amherst as the new commander in chief."

Athena's eyes widened. "Has General Abercromby been replaced?"

Aunt Amelia gave her niece an impatient look. "I really haven't the faintest idea, child," she said, her tone indicating clearly that Athena shouldn't be troubling herself over such matters.

But Athena was already wondering if the strict military security she had encountered in Albany had had anything to do with Jeffrey Amherst's appointment and what General Abercromby's demotion would mean to the war effort itself. She shivered, suddenly afraid for Jeremy and Colm, who might soon be marching across the mountains to confront the French in Canada, and for Fletcher, who was serving in an unknown outpost somewhere in the maritime provinces.

"Many of the general's officers and adjuncts will also be honored at the ball," Aunt Amelia went on eagerly, scanning the few lines Mistress de Vries had penned at the bottom of the formal invitation. "Oh dear, Athena, I do hope your new gowns will be ready by then, for 'tis obviously meant to be quite an affair."

Athena could tell by the faraway expression on her aunt's face that she was already dreaming of the dashing young officers who would be present that evening. She scowled to herself, certain that she would be expected to conquer as many hearts as she could. And if she were to receive an offer of marriage that very night—why, nothing on earth would make Aunt Amelia happier.

"I'm certain we'll never have enough time to prepare," the older woman added fretfully. " 'Tis vexing that I didn't give Mynheer van Ties a more definite deadline!"

"I could always wear one of my old ballgowns," Athena offered, yet her suggestion was met with an exclamation of horror.

"I will not have you wearing one of those . . . those outdated rags,

Athena Courtland, especially not when you'll be meeting Katrine de Vries face to face in the receiving line!"

Athena rolled her eyes at Prudence, who had come in with Wills, the Courtlands' only footman, to oversee the removal of the breakfast dishes. The round-faced cook, a plumper version of her redheaded daughter Mercy, tried hard to conceal a giggle behind her hand. It was common knowledge at Courtland Grace that Amelia Bower considered the de Vries's eldest daughter to be Athena's most formidable rival. Aunt Amelia was almost fanatical in her determination to see her niece married off before Katrine de Vries, and the unspoken rivalry between the young women had only increased since Stephen Kensington had returned from England.

Athena didn't really care if Katrine was the first to snare a husband. In fact, Katrine was heartily welcome to any young man who captured her fancy—which seemed to include any male in the area old enough to be out of short pants. Katrine considered Athena her best friend, yet Athena had never come across a more fickle creature. Her affections could turn at any imagined slight. With her vitriolic tongue she had spread more damaging gossip than anyone else in the colony.

Privately Athena considered Katrine de Vries the dullest of living creatures, yet for Fletcher's sake she did her best to be kind to the girl. Egon de Vries doted on his daughter, and Egon de Vries was one of the most influential men in the colony. He was an important business ally for Fletcher to have, and Athena was not about to risk her brother's chances of stepping smoothly into his father's shoes by alienating either Egon de Vries or poor, silly Katrine.

"I believe I'll send Tykie to Albany at once," Aunt Amelia announced decisively. "He can fetch your gowns himself, and you, Athena, must go through your wardrobe with Mercy to make certain you have the proper gloves and accessories for the ball." Her thin lips tightened irritably. "Oh, if only they'd sent those invitations round before we left for Albany! I'm certain you'll need a new fan, and last I looked every one of your stockings had holes in them! Athena, you'll simply have to—"

"Why don't I send Tykie to Albany for you?" Athena volunteered, knowing how much her aunt hated giving orders to the hulking Scotsman. "That way you can go through my things yourself and personally make sure everything's in order."

This seemed an excellent idea to her aunt, who suspected that Athena would make a less than satisfactory inspection of her belongings. Calling loudly for Mercy, she vanished amid a rustle of stiff black skirts while Athena hurried out to the stables, her eyes sparkling with anticipation. If Aunt Amelia found even half the disorder in Athena's drawers and clothespress that her niece expected, she could count on at least a good half-hour's ride before her absence was noticed.

"Aye, I'll bring back your dresses for ye, Miss Athena," Tykie agreed promptly when she told him of Aunt Amelia's plan. " 'Twill gie me a chance tae learn if thot brother o' yours still be i' town." He helped her saddle Ballycor and gave her a disapproving look as he led the stamping animal to the mounting block. "Ye'll no be riding in them skirts, Miss Athena?"

"There wasn't time to go upstairs for my habit." She smoothed the folds of her black silk gown, wishing that she didn't have to wait until her new wardrobe arrived before Aunt Amelia would permit her to put aside her mourning attire. How sick and tired she was of wearing black!

"You'd best wear your cloak, miss," Tykie insisted, refusing to relinquish Ballycor's reins. " 'Tis chilly this mornin', an' 'twill help keep the beastie smell frae your dress as well."

Athena twinkled at him. It was true that Aunt Amelia had a sharp nose.

The cloak hung on a peg near the front door, and as she reached for it, Athena could hear loud thumps coming from her bedroom above. She smiled to herself. Obviously Aunt Amelia was forcing Mercy to empty out the contents of every one of her drawers for inspection. 'Twould take quite a bit of time before they were finished.

A few minutes later, she had set off astride Ballycor. The cool autumn wind stirred the tendrils of golden hair that framed her lovely face. Her peacock-blue velvet cloak, in bright contrast to her somber mourning gown, fell in graceful folds from her slender shoulders, the hood thrown back so that its lining of silver fox fur brushed lightly against her jaw.

Almost overnight the woodlands had been transformed into a blaze of scarlet and gold, and Athena breathed deeply of the fragrant scent as Ballycor thundered off through the trees. How she loved the solitude of the forest, and her expression grew wistful as she recalled the many hours she and her brothers had spent roaming through them. There had never been any reason to be afraid, for they had always carried muskets to protect themselves from the bears that prowled the mountains, and the Iroquois that lived in the region had always been friendly.

Athena still enjoyed coming here alone despite the fact that the colonies were at war. No matter what Aunt Amelia believed, she was in no danger from roving Indians, for most of the tribes belonging to the Iroquois nation fought on the side of the English, while the treacherous Algonquins, the ones to be feared, had gone farther north to aid the French in their battles. Now that Jeremy, Colm, and Fletcher were gone, Athena found she needed the solitude of the mountains more than ever. It was well worth risking Aunt Amelia's wrath to slip away for a time and forget the loneliness that weighed so heavily upon her.

A half-hour was barely enough time to put Ballycor through his paces, and the big stallion obeyed only reluctantly when Athena at last turned him homeward. She laughed as she patted his sleek neck, her eyes lit with merriment.

"You might not care if I get punished for taking you out today, my fine fellow, but I can assure you that I wouldn't enjoy it."

Aware that it might be some time before she could ride him again, Athena urged him into a gallop, hoping to spend a little bit more of his boundless energy before they reached the stables. Her velvet cloak billowed behind her as she charged off through the trees, the sunlight turning her glossy curls into molten gold.

"Lord, lads, did ye see her too, or was I under some enchantment?"

The question came from a bearded soldier wearing the uniform of His Majesty's Highlanders who had stepped out from the trees in time to witness Athena's whirlwind departure.

"She were real, all right," one of his companions assured him, setting his heavy pack down with a sigh. "Did ye see them breasts of hers?" he added, smacking his lips at the brief glimpse he'd caught of the enticing body wrapped in the folds of the flowing cloak. "Like two captive dove waitin' to be set free."

"By the likes o' yourself, eh, Skelley?" another soldier said with a laugh, giving his companion a dig in the ribs.

"Couldn't ye see that was a lady?" the bearded man demanded angrily, haunted by the vision of the beautiful young woman plunging into the forest astride her gleaming white horse.

"Och, go on wi' ye, Hugh," he was teased for his defensive words. "You're always dreamin' of fairies an' enchanted creatures! That one looked too delectable to be a nymph or some will o' the wisp!"

A quiet but authoritative voice interrupted the angry protest Hugh was about to make. "Here, corporal, that's enough. We're supposed to be scouting the area, not arguing over the local lasses."

"Didn't ye see her, sir?" Hugh persisted, turning eagerly to his senior officer.

"I didn't get a good look at her, corporal," Major Blackmoor admitted, a small frown creasing the bridge of his straight Roman nose, "but I did see enough to realize that she must be something of a fool to be riding alone."

"I'd love to gie her a sound spanking to show her the error o' her ways," the blond soldier remarked with a laugh, only to be rewarded for his wit by a piercing glance from his senior officer, who indicated the knapsack he had set down at his feet.

"Is your pack too heavy for you, Skelley? Shall I have someone else carry it back to town?"

Davie Skelley flushed to the roots of his sandy hair while the rest of the men snickered. "No, sir, I'll manage," he said and hastily slung the heavy canvas bag over his shoulder.

Athena, meanwhile, had returned home to find that her absence had thankfully not been noticed and that Aunt Amelia was more than satisfied with the shawl, gloves, and fans Mercy had uncovered in a big cedar trunk in the attic. Her excitement was oddly infectious, and Athena had to admit to herself that she was beginning to look forward to the de Vrieses' ball. If she were lucky, perhaps she might even find the chance to speak privately with General Amherst concerning the whereabouts of her brothers' regiments. Surely that in itself would make the evening worthwhile!

Athena had long suspected the de Vries family of holding formal assemblies merely to display their wealth, and the officers' ball was to prove no exception. An excessive number of candles blazed in the crystal chandeliers in Bountiful's magnificent withdrawing room, and the priceless silver appointments glittered with rainbow prisms of reflected light. Servants in shimmering scarlet livery moved among the milling guests bearing trays of fluted glasses filled with several choices of libations. No fewer than four violins, a bass viola, and two German flutes played sweet melodies that floated softly to the plaster ceiling, while the black-coated musicians remained discreetly hidden in a small alcove.

A bewigged Egon de Vries stood at the head of the receiving line, resplendent in a dark gray Geneva serge suit, his waistcoat of Mecklenburg silk shot with silver threads. His wife stood beside him in a gown of mauve silk, her heavily powdered curls piled high.

"My dear Athena, 'tis a pleasure to see you," Egon de Vries said heartily as the lovely young girl paused before him, for he was genuinely fond of Foster Courtland's high-spirited daughter. Introducing her to the Earl of Loudon and General Amherst, who stood together behind his wife, he wondered what it was about Athena that seemed special to him that evening. She had always been enchanting, yet tonight she seemed to sparkle, to radiate some inner fire that had been lacking for quite some time. Egon wondered to himself what had brought about the change.

Marianne de Vries knew the cause the instant she clapped eyes on the young woman moving gracefully into the glittering hall with her aunt behind her. Athena was no longer in mourning, and Marianne guessed at once that Amelia Bower had deliberately planned her niece's reemergence into society to coincide with the ball. Athena was wearing a gown that would have drawn attention even if one hadn't been accustomed to seeing her in somber black for the last twelve months. It was of shimmering silver, as bright and lustrous as a newly minted coin. Ruffled petticoats, the color of a brilliant autumn sky, were revealed by gold ribbons that artfully caught and lifted away the pleated front of her skirts. Dainty slippers of Morocco kid, adorned with silver thread, peeped from beneath the ruffled hem, and Athena carried a silver-handled fan of dark blue silk in one slim hand.

Silver and blue were simple colors in contrast to the stunning, jewel-toned gowns worn by the other women present that evening, yet they heightened Athena's dramatic looks so that it was impossible to take one's eyes off her. Her unpowdered curls gleamed in the candlelight, and her eyes seemed even darker in contrast to the cerulean blue of her petticoats. Wide and expressive, they sparkled with lively interest, while a knowing smile played on her soft lips as she took Marianne de Vries's offered hand.

She chatted easily with both Lord Loudon and General Amherst, all the while aware of the glowering looks of Katrine de Vries, who stood with her small hand resting possessively on the general's arm. It galled Katrine to see her archrival in silken finery that complemented to perfection her golden beauty. She had expected Athena to attend in one of the tired black outfits everyone had grown accustomed to seeing her in, and she was furious not only because Athena looked so beautiful, but because convention would allow her to dance this evening.

"Your new gown is most becoming, Athena," Katrine said with a smile that looked as if she had been sucking lemons. "I'm so glad you're finally out of mourning!"

She'd rather see me roasting in hell, Athena thought cheerfully to herself, deliberately allowing her hand to linger in the general's big, callused one simply to annoy her. Katrine was wearing a gown of maidenly white, the sleeves and neckline edged with fine Bruges lace. Sapphires sparkled at her throat and in her ears and were worn, Athena suspected, to draw attention to her delft-blue eyes. Doubtless the white was also a calculated choice to remind any eligible officers in attendance that Katrine de Vries was unmarried and therefore quite accessible.

Unfortunately the color choice was poor, for Katrine seemed paler than ever, and in the bright light of the chandeliers her powdered blond curls seemed dull and lifeless. Athena fled the receiving line as quickly as she could, leaving her aunt to chat with Mistress de Vries. She herself was soon surrounded by acquaintances she hadn't seen for quite some time.

As she talked and laughed with them, she kept her attention on the front door, and her interest quickened when she saw General Amherst excuse himself from the ladies and disappear with Egon de Vries into the back of the house. The last guests must have just arrived, and Athena felt certain the men had gone off for a private talk before the general returned to the drawing room to open the dancing.

Excusing herself from the small ring of admirers who had gathered around her, Athena hurried down the corridor after them. Surely Master de Vries wouldn't object if she asked General Amherst a few questions. If she waited until later, he would doubtless be monopolized.

The last door at the end of the corridor was closed. Athena had been to Bountiful often enough to know that this was the study, and she hesitated before knocking, not really wishing to interrupt them here. No answer was forthcoming, however, and when she tested the latch and discreetly opened the door, she found the room empty. A lamp glowed softly on the enormous oak desk, illuminating the heavy brocade drapes and the Hogarth engraving that hung above the mantel.

Disappointed, she turned to leave only to find that her path had been blocked by a gentleman in scarlet satin.

"Oh!" she exclaimed, feeling guilty at having been caught out.

"Good evening, Athena," he said with a mocking smile. "Don't tell me you've already grown tired of the ball? The evening hasn't even begun."

"Did you follow me here?" Athena asked suspiciously, recovering her composure as she recognized Stephen Kensington.

Stephen shrugged. " 'Twas impossible to get anywhere near you out there in the ballroom. I must admit I was more than a little annoyed by the number of pups who were panting at your heels. 'Twas a stroke of luck for me when I saw you slip away." He indicated the study with an affected wave of his hand. "Why did you come here?"

"I was looking for someone," Athena murmured. She had no desire to tell him what she'd been up to, and she certainly didn't want to spend another minute alone with him. "If you'll excuse me, please, Mr. Kensington."

He caught her arm as she tried to brush past him. Her golden beauty had captured his interest, and the dusky satin of her skin in the lamplight was nearly as seductive as the warm, steady throb of her pulse beneath his hand. Innocent, his mind whispered, innocent she could not be, for he had never come across a woman whose beguiling eyes seemed to be telling him exactly what she wanted. The subtle fragrance of her hair tantalized him, and he felt again the heady desire that had coursed through him when he had taken her soft body into his arms on his parents' terrace.

"Athena," he murmured huskily. His hand slid from her arm to her waist, caressing the curve of her hip.

"Let me go!" Athena commanded through clenched teeth. She wasn't about to tolerate a repeat of the last night they had been together.

"You've grown even more beautiful since I've been away," he told her, bending his head so that his hot breath stirred the tendrils of hair that curled across her brow. "I wouldn't have thought it possible, but . . ." His words trailed away as he moved even closer, lowering his dark head to kiss her.

Athena uttered a strangled sound of disgust and twisted away from him. Silken petticoats swirling about her ankles, she reached behind her where a letter opener lay on the desktop. Though it was blunt, the blade was long, and the look in her dark eyes when she turned to face him informed a suddenly wary Stephen that she wouldn't hesitate to use it.

"You're a wild little thing, aren't you, Athena Courtland?" he inquired mildly, though Athena noticed that he remained well out of reach of her raised hand. It pleased her that the tables had at last been turned.

"Mayhap I am," she conceded, beginning to enjoy herself, "but I cannot think of a better way for a helpless young woman to defend herself against the unwanted attentions of a gentleman." She gave the last word a soft, derisive emphasis and tossed her head as she gazed up at him, daring him to contradict her.

Stephen gazed at her thoughtfully for a moment. It was going to prove harder than he'd anticipated to seduce this passionate beauty, yet his appetite for the chase had been thoroughly whetted. He would concede her the victory this time, but the battle wasn't over yet.

"My apologies, Athena," he said at his most gallant best. "I regret that my behavior has warranted you to feel that you must arm yourself against me. I shall attempt to handle myself more discreetly in the future."

With a deep bow and a playful smile on his lips he retreated, leaving Athena to gaze after him with a puzzled look on her face, the letter opener still threateningly poised before her. Was he genuinely sorry or was this some new ploy to confuse her? Her lips tightened grimly as she turned to lay the brass tool back on the desk. She didn't relish at all the idea of becoming the object of Stephen Kensington's attentions. Her eyes blazed mutinously. He would never have attempted something so bold if Fletcher were still at home, the arrogant sod! She'd show him exactly what she thought of him if he continued to annoy her.

Without warning the study door opened behind her. Reacting instinctively, Athena snatched up the letter opener and whirled, the gleaming handle clenched tightly in her fist. "I wasn't making idle threats, sir!" she snapped. "Get out!"

"I've yet to set foot in the door, mistress. Surely you'd not run me through for that?"

Athena lowered her hand at the sound of the deep voice that addressed her. She bit back a gasp as she found herself looking into a pair of eyes as gray as slate, the surprise within them tempered by amusement. "My poor mother wept the day I sailed for the colonies, convinced I'd be scalped by a savage redskin. What do you think she'll say, mistress, if she learns I lost my life, and my boyish curls, to a fierce female wielding a letter opener?"

Athena did not respond to his insolent remark. Her disbelieving gaze took in the scarlet tunic with its black lapels and the span of the shoulders it encased. White military dress breeches and gold piping completed the outfit, but it wasn't the impressive uniform that took her breath away. It was his face, which Athena had seen only once in her life on a warm, moonlit night, yet had never forgotten.

His regulation wig emphasized his wide, noble forehead, while his unnerving eyes gazed back at her steadily from beneath dark brows, one of them arched in a manner that gave him a perpetually mocking expression. His features were sharply defined, almost hawkish in appearance, and Athena didn't care at all for the sardonic twist to his finely chiseled lips or the arrogant way he carried his long, muscular body.

She swallowed hard and cursed her ill fortune. What would he do now that he'd recognized her? Reveal her folly to the entire assembly? Oh, how Katrine would seize upon such a merry tale! She could have groaned aloud, so vexed was she that fate had been cruel enough to bring her face to face with the one man who had caught her trying to sneak into Albany's fort.

He had recognized her, hadn't he? She bit her lip and bravely raised her chin, refusing to turn away from the inevitable. She could not know that Major Lochiel Blackmoor had forgotten about the young girl he had caught that night on the parade grounds and was thinking instead of the wild, golden vision that had fled before his eyes on horseback several mornings ago.

Though he had gotten only a brief glimpse of silken hair the color of sun-ripened wheat, he sensed instinctively that this defiant young woman was the same one he had seen. Lochiel could not credit the fact that she could be so beautiful. Never had he been confronted by such a wild, alluring creature whose dark blue eyes seemed to glow with inner fire as she boldly returned his gaze. He was aware of a haughty, straight little nose and a square jaw that gave her oval face immense character and a curiously piquant expression. Her cleavage and narrow waist, artfully revealed by the curve of the skirts at her hips, were a delight to any gentleman's roving eye. But Lochiel found himself studying instead the glinting blade she held in one small fist, for the determined look on the young lady's face made it obvious that she was prepared to use it.

A wicked light entered the silver eyes. "I've been told colonials are an impetuous lot, and I'm inclined to agree after sharing barracks with Provincial soldiers, but I hadn't thought the same held true for colonial ladies."

The deep voice with its faint trace of northern Scotland was tinged with amusement, and Athena scowled, aware that he was making fun of her. Did he intend to toy with her before revealing that he knew who she was? Well, she was in no mood to indulge him.

" 'Tis the sorry state of military affairs in our colonies that cause us to turn to ourselves for protection, sir," Athena informed him coolly.

The dark brows rose in surprise. "Are you intimating that you were defending yourself against the attentions of one of the officers present this evening?" He had suddenly remembered the words this wild-eyed vixen had flung at him when he'd first stepped inside the study looking for General Amherst. If this were the case, 'twould be his duty to intervene, though he didn't exactly relish the fact.

Athena was taken aback by the sudden change in him. Where moments ago she had been defending herself against his gentle mockery, she now found herself facing a stern inquisitor whose manner almost frightened her. "No," she admitted at last, " 'twas not an officer."

She didn't seem prepared to say anything more, and Lochiel permitted his harsh expression to soften. He wasn't surprised that some unknown guest had tried to take liberties with her. In fact, he found it rather odd that she had tried to resist his attentions at all. There was a wanton sparkle in her eyes that belied the innocent flush that had crept to her cheeks, and he could well imagine that she enjoyed playing the role of seductress.

"Perhaps I should escort you back to the withdrawing room," he suggested, thinking it might be wiser to return her to her parents before her gentleman admirer had second thoughts and came back for her. Egon de Vries did not seem the sort of man who would appreciate a murder in his study, especially not a brutal one involving a brass letter opener.

"I imagine you'd enjoy exposing me before the entire assembly, wouldn't you?" Athena demanded fiercely. Her eyes were so dark with fury that he could see the indigo rims of her irises. Thick black lashes fringed their tilted corners and were dusted, Lochiel noticed for the first time, with gold. "If you have anything to say to me concerning my behavior," she added hotly, "I suggest you do so here in private!"

"I have no intention of gossiping over your personal habits with anyone," he told her coldly. "If you choose to compromise your honor in Egon de Vries's study, then I consider that your own affair."

His words brought a cry of outrage from Athena, who flew at him, aching to slap that arrogant face of his. Lochiel, thinking she intended to make use of the letter opener after all, lunged forward to intercept her. Iron fingers wrapped themselves about her wrist, squeezing relentlessly until the weapon clattered to the floor. Satisfied that he had subdued her, Lochiel let her go, but Athena was not about to allow such an insult to go unavenged. Her hand lashed out, balled in a small but potent fist, which caught the unsuspecting Lochiel square in the belly. He emitted a startled grunt while Athena gasped in pain, her throbbing hand having come in contact with a wall of solid muscle.

Lochiel straightened with a groan, thinking to himself that colonial women must be thoroughly mad. First there had been that brazen prostitute in Albany whose well-aimed kick had left an impressive purple bruise on his leg, and now he was forced to contend with this silk-clad barbarian who must have learned the rudiments of boxing from a professional!

He lifted his head to look at her and was surprised to find her glaring back at him as though daring him to ask for more. There was no sign of contrition on her beautiful face, only mutinous determination as she raised her square jaw and regarded him defiantly. Lochiel's temper snapped. In two long strides he had crossed the distance between them and had her by the shoulders. He shook her cruelly, his hostility increasing when he couldn't help noticing how soft her bare skin felt beneath his hands.

"I wager you needs be taught some manners, mistress," he said, shaking her until her carefully arranged curls began to work themselves loose. One long, silken strand fell to her shoulder, wrapping itself about his wrist. "I've half a mind to turn you over my knee here and now," Lochiel continued harshly, ignoring its seductive softness. "Though I believe I'll leave the pleasure to your father or husband, if you have one. The unfortunate fellow," he added, giving her another shake for good measure. "I only pray he isn't the sort to humor your roving ways."

Athena was trying frantically to push him away. He was mad, she decided, striking him fruitlessly, his wide, scarlet-covered chest totally unyielding. She was panting, her cheeks flushed with exertion, but she refused to beg for any quarter. She would show him what happened to people who dared speak to her like that! She would—

"Goodness gracious, Athena! What's going on here?"

The startled cry came from the study door and was uttered by a thoroughly alarmed Katrine, who, having noticed Stephen Kensington's absence from the drawing room, had been making a discreet search for him.

In the first, disbelieving moment when she had opened the study door, she thought it was Stephen who was holding Athena in his arms, but she saw now that the broad back turned toward her was covered with the brilliant scarlet of a military tunic. Katrine breathed a sigh of relief while a calculating look stole across her thin face. It was quite obvious that both had agreed to a clandestine meeting here in her father's study. Why else would Athena's cheeks be so rosy, her eyes glittering, if not from the heat aroused by passionate kisses? Katrine cast an admiring glance at the strong, sun-browned hands that were gripping Athena's white shoulders. Why, he'd even left marks on her flesh, she thought with a delicious shiver.

At the sound of Katrine's voice Athena froze in dismay while Lochiel obligingly released her. Calmly he turned around, prepared to make a comment that would spare her embarrassment, although he was thinking to himself that it would serve the little witch right if she was forced to explain herself alone. A small cry of pain from Athena and a tug on his sleeve prevented him from saying a word. Turning back to her, he saw that several strands of her hair had become entangled in his brass buttons.

"You needn't hurry," she hissed at him as he began to work them free. "Katrine's gone, doubtless to spread the tale throughout the assembly!"

"Believe me, I'm in no hurry at all," Lochiel assured her casually. "If I'm tugging a wee bit 'tis only because you deserve no better treatment."

She tried to jerk away at his mocking words, only to pull her tangled curls painfully. She heard a deep, amused chuckle rumble in his chest, and she clenched her teeth, willing herself to remain still. Inwardly she was trembling with frustration. Ooh, how she'd love to claw Katrine's whey face to shreds, and as for this . . . this insolent wretch, she'd love to bash his head in with the heavy glass paperweight sitting so invitingly on Master de Vries's desk!

It was fortunate that Lochiel could not see the murderous look on Athena's lovely face, for it would only have served to reignite his own volatile temper. Instead he was thinking to himself how dull his polished brass buttons appeared in contrast to the shimmering gold strands that were wrapped about his sleeve. Freeing them at last, he allowed them to play through his fingers, admiring their satin softness.

Athena, thinking he was still trying to untangle her, was standing quietly before him, her head obediently bowed. Becoming aware of his silence at last, she looked up, only to find him staring thoughtfully down at her, his sharply chiseled features only inches from hers. A long golden curl was captured between his big thumb and index finger, and Athena snatched it free, blushing furiously at the unnerving nearness of those silvery eyes.

"Wait just a moment, mistress!" Lochiel commanded as she pushed past him without a word, her skirts brushing against his booted legs.

Athena turned in the doorway, her disdainful gaze upon him. Lochiel had to admit that he'd never been confronted by such a blazing beauty, and felt a moment of regret at having been instrumental in what, for her, would doubtless prove an unpleasant return to the drawing room.

"Surely you don't intend to leave your hair in such disarray?"

Athena's lips tightened, well aware that she mustn't rejoin the other guests looking for all the world as if she had just indulged in wanton lovemaking. Ignoring him, she deftly twisted her hair into a thick golden rope and pinned it carefully to her head. Lochiel watched her solemnly, refusing to admit to himself that there was something seductive about this intimate scene. His brows came together when Athena adjusted the rumpled bodice of her gown, and he saw the angry welts his fingers had left on her bare shoulders.

"Perhaps it isn't too late to explain to Miss de Vries what really happened," he said, feeling a twinge of uncustomary regret and deciding the only proper thing to do was to prevent uncharitable gossip about this golden beauty.

Athena's winged brows rose in mock astonishment. "Faith, do you profess to gentlemanly impulses, sir? I'd not have thought they governed your conscience."

She was gone before he could reply, a vision of silver and gold, her petticoats rustling softly and her small head held high. Lochiel, doubting she truly had the courage to return to the drawing room alone, was astonished to find her whirling across the dance floor in the arms of a smiling young officer. He cast a narrowed glance at Katrine de Vries, who was dancing with Lord Loudon, but when their gazes chanced to meet, he saw nothing save studied indifference in hers.

Athena had also been surprised by the fact that no knowing stares or whispers accompanied her return to the drawing room. She hadn't really wanted to go back, but she was determined not to let Katrine or the despicable Highlander ruin her evening. Yet as the dance ended and another young swain hurried forward to beg for her hand, Athena had to admit to herself that it truly seemed as if Katrine hadn't said a word to anyone. She cast a puzzled glance at the other girl as she swept past on Lord Loudon's arm while the music swelled in a popular reel. Could it be possible that Katrine had given up her vicious ways?

In truth Katrine hadn't. She had deliberately kept her discovery to herself despite the fact that she was bursting to tell someone. Before making Athena Courtland's shocking behavior public, she planned to make certain first that the tale wouldn't prove more valuable if saved for a more opportune moment. A catlike smile of contentment passed across her lips. Such information was far too significant to waste as mere gossip and Katrine firmly suspected that the chance would eventually come for her to put it to good use. Until then Athena Courtland could just worry herself into a state of utter despair.

Yet Athena did not. In fact, she found that she was enjoying herself immensely once it became obvious that Katrine wasn't going to say a word and that Major Lochiel Blackmoor wasn't going to reveal to everyone the folly of her attempted break-in at Albany fort. She danced with countless officers whose compliments would have turned any young girl's head silly enough to take them seriously, and she was able to ask enough discreet questions to learn all she needed to know concerning the whereabouts of her brothers' regiments.

She even managed to hold General Amherst's interest long enough to be guided through two subsequent dances, and though he proved vexingly uninformative, she was able to glean enough information about his plans to form the opinion that he was a capable military strategist.

At the conclusion of the dance General Amherst led her back to her aunt, who was fanning herself vigorously beneath the tall glass windows. Passing Katrine de Vries, who was just heading out onto the floor on Stephen Kensington's arm, Athena responded to the younger girl's envious glower with a guileless smile. She was secretly amused that Katrine believed her guilty of having had an assignation with Major Lochiel Blackmoor of His Majesty's Seventh Highland Company.

Oh, yes, Athena knew exactly who he was by now. His dark good looks and broad-shouldered frame had quickly made him the object of lively feminine interest. Athena had already listened to numerous sighing discourses concerning his masculine attributes, and his name had come up several times while discussing the war with her dancing partners. She herself was not particularly impressed with Major Blackmoor. Oh, she would go so far as to concede that he was somewhat good-looking, if one cared for the arrogant, eagle-featured sort. Yet she had found him to be ill-mannered, foul-tempered, and not at all pleasant. She wasn't the least bit inclined to feel charitable toward him, regardless of the fact that he had chosen not to expose her before everyone present that evening.

Athena heartily suspected that he was saving such information for a more opportune time, and she chafed beneath the feeling of unease this knowledge gave her. She didn't trust Lochiel Blackmoor in the least, and she hated the thought that he was privy to a secret about her she never wished to have disclosed. She should have confronted him with it in the study instead of allowing herself to become rattled by his presence. Damn him! What right did he have to play games with her? She was only glad that he hadn't asked her to dance, for there was no telling what she might have said to him!

"What a grand party it was," Aunt Amelia said with a sigh at the conclusion of the evening as Wills closed the carriage door behind them and the vehicle rumbled off into the night. "I'm very proud of you, Athena. I received countless compliments concerning your looks and behavior." Her fan fluttered excitedly in her thin hands. "Why, even Lord Loudon took time out to inform me how charming he found you."

"How nice of him," Athena murmured. Her eyes were closed as she rested her head against the leather cushions. She didn't care in the least what the earl had thought of her.

"Your mother would have been proud of you tonight," Aunt Amelia added, knowing she herself was largely to thank for her niece's success. After all, one had to consider the great deal of work she had put into correcting Athena's negligent upbringing. Having watched Athena closely all evening, Amelia was delighted that she'd been unable to find a single fault with her. Only one incident marred her pleased perception of the ball, and that had been an exchange between Katrine de Vries and Stephen Kensington that had taken place on the dance floor shortly before the festivities ended.

Actually, Amelia might never have noticed it if she hadn't been watching the young couple so closely. She had wanted to make certain that Stephen Kensington wasn't showing signs of interest in Athena's archrival, and she had seen Katrine stand on tiptoe and whisper something in Stephen's ear that had brought a startled look to the young man's face. Then both of them had turned to look at Athena, who had been whirling past in the arms of a senior officer. There had been a triumphant gleam in Katrine's eyes and a thoughtful frown on Stephen's lips that had convinced Amelia that the spiteful girl had whispered in his ear some foul and untrue piece of gossip about Athena.

She sighed and stirred restlessly on the seat. Athena would have to pay a great deal more attention to Stephen Kensington if she intended to win him. Opening her mouth to say as much, she thought better of it. 'Twas late and both of them were tired, and doubtless Athena's head was stuffed with thoughts of the upcoming race that Egon de Vries had announced would be held the day after tomorrow.

Amelia abhorred the fact that her niece could interest herself in such a dangerous sport. She had tried to prevent her from attending the matches that took place monthly at the various estates in the area, but Athena was so adamant in her refusal to obey that Amelia had quickly given up. To make matters worse, Athena insisted on taking Tykie Downs with her every time she went, and Amelia hated the thought of her niece appearing in public with that hulking Scottish fellow. She suppressed a nervous shudder. The best she could hope for was that Stephen Kensington would marry Athena quickly and persuade her to give up the races. Even better was the possibility that Stephen would force her to get rid of Tykie Downs once and for all. With this optimistic thought in mind, Amelia closed her fan with a snap and began to dream of the downy bed that awaited her at home.

Four

It was the beginning of a crisp autumn day, the sort that never failed to make Athena's wild blood sing. October had arrived in breathtaking splendor, and the maples dotting Courtland Grace's sweeping lawn were crowned in scarlet. As Athena crossed the dew-touched grass, she heard the stirring cry of geese winging south through the deep blue sky. Her cheeks were pink with cold and her eyes sparkled as she wrapped her forest-green velvet cloak tightly about her and hurried into the stableyard. Ballycor, finding the weather just as stimulating, was prancing nervously at the end of his lead and refused to be quieted by Tykie's experienced hand.

"If he ain't ready tae run, I'll retire frae racin', Miss Athena," the big Scotsman announced.

Athena smiled as one of the stablehands darted out of reach of the skittish stallion's flashing hooves. It did appear that Ballycor was more than eager to be put through his paces. "We can thank the cold for that. 'Tis fortunate the weather turned."

"Aye, miss." Tykie's coal-black eyes appraised her, taking in the forest-green cape and the yellow skirts trimmed with black ribbons visible beneath it. "Will ye be ridin' him tae town yourself?"

Athena's young face fell and a pout pulled at the corners of her mouth. "I can't. Aunt Amelia found out about the last time and has expressly forbidden me to do so again."

"We'll take him behind the trap," Tykie said heartily, seeing how disappointed she was. If Master Courtland were still alive and none of those silly rules of Mistress Bower's were hanging over Miss Athena's head, why, the wee lass would be permitted to ride her horse in the stakes herself instead of settling for the ride to the track. Sure, 'twould cause a furor among West York's more avid gossips, but then tongues were always waggin' about Miss Athena. As it was, young Evan Whistler rode Ballycor in the races while Miss Athena perched on the rails by the finishing line with a wistful look on her bonnie face.

"Get the tack together, lad," Tykie growled to his stablehand, feeling a familiar softening in his heart. He'd never be able to understand how Athena Courtland managed to worm her way into his affections, when in truth she was such a difficult brat. He shouldn't be feeling sorry for her. He should be wishing Master Fletcher were home so that someone whose authority Miss Athena respected was looking after her properly.

A sizable crowd had gathered at the track by the time Athena and Tykie arrived, Ballycor trotting restlessly behind their high-wheeled trap. This was the second day of the annual autumn fair, and the streets were filled with horses, oxen, and sheep being offered for sale. Stalls had been set up to display numerous wares, and a medicine hawker's dramatic presentation had attracted quite an audience to his colorful wagon. The smell of molasses, sweetmeats, and smoked sausages mingled in the air with the fragrant scent of the hay spread on the ground for the livestock to consume.

The fairgrounds and race course had been set up on the wide expanse of grass known as the village common. Beyond them lay the meeting house with its pillories and stocks serving as dire reminders to West York's citizens that the town would tolerate no abuse of the law. Whitewashed houses lined the pleasant streets, the oaks and maples flanking them crowned in blazing autumnal colors.

Nestled amid the foothills in an emerald valley, West York was a picturesque town, and Athena dearly loved it. Yet today her mind was not on the splendor of the scenery or the lure of the fair. She was thinking about the race, as was everyone else who had gathered, not to watch the cudgeling bouts and greased pig chases that would take place later, but to see Athena Courtland's white stallion take on Egon de Vries's mysterious colt, Hyperion. Gaming was a consuming passion with colonial folk, and horse racing was by far the most popular choice of diversions. Normally, matches such as this one were private, attended by invitation only, yet General Amherst had asked if his enlisted men might be permitted to watch, and after some debate, Egon de Vries had agreed to open the meet to the public.

Athena didn't care at all where Ballycor was expected to run. She was confident that her stallion would win, and her eyes were shining with excitement as she stepped down from the trap on Tykie's arm. Ballycor was instantly surrounded by men eager to judge his condition, and approving murmurs were exchanged as the skittish animal tossed his head and snorted, disliking to have strangers press so close.

"Here, gie the lad some room," Tykie commanded, using his imposing bulk to disperse the curious, one big hand wrapped firmly about the stallion's halter.

Athena followed him with her head held high, oblivious of the admiring glances turned her way. Her sweeping green cape, trimmed with dark beaver, fluttered in the cool wind and revealed her slim, curving hips. A small hat with seed pearl netting covered her glossy curls, while the black plume that adorned it curled jauntily against one cheek. It was obvious that many of the men who had hurried forward eagerly when the carriage had arrived had done so to catch a glimpse of this golden-haired vision and not the impressive white stallion that pranced at her side.

While Tykie and Evan led Ballycor away to be saddled, Athena approached the whitewashed stand where the men who served as the race officials had gathered. Tipping their hats politely, the spectators milling nearby made room for her, and Athena lifted her heavy skirts to climb the short flight of steps leading into the small, covered enclosure.

An insistent tug on her hem brought her to an abrupt halt. Turning her head, Athena saw that a careless boot had planted itself directly upon her petticoat, preventing her from moving without ripping it. Allowing her gaze to travel up the length of polished black leather past lean, muscled thighs, she opened her mouth to deliver a cutting remark to the negligent individual responsible. The words died on her lips as she found herself staring into the sharply chiseled features of Major Lochiel Blackmoor. Sunlight reflected on his thick black hair, making him look younger than he had two nights before in a wig and regulation tunic—and more disturbingly handsome than Athena cared to acknowledge. Her small foot began to tap impatiently on the wooden step until Lochiel, dismissing the man with whom he had been conversing, chanced to look up and see her staring down at him.

His first impression was of an incredibly lovely face, framed in luxuriant fur, and a black plumed hat tilted pertly on top of a softly gleaming mass of rich golden curls. Eyes as blue as the autumn sky were staring boldly into his, the winged brows above them haughtily raised.

"Miss Courtland," Lochiel said, inclining his head politely as he recognized her. Who else but the beautiful Athena Courtland could manage such a scornful look merely by raising her straight little nose in the air? "I trust you've recovered from the late hours kept at Master de Vries's soirée?"

Athena was in no mood to respond to his polite attempt at conversation, nor did she wish to be reminded of their embarrassing encounter in the study at Bountiful two nights ago. As far as she was concerned it had never happened, and just because Major Blackmoor intended to keep her foray into Albany fort a secret didn't mean she owed him anything.

"Sir," she said frostily, "you are standing on my gown."

A wicked grin crossed the sun-bronzed face, and Lochiel obligingly removed his boot from the frilly bit of petticoat trapped beneath it. "My apologies, mistress. 'Twould seem I am destined to inflict some form of damage upon your person whenever we chance to meet."

But Athena had already turned away, and Lochiel received nothing more than a brief glimpse of her impudently swaying backside before she was surrounded by the waiting gentlemen. He could see the tip of the black plume bobbing among their powdered heads and, hearing her soft, musical laugh, knew that she was doubtless charming them with little more than a saucy glance from her gold-fringed eyes. Athena Courtland was an accomplished seductress, Lochiel Blackmoor thought to himself, easing his way back into the gaily conversing throng, and he was greatly relieved that her magic had no effect upon him whatsoever.

"Is your stallion fit this morning, Miss Courtland?" the Earl of Loudon asked jovially. He had put quite a bit of money on Egon de Vries's colt, but he was not above wishing success to the blue-eyed beauty smiling up at him so beguilingly.

Athena's smile widened. "Ballycor is always fit, your lordship. Today is no exception." She was admiring the enormous silver punch bowl on the table behind him as she spoke, thinking to herself how nice it would look amid Ballycor's other trophies in the parlor back home.

"Here you are, Athena! Isn't the weather grand today? Oh, excuse me," Katrine exclaimed, blushing prettily as she became aware of the number of handsome, uniformed men gathered around. "I didn't mean to interrupt," she added with demurely lowered eyes, though Athena was quite certain she had bowled people over in her haste to reach the stand. Lifting her chin in order to provide everyone with a better view of her new hat, she batted her eyelashes coyly.

"Is your father here, too?" Athena asked crisply, impatient with Katrine's flirtatious behavior.

"Mama and I didn't wait for him. He wanted to bring Hyperion over himself. I expect he'll be along shortly." Katrine was paying her words little mind. It was taking most of her concentration to keep the enormous plumes adorning her hat from falling into her eyes. Perhaps Mama had been right after all, she thought to herself. 'Twas a bit too grand for a gathering like this. She only hoped the wind wouldn't pull the feathers out.

Excusing herself from Katrine and her admirers, Athena joined Tykie, who was leaning casually against the trunk of an oak tree watching Evan warm up Ballycor in the nearby field. His gold earring flashed in the sun as he turned to give her a wide grin.

"Hae ye seen the de Vries colt, lass? Yonder he stands."

Amid a crowd of curious onlookers Athena could see the gleaming chestnut hindquarters of a nervously prancing horse. Her eyes widened as the animal unexpectedly balked, whirling and snorting while his groom held grimly onto the lead shank.

"He's beautiful," she murmured admiringly.

"Feisty, too," Tykie added. "Master de Vries will hae his hands full for a year or twa before the beastie settles doon."

"Ballycor was the same way," Athena remembered with a smile. "Do you think he's fast?"

Tykie nodded. "Bred for speed an' little else. I'm na wonderin' why de Vries kept him a secret."

Athena's slim jaw jutted. "I still think Ballycor can beat him."

Tykie's hand settled reassuringly on her shoulder. "I've some gold on him says the same, miss."

The race was to be run over a mile-and-a-quarter course, the winner taking two out of three scheduled heats. While the horses and their youthful jockeys were led to the starting line, the spectators eagerly dispersed along the length of the track, pressing forward to get a good view. Athena watched with bated breath as General Amherst lifted the pistol that would signal the start of the first heat. Her eyes were on Ballycor and fourteen-year-old Evan Whistler, who looked small and insignificant in the saddle. Yet Evan was a gifted rider and one of the few people Ballycor would tolerate on his back.

The pistol cracked and both horses thundered off across the turf. The English colt, distracted by the roar that rose from the crowd, lost valuable ground as he hesitated, while Ballycor, familiar with what was expected of him, surged ahead. A gleaming white blur as he streaked past the scarlet and blue uniforms of the watching soldiers, the big stallion managed to win by a full three lengths.

"I don't know why I put my money on that English beast," Athena heard a disgusted field worker complain behind her.

"You should've known better," his companion agreed smugly. "That colt might be pretty to look at, but he sure as hell can't run."

Athena knew better than to pass judgment on the colt so quickly. Hyperion would be more accustomed to the noise and crowds by the second heat and would prove harder to beat. She spent the time until then chatting with acquaintances and exchanging greetings with Egon de Vries. She was relieved that Katrine chose to stay in the stand with her mother, where she remained surrounded by no fewer than half a dozen interested males. One of them was Stephen Kensington, Athena noticed, and she turned away quickly lest he should see her. She was glad that he hadn't taken the time to seek her out and that Major Lochiel Blackmoor seemed to have disappeared as well after their unpleasant encounter earlier.

When Hyperion was led to the starting line a second time he was far more collected, and Athena's heart began a nervous beat. She knew enough about horses to realize that Ballycor was pitted against a formidable rival. Joining Tykie at the finish line, she held her breath as she heard the pistol crack. Craning her neck to see what was happening, she uttered a cry of dismay when the horses charged into view and she saw Ballycor trailing by half a length. Hyperion was running superbly, his strides long and sure, easily passing the finish just ahead of the big white stallion. The wild gesticulations of the crowd seemed to throw him into a blind panic, however, for he suddenly shied to the right and barreled directly into Ballycor, causing the unsuspecting Evan to be thrown.

With a cry of alarm, Athena pushed her way past the gathered spectators, while Tykie, who had reached Evan first, bent anxiously over the lad's inert form. Ballycor was cropping grass a short distance away, yet at the sight of his mistress he came trotting toward her, and Athena slid her arm about his glossy neck, relieved that he wasn't injured.

"Oh, Evan, are you all right?" she asked anxiously as Tykie lifted the boy to his feet. Evan gave her a shaky grin but winced painfully when Tykie made a careful examination of his left arm.

" 'Tisn't broken," Tykie announced with relief, "but I canna let you ride i' the last heat, lad."

Evan's expression was filled with disbelief. "What about the race?"

Tykie shook his head. "I'm sorry, lad."

" 'Tisn't important, Evan," Athena said soothingly. "What matters is that you weren't badly injured."

Evan blinked as he fought back threatening tears. "My arm don't hurt that bad, Miss Athena. I can still beat the colt, I know I can."

"Not wi' your wrist already swellin'," Tykie said gently. "We'll hae Dr. Nolan take a look at it."

"But what about the last heat?" Evan persisted. He gave Athena a pleading glance. "You aren't going to let Hyperion win by forfeit, are you, miss?"

"There isn't much we can do about it," Athena pointed out, though she hated to admit defeat as much as Evan did.

"You could ride him yourself, miss," Evan said eagerly, forgetting his pain as his hopes rose anew. "Ballycor knows you better than he does me, and Tykie says you ride better than most. Why don't you run the last heat?"

"I couldn't possibly," Athena said promptly. "Tykie, 'tis out of the question," she added, seeing the calculating gleam that entered the Scotsman's black eyes. "My aunt would never approve, and moreover, I can't ride a race in skirts."

"The race will be over afore your aunt ever hears o't," Tykie pointed out with a grin, "an' as for breeks, I'm certain they can be borrowed frae someone i' town."

Athena hardened herself against his words and the pleading look on young Evan's face. "I'm sorry," she said firmly. " 'Tisn't possible. We'll simply have to extend our regrets to Master de Vries and withdraw from the competition."

In the stands, meanwhile, a curious Katrine had broken off her flirtatious conversation with Stephen Kensington and Major Lochiel Blackmoor. "What could be going on at the finish line?" she wondered, becoming aware of the unruly crowd. "Hyperion won the last heat, didn't he?"

"The results are official," Stephen assured her. "The second heat belongs to your father's entry."

Katrine scowled darkly. " 'Twouldn't surprise me if Athena Courtland is at the bottom of whatever disturbance is going on out there. I warrant she's challenged the results. You know what a bad loser she can be."

Lochiel, having grown quite bored with Katrine's empty-headed chatter, found this a good time to make his excuses. He was sorry now that he had allowed her to detain him on the pretext of introducing him to a few of her friends. One of them had been a fellow by the name of Kensington whose unusually hostile scrutiny had put Lochiel immediately on the defense. He had no idea what Kensington wanted from him, nor did he care, and he dismissed both the arrogant dandy and his scatterbrained companion from his thoughts as he headed toward the track.

Ignoring the blushing smiles of the young girls standing near the finish line, the tall Highlander swept his narrowed gaze across the crowded field. Egon de Vries, he saw, was talking earnestly with his jockey while making a careful inspection of his colt's legs. Farther downfield stood the magnificent white stallion belonging to Athena Courtland, his bridle being held by a man with arms as thick as young oaks. Long dark hair curled about his corded neck, and when he turned his head, Lochiel could see a gold earring glittering in one ear. He was a giant of a man, and it was obvious from the manner in which he was spoken to that he was extremely well respected by the people of West York. Lochiel's interest was aroused despite himself. Was this one of Miss Courtland's grooms? If so, she certainly conspired with curious individuals.

Just then a murmur arose from the crowd, attracting Lochiel's attention to the far end of the track where Ballycor's jockey was being led onto the field. A small contingent of admirers was acting as escort while spectators thronged forward to thump the lad on the back and wish him luck. Lochiel searched the crowd for a sign of Athena, thinking it odd that she wasn't among the well-wishers, yet he could find no smartly plumed little hat or green velvet cape in evidence anywhere.

Approving shouts from the crowd brought Lochiel's attention back to Ballycor's jockey, who was being tossed bodily into the saddle by the earringed giant. Cheers and gay laughter followed both horses to the starting line, and Lochiel watched with interest as they passed him, his arms folded impassively before his broad chest. Ballycor's young rider was sitting tall in the saddle, his booted feet swinging idly in the stirrups. Feeling Lochiel's pensive eyes upon him, he turned his head, and his gaze chanced to meet the tall Highlander's. A flush of recognition crept to the hollow cheeks, and he looked hastily away, but not before Lochiel had recognized him.

"Blood and fury!" Lochiel cursed softly to himself. Though he had suspected from the first that she was a rather fey creature, he would never have credited Athena Courtland with the courage—or the foolishness—to don masculine attire and compete astride in a horse race!

But it wasn't her brazen behavior that shocked Lochiel Blackmoor so or brought a dangerous gleam to his silver eyes. It was the way she had looked, her blue eyes wide, her hair hastily tucked beneath a hat—just as on that moonlit night in Albany. Although Lochiel would never have made the connection between the rebellious prostitute he had apprehended on the fort parade grounds with the glittering beauty of Athena Courtland, he did recognize this impudent lad clad in breeches and boots. There was no shred of doubt in his mind that they were one and the same.

Lochiel's handsome face darkened as he watched Athena guide her big stallion to the post. It didn't surprise him that she had found the nerve to steal into the fort, for her reasons for doing so were obvious to him now that he knew a bit more about her. Athena Courtland had a lover among the soldiers who had been quartered in Albany that night—probably one of the Provincials who had shared the barracks with his own Seventh Highlanders. If he remembered correctly, that same troop of Provincials was scheduled to march through West York within the next day or two.

His thoughtful gaze came to rest on the young face visible beneath the brim of the soft felt hat. Athena had the reins wrapped tightly about her slim fingers, and she was leaning low over Ballycor's neck, awaiting the starter's signal. He wondered if she would try to meet her lover again despite the fact that General Amherst intended to maintain tight security by forbidding interaction between soldiers and civilians. Of course, Lochiel wouldn't be at all surprised if Athena simply ignored such orders.

His lips tightened grimly, deriving no enjoyment at having become recipient of the irascible young beauty's most carefully kept secret. Small wonder she had been so furious with him at the de Vrieses's ball. She had known exactly who he was. How it must have puzzled her that he hadn't chosen to expose her! Lochiel's eyes narrowed. Though he hadn't been aware of the truth at the time, he wondered what to do with the information now that it had fallen so innocently into his hands.

The sharp report of the starting gun and the wild roar of the crowd brought his thoughts back to the present. Turning his head, he saw the white stallion and the chestnut colt explode from a standstill amid clods of flying turf. Athena's slim figure passed by him in a blur, and Lochiel could see at once that she was by far the better of the two riders. She was leaning low in the saddle, knees well forward, her slim body pumping in rhythm with the stallion's. A moment later he saw her sweep across the finish line well ahead of the colt, her golden hair spilling untidily down her back.

The spectators shouted their approval and a tide of them surged toward the finish line to congratulate her. Lochiel stood watching as Athena pulled the cap from her head, her gilded curls tumbling free as she leaned down to embrace the lathering stallion's neck. The enormous fellow with the gold earring had waded to her side, scattering people in his wake, his lusty grin reminding Lochiel of a pirate who had just captured a galleon loaded with precious plate. An enigmatic smile curved Major Blackmoor's lips. He had not bargained for the interesting developments of General Jeffrey Amherst's latest campaign.

Five

Stephen Kensington swept off his hat and tossed it rudely at the manservant who had appeared from the shadows of the glittering foyer. The great riding coat with its gold braid and brass buttons followed, hitting the unfortunate fellow in the face. Stephen offered no apology. In fact, he hadn't even noticed, and his handsome face was set in a cold mask of rage as he slammed the door of his father's study behind him. God be thanked that his parents and sisters were still out. He was in no mood to listen to his sisters' squealing descriptions of the things they had seen at the fair or to be offered the sticky remnants of the sweets they had saved for him. He wanted to be alone to think and was not about to tolerate any interruption.

"Would you care for supper, sir?" came the polite inquiry of another manservant from the doorway, totally disregarding Stephen's wish for privacy.

"No," was his curt reply. "I wish to remain undisturbed."

The manservant wordlessly inclined his head. His expression betrayed none of the dislike he felt for the Kensingtons' only son, whose year-long absence from home had been heartily welcomed by everyone on the staff.

Alone in the study, Stephen splashed rum into a glass and settled himself into his father's plush leather chair. Crossing his booted legs before him, he stared at the rows of books lining the shelves, his scowl deepening. He was in a foul mood, and thinking of the guineas he had lost wagering on Egon de Vries's useless colt didn't improve his frame of mind any. What annoyed him most was his brief encounter with Major Lochiel Blackmoor at the race earlier, and the more Stephen thought of the officer who was Athena Courtland's lover, the angrier he became.

"Cursed wench!" he muttered, pouring himself more rum. How dare she rebuff him in favor of a common soldier? Had she been dazzled by his uniform or the stories about him? Surely she hadn't been stupid enough to believe them! Stephen had made it a point to learn everything he could about Major Lochiel Blackmoor after Katrine had whispered her shocking disclosure to him the other night. He had learned about the good major's bravery on the battlefields of Oswego and Fort William Henry. He had heard naught but praise for a highly respected leader and an able soldier who had distinguished himself even as a young captain in the conflict over the Austrian succession ten years ago.

Stephen had considered the tales utter nonsense and dismissed with a laugh the warning that Lochiel Blackmoor was not a man to be crossed. 'Twas true he was extremely well built and seemed a callous enough fellow, yet he was a Scotsman, a Highlander at that, and 'twas common knowledge that they were a heathen folk. It wasn't possible that Athena Courtland preferred a barbaric foreigner over himself!

Stephen's hand tightened about his glass. In his mind's eye he could see Athena as she had appeared at the race track dressed in tight-fitting leather breeches, her small derrière swaying when she walked, her curving hips all but beckoning a man to slide his hands about them. His loins tightened at the thought. By God, he wanted Athena Courtland, burned to possess her, and 'twas a torment to learn that she had willingly given to a lowborn Scotsman what she had blatantly denied him. He could almost picture the smooth perfection of her ivory body as she lay with her thighs spread, begging her lover to take her as his dark head bent over her heavy breasts and his hands roved the hidden curves that Stephen himself ached to plunder.

The chair creaked as he jerked upright. " 'Tis time to put a stop to all of that!" he vowed drunkenly beneath his breath. He would find a way to drive the lovers apart, to leave Athena no recourse than to turn to someone else to quench the womanly fires burning within her.

A vicious gleam entered Stephen's eyes. Athena would pay for having spurned him. She would pay for having given freely to a soldier what should have been saved for him. And the weapon he would use? Athena's own brother, Jeremy Courtland. Idle conversation with General Amherst at the track had revealed that several Provincial regiments were expected to arrive in West York some time after midnight tonight. When Stephen had casually mentioned to the general that Athena's brother would be among them, the general had been delighted. All newly arrived troops would be confined to their barracks, he had told Stephen, yet in view of the fact that Miss Courtland was such a charming creature, he would permit young Jeremy to spend the night at home. 'Twould be a surprise for her, he'd added with a wink, and Stephen had assured him that he would say naught to Athena about it.

A plan began to form in Stephen's mind as he came unsteadily to his feet, one that would depend a great deal on chance, yet ought to reward him richly should it succeed. Not only would he have his revenge on Athena for her faithlessness, but the resulting scandal should leave her wide open to his attentions. His visage darkened as he remembered how she had refused his advances in de Vries's study, while an eager Major Blackmoor waited in the shadows to take his place.

"Soon you'll be mine, my beauty," Stephen whispered to himself, tugging at his breeches to relieve the pressure of his erection. The thought of what he planned to do excited him, and he called loudly for his coat as he pulled open the study door. 'Twould be a pleasing bonus if Major Blackmoor were courtmartialed for this, he reflected with an evil smile.

Although a few lights continued to burn in the manor house of Courtland Grace, the bedrooms in the small west wing were dark, and Stephen scowled to himself as he drew his mount to a halt before the imposing front door. Riding through the crisp night air had cleared the fog from his brain, yet he was still determined to go through with his plan no matter how slim the chances of success. If Athena were already abed, all would come to naught, yet Stephen was not about to let the darkened house discourage him.

A startled Wills answered his bold knock on the door. "I'm afraid Mistress Bower retired some time ago, sir," he said before Stephen could utter a single word.

In truth Amelia was heavily sedated, having swallowed several doses of powder upon hearing from Athena what had transpired at the race track earlier that day. After a dramatic collapse on the sofa, Amelia had revived sufficiently to berate her niece in a voice that had carried clear to the servants' quarters. Tykie would be dismissed first thing in the morning, she vowed, and plans would be made for Ballycor's sale on the auction block. Athena herself would be enrolled immediately in Miss Mason's school in Boston, where she should have been sent long ago. Perhaps 'twasn't too late to save her entirely from ruin!

Athena had grown impatient with all of this at last, and Mercy had been dispatched to fetch her aunt's bottle of medicine. Amelia had accepted it gladly, and her last coherent words had been to the effect that no one, least of all Stephen Kensington, would ever marry Athena now. Peace had descended upon the house with the closing of her bedroom door, and Wills, who was just beginning to enjoy it, found the intrusion of a visitor, particularly Mr. Kensington himself, thoroughly unwelcome.

"I've come to see Miss Courtland, not Mistress Bower," Stephen said coldly, certain that the surly fellow was aching to slam the door in his face. "I've received news concerning her brother Jeremy, and I thought perhaps she might like to hear it now rather than in the morning." His tone had grown apologetic to prove to Wills that he had naught but Athena's interests at heart.

"What's this about Jeremy?" he heard her soft voice inquire worriedly from the darkened stairway.

Wills opened the door wider, looking less hostile of a sudden, and Stephen wasted no time stepping inside. Then Athena was standing before him in a gray kersey gown that, despite its maidenly simplicity, served to enhance the wanton loveliness that was hers alone. Stephen feasted his eyes on the slim hips and the roundness of her firm young breasts revealed by the nipped waist. His senses reeled, for he had never seen her with her hair unbound, the glorious gold spilling across her shoulders and tumbling down her back.

He had forgotten completely his purpose for coming until she laid her hand on his sleeve. Her blue eyes were wide, her breath came softly through parted lips.

"You said you had news of Jeremy. What is it? Is he all right?"

"Pray forgive me for worrying you," he begged her. " 'Tis good news actually, and I was certain you would want to hear it now instead of waiting until morning."

Athena's expectant smile caused his pulses to pound. Never had she looked at him so kindly before. He cautioned himself to be careful not to arouse her suspicions. She was no scatterbrain like Katrine de Vries. In fact, she was unfashionably unafraid to demonstrate her intelligence. 'Twas one thing about her Stephen had always resented.

"Let's go into the study," Athena suggested, taking him firmly by the arm and ignoring Wills's disapproving glance.

Stephen spared little attention to the beautiful interior of Foster Courtland's former domain. His eyes were on Athena, who had closed the door and was turning around to face him, a golden curl brushing enticingly against her shoulder. "Your brother," Stephen informed her when she asked, "is due in West York sometime tonight with his regiment. General Amherst told me himself that no leave will be granted any of them, yet I believe there's a way around that." He paused dramatically, giving her a chance to understand that he intended to help her.

Athena said nothing, her dark eyes resting expectantly on his face, and her expression would have been enough to stir the conscience of any man —but not Stephen Kensington. He found himself barely able to think for want of her. Her nearness and the subtle fragrance of her hair drove him to distraction.

"I can't make any promises," he went on, "but I believe I may be able to get a message to him. My father has opened our house for billeting, and I'm certain Jeremy's regimental commander will be staying there. 'Twould be easy enough to obtain his permission to deliver a letter, provided you would like to send him one."

Athena's eyes were shining like stars, dazzling him with their beauty. "Of course I would! Oh, Stephen, would you really be able to give it to him?"

"I'll do my best," he promised. He watched as she bent over the desk to scratch a hasty message with the quill, oblivious to the fact that she was providing him with a tantalizing view of the shadowed cleavage of her breasts. The gratitude on her small face as she handed him the folded note elated him. No matter what the outcome, he knew he had earned a special place in her heart this night.

"I'll bring you a reply in the morning," he promised, unaware that Athena was already plotting how she might get around Jeremy's enforced house arrest without him. She scarcely noticed when he took his leave, her mind too full of plans. If Jeremy hadn't sent a reply by morning, she'd ride over to the Kensingtons herself, she decided, despite Aunt Amelia's intention to leave right away for Boston. And just in case he managed to sneak away tonight, she'd leave her bedroom window open so that she'd be sure to hear him. Blowing out the lamps, she danced across the floor, unable to contain her happiness.

Drawing his horse to a halt on the road that led to town, Stephen was hard put to hide his own glee. As a precaution, he had ridden out of sight of the imposing white house before unfolding the parchment Athena had given him. Squinting in the faint starlight, he read the words she had written, unable to believe that she had played so well into his hands.

"Dearest," the note read, "come at once for I miss you so! 'Tis lonely here without you! Always, Athena."

Stephen began to chuckle. Kicking his horse to a gallop, he threw back his dark head and gave a full-throated laugh. All he had to do was deliver this yearning note to the person 'twas really intended for and then sit back and wait for Jeremy Courtland to return home from the wars.

Major Lochiel Blackmoor massaged the back of his neck as he dismounted and turned his horse over to the sleepy groom who came out of the stables to meet him.

"Ach, I'll be glad tae turn in," Sergeant-Major Andrew Durning sighed as he limped painfully to Lochiel's side. "These campaigns are beginnin' tae tell on me, lad. 'Twas a time when nightly summons frae the general had me ready tae leap tae attention, but the noo . . ." His words trailed off and he shook his grizzled head. " 'Tis my last war, lad. If the Frenchies dinna lift my scalp, I'll be off for hame an' a princely pension when all o' this be over."

"You'd be bored to distraction in two weeks' time," Lochiel remarked with a smile. Though he complained often about his difficult lot as a soldier, Andrew Durning was devoted to his regiment and asked for little more in life than to die with his boots on. Actually, Lochiel thought to himself, if the impromptu meeting from which he and the sergeant-major had just returned was any indication of the state of affairs, the war might indeed be over soon. The massive assault General Amherst was planning on Quebec just might succeed in seeing Andy home by summer.

"I've whiskey i' me locker," the sergeant-major said with a wink as the two men strode toward their tents. "Will ye be sharin' a dram wi' me?"

Lochiel's white teeth gleamed in the darkness. "Only a minute ago you were telling me how exhausted you were."

"Aye, but Scotch is meant tae help a mon sleep."

"Some other time, Andy, thanks," Lochiel said.

"Ye've a narrow cot tae sleep in," the sergeant-major reminded him shrewdly. "An' 'tis yer ain fault for turnin' doon a room i' the de Vries house. I hear 'tis satin coverlets an' goose down mattresses they be havin'," he added longingly, "not tae mention the bonnie Miss Katrine tae serve ye tea i' the mornin'."

Lochiel uttered a short laugh. If there was one person he didn't care to encounter first thing in the morning, it was Miss Katrine de Vries, whose silly prattle could surely drive a man mad in record time. 'Twas mainly his desire to stay away from her that had prompted him to turn down Mistress de Vries's offer and seek his own tent for the night. Moreover, he had no intention of growing soft sleeping in a bed with a roof over his head.

Bidding the sergeant-major good night, Lochiel headed across the field where Egon de Vries had permitted the collected regiments to erect their camp. Dried oat stalks crunched underfoot as Lochiel made his way to his own tent, where Barrett, his fastidious aide, had left a lamp burning for him. As he pushed the flap aside, Lochiel's handsome countenance darkened when he saw the strange man seated on the footstool in front of his cot.

"Major Blackmoor?" he asked, rising quickly to his feet.

Lochiel inclined his head suspiciously. What the devil did this fellow want?

"I've been waitin' for you to return, sir. I've a message to deliver to you."

A creased piece of parchment was held out to him, but Lochiel made no move to take it. His narrowed gaze took in the round face and work-roughened hands. Though the speech was rough, the dialect was obviously local. "Who sent you here?" he asked quietly.

"Miss Courtland, sir. I'm one o' the field hands at Courtland Grace.

She asked me to deliver this to you right away. I been waitin' for some time, sir."

A flicker of surprise crossed Lochiel's face. What in hell did the uncivilized witch want from him now?

"She said to make sure it came to you personal," the fellow in homespun continued. His voice had taken on a pleading edge, for Lochiel still hadn't made a move to take the parchment from him. In fact, he was beginning to make Asa Brewster a little nervous, what with those pale eyes studying him intently.

"I'd be pleased if you'd take it, sir," he added, hoping he sounded polite enough. Damn the pulin' foreigner, what was he waitin' for? Kensington wouldn't pay him unless the major actually took the thing from him. " 'Tis late and I needs be getting back."

"Miss Courtland expects no reply, then?" Lochiel inquired, taking the missive from him at last.

Asa tried hard to hide his relief. "She didn't say, sir."

"I'd suggest you wait, in any case," Lochiel said coldly, certain that he'd have something to say to Athena Courtland after learning what sort of mischief she was up to.

Asa seated himself with an indifferent shrug on the footstool, his eyes on Lochiel's face as the tall Highlander unfolded the parchment and gave it a cursory glance. He saw the gray eyes narrow to slits and a muscle in the lean cheek twitch.

"Surely this was not intended for me," Lochiel said, and something in his tone sent a shiver down Asa Brewster's spine.

"You be Major Lochiel Blackmoor, right?" he said sullenly. "Miss Courtland said 'twas for you and none other."

He gave a startled yelp as a pair of iron hands grabbed his shirtfront, lifting him bodily off his feet. "By God, I'll cut out your tongue if you're lying," an ominous voice intoned harshly in his ear.

The thought of the money awaiting him bolstered Asa's courage. He was not normally a timid man, and Stephen had chosen him to deliver Athena's letter because he was not the sort to allow himself to become easily rattled. In fact, he was quite willing to suffer the indignity of being manhandled by a hated foreigner simply because gold was more important to him than ruffled pride.

"Why would I lie?" he whined convincingly. "Why would I bring the letter to you if 'twere meant for someone else? I'm only followin' Miss Courtland's orders."

Slowly Lochiel released his grip. Was it true that Athena had intended the note for him? To what purpose? Surely not for the reason so subtly stated! As a joke, perhaps? To make him look the fool after the way he'd treated her both in Albany and at Bountiful? Damn her eyes, 'twas impossible to guess!

"Get out," Lochiel rasped, thrusting Asa away from him. The other man's relief was obvious as he vanished into the darkness. For a moment there was silence in the tent while the lamplight flickered over Lochiel's rigid countenance. Straightening abruptly, he tucked the parchment into his vest and stepped outside, his expression set in a mask of carefully controlled anger. Athena Courtland had played her wicked games long enough, he decided. Though other men might be willing to let her go unpunished, captivated as they were by her seductive beauty, Lochiel was not. He would show her just how dangerous it could be to play with fire. She was a spoiled brat in dire need of a sound thrashing, and Lochiel, ordering the startled groom to resaddle his horse, wasn't at all sure that he didn't intend to give it to her himself.

A chill October wind blew in his face as he sent the well-schooled beast galloping through the darkened countryside. Daily marches with his men had familiarized him with most of the estates in the area, and he turned toward Courtland Grace without hesitation. By the time the elegant front facade appeared in the starlight, Lochiel's temper had begun to boil. Would Athena be waiting for him outside, or was she watching his approach from the darkness of her room giggling at the success of the joke she had played on him? His lips tightened ominously, relishing the thought of putting an end to Athena Courtland's foolish games.

He left his horse tethered to a post a good distance away from the stable. No sense in waking any dogs or grooms, he thought to himself, though he made no attempt to conceal his presence as he strode across the brittle lawn. A low whistle, the sort children might use to signal one another, came to him from the far side of the garden wall. Lochiel halted obligingly, his arms folded impassively across his chest. Hearing soft, female footfalls behind him, he turned expectantly, relishing their pending confrontation. Yet his breath caught when he saw her, for he could never really be sure in that one moment that she was not the enchanted creature Hugh Martin believed her to be.

It was a moment frozen in time for Lochiel Blackmoor as Athena Courtland danced toward him in a gossamer nightgown washed silver in the starlight. Her unbound hair floated wild and untamed about her slender shoulders and her arms were outstretched, revealing to him the achingly desirable curves of her body. He saw the silken gleam of the bare skin at her throat and the outline of a long, graceful leg as the wind blew the milky material against her. This was Athena set free of the artificial settings in which he had seen her, her mystical beauty coming alive in the night without the trappings of convention and the propriety of a wardrobe to confine her.

Lochiel Blackmoor, who had thought himself immune to her womanly charms, could not admit the effect her ethereal appearance had upon him. She was close enough now for him to see the sweet curve of her lips and hear the delighted laughter bubbling in her white throat.

"I knew you'd come! I just knew it!"

Slim arms wrapped themselves about his neck and a warm body was pressed against the length of his, while her subtle fragrance enveloped him, making his senses reel. She wiggled closer, insinuating herself against him so that he could feel the curve of her hips and her round, womanly breasts brushing him intimately beneath the nearly nonexistent nightgown. Her breath was warm and sweet as she stood on tiptoe to press a kiss to his lean cheek.

" 'Twas my letter, wasn't it? I knew you'd come once you got it! I've been waiting here since midnight!"

Her words broke off in a happy sigh and she laid her head on his shoulder, nuzzling him lovingly while her arms tightened about his neck. Lochiel found himself powerless to fight the wave of desire that washed over him, his manhood rising hot and ready, as Athena made no move to break the intimate contact between them. His anger was gone, replaced by an ache so fierce that he trembled with it. Why such a desperate, elemental need should suddenly hold him powerless was beyond his ken, for he had taken his pleasure with camp followers often enough since the campaign had begun. Yet there was no denying that he was in the grip of some heady, primal passion, and that the fires kindling hot within him burned for Athena alone.

His hands came up to capture her face so that his lips could plunder the yielding sweetness of hers. But by then Athena had gone rigid in his arms, her joy fading with the dawning realization that something was different about her brother. Tilting back her head she looked full into his face and her breath caught in her throat as the starlight illuminated not the familiar features of her beloved Jeremy, but sharply chiseled cheekbones and silver eyes glittering with passion.

"Y-you!" she gasped, and Lochiel could hear the horror in that one simple word. He knew at once that he was not the man she had been waiting for.

In a saner moment he probably would have stopped to consider who had played such a vicious joke upon him. He might have spoken reasonably to Athena, calming her so that she would admit to him the name of the person she had entrusted her letter to. Yet the look on her face as she backed away from him unleashed his long-simmering rage and fanned the heat consuming him.

"Perhaps I'm not the lover you were expecting," he grated, pulling her roughly into his arms, "but I vow I'll satisfy you better."

"You must be mad!" Athena breathed, struggling against his hold. "How dare you come here expecting to—to—"

"If you choose to send tempting invitations such as the one I received by mistake tonight, 'tis entirely possible that you might end up with more than you bargained for."

Athena gasped. Her note, the one she had given Stephen! How could it have been delivered to Major Blackmoor instead of Jeremy? What was she to do now that he had entirely misconstrued its meaning? "Please, you don't understand," she panted, shying away from the strong hands that continued to hold her fast, trying to free herself from the wild and intoxicating pounding of her heart. She was frightened of this man who was a stranger to her, frightened, too, of the realization that something more than fear was causing her pulse to beat madly in her throat. She felt herself being swept on a dizzying tide toward some unknown end, Lochiel Blackmoor's touch filling her with sensations that were new and dangerously irresistible.

"You don't understand," she repeated, her words sounding unsure even to her own ears. "That letter was never meant for you. 'Twas—"

"It doesn't matter, Athena," Lochiel said roughly. Jealousy had ripped through him as he gazed down into her exquisite face, finding the thought intolerable that she could desire someone else. "Fate did not bring your lover tonight, and I don't intend to let you go."

Even as he spoke he knew the growing hunger within him would never be satisfied unless she gave herself to him willingly, allowing him to experience her own wild abandonment. "Athena," he murmured when she didn't speak, and a groan escaped him as he stared down into her upturned face, her eyes wide in the starlight. She was poised before him as though on the verge of flight, and he could feel the quiver that fled through her as he clasped his strong hands about her waist. Drawing her unresisting body to him, he lowered his head until his lips found hers.

Lochiel's hard, male mouth seemed to draw the very breath from Athena's body. A tremor fled through her, centering in that secret, womanly place between her legs. A compelling yearning, as ancient as time itself, began to throb through her blood. She did not know if it was the night or the starlight or the wild, intoxicating touch of this virile man's mouth against hers that awoke within her for the first time in her life the realization of what she wanted, of what she was born for.

With strong, sure fingers, Lochiel untied the front of Athena's nightgown, drawing the filmy material impatiently aside so that his hands could slide about her curving hips. The nightgown fell away from her shoulders and she was standing naked before him, bathed in silver, her unbound hair falling wildly down her back. Her eyes were closed, her head tilted in anticipation of another kiss, and to Lochiel she was like some pagan goddess, too wildly beautiful to be a mortal woman.

But the pulses that throbbed through her were warm and real, and with a groan he captured her lips with his. He drew her closer so that Athena knew for the first time in her life what it meant to be held by a man who burned to possess her. Between her slim thighs she could feel the insistent hardness of his manhood, the pliant leather of his breeches rough against her skin. She arched against him, uncertain of what she wanted yet sensing instinctively that its fulfillment lay here, in Lochiel Blackmoor's arms. The essence of his maleness, its bold, hard touch, was like a brand against her, and she ached for the sweet release she sensed he could give.

Lochiel laid her back into the grass, his kisses continuing to lead her toward some tantalizing end while he shed his clothes above her. Shirt, breeches, and boots were tossed aside without ceremony, and only once did Athena open her eyes to look up at him, and that was when he paused, his task finished, to admire her mystical beauty. Though she had never seen a man's body before, Athena sensed that he was endowed with an exceptional physique. Wide shoulders and whipcord arms accentuated his maleness, and muscles rippled along his chest and down his hard, flat belly. Her gaze lingered unashamed on the dark patch of hair between his lean thighs, his desire for her evident in the bold length of his manhood.

Her eyes traveled back to the harsh contours of his face. If a man could be called beautiful, Athena found herself thinking, then Lochiel Blackmoor was beautiful, and the classic perfection of his hard, driven countenance made her shiver. She remembered the night she had first looked up into those handsome features, her heart thundering, unnerved by the compelling nearness of those silver eyes. She knew now that she had merely been responding to the primal call of his maleness, though she had interpreted her reaction as confusion and fear. And what she had felt for him during their tense encounter in the de Vries's study had not been dislike but an attraction older than the sea and too powerful to deny.

Lochiel, too, was thinking of the night he had first laid eyes on Athena. He remembered how he had stared down at her for a timeless moment, something about her stirring him to the very soul. Now that nameless, elusive sensation was rekindled within him as her dark eyes gazed unafraid into his. Lochiel knew he must possess this woman or be damned as a man.

With a groan he came down upon her, capturing her slim thighs between his. His manhood throbbed against her belly while his lips found hers in a hot, demanding kiss. His strong hands slid down the long, luxurious length of her, leaving her weak with his practiced caresses. His tongue slipped between her lips, plundering the sweetness of her mouth, and Athena tasted it with her own, feeling him quiver in response. Her arms entwined themselves about his broad back and she allowed him to press her even closer, his hard muscles rigid with the forces that shook him.

With his hands at the curve of her hips, Lochiel shifted her body beneath his. Athena gasped as she felt the tip of his manhood touch her intimately, and she spread her thighs to accommodate him, to allow him to fill the aching void within her. She arched herself up to meet him, her slim buttocks lifted into the air as Lochiel cupped his big hands about them. The force of his entry drove the breath from her body, but the pain Athena experienced as he thrust deep inside only heightened the sweet ecstasy of that precious moment.

She clung to him, luxuriating in the wildness of their mating, every thrust taking him deeper into the essence of her womanhood. She could feel herself being carried away on a tide of sensation, rising higher and higher, until the splendor of Lochiel's lovemaking coursed like wildfire through her being. Her lips parted beneath his in a soft moan and she felt him surge against her, his ultimate possession sending both of them soaring on peak after peak of ecstasy.

Athena's long white legs were entwined with Lochiel's, his lean body fused to hers, and even when both shuddered and grew still they remained unmoving, awed by the wonder of it all. Eventually their ragged breathing quieted and they were silent, neither willing to shatter the intimacy that surrounded them by speaking.

For Athena, words weren't necessary. Her heart was in her eyes as she gazed into the handsome face above hers. A smile curved her soft lips as she traced the lean contours of his features with a tapering fingertip. Lochiel's own heart constricted oddly, and he found himself unable to explain why this innocent gesture should move him. Lowering his head, he caressed her lips with his. Athena responded by clinging to him and tightening her hold about his neck. Her body moved languidly, sensuously beneath his, and Lochiel felt his manhood beginning to stir within her.

Gently, a hand entwined in the silky softness of her hair, he eased himself away from her. Though 'twould prove too temptingly sweet to have her again, he knew he must not. He had lost all sense of reason in his heated possession of her the first time, and Lochiel was clear-headed enough by now to realize how great the danger was of losing his heart if he did so again. He could not afford to fall victim to one of Athena Courtland's bewitching spells.

"Must you go?" he heard her whisper as he reached for his shirt. The disappointment in her voice touched him, yet he refused to respond to it.

"Indeed I must. I've several reports to finish before reveille."

The indifference of his tone startled her and she sat up, reaching out her hand to brush his lean cheek in a shy caress. She felt him flinch at her touch, and she gazed at him wordlessly, unable to understand why he had withdrawn so abruptly from her. Lochiel himself was grappling with the urge to take her into his arms, for she looked breathtakingly beautiful kneeling before him, her long, golden hair tumbling over her breasts to her curving hips. What harm could there be in taking her again if both of them desired it?

Yet he could not. He must put an end to the madness of wanting her, for that was a torment he could ill afford. He was sure he was but one of many lovers Athena had doubtless taken in the past, and there would be others once he was gone. The thought caused a pulse to throb in his temple, and he drew on his breeches without giving her another glance.

"Lochiel, please," Athena whispered, his name falling for the first time from her lips. Its soft utterance and the pain in her voice made it impossible for him to ignore her. Drawing his shoulder plaid across his broad chest, he gazed at her questioningly, his eyes fastened deliberately to her small face and not the tantalizing smoothness of her body.

"What have I done?" she asked, coming to her feet beside him. "Why are you angry with me?"

He had not expected such a question or to fall victim to the confusion in her eyes. He looked away from her abruptly only to find his gaze drawn to the shadowed vee between her thighs. A hot, futile ache began to grow within him.

"Why, you've done naught, my dear," he told her blandly, "save offer me a most pleasant diversion on an otherwise dull night. My thanks for that."

It was fortunate that he turned his back at that moment and could not see the stunned look that crossed Athena's face. Like a child unfairly struck she recoiled, unable to believe that the gentle lover who had all but stolen her heart had, for no apparent reason, become this hard and callous man. She bit her lip as tears spilled to her eyes, thinking to herself that she deserved little better. What did she know of Lochiel Blackmoor save that he was something of a military hero, a career soldier who, like Tykie, had lost everything with the downfall of the Stuart dynasty in 1745 when the Scottish Highlands had been overrun by bloodthirsty Englishmen out for revenge? Tykie had turned to pirating to escape the grief of losing his family. Had some similar tragedy soured Lochiel Blackmoor's heart so that he could, without conscience, hurt her like this?

Lochiel had finished dressing, and the sharp planes of his face were set in rigid lines as he turned back to Athena. She could not know that years of discipline, of learning to hide his emotions behind a strict military bearing, enabled him to regard her with a slightly mocking expression, as though little more weighed on his mind than the brandy he would drink when he returned to camp.

"Good night, m'dear," he said casually. "I trust you'll number me among your fonder memories."

He was not prepared for the sharp crack or the pain that exploded in his head when Athena's palm connected solidly with his cheek. Cold rage washed through him, his nerves every bit as brittle as hers, yet he forced himself to keep his anger in check.

"I suppose I deserved that," he conceded before turning away. Behind him he heard something he hadn't expected to, a choked sob quickly muffled behind her hand. He might have relented then, yet the sound of her footsteps as she fled across the grass informed him that she was gone. For a moment he stood without moving, the struggle evident in his hard face, then he strode quickly toward his tethered horse and savagely untied the reins. He froze abruptly as his horse lifted its head, ears cocked in the direction of the drive. Quietly he guided the obedient mount into the shadows of a towering chestnut, his hand going instinctively to his saddle bag. Like all Scotsmen, Lochiel never went anywhere without his dirk. His long fingers tightened about the carved handle as he saw a man coming up the drive on foot, canteen, musket, and pack slung over his shoulder. Though the load was a heavy one, the traveler seemed not to notice, and his steps quickened as he caught sight of the house through the trees.

Lochiel watched him disappear through a small door on the west side, an entrance he himself hadn't noticed but which the newcomer was obviously accustomed to using. His lips tightened grimly and he kicked his startled horse into a savage trot. Apparently he'd been right about Athena Courtland. No sooner had she sated her passion with one lover than another was summoned to take his place.

"Damn the wench," Lochiel grated to himself. He had been a fool to come here, a fool to succumb to her seductive ways. He would simply have to forget her, he thought harshly, whipping his horse into a gallop as the house fell from view behind him. 'Twould prove hard to do, he realized, for despite the anger burning within him he could think of naught save the silky perfection of the body she had offered him and the banking fires in her sultry eyes as she had gazed wantonly into his face.

Lochiel gritted his teeth, disgusted with himself for behaving like a schoolboy besotted by the object of his sexual dreams. Athena Courtland was by no means a virgin, despite the small cry of pain and the quiver that had fled through her when he had driven into her that first time. Though he had been on fire for her then he had held himself in check for a brief moment, sobered by the possibility that he had made some terrible mistake. Yet now he suspected that all of it had been part of an act and that it probably heightened her own pleasure to behave as if she were being robbed of her maidenhead for the first time.

Damn her! Why had Athena Courtland ever come into his life? What had he done to deserve the torment of envisioning her lying beneath the man he had seen coming up the drive, her hair spilling in a gold ribbon across the bed, her white legs spread, soft lips parted as she moaned with passion? He could only pray that General Amherst ordered troop mobilization quickly so that West York and Athena Courtland would soon be little more than a dim memory in his mind.

Dismounting in the stableyard, Lochiel ran an agitated hand through his dark hair. A subtle yet maddeningly provocative fragrance drifted to him as he did so, and he recalled how he had held Athena against his shirtfront when he had first kissed her. Aye, 'twas a torment, he told himself, remembering how he had breathed deeply the fresh, clean scent of her hair, which clung to him now, mocking his determination to forget her. His face a thundercloud of rage, Lochiel strode back to his tent, vowing to drive Athena Courtland from his mind forever.

Six

"Miss Athena, wake up! Oh, please, wake up!"

"What is it, Mercy?" Athena whispered, opening an eye to find the redheaded maid gesturing frantically from the doorway. Her entire body ached and her lips felt bruised from the passion of Lochiel Blackmoor's kisses. She inhaled sharply, tears stinging her eyes, reminding herself fiercely that she had sworn never to think of him again. Yet how long had she lain awake last night trying to find a reason for the pain that filled her heart, for the aching longing she had been unable to deny?

" 'Tis Master Jeremy!" Mercy announced. "I went into his room to put fresh linen on the bed, and there he was lying fast asleep on the counterpane!"

Athena's jaw dropped. "What?"

Mercy bobbed her head vigorously, her frilly mobcap threatening to tumble off. " 'Tis true, miss! Why, he hadn't even taken his boots off, and I doubt he's had a good wash for days!" She blushed furiously. "I mean, 'twas obvious from what little I could see from the doorway, miss."

Athena knew perfectly well that Mercy had made a thorough and quite worshipful study of the sleeping Jeremy before hurrying off to report his return. Yet she felt no inclination to tease her this morning, and she winced as she rose from the bed to stretch before the pier glass. There were bruises on her flesh, and her lips felt tender from the pressure of Lochiel Blackmoor's insistent mouth. 'Twas a relief to her that she looked the same despite how different she might feel inside, and some of her self-assurance returned as she turned to face her expectant maid.

"We're not going to wake him, Mercy."

"We're not?" Mercy could scarcely conceal her disappointment.

"No. He has obviously marched a long way and needs to rest. Go downstairs and inform the household that they're to make as little noise as possible. And tell Prudence to have some plum tartlets in the oven when he wakes. You know how much he loves them."

Mercy dimpled. "Of course, miss! I haven't fogotten." Her smile faded suddenly and she cast a hesitant glance over her shoulder. "What about

Mistress Bower? She's still abed, but I believe I heard her stirring when I went past her room."

"I'll tell her about Jeremy myself."

" 'Tisn't what I meant, miss," Mercy said uncomfortably. "I was wondering what this'll do to her plans."

One winged brow rose questioningly. "What plans?"

"To leave for Boston, miss. She gave Wills the order to let Tykie go first thing this morning and told me I was to make certain you had your trunks packed before breakfast."

Athena gave an unladylike snort, her back turned as she began to brush her hair with vigorous strokes. "I'd like to see anyone try to dismiss Tykie! Why, I couldn't even vouch for my own safety were I to attempt such a thing!" She chuckled despite herself, delighted that Jeremy was home at last. Dismiss Tykie, indeed! She felt quite certain her brother would have a thing or two to say about that.

And as for Lochiel Blackmoor, she thought with a defiant toss of her head, that was one arrogant cad she'd prefer never to lay eyes on again. She was only glad that she had discovered what a conscienceless scoundrel he was before she succumbed to some foolish female whim such as falling in love with him merely because he was the first man to have lain with her.

Bah! She didn't care a whit for Major Lochiel Blackmoor, and she only hoped that her behavior last night hadn't convinced him otherwise.

"Is something wrong, Miss Athena?" Mercy asked, pausing in her search for a suitable gown for her mistress to wear. 'Twasn't like Miss Athena to be so silent, not with Master Jeremy home and all!

"I'm perfectly all right, Mercy. As a matter of fact, I'm quite looking forward to the opportunity of telling my aunt that we are not moving to Boston and that Tykie Downs is not leaving Courtland Grace."

Seeing the determined tilt to her mistress's square jaw, Mercy gave a sigh of relief. Miss Athena certainly seemed to be her old self, she thought, turning back to the rustling gowns hanging before her and missing the fleeting expression of pain that crossed Athena's small face as she dismissed Lochiel Blackmoor once and for all from her heart. Athena couldn't deny that what had happened between them last night had changed her, yet her pride made it impossible to ignore the humiliation of his abrupt rejection. 'Twas something she'd never forgive him for.

Damn you, Lochiel Blackmoor, Athena breathed to herself. I shan't forget what you've done!

There was a festive bustle in the air when Athena came downstairs a few minutes later, something that had been missing from Courtland Grace for quite some time. Dour Wills was actually whistling as he went about his tasks, while Nancy, the village girl who came to help Mercy and Prudence during the day, hummed as she gave the silver teapot a vigorous buffing. Through the opened casement window Athena could hear Tykie's deep voice bellowing out a Scottish song from the darkness of the stables, slightly off-key but joyous nonetheless.

A gentle smile curved her lips, and some of the pain in her heart began to fade. Jeremy was home, and though his stay might be brief, 'twould be enough to bring some happiness and order back into the confusion of her life. Surely his presence would help drive Lochiel Blackmoor's memory away and bring back those innocent times when her father was still alive and naught but childhood pleasures had occupied her thoughts.

"Here you be, miss. Muffins hot from the oven and a new crock of blackberry jam right out of the cellar." Prudence's round face glowed as she bustled into the room, the plate of muffins wrapped in her voluminous apron to keep them warm. "I've a dozen tartlets baking now, and Mercy's on her way to the spring house to fetch fresh buttermilk. 'Tis Master Jeremy's favorite, you'll recall."

She was gone before Athena could reply, muttering something about sending Wills outside to select a plump baking hen for dinner. Athena leaned back in her chair with a smile, sharing Prue's happiness yet feeling grateful for the chance to be alone. She needed time to collect herself before Jeremy made an appearance or, heaven forbid, Aunt Amelia swept downstairs to resume her ranting and raving of the day before. What would she say if she knew what had transpired between her sheltered niece and a virile Highland officer last night? 'Twould certainly lend an element of truth to her claim that Athena was ruined forever.

Athena's slim jaw tightened. 'Twas no joking matter, and she suddenly found herself feeling uneasy. Her letter had been delivered to Lochiel Blackmoor by someone who must have been fully aware of what he was doing. But who? Stephen? 'Twasn't likely since Stephen had known all along the letter was intended for Jeremy. How, then, had it wound up in Major Blackmoor's possession? And was the person responsible for delivering it also aware that Lochiel had ridden to Courtland Grace in response to its summons?

Athena swallowed hard. She didn't care a whit if gossip linked her name with Major Blackmoor's, despite the fact that her reputation might be forever blackened in the eyes of the local townsfolk. Yet something like this would prove impossible for her to explain away, and she wondered how her brothers were going to weather the shame of knowing that their sister had entered into an impassioned liaison with a Scottish officer. She felt sickened at the thought of what Katrine de Vries could do with such a malicious weapon in her hands. Her eyes grew hard and her slim fingers tightened about the handle of the knife she was using to spread jam on her muffin. If that little witch so much as—

"Mmm, you're a delicious sight, my wee bonnie bairn!"

A pair of muscular arms slid about her neck as a deep voice addressed her much as Tykie had always done when Athena was small. Uttering a joyous cry, Athena leaped to her feet, and for a moment brother and sister embraced tightly until Athena pushed him away, laughing and crying as she studied the beloved face before her.

"Oh, Jeremy, how you've changed!" she breathed, overcome with admiration. Though she was tall herself, he now stood a good six inches above her. His golden curls were worn carelessly long, brushing the collar of his Holland shirt. Broad shoulders, sun-bronzed arms, and a muscular torso gave evidence of the hard training that he had undergone during the past year. Athena gave his filled-out frame a sweeping glance before her eyes settled again on his face, searching anxiously for a sign that he had suffered, that nearly eleven months of war had left an indelible stamp of tragedy upon him.

But there was no mistaking the old twinkle in those bright blue eyes or the mischievous grin he could not contain. Both of the twins had always tackled life in a boisterous fashion, never allowing sadness to defeat them. If there was pain in their hearts, they hid it behind silly antics and careless charades, yet there were few individuals who were more loyal, giving, and deeply caring than Colm and Jeremy Courtland. Though the horror of the battlefield had taken its toll, Jeremy had refused to allow the memories to haunt him, thereby managing to present to his sister the swaggering countenance and ready smile she expected.

Athena hugged him again, tears of relief splashing his shirtfront as she realized that he was unharmed, unscathed, and still the mischievous scoundrel she had bidden farewell to so long ago. Jeremy in turn embraced her warmly, his cheek resting against the top of her head.

"You've changed too, sweeting," he murmured. Though she had always been a beautiful child, he saw now that the past year had taken away much of the coltish awkwardness of girlhood, leaving her with a womanly grace that even he, her own brother, found difficult to ignore. The dove-gray wool gown she wore was new, and there was no mistaking that the narrow waist and rustling petticoats of pearl satin peeking from beneath the hem were the attributes of a woman of fashion and not the little girl in pantalets and embroidered apron he remembered. He felt an uncustomary tightness in his throat, wondering if he and Colm had done the right thing to abandon her as they had, forcing Athena to experience the difficult transformation from child to woman alone.

"Have you been well?" he inquired with a thread of concern in his voice that made her tears flow faster. "Has it been hard for you trying to run the farm with that harridan in your hair?"

Athena giggled despite herself. "Do you mean Aunt Amelia? We've had our disagreements, but I—oh, Jemmy, must we talk about it now? You must be starving, and there's so much more to tell you. Come, sit down. Prudence has made plum tartlets."

She pulled him to the table, and he seated himself with a contented sigh. "I've eaten naught but undercooked game and pemmican the past few weeks," he confessed. "You'll never know how much I've been yearning for a breakfast served Courtland style."

Athena's smooth brow furrowed. "Haven't they been feeding you properly? Why, I overheard the governor boasting to Lord Loudon that the New York Provincials ate better than any of the other militias."

Jeremy waved his jam-laden muffin by way of answer, his mouth full. "I'm not with the Provincials anymore," he informed her when he could speak. There was a hint of pride in his voice. "I'm with the Rangers, now."

Athena's eyes widened. "Rogers's Rangers? Oh, Jeremy, how wonderful for you! 'Tis what you were hoping for all along!"

The Rangers, as Athena well knew, was an elite group of fighting men handpicked by the famous Indian scout Major Robert Rogers. Unlike the Provincial militias, which were poorly trained and bad at bush fighting, the Rangers were crack shots and their stealth in the forests had earned them the reputation of being the eyes and the ears of the army.

"I couldn't have asked for anything better," Jeremy agreed, "and I'm hoping they'll accept Colm before long. 'Tis a different way of life, Athena, being a Ranger. When Colm and I joined the Provincials we found out just how bad things were. I hate to say this about New England," he added with a shake of his curly head, "but our militias have the poorliest trained soldiers I've ever seen. Most of my company consisted of homesick youngsters who bawled for their mamas every night. The food was terrible, the pay nonexistent, and you don't want to hear the excuses for weapons they issued us."

Athena listened to him speak with a sense of mingled wonder and dread. What few letters she had received from Fletcher and the little the townsfolk knew about military campaigns hadn't given her a real idea of what the war was like. Oh, she could quote the dates and locales of every battle that had taken place on New England soil since the war began, but no one had ever really bothered to answer her questions. Even Lord Loudon and General Amherst had laughed at her the other night, informing her with indulgent smiles that a young lady needn't trouble herself over the technicalities of warfare, and assuring her that the Provincial army was well trained and exceptionally well cared for.

"Even the Regulars," Jeremy continued, referring to the British troops that had been sent from England to assist the colonies in their fight for freedom, "don't know a thing about engaging Frenchmen in hand-to-hand combat, especially now that the Indians have taught them to scalp from behind." He took another bite of his muffin and washed it down with a sip of hot tea. "Haven't we got any buttermilk?" he asked, pulling a face.

"Mercy's gone to the springhouse to fetch some," Athena assured him.

Jeremy grinned. "Dear little Mercy. Has she pledged her heart to another since I've been gone?"

"Don't you tease her," Athena warned, aware that her brother was quite oblivious to the fact that what Mercy felt for him had far outgrown the hero worship of the past. Mercy, too, had been doing quite a bit of growing up in the year the twins had been gone. Athena wondered what her brother would say when he found himself confronted by a pretty young woman totally unlike the child he remembered.

"We call them lobsterbacks and furriners," Jeremy added.

"Who?"

"The Regulars. That's what the Provincials call them anyway, and I promise you there's little love lost between them. The Provincials complain that the Regulars don't know a thing about fighting. They object to all the parades and military precision, even the scarlet uniforms they wear. The Regulars, on the other hand, claim that the Provincials are an undisciplined bunch of backwoods boys unfit to be wearing uniforms. I'm only glad I'm with the Rangers. No petty jealousies there. We're the best and we know it."

Athena laughed with him, deeply glad that he could lounge so casually before her in his buckskin breeches and unruly curls, behaving as if he'd never been away. Only now could she begin to understand how terrified she had been of losing him, not only to some Frenchman's musketball but to the damage war could inflict upon a man's soul. She wanted to ask about Colm and if there was news of Fletcher's regiment, but sensed that he needed to talk. She would ask her own questions later.

"I've no objections to the Regulars myself," Jeremy was saying. "An army needs discipline, and they've surely got it. As a matter of fact I've really come to admire the Highland regiments. Everything Tykie ever said about his people is true. They're a fearless bunch, Thena, and I've seen them leap into a line of Frenchies armed with naught but their swords—claymores they call 'em—and fell them like trees even though the Frenchies were carrying loaded muskets."

There was a sudden tightness in Athena's throat. "The Seventh Highland Company has been here in West York the past few days. In fact, most of them are camping on Egon de Vries's land. Do you know any of them?" She couldn't help asking. The words seemed to fall without warning from her lips.

"As a matter of fact, the Seventh was quartered in Albany with the New York Militia last week, but I wasn't—"

"The good Lord be praised! You've really come home, then, Master Jeremy!"

Prudence beamed as she bustled into the room, then gave a startled squeal as Jeremy rose and swung her into his arms.

"Oh, put me down, you wicked lad!" she protested

"I can't tell you how much I've missed your cooking, Prue," he said as he obliged her, his eyes twinkling.

"I've baked some plum tartlets and whipped some cream for you, too," the portly little woman stammered, hastily adjusting her mobcap, which was hanging over her eyes. Setting the steaming tarts on the table, she clucked with relief that none of them had spilled.

"And I've brought the buttermilk," came Mercy's shy voice from the doorway. She hastened in, her dark skirts billowing, an earthenware jug in her hands. Athena had never seen her look so pretty, the brisk October wind having worked her red curls loose and bringing a pink blush to her freckled cheeks. Jeremy, she noticed with satisfaction, seemed quite startled by the ravishing little creature, whom he remembered as a timid child whose enormous eyes had followed him worshipfully wherever he went.

He would have spoken to her, said something that might have fueled her dreams in her lonely little room below the eaves, yet at that moment a foul-tempered bellow rent the air, causing all of them to whirl about.

"Master Jemmy's hame, is he? Well, no ane thought to tell Tykie Downs! Had tae figure it oot for meself wi' all the noise an' confusion frae the kitchens this mornin'!"

Tykie's expression was terrible to behold as he lumbered into the room, and his black eyes narrowed even further as he took in the small crowd gathered around the table. Wills and Nancy had accompanied Mercy inside in order to greet their long-absent master, and to Tykie the reunion seemed staged to deliberately exclude him.

"Celebratin', are ye?" he shouted, red-faced with what a terrified Mercy and Nancy thought was anger but which Athena knew perfectly well was mere bluster to hide his joy. "Fine, hae yer fun while poor auld Tykie gaes back tae cleanin' harnesses! 'Tis clear I'm no welcome here!"

" 'Tis clear that poor old Tykie has grown more unmanageable than ever," Jeremy remarked with a devilish laugh as he came forward to embrace the man who had been a second father to him. Big as Jeremy might have grown, Athena was amused to see that Tykie nearly swallowed him up in a bruising bear hug. There were tears in Tykie's eyes, though the Scotsman would probably deny on his deathbed having shed them. There was little for him to be ashamed of, however, for everyone seemed to be a little misty-eyed, and even dour Wills was forced to fumble for a handkerchief before turning away and energetically blowing his nose.

"What on earth is the meaning of this!"

Though Amelia Bower made it a habit never to raise her voice, she had perfected a manner of speaking that, when sharpened with disapproval, could send chills through any noisy company. Instant silence fell over the room, and even fearless Tykie was startled into momentary obedience.

"Well, Athena?" Amelia asked frostily. Her disapproving eyes mustered her niece from either side of her hawklike nose, thin lips tightly compressed as she wondered to herself if there was any hope left for Athena at all. "What is the meaning of this . . . this rowdiness? I've told you countless times that servants are not permitted—"

"Calm yourself, auntie. 'Tis a celebration and you're welcome to join in."

Amelia gasped as a wet kiss was deposited noisily on her withered cheek. The eyes that twinkled boyishly back at her were so like Fiona's that she went white. Uttering a strangled sound, she slid forward in a faint, rescued at the last possible moment by the lumbering Tykie, who could move quite swiftly despite his great size.

"Lay her down in the salon," Athena directed while dispatching Mercy upstairs for the smelling salts. Prue and Nancy clucked anxiously over their swooning mistress while Athena's gaze met Jeremy's across the room.

"I never knew I had such a dramatic effect on unmarried women," he teased, thinking she was upset and hoping to calm her. To his surprise she gave a shout of laughter, gay and free of cares, like a little girl, and her slim arms wrapped themselves tightly about his neck.

"Oh, Jeremy, I'm ever so glad you've come home! 'Tis obvious you know just how to deal with our dear Aunt Amelia!"

Athena could not keep the amusement from her expression as she swept into the parlor that evening to find her brother standing stiff and uncomfortable before the fireplace. The brown wool suit and tight-fitting waistcoat were obviously not to his liking, and he scowled as Athena leaned down to admire more closely his silk hose and polished shoes.

"Don't say a word, Thena," he warned. "I've half a mind not to go tonight. I vow I feel exactly like one of Prudence's trussed game hens about to be slid in the oven!"

Athena laughed merrily at this. "Apparently you've forgotten the lengths a gentleman must go to in order to be fashionable." She put her finger to her lips and regarded him with thoughtfully arched brows. "And yet there seems to be something missing. Dashing as you look I can't seem to place it—ah, of course! Where's your wig?"

Startled, Jeremy ran a hand through his untidy blond curls. "My what? My wig? Are you mad? I'm not going to wear one of those hot, itchy things in public!"

"Aunt Amelia will insist, I'm afraid. You know how important appearances are to her, especially where the Kensingtons are concerned."

" 'Tis just my luck to have leave on the same night Leda Kensington decides to give a dinner party," Jeremy lamented. "Not only do I not care that Stephen has braved the voyage back from England through French-infested waters, I heartily resent having to congratulate him on his return. I never did care much for the pompous fellow, and as for wearing a wig—"

His eyes narrowed when Athena burst into helpless giggles. "Pulling my leg, were you? Cheeky wench, 'twill go bad with you now."

He reached for her, encircling her with a powerful arm and tickling her unmercifully. Athena squealed and tried to squirm free, her carefully arranged locks tumbling in total disarray about her shoulders. She was unable to break away until Jeremy, hearing his aunt clear her throat in the doorway, released her abruptly. Athena scowled defensively as she pushed the hair from her eyes, but Jeremy merely sketched his aunt a mocking bow.

"We are in roving high spirits tonight, as you can see, auntie dear, and quite ready to depart. Shall I see if Wills has brought the carriage round?"

Amelia nodded her head, not quite certain what to make of Fiona's youngest son. He was never rude or disrespectful, yet she couldn't help feeling that he made a constant mockery of everything. Small wonder Athena herself was so wild. 'Twas impossible for an impressionable young girl not to grow into a hoyden when raised with such unmanageable brothers.

"Athena, see to your hair while your brother fetches the carriage," she said, choosing not to chastise either of them for their horseplay, distasteful as she might have found it. Brushing specks of lint from her immaculate russet-colored gown, she waited while Athena dutifully retreated to the hallway, where a mirror hung above the graceful cherry sideboard.

"Is she always this bad?" Jeremy whispered as he stepped back inside.

Athena giggled, for nothing could dampen her spirits this evening.

"Sometimes she's far worse. I've a feeling she's restraining herself tonight simply because you remind her so much of Mama."

"Or because she's been quite taken in by my boyish charm." Jeremy's eyes twinkled. "Stop fussing with your hair, will you? 'Tis perfect, and you, my bonnie wee bairn, are a vision of loveliness." He took her hands in his and whirled her about until her jade-green skirts belled about her, revealing her slim ankles and the tips of her emerald satin slippers.

Athena's soft lips were parted, and she laughed as he whirled her even faster. She was beautiful, he thought to himself, more beautiful than a girl had a right to be, and he felt a sudden rush of fierce, protective love for her. With her wild, impetuous ways and her distracting loveliness, Athena was more vulnerable than most to the roving eyes of unscrupulous men.

Though he'd be able to act as her escort tonight, he'd not be here to protect her come morrow, and he resolved to speak to her earnestly before he returned to the Rangers. Three short years might separate them in age, yet she was a child still, and innocent to the ways of the world. With their mother dead and Fletcher, the oldest, so far away, 'twould be up to him to make certain that his sister would not suffer the cruel fate that was all too often the reward for uncommon beauty.

"What is it, Jeremy?" Athena asked, wondering why he scowled so abruptly.

He shook himself free of his thoughts and slung his arm about her bare shoulders. "I was wondering how a single man, acting alone, is going to fend off all your ardent beaux tonight without resorting to violence."

"Mrs. Kensington assured us 'twould be an intimate gathering. Surely your task won't prove too difficult." Athena picked up the gloves that lay on the sideboard and allowed him to lay her cloak over her shoulders. "Let's not keep Aunt Amelia waiting."

The air was crisp and cold, the autumn heavens bright with stars as the three of them stepped outside. From a window in the main wing Athena could see Mercy peering down at them, her attention no doubt centered on the imposingly attired Jeremy. Her brother did cut quite a dashing figure, Athena thought to herself, and she was reminded again of the resemblance between her handsome brother and the portait of the beautiful Fiona that still hung in her father's library.

Colm and Jeremy had always resembled their mother, while she and Fletcher had inherited the square jaw and slightly aquiline nose of their father. Yet of all four Courtland children only Fletcher possessed his father's dark coloring, which Athena had always secretly believed gave him a distinguished air.

"You call this an intimate gathering, Athena?"

Startled from her thoughts, she peered from the carriage window to see that they had already completed the short drive to the Kensingtons'. Wills had been forced to slow the vehicle almost to a complete halt in order to avoid the traffic snarl that was inching its way up the winding drive leading to the manor house.

"I'm not surprised that Leda Kensington chose to invite so many guests," Aunt Amelia remarked. "I understand she was quite miffed that Marianne de Vries hosted Lord Loudon and General Amherst while they were here."

"Still squabbling like barnyard hens, are they?" Jeremy asked. "I would have thought by now that one of them would've been proclaimed Hostess of the Colony."

Athena hid a giggle behind her hand, glad that her aunt was sitting on the opposite seat and couldn't hear Jeremy's remark. Unkind words about one's acquaintances were not permitted, even though 'twas common knowledge that Leda Kensington and Marianne de Vries were archrivals in the social world. Thanks to the income generated from renting farmland to tenants, a practice the Courtlands abhorred, Leda Kensington was able to maintain her wildly frivolous life, her entertainment extravaganzas rivaled only by the wealthy Dutch matron living upriver.

All of New York enjoyed this continuous competition, for the parties and balls that resulted were festive indeed, and not a one was held at Bountiful without another, grander one taking place at the Kensingtons' the following month. Athena found this subtle class warfare extremely tiresome, especially since, for all outward appearances, the two archrivals considered themselves the best of friends.

Yet tonight she did not ponder the antics of two vain and rather foolish women, which normally offered her a source of considerable amusement. She was staring up at the house, its windows ablaze with lights, and at the number of guests that were being admitted inside. Her pulse began to beat uncomfortably in her throat. With so many people invited 'twas entirely possible that she might come face to face with Lochiel Blackmoor, a prospect that entirely unnerved her. She had been so certain that this gathering would include only the Kensingtons' acquaintances and not the British officers staying at Bountiful. What was she to do if Major Blackmoor was there? She knew she couldn't face him, not so soon after what had happened!

"What's wrong, love?" Jeremy asked as her hand slipped into his. The interior of the carriage was dimly lit, and he couldn't see her face, yet he sensed that something was troubling her.

"Athena, you're to be on your best behavior tonight," Aunt Amelia interrupted sharply. "I only hope you haven't done irreparable damage to your reputation with your shocking antics at the race track yesterday! 'Twould suit me better if you didn't make an appearance in public so soon afterward, but I accepted this invitation days ago. Perhaps," she added hopefully, "this will give you the opportunity of showing everyone that you still possess proper manners regardless of your past indiscretions."

"Yes, aunt," Athena said quietly, not feeling the least inclined to argue with her at the moment.

Jeremy's hand was beneath her elbow as they entered the glittering hall. The floor was of beautifully buffed slate, quarried in the colony, the wainscoted walls lined with gleaming brass sconces. Leda and Ambrose Kensington stood near the doorway greeting their guests, their daughters standing dutifully beside them. Wearing identical pastel gowns, one pink and one blue, and stiff petticoats adorned with rosettes, Aramintha and Eliza Kensington might have passed for twins despite the fact that Eliza was two years older. Their similarity was made even more striking by the fact that both girls were exceedingly plain and as plump as their parents.

Eliza's fan began to flutter furiously as she caught sight of Jeremy, and she brought it discreetly to her lips as she leaned over to whisper something to her sister. Aramintha's pale brown eyes widened appreciatively as she, too, became aware of the handsome young man acting as Athena Courtland's escort. Neither of them spared Athena so much as a glance, though the same could not be said of the males, both young and old, conversing nearby.

Athena was dressed in rich emerald velvet, her petticoats of satin ivory rustling seductively as she moved. Mercy had arranged her hair to fall in ringlets to her white shoulders, and the disarray caused by Jeremy's earlier roughhousing gave her an unconsciously wanton look. The three-quarter-length sleeves, adorned with ivory ruching, revealed the slimness of her arms, while the plunging neckline left Athena's creamy throat delightfully exposed.

Yet Athena was unaware of the admiring glances that were turned her way. She was searching the crowded drawing room before her, and she breathed an inaudible sigh of relief when she noticed that not a single military uniform was in view. 'Twas obviously Leda Kensington's strategy, for tonight the citizens of West York were expected to pretend that their colony was not overrun with soldiers and that the threat of a French invasion hadn't been hanging over them for the past three years. Even discussions about the war were not permitted except in the private rooms set up for the gentlemen's use. It was a master stroke of planning, and Leda Kensington had proven once again that she was not so easily outdone.

Greeting Jeremy with effusive warmth, seeing in him a potential suitor for one of her daughters, Leda paid little attention to Athena. There was no sense in cultivating a close relationship, Athena knew, with a young woman considered an unworthy choice for Leda's beloved Stephen.

The feeling was heartily reciprocated, Athena thought to herself, yet even as she extended her gloved hand to Ambrose Kensington, she was already searching the drawing room for his son. She was determined to learn how Lochiel Blackmoor had gotten hold of her letter, and Stephen was the only one who could tell her.

"Jeremy, Miss Courtland, how good to see the two of you together again!"

Stephen had come up behind them, a blood-red ruby glittering in his snowy stock. In gold silk hose and peacock-blue waistcoat, he was obviously playing the part of a dandy. Seeing him so overdressed, Athena felt all of her previous dislike for him resurfacing. How could she have entrusted him with Jeremy's note? Could it be possible that he was responsible for its delivery to Major Blackmoor? Blood and thunder, there'd be hell to pay were that the case!

"Good to see you again, Stephen," Jeremy said with a heartiness he was far from feeling. None of the Courtland brothers had ever been overly fond of Stephen and the gaming and wenching that filled his days.

"Glad to see you've got some leave," Stephen went on, his interested gaze traveling from Athena's face back to her brother's. "When did you get in?"

"Late last night. I hitched a ride on a farm cart from Albany and then walked the rest of the way home."

Stephen's satisfied gaze rested on Athena's rosy lips. "I imagine you caused quite a stir when you came in unannounced."

Jeremy shook his head, his hand beneath Athena's elbow, already pulling her into the drawing room. "Actually I took great care not to awaken anyone in the house."

"No one discovered his presence until this morning," Athena added, wondering why Stephen frowned when she said that. She would have liked to question him further, but Jeremy was by now tugging openly on her sleeve.

"There's Trey Warwick, Thena. I haven't seen him since I left home. Who's that pretty lass beside him?"

Athena had to smile. "His wife."

Jeremy's eyes widened. "Trey's married? Good God, never thought I'd see the day! Excuse us, Stephen."

"Certainly. I'll speak to you later, Miss Courtland. Perhaps you'll spare me a dance after dinner?"

"Of course."

The meal was sumptuous, consisting of several choices of wild fowl and other game taken from the surrounding forests. Soup and a hearty hunter's stew dispelled the chill of the October evening, and wine, champagne, and mulled cider flowed freely. It was a festive occasion, Leda Kensington's planning and the talents of her kitchen staff, all domestics imported from England, assuring a grand success.

Athena could hardly wait for the meal to end. Usually she cared little for the dancing that took place afterward, yet tonight she was eager to question Stephen about her letter. When the opportunity finally arrived, she wasted no time in flatly demanding to know what he'd done with it.

"I entrusted it to one of my footmen with the strict order that 'twas to be delivered to your brother as soon as his regiment arrived. As you heard from Jeremy yourself, he went straight to Courtland Grace and didn't accompany his regiment here. Charles probably still has the letter in his possession. That's him over there serving champagne to your aunt. Shall I ask him to return it to you?"

Athena could feel the heat rise to her cheeks and she bit her lip in vexation. She never blushed, and here she was behaving like a rattled ninny merely because he was looking at her so expectantly.

" 'Tisn't necessary," she said, recovering her composure enough to lie quite gracefully. "Jeremy's home, so what purpose would the letter serve? Simply throw it away and we'll have done with it."

For a moment Stephen glanced at her thoughtfully, annoyed by the fact that those deep blue eyes of hers could look so guilelessly into his. Damn the wench, what was she thinking? Was she hiding something from him, or had Lochiel Blackmoor failed to respond to the missive Asa Brewster had delivered?

At any rate, it no longer mattered. Jeremy Courtland had crept into his house unseen last night without stumbling upon the two lovers as Stephen had hoped. His plan had failed, yet he wasn't about to lament the fact. There would be others to teach the wayward Miss Courtland that it didn't pay to take a soldier to bed.

Stephen's hand tightened unconsciously about hers as cold rage consumed him. By God, he was still mad with want for Athena, and 'twas all he could do at the moment to keep from leading her out into the garden, tearing her bodice in two, and planting his lips upon her breasts.

He forced his thoughts elsewhere, aware that his manhood was beginning to stir and that 'twould quickly become obvious, thanks to the tightness of his knee breeches. Swinging Athena across the dance floor, he smiled benevolently into her face, yet Athena felt an uneasy prickle flee down her spine. Something was amiss here, yet she couldn't for the life of her guess what it might be. Regardless of Stephen's kindness and his seeming ignorance of the fate of the letter she had entrusted him with, Athena was determined never to take him into her confidence again.

"Thank God that's all over," Jeremy sighed when he collapsed onto the carriage seat sometime after midnight. "I didn't think the evening would ever end!"

"I'm proud of you both," his aunt informed him, smoothing down her skirts and drawing her cloak more tightly about her shoulders. The night air was cold and damp, and she was already thinking of the warm fire that would be waiting for her in her bedchamber back home. "I must confess you've got all the charm of your devil-may-care father, and you, Athena, seem to have emerged once again with your reputation intact."

"Thank you, aunt," Athena murmured, knowing full well that what had pleased the older woman so was the fact that Stephen had danced with her twice, an honor he hadn't bestowed upon anyone else that night.

"I've got to be up early tomorrow," Jeremy added with a yawn, not caring to enter into a discussion of his merits with his aunt. He had enjoyed being reunited with several of his old school chums and in playing the part of a military hero in the eyes of the young girls he had danced with. Yet the evening's pleasures had quickly grown dull, and he had to admit to himself that, like Athena, he cared little for socializing. This clannish dislike for pomp and pageantry was clearly a Courtland trait, he thought with a smile.

"Are the Rangers leaving tomorrow?" Athena asked, striving hard to hide the disappointment in her voice. She didn't want him to know how much she hated the thought of his leaving.

"I've got to report to Major Rogers and find out. Ambrose Kensington told me tonight the Seventh Highland Company and the rest of the Regulars quartered in West York are marching out at dawn. I imagine we'll be next."

Athena's breath caught painfully in her throat. So Lochiel was leaving tomorrow. She should have realized, for Jeremy had told her that another assault on Quebec was being planned by General Amherst. A numbness unlike anything she had ever experienced crept into her heart. The Rangers would undoubtedly be taking part in that assault, and Fletcher's regiment would probably be sent to join them.

For the first time in her young life Athena knew what it meant to be in the grip of mortal dread. 'Twas entirely possible that all of the men she loved might assemble together on that great battlefield, for General Amherst had assured the citizens of West York that this campaign would be the last one of the war. She didn't think she'd be able to bear it if she lost any one of them.

Except Major Blackmoor, she told herself angrily. She might have come to care for him, given time, but he had behaved so callously towards her that she'd gladly send him off to Quebec to meet the French with all her blessings.

"Don't be so somber, sweeting," she heard Jeremy whisper under cover of the gentle snores that were issuing from her aunt's corner of the darkened carriage. "I'll keep my visit with Major Rogers brief so we can spend the evening together. I'll find out if he's heard anything about Colm and Fletcher, too."

"Oh, would you really?" Athena asked, some of her fears evaporating.

"Anything for you, my pet," he told her with a chuckle, hoping to leave her with some happy news to cling to. In truth he, too, was concerned about Fletcher, whose regiment seemed to have taken some brutal abuse on the Canadian border of late. 'Twould ease his own mind as well as Athena's if he could discover what had happened to their absent oldest brother.

Bidding Jeremy a sleepy good night, Athena entered her bedchamber to find a single candle glowing on the dressing table. The soft, golden light it shed illuminated the sleeping Mercy curled up on the counterpane of the big four-poster bed. Shaking her awake, Athena obligingly described for the groggy girl the events of the evening while Mercy unfastened the whalebone corset that Athena had suffered to wear.

"I vow 'tis a pleasure to breathe again," Athena remarked, stretching her arms in relief. "Breeches are by far the most comfortable things to wear, and I'm beginning to wish I'd been born a lad like my brothers!"

"Listening to Mistress Bower, one would think you're already too much like them!" Mercy giggled, hanging the magnificent ballgown away. "Tell me again who Master Jeremy danced with," she begged, though Athena had already run through the list twice.

"Tomorrow," Athena promised with an unladylike yawn. "I'm too tired to remember now."

Indeed, she was asleep the moment her head touched the pillow, and she dreamed of the dancing that had taken place at the Kensingtons' that night. She was being partnered by Stephen, who was holding her far more intimately than the discreet steps of the dance permitted. Yet Athena didn't mind, and when she glanced past his wide, satin-covered chest, she found that his eyes were warm as they gazed into hers and that it was not Stephen but Lochiel Blackmoor who was sweeping her off her feet.

Athena's soft lips curved in her sleep, and she burrowed deeper into the feathery depths of her bed. Yet something disturbing had insinuated itself into her dream, and the smile faded when she realized that it was Ballycor's insistent whinnying. 'Twas an odd sound to be mingling with the soft strains of violins, and Athena came wide awake when it dawned on her that the stallion's angry cries were, in fact, real.

She rose from the bed and ran barefoot to the window. Pushing the hair from her eyes, she peered through the frosted glass, startled to see the grayish glow of dawn stealing across the horizon. Was it morning already? She couldn't believe she had slept for so long.

All was silent in the stables below, and no light burned in the small rooms above them where Tykie lived. Yet Athena knew that she hadn't imagined the stallion's nervous stamping and snorting. Pulling a wrapper over her shoulders, she quietly descended the stairs, knowing Ballycor wouldn't sound an alarm without reason. She decided against awakening Jeremy or Wills, yet as a precaution took Fletcher's aged but trustworthy Brown Bess from the gun cabinet. The musket gave her a feeling of security, though she had no real need for it, not with Tykie nearby.

The dawn air was chilly, and Athena shivered in her thin cotton wrapper as she hurried across the lawn. The whitewashed stables loomed eerily through the graying light, and her breath caught fearfully in her throat as she came close enough to hear the low murmur of male voices coming from within.

What was going on? Where was Tykie? She couldn't distinguish his deep Highland dialect among the voices she heard. Leaning against the tack room door, she wondered if perhaps she shouldn't go back for help. Horse thieves abounded in the colonies, thanks to the princely sum the army paid for any animals not already confiscated in the name of the war effort. The thieves were usually desperate men out to make money, and Athena had no desire to confront them alone.

Yet the sound of Ballycor's angry squealing instantly made her forget her caution. The thieves would be long gone by the time she managed to rouse Jeremy and Wills. She knew that she would have to stop them herself if she intended to save her beloved stallion, and with the musket held firmly in a white-knuckled grasp, Athena stepped inside.

The sight that met her eyes made her stop short in astonishment, for never in her life had she expected to see anything like this. There on the hay-strewn floor lay Tykie Downs, his hands and feet bound by leather thongs while three men in Provincial uniform were doing everything short of sitting on top of him to keep him subdued. Two other soldiers, meanwhile, were trying to put a halter on Ballycor, who chased them out with teeth and hoofs whenever they entered his stall. It was difficult to tell who was having the worse time of it, the trio battling the struggling Tykie or the two who had chosen to halter the big stallion.

"If you don't all stop this minute I'll go ahead and shoot."

Five startled pairs of eyes swung around at the sound of that clear, hard voice to find a determined young woman standing before them in little more than her nightrail. There was a muzzle loader in her hands, and the easy way in which she hefted it against one hip made it obvious to them that she knew how to use it.

"I want you to untie him," Athena continued, jerking her head in Tykie's direction without taking her eyes off the one in the corporal's uniform, who was obviously in charge.

"You can't be serious!" he burst out. "Took all five of us to tie him up in the first place!"

"Untie him," Athena repeated. Her finger tightened about the trigger.

"C'mon, corporal, surely you ain't scared of that one. She's little more'n a girl."

"A real beauty, too," another soldier stated.

All five of them had come to their feet by now, and Athena didn't care too much for the gleam in their eyes as they studied her. Neither, apparently, did Tykie, who resumed his frantic thrashing, muffled curses issuing from the gag stuffed in his mouth.

"Keep your distance," Athena warned as the two biggest soldiers began a slow advance. One of them was all but leering as he studied her, his eyes on the gaping neckline where she had neglected to tie the wrapper shut. The tops of her breasts were visible above the embroidered edging of her nightgown, a sight that made it easy to forget the cold metal barrel of the Brown Bess.

"We've come to take your horses, miss. We don't aim to do you no harm."

"What about him?" Athena demanded, indicating Tykie. "You've bound and gagged a loyal citizen of the colony, and you don't call that doing him harm? Furthermore you're stealing horses belonging to provincials like yourselves. I thought we were supposed to be fighting the French, not each other."

"Saucy-tongued wench, ain't you?" the biggest of the soldiers, a middle-aged individual with something of a potbelly, inquired interestedly. "Seems to me she could use a lesson in manners, eh, corporal?"

"Take it easy, private," the corporal pleaded. It was obvious to Athena that he didn't have the authority to command the older man's respect.

"You stay where you are," Athena repeated, swinging the musket in the big soldier's direction. She was fairly certain that he took orders from the corporal only if he wanted to. "I'll shoot if you come one step closer."

"Will you now?' he asked, unimpressed by her bravado. His grin was rather frightening, and Athena wet her dry lips, wishing she had roused Wills and Jeremy after all.

"How do you intend to stop me, girl? Surely someone as pretty as you wouldn't dream of shooting one of your own kind, would you? Like you said, I'm not a Frenchie."

"I take considerable offense at the comparison of your ownself to someone of Miss Courtland's caliber," came a low yet decidedly threatening voice from the doorway.

Athena's head came round and she stifled a gasp as she saw Lochiel Blackmoor lounging against the door, hands thrust casually into his belt, a smile playing on his lips. Yet there was nothing pleasant about the way his eyes were mustering the men gathered before him, and perhaps they sensed as much, for they began to give the corporal uneasy glances.

All save the overweight private, whose sneer grew even nastier when he noticed Lochiel's green plaid kilt. "Have I offended you, girlie?" he asked contemptuously.

"Peters, you're talking to a major," the corporal reminded him nervously.

Private Peters uttered a short laugh. "You think I'm gonna show respect to a lobsterback, especially one wearin' a dress?"

Athena's heart gave a fearful leap as she saw the look that passed across Lochiel's face. She didn't mind admitting to herself that her knees had grown weak at the sight of him, yet her joy turned instantly to fear as she began to suspect the violence he was capable of. Apparently Peters also seemed to realize that he had broached a temper better left pacified, and the change in him from surly troublemaker to respectful subordinate was almost laughable.

"We're under orders, sir," he reminded the Highland officer, whose menacing expression had unnerved him. "General Amherst needs horses for the march north, and we're to round up anything in the area that looks halfway decent."

"I'm well aware of the general's order." Lochiel's voice was smooth, yet a shiver fled down Athena's spine. As yet he hadn't spared her a single glance or made a move to step away from the timbered wall against which he leaned. Didn't he know she was here, or was he ignoring her intentionally?

She could not know that he was aware of her to the depths of his man's being, that every sense within him was attuned to the seductive wildness of her unbound hair and the graceful curves revealed by the clinging muslin wrapper.

"I realize you have orders to follow," Lochiel went on reasonably, "but I see no need for a white horse in our army since we are often forced to travel by stealth. Furthermore, a stallion as unmanageable as this one could prove dangerous to the other horses. Your Captain Hitchcock agreed with me when I took the matter up with him and allowed me to intervene on his behalf."

He was not unaware of the gratitude shining in Athena's beautiful eyes when he finished speaking. Deliberately continuing to ignore her, he sauntered across the floor, his polished boots nearly touching Tykie's prone form.

"I want this man untied and apologies made to Miss Courtland," he added quietly.

"Oh, please, sir, couldn't you untie him for us?" the corporal begged. "I've seen that crazed look in a man's eyes before, and I can't vouch for our safety were we to try it."

Lochiel's lips twitched. "I understand, corporal. I would suggest, however, that you take yourselves away from here with utmost haste, as I doubt Miss Courtland and I will be able to restrain him once his bonds are removed."

All five soldiers were hard put to hide their relief and were quick to make their apologies.

"Thank you, sir."

"Begging your pardon, Miss Courtland."

"The major's right, miss. A white horse'd be hard to hide from the Frenchies. Sorry we tried to take him from you."

Silence fell in the raftered barn as soon as they were gone. Only Tykie continued his thrashing and ranting, and Lochiel, his eyes twinkling with amusement, waited a moment before he bent down to cut the leather thongs with his dirk.

"The bastards!" Tykie roared as soon as he was free. "Did they hurt you, lass?" he demanded, lumbering to his feet.

"I'm fine," Athena assured him.

"Pulin' little soldiers leaped on me when I came doon tae stop the beastie's fussin'!" the big Highlander exploded, referring to the now complacent Ballycor. "Mayhap it took a' five o' them tae pin me, but, by God, 'tis an insult I willna leave unavenged! You, lad!" His thick forefinger poked Lochiel's wide chest. "I've a debt tae repay ye, but I maun be after 'em the noo."

He was gone before another word could be said, a fierce battle cry echoing through the still dawn air. Lochiel and Athena exchanged startled glances, and then both of them burst into helpless laughter.

"Thank you for coming," Athena said when she could speak. "I don't know what would have happened if you hadn't."

Her words caused the amusement to vanish from Lochiel's face. For a moment he stared down at her, an enigmatic expression in his silver-gray eyes. Color rose high in Athena's cheeks, and she retreated to Ballycor's side, trying to recover her composure while she stroked the stallion's velvety muzzle.

"I couldn't allow Ballycor to wind up on the front," Lochiel said. "He's a hunter, not a war-horse."

Athena couldn't see him over the high door of the stall, but his voice sounded cool and detached. She hated herself for the pang it caused her. She could not know that he was unable to admit to her the real reason for his coming, that he had wanted to spare Ballycor for her sake . . . and to see her again.

He had told himself that he had intervened simply because he could not allow a magnificent animal to succumb to the cruel abuse of being an army mount. Yet watching the achingly beautiful profile that was Athena's as she whispered with seeming absorption into Ballycor's ear, he knew that he had only been fooling himself.

"Athena," he said abruptly and saw her flinch at the curt utterance of her name. Her large blue eyes were on his face, and he felt enraged by the distance that separated them.

"Come out of that stall," he commanded. "I don't like speaking to people I can't see."

To his surprise she obeyed, closing the door behind her as she came to stand before him. Her wrapper was untied at the throat, and he could see a pulse beating wildly in her throat. Was it fear that caused her breasts to rise and fall in such rapid rhythm or something else? Could it be possible that she, too, was aware of the current that crackled like wildfire between them?

By God, he had to know. He had to touch her one last time, to feel the sweetness of her lips beneath his before she was gone forever. Distant memories taunted him as he reached for her, of the promise he had made to himself on the ride over not to forget where his duty lay.

As his hands slid about her waist she uttered a soft moan and her lips parted. "Oh, Lochiel," she whispered, trembling with the need to feel his mouth touch hers.

He lowered his dark head, his strong, brown arms capturing her in a savage embrace. Her nightgown became entangled between his booted legs as he pulled her close against the lean length of his body.

"Athena! What the devil's going on here?"

They broke apart at the sound of Jeremy's voice coming from outside. Athena gazed up at Lochiel to find him regarding her with a sorrowful shake of his head, his expression inscrutable.

"I see I've been a fool again," he said with cold finality. "I should have realized you wouldn't be content with what I could give you."

She stared at him uncomprehendingly. "What do you mean, Lochiel? What have I done?"

He uttered a harsh laugh. "Please don't play the innocent with me, my dear. It doesn't become you."

"Athena!" Jeremy called again. A moment later he had appeared in the doorway, barefoot and in cotton long johns, still tousled from sleep. "I heard Tykie storm out of here like a bull on the charge. What's happened?"

His words trailed away as his gaze traveled from the tall, raven-haired Highlander to his sister's stricken face. "Thena?" he questioned, placing a brotherly arm about her shoulders. "What's happened? Are you all right?"

"I'll be taking my leave now, Miss Courtland. There seems to be naught else I can do for you."

With a curt bow in Athena's direction, Lochiel strode out, ignoring the handsome young man whose casual embrace seemed so familiar to her. His expression was rigid as he mounted his horse and galloped off toward town. Bitterness, more galling than any he'd ever experienced, overwhelmed him. What a fool he'd been! In rushing headlong to protect Athena's horse and to see her again, he hadn't even paused to consider that her lover might still be with her.

Fool! he cursed, aware that he had almost bared his heart to a woman more cold and calculating than any he had ever met. Athena Courtland had shown him the meaning of deception once before and he had been stupid enough to allow himself to be duped a second time. Never again, Lochiel Blackmoor vowed to himself, turning his back on Courtland Grace forever.

Seven

Major Lochiel Blackmoor stepped from his quarters, the cold April wind hitting him full in the face. Frozen grass crunched beneath his boots as he paused to survey the empty parade grounds before him and watch the dark smoke coiling skyward from a fire several soldiers had built near the main gate. A brief thaw had swollen the brook that ran past the fort's outer ramparts, and even from here Lochiel could hear the dull roar of the whitewater.

"Major?"

He turned to find his orderly hurrying toward him with a sheaf of papers in his hands.

"I've orders from Albany, sir."

"Thank you." Lochiel's lips twitched as he took the folder from the younger man, who immediately thrust his hands into the pockets of his worn greatcoat and stamped his feet.

"Cold, Barrett?"

"I haven't been truly warm since we spent Christmas in Albany, sir." His wind-reddened features took on a wistful look as he recalled the barracks where the Highland Regiment had spent the holidays. Fires had blazed night and day in the enormous stone hearths, and there had been little reason for anyone to venture outside.

Though Piers Barrett had loathed those endless hours of inactivity, he would gladly have traded this frozen existence for the comforts of Albany all over again. He shook his head, recalling how excited he had been when the orders to march had finally come through. If only the company had been sent somewhere besides the frozen hills just south of Lake Ontario!

"I'm not a Highlander like yourself, sir," Piers went on, wondering how the major managed to remain unaffected by the brutal cold. He was wearing naught but his uniform and a shoulder plaid, and his dark head was bare. Most of the Highlanders were oblivious to the cold, Piers thought enviously to himself. He had seen them drop exhaustedly to the ground at the end of a long day's march, wrapped only in their plaids, and fall instantly asleep despite the fact that they were lying in mud or snow.

"Colonial winters are tame compared with those back home," Lochiel told his young adjunct with the trace of a smile. 'Twas easier these days to think about the isolated mountain glen where Blackmoors had lived for the past three centuries. Time had dulled the pain of losing everything to the vengeful English who had defeated the Scots over a dozen years ago after Prince Charles Edward Stuart had rallied the clans in an effort to reclaim his throne from the German King George, whom the Scots called the true pretender.

Lochiel Blackmoor's harshly chiseled countenance took on a bitter expression. Bonnie Prince Charlie they had called him, and how eagerly the clans had pledged him their hands and hearts. He himself, an impressionable lad of barely eighteen, had taken up arms for the Stuart cause, and even now he could remember the patriotic fervor that had burned within him. How swiftly his innocence had died in that terrible defeat on Culloden Moor, when the clans had been slaughtered by King George's butchering son!

Lochiel had become a fugitive, his one driving need to return home to the safety of his remote Highland glen. He and a handful of other survivors had been hunted like animals, but by traveling at night over rocky paths known only to them, they had managed to elude capture.

The bitterness in the silver eyes deepened. There had been no home for Lochiel to return to, only a smoldering ruin to mark the boundaries of the once magnificent lodge the Blackmoors had owned. The sheep and cattle had been driven off, the loyal servants and clansmen killed, and his own mother and sister had barely managed to escape the carnage with their lives.

The shock had caused his sister to lose her unborn child, a bitter blow since her husband had fallen at Culloden despite Lochiel's efforts to save him. Both his mother and sister were living in the Lowlands now and his sister had remarried, but Lochiel knew that the scars had never quite healed for any of them. Yet they were luckier than most, Lochiel's mother was always fond of saying. Many of their fellow clansmen hadn't made it out of the Highlands alive.

Lochiel often wondered if the Blackmoors could truly call themselves lucky. Their ancestral home was gone, they had been forced to turn to indifferent relatives for help, and he himself had turned his back on everything the proud Highlanders stood for by enlisting in the British Army not a year after the bloody defeat at Culloden.

Many of the loyal men who served under him now were also survivors of that bitter conflict, Lochiel knew, recalling his thoughts to the present.

Most of them had joined the Highland Regiment for the sole purpose of coming to the New World to fight the French, Scotland's supposed allies in the Stuart conflict, who had failed them miserably despite their pledged support of the Bonnie Prince.

Oddly enough, Lochiel's motives were different. He felt no bitterness toward the French and instead found himself haunted by memories of the cruelty of the English soldiers who had murdered his uncles, his cousins, and his closest friends on the blood-soaked moor of Culloden. The victors had taken no prisoners, and Lochiel had never forgotten how they had chased the wounded survivors into the hills, cutting them down as they ran and then, thirsting for more, launching themselves upon the innocent women and children of the various clans.

As a major in the Seventh Company he was known for his courage and cool nerves on the battlefield. He expected and received the unswerving loyalty of his men, and if rules were broken, punishment was meted out in a swift and terrible fashion. Yet Major Lochiel Blackmoor was just, and this above all had earned him the respect of his men and the officers who served with and above him. He had made enemies for his unshakable convictions, yet they were greatly outnumbered by those who admired him.

"The sergeant-major asked me to bring these to you," Piers Barrett said, wondering why the major hadn't made a move to open the thick pouch of papers he held in his hands. He was curious about their orders, secretly hoping that someone with authority had decided the wilderness surrounding Fort Shuyler was no place to winter an army. Mayhap they'd be sent back to Albany until spring to wait out the arrival of the English warships that would participate in the final assault on Quebec.

The winter had been quiet enough, what with Montcalm in Quebec and most of the French Regulars and Canadian troops holed up in their various forts. No unusual activity had been reported by any British regiments stationed along the chain of great lakes and the St. Lawrence River. Throughout the long, snow-filled days of February and March, Piers Barrett had performed his duties without complaint despite his impatience to leave the primitive conditions of Fort Shuyler behind. Now that a new set of orders had arrived from Albany, Piers was intensely curious to find out what they were. Why didn't the major seem to share his hope that they'd been recalled?

"Bring me some tea, please," was all Lochiel said as he vanished into the small room that served as his office.

When Piers returned several minutes later with the steaming teapot, he found the papers lying in a neat stack on Major Blackmoor's desk. There was no indication that he had even read them, yet Piers was quick to note the thoughtful expression on the officer's face.

"Corporal Martin's wagering we're being sent south," Piers remarked conversationally, transferring the fragrant tea into the mug he had brought with him. Major Blackmoor's deep chuckle came from behind him.

"Are you hoping the same?"

Piers's eyes met the major's unflinchingly. "Aye, sir." Having been the major's adjunct for the past two years, he had learned that it didn't pay to be dishonest with him. In truth, Piers all but worshiped Major Lochiel Blackmoor and secretly hoped that someday he'd make as fine a soldier. He was eighteen years old, young enough to still have heroes, and there were few men he respected as much as the soft-spoken Highland officer.

A tired smile lit the harsh features as Lochiel reached for his tea. "I wish I could tell you as much, lad, but I'm afraid that's not the case."

"Then we do have new orders?"

"Aye, and Mr. Martin isn't going to like them. Colonel Hambrick of the Massachusetts Provincials has reported increased movement among Canadian troops near Fort Oswego. Bands of Christian Iroquois have been spotted heading north from Fort Niagara to join them."

Piers Barrett's youthful face went pale. "Do you think Montcalm is planning an assault on New York, sir?"

Lochiel's own expression was grave. 'Twas entirely possible that the Canadians were being assembled for just that purpose. Deep snow and bitter cold wouldn't stop the Marquis de Montcalm from attempting a repeat of his crashing victory at Fort Ticonderoga last June, especially not with rumors running rampant that General Amherst was planning an English attack on Quebec. As soon as the Atlantic was free of winter storms, a fleet of British warships would be dispatched from Portsmouth to lend their aid, and Montcalm, obviously aware of it, wasn't content to quietly await their arrival.

The marquis was a seasoned soldier who would not hesitate to sweep south across snow-covered mountains in order to capture Albany. It was a chilling prospect, Lochiel knew, and one that had plagued the English commanders headquartered there since the war had begun. Lochiel's expression was savage. He had forced himself time and again during the last six months to remember that the citizens of New York could look after themselves. There was no reason in hell he should concern himself over the welfare of the people who lived there.

He became aware that young Piers Barrett was watching him intently and forced himself to smile, his stern features relaxing. "We've orders to make room for houseguests, lad. General Prideaux's Regulars are planning an advance on Lake Ontario to counter the French escalation at Oswego, and some of the Provincial militias are coming up to help. As yet a confrontation seems unlikely," he added, "so you've naught to worry about for the moment."

"Always keepin' us guessin', eh?" came the disgruntled voice of Sergeant-Major Andrew Durning from behind them. Like Lochiel, he wore a plaid over his tunic, pinned at the shoulder with a cairngorm brooch. Nothing kept a Highlander warmer, the sergeant-major was fond of saying, than a claymore at his side and a wool plaid to wrap himself in.

"Should've used yer influence wi' Jeff Amherst to request that the Seventh remain behind in Albany for the winter," the grizzled officer complained, making a face at the tea that had grown cold in the ironware kettle. "Instead ye've let them send us frae one place to another playin' peacekeepers an' scouts like them filthy Rangers."

"You told me yourself that three months of idling away in Albany nearly drove you mad," Lochiel reminded him, unable to hide his fondness for the belligerent old soldier. "Why would returning there now be any different?"

"Because at least down there we willna be freezin' our arses off waitin' for the bloody Frenchies tae do summat," the sergeant-major grumbled. "I've a mind they ain't payin' us enough for this," he added, stretching his hands toward the warmth of the small stove that stood in the center of the room. "When I hae me pension I'll write a long letter tae—"

"Would you care for tea, sir?" Piers interrupted politely, hoping to halt what was bound to be an endless tirade. "I can reheat what's left in the pot."

"Och, very well."

No sooner were the two officers alone than Sergeant-Major Durning fixed Lochiel with a sharp eye and demanded bluntly, "Wha' be ailin' ye, laddie? Ye've no been quite the same since we spent Christmas i' Albany. New Year's Eve was the last time ye agreed tae drink a dram wi' me, an' thot bonnie camp follower ye cast yer lecherous eye on last summer hae pined awa' of a broken heart for want o' ye. Furthermore my men'd rather face a battalion of Frenchies than your temper at inspection. What's happened to ye, eh?"

Lochiel's expression was unreadable as he moved to the window to study the smoke from the fires of the camp followers whose tents were erected on the south side of the fort. Even the terrible cold and the drifting snow hadn't daunted the soldiers' wives, the prostitutes, and the general riffraff who had followed them from Albany. To most of the soldiers at Fort Shuyler their presence was welcome. Camp followers performed services for the men, such as cooking, laundering, and sewing, and there was always a willing lassie to warm a lonely bed at night. Though Lochiel had never given a second thought to availing himself of their services, he had found his appetite for the so-called blanket girls diminished of late.

"Some of the lads, Hugh Martin in particular, hae the feelin' ye left yer heart back yonder in New York," Andy added shrewdly. " 'Twould explain why ye've been so surly."

"There's been a great deal on my mind recently," Lochiel informed him, his silver-gray eyes resting impassively on the sergeant-major's leathery face and revealing nothing. "One of my problems has been wondering what to do with a certain regimental sergeant-major who can't seem to keep from wasting time involving his men in idle speculation."

"I should've expected summat like that." The older man threw up his hands in disgust. "Never can expect a straight answer frae ye when the matter be personal." He shook his grizzled head as he studied the broad back turned toward him. " 'Tis wha' the lasses find sae irresistible aboot ye, Lochiel—the air o' mystery ye like tae cloak yersel' behind. Well, perhaps ye do ken how tae make those young hearts flutter, but tae me 'tis damned annoying."

Lochiel could not keep the grin from his face. Andy's tirades, whatever their nature, never failed to amuse him. Furthermore, he had no reason to take offense at the older man's words. The winter had been long and hard, and he was growing tired of the endless marches and the nerve-racking hours of idleness that were part of army life. He couldn't be expected not to become "surly," as Andy put it, not when the final confrontation with Montcalm still lay far in the future.

Surely Andy, who knew him better than most, must realize that. What bloody nonsense to suspect that a woman was the cause of his irritable nature! Perhaps he might have allowed himself to think a little too often of a pair of bright blue eyes and an impossibly arrogant, tilted chin—but that had been months ago, and Athena Courtland had become little more than a distant memory in his mind.

"Don't worry about me, Andy," he advised, clapping the sergeant-major on the shoulder. "If I've been unduly hard on your men I'll make it up to them. I always do." He turned at the door with a devilish smile. "And as for pining after a woman, you ken damned well I've yet to meet one that can hold my attention for the space of half an hour, let alone six long months."

Ironically those mocking words were to come back to Lochiel not a fortnight later, when a weary band of Provincials marched into the fort. Fresh snow had fallen the night before, making the long trek even more difficult, and it was obvious to the watching Lochiel that the men were tired and in need of sleep. Accompanying the fort commander out to meet them, he noticed how warm the pale April sun felt on his back despite the fact that a fresh layer of snow powdered the hemlock trees beyond the bastion walls. Spring was in the air, yet few save the winter-seasoned Highlanders seemed aware of it.

"We're going to have a devil of a time putting all these men up," Major Eure remarked. He was an amiable man with an excellent sense of humor, and Lochiel had come to respect him since the Highlanders' arrival at Fort Shuyler.

"I don't think my men will object to doubling up," he remarked, watching the cold, weary soldiers in their blue and red uniforms file past.

"Looks like we picked up some Rangers, too," Major Eure remarked, catching sight of the canvas gaiters and familiar green shirts. He sighed. "Gonna be hard to keep 'em from fighting with the Provincials and the Provincials from fighting with your Regulars. I sometimes wonder how come the French haven't stomped all over our divided ranks. I suppose I'd better receive the company commander and get his orders. Coming, Major Blackmoor?"

Lochiel's reply was a nearly imperceptible shake of his head, for his attention had been caught by one of the Rangers who was striding toward the barracks with his companions. His silver eyes narrowed as he took in the familiar blond hair and the square, clefted chin. It was a face he hadn't seen for quite some time but one that he had never forgotten.

Feeling those disconcerting eyes upon him, the Ranger lifted his head, and although no recognition passed across his face, he came forward to address the silent Highlander. "You got something on your mind, sir," he asked in his broad, New England drawl, "or were you just staring at me for fun?"

Lochiel's frown deepened. The cocksure young man before him could use a lesson or two in discipline. With his thumbs hooked in his belt and a smile playing on his lips, he didn't seem to care at all that he was addressing an officer.

"So you've joined the Rangers," he remarked, the coldness of his voice causing the younger man to lift a brow in surprise.

"Do we know each other, sir?"

The puzzled look in those youthful blue eyes inadvertently fanned Lochiel's anger. "We were never formally introduced," he grated, recalling the hot brand that had twisted through his guts when this half-clothed young pup had appeared behind Athena in the stables at Courtland Grace, his hand resting intimately about her slim shoulders. "I happened to see you in West York last October. You—"

The Ranger interrupted him by throwing back his head and uttering a hearty laugh. Merriment danced in those blue eyes, which reminded Lochiel all too annoyingly of another. "That must have been my brother, sir. He has a way of getting himself in hot water and causing me all the grief when it comes to mistaken identities."

Lochiel didn't care overly for the fact that this insolent whelp seemed to have the advantage of him. "Your brother?" he inquired softly.

Instantly the Ranger's merriment vanished. Perhaps he sensed that the whipcord-lean man before him was dangerous. "Yes, my brother Jeremy," he said cautiously. "We're twins. You say you met him in West York last autumn?"

Lochiel's anger began to fade. It wasn't fair to condemn this lad because his twin brother was Athena Courtland's lover . . . yet thinking about that only served to make his blood boil anew. "Your brother and I," he said coldly, "have a mutual acquaintance, a young woman by the name of Athena Courtland."

The Ranger's hands were suddenly entwined in the rough material of Lochiel's blue coat. "Athena?" he rasped. "You've seen her? When? Did you find her well?"

Though there was uncommon strength in the eagerly clutching hands, Lochiel easily pushed the excited Ranger from him. His mind was reeling. By God, had Athena taken both of them to bed? There was no mistaking the emotions that blazed feverishly in those bright blue eyes. Blood and fury, how many men in the colonies were living testament to Athena Courtland's sexual appetites? How many more of her lovers was he to encounter before the war was over?

"I met Miss Courtland at Egon de Vries's home in October," he remarked in a voice that caused Colm to retreat a hasty step, wondering what Jeremy could possibly have done to make such an enemy of this man. "She appeared well and seemed perfectly content to be in the company of your brother."

No jealousy flared across the pleasant features at this statement, but Lochiel wasn't about to answer any more questions. Let him find out for himself how Athena was faring. He could always write his brother and ask, Lochiel decided, striding away with his features set in anger. If he and his twin shared the same woman, then surely they wouldn't mind sharing the same information about her.

Near the barracks he was hailed by Corporal Hugh Martin, who had been sitting cross-legged on a narrow bench polishing his beloved dirk. "I hear we've got new orders, sir," he remarked, coming to his feet. "Will we be seeing any action soon, do ye think?"

"The only action you'll be seeing, corporal," Lochiel grated, "is an extra eight hours of sentry duty tonight if you don't learn to stop questioning your superiors."

"What in hell was that all about?" Davie Skelley demanded, staring in puzzlement after the dark-headed officer. "He's never refused tae discuss our orders wi' us openly before!"

"I keep tellin' ye, Davie," Hugh Martin replied, rubbing his beard, "there be a woman behind the major's troubles."

"Stuff it, Hugh," Davie snorted scornfully. "Why, the major'd na sooner let some schemin' lassie worm her way into his heart than he'd gie up the pleasures o' takin' a different one tae bed each night!"

"I'd no be sae sure," Hugh protested softly, looking thoughtfully in the direction Major Blackmoor had vanished.

Davie gave him an impatient punch. "Ye be an incurable romantic, Hugh. There's no but military matters on the major's mind, an' if some bonnie lass did catch his fancy, ye can bet he'll hae forgotten her name come tomorrow."

Eight

Athena's face was scarcely visible beneath the fur-edged hood of her cape, yet the frown that marred her smooth brow was difficult to conceal. Her attention was centered on the slate rooftop of Courtland Grace, which had appeared over the snow-covered hill ahead of her, and she was thinking to herself how much she loathed returning to that dark and gloomy place.

Tykie Downs, who rode behind her, sighed as he caught sight of her wistful expression and morosely scratched his head. The winter had been hard on all of them, but Miss Athena seemed to have weathered it worst of all. How could she not come to dread living in her own home with that sea-serpent aunt of hers growing more difficult and demanding by the day? Illness had forced Amelia Bower to her bed during the holidays, and for the last few months she had languished, refusing to let anyone but her niece take care of her.

"Wha' the auld termagant needs is a good, swift kick in the arse to cure her," Tykie mumbled to himself. "Nothin' but a thirst for pampering be ailin' her!"

His dour thoughts were interrupted by Stephen Kensington, who had trotted his gray mare to Ballycor's side. "Have you had enough, Athena?" he called. "I vow I'm chilled to the bone."

"Just one more turn around the fields," Athena begged.

Stephen's ears were red with cold beneath his beaver hat, and the expensive serge coat he wore was better suited for a drive in a covered coach than a brisk gallop through the frozen winter air. In truth he hadn't expected to go riding when he paid a call at Courtland Grace, but then he hadn't expected to fall victim to Athena's skill at manipulation, either.

"Oh, very well," he agreed, unable to resist the little face that pleaded with him from amid the fringe of glossy marten fur.

Tykie watched with a satisfied grin as Athena kicked Ballycor into a run. The big stallion's hindquarters pumped rhythmically as he took off across the frozen snow, Stephen's small mare floundering behind. 'Twas good to see the wee lassie in the fresh air for a change instead of fetching for her aunt, who spent her days on a settee with a shawl wrapped about her shoulders, querulously demanding that this and that be brought to her.

Young Kensington didn't seem to relish the exercise as much as Athena did, and Tykie was surprised that he had even agreed to it. Usually his visits consisted of long hours spent on the sofa under Amelia's watchful eye while poor Athena chafed with obvious boredom at the small talk they exchanged. Stephen's appearances had increased lamentably of late, Tykie had noticed, and he had railed at Prudence just the other day for daring to suggest that the arrogant pup was seriously courting Miss Athena.

Tykie was shrewd enough to realize that Kensington had other things on his mind than marriage. For that reason he had been quick to insist on accompanying the young couple out riding. 'Twas obvious to Tykie that if anyone needed a chaperone, Miss Athena did. Being no fool, he could easily read what was on Stephen Kensington's mind, and he would sooner kill the fellow with his bare hands than allow his beloved mistress to come to harm.

"I dinna ken why the lassie's puttin' up wi' him!" Tykie grumbled to himself, watching as the slim figure in dark blue velvet disappeared into the bare trees while Stephen's mare fell farther and farther behind. "She'd no hae hesitated tae send him packin' before! Och, everythin' be changed since Master Jem went awa' an' the winter came sae hard an' cold!" He sighed deeply, wishing things were as they had been before the war, when the Courtland brothers had all been home and the sparkle hadn't faded from Miss Athena's beautiful eyes.

Reaching the stables ahead of Stephen and Tykie, Athena dismounted and bent to warm her hands in front of the small Franklin stove in the tack room. She was grateful for a few minutes alone, for it seemed that she never had time to herself anymore. Aunt Amelia was always asking her to fetch for her or to read to her, and Stephen had been coming round nearly every day since the February drifts had given way to the frozen wastes of March and April.

Why didn't she simply tell him to go away? She didn't particularly enjoy his visits, finding him thoroughly dull and self-centered, nor did she care for the lecherous way he always stared at her whenever her aunt wasn't looking.

"You've grown into such a spineless creature, Athena Courtland," she admonished herself. 'Twas true that her happiness seemed to have fled with Jeremy's departure last October, and she hadn't been able to bury the pain of her loss during the usually hectic holiday season.

Even though the people of New York seemed determined to forget about the war and an overwhelming number of balls and soirées had been held throughout the winter, Athena had been forced to turn down every one of them. Her aunt wasn't up to attending, and it wouldn't have been proper for her to go alone. The invitations that had arrived from Albany had been particularly difficult for the bored and restless Athena to refuse. Few people in West York had any real idea how the war effort stood, and Athena had wanted very much to question the officers in Albany themselves.

"Mayhap Aunt Amelia's illness was for the best," she told herself now, rubbing her cheek against the soft marten fur that trimmed the hood of her velvet riding cloak. The British Regulars were among the troops that had been quartered in Albany throughout the winter, and it was entirely possible that Major Blackmoor had been invited to many of the same functions Athena and her aunt had.

In fact, according to Katrine de Vries, who had spent the entire holiday season there, Lochiel Blackmoor had become something of a hero to the ladies of Albany. Her giggling descriptions of the major's numerous liaisons made it obvious to Athena that he hadn't spared her a single thought since he'd ridden out of her life last October. She told herself it didn't matter, although in moments of painful honesty she had to admit that the memory of his kisses and the possessive gleam in his silver eyes still haunted her sleep.

It would have galled her to learn that Katrine's tales were total fabrication. In truth Lochiel Blackmoor's public appearances had been noticeably rare and were intended merely to please General Amherst, who greatly enjoyed the young officer's company and personally requested his presence at every gathering held.

Moreover, Katrine had taken quite a fancy to the handsome Highlander herself, yet she would never admit as much to Athena, not when Major Blackmoor had all but refused to acknowledge her presence whenever they chanced to meet. Since Katrine thrived on attention, she found his attitude vexing to the extreme, every failed attempt to coax him into conversation or plead a dance serving to remind her of how Athena had successfully managed to lure him into her father's study for clandestine lovemaking last autumn.

"Thank goodness she doesn't know what really happened between us," Athena murmured aloud, pushing back the hood of her cloak as the heat of the stove began to warm her. 'Twas hard enough for her to feign indifference whenever Katrine came rushing over with yet another vivid description of the latest beauty Major Blackmoor had been seen dallying with.

"I'll box her ears the next time she's here," Athena vowed, her patience wearing thin. How much longer was she to pretend that what Katrine had to say held no meaning for her at all?

A hand settled on her sleeve, startling her from her thoughts, and she whirled about, fearing for a moment that Stephen had caught her in the tack room alone.

"Oh, 'tis you, Tykie," she breathed.

"Aye, 'tis only Tykie," the big man growled, stretching his own hands toward the stove. "Na the Kensington pup as ye feared. I left him behind the byre cursin' an' knockin' ice frae his wee beastie's shoes. 'Twill take him a while tae get back here, especially if he canna ride her."

"You should've offered him your horse and led his mare back yourself," Athena chided softly.

"Aye, I should hae," Tykie agreed, peering down at the square-jawed profile that was turned to him. Athena's cheeks were flushed from the heat of the stove and her eyes were downcast, but he could see the faint outline of a smile curve her lips. "Why do ye let him come, lass?" he demanded, encouraged by this. "Will ye no tell him ye've na interest in lettin' him court ye?"

Athena stirred restlessly, and for a moment he didn't think she'd answer. "Oh, Tykie," she said at last, her soft voice hollow with despair, "it doesn't matter one way or the other if Stephen comes to see me. Nothing seems to matter anymore." She gave a bitter laugh. "Sometimes I think I might even accept if he asks me to marry him."

"Och, lass, dinna say thot!" Tykie burst out.

The blue eyes that were turned upon him were filled with anguish. " 'Tis useless to go on pretending, Tykie. Everything's changed. Father's gone and Colm and Jeremy are soldiers now, not the boys they used to be. Fletcher hasn't written in four months and"—her voice broke but she continued stubbornly—"and even Major Rogers hasn't been able to locate the whereabouts of his regiment. He may be dead for all we know," she added flatly.

Tykie was aghast. This hopelessly unhappy young woman couldn't be his brazen Athena! How could she have been harboring so much sadness without his being aware of it? " 'Tis na reason tae marry Stephen Kensington," he pointed out angrily. "The war willna last forever, lass, an' yer brothers will come hame eventually. Ye maun think o' the future!"

"I am thinking of the future," Athena replied, bitter tears stinging her eyes. "Suppose none of my brothers survives the assault on Quebec? Suppose I have to spend the rest of my life caring for my aunt, who seems to have found enjoyment in playing the role of invalid, though both of us know she's healthy as an ox?

"I am thinking of the future, Tykie," she repeated more softly, as though she were finally making up her mind to turn her back on something she had been clinging to. "Mayhap marriage to Stephen Kensington won't be as horrible as both of us think."

She was gone before he could reply, brushing past him amid a whisper of flounced skirts. The echo of her boots on stone and the sound of the outer door slamming shut made Tykie wince. Collapsing on a three-legged stool, which groaned beneath its heavy burden, he put his face in his hands and wondered what he could do to mend the pain in her heart and give her new hope to cling to.

The first thing he could do was get rid of that addlepated Kensington fellow, Tykie decided, in case Miss Athena was really daft enough to marry him. 'Twould take a bit of planning, he decided, and in the meantime the least he could do was give the poor lass a wee bit of time to herself. She was in such a sorry state of mind at the moment that Kensington was bound to notice. Being the worm he was, he'd doubtless take advantage of it by pressing for her hand the moment he came back into the parlor—and Miss Athena might just be unhappy enough to accept.

"O'er my dead corpse," Tykie muttered to himself, the expression on his bearded face so ferocious that Hale, his assistant, took one look at him and hastily shut the tack room door without asking for the afternoon off as he had planned.

Stephen's mood was foul by the time he returned, for he was badly frozen as a result of having been forced to lead his mare by the bridle the last quarter-mile to the barn. An ill-tempered throbbing began to pulse in his temples when he was informed by a regretful Tykie that Mistress Athena had been taken ill unexpectedly.

"She was coughin' badly an' shakin' wi' the chills," Tykie told him gravely. " 'Twas best she went straight to bed."

"Perhaps we should send for the physician," Stephen said with a forced show of concern. Inwardly he was thinking that it served Athena right for having ridden out in such frigid weather.

"A mustard plaster an' a wee bit o' rest be all Miss Athena needs," Tykie assured him.

Stephen debated whether or not to believe him. He had hoped to find Athena alone in the parlor when he returned, her whining aunt for once retired to her rooms. 'Twas vexing enough to have endured an hour of riding in the brutal cold and being abandoned on the hillside by this grinning giant! Surely his sacrifices weren't about to come to naught? Was Athena truly ill or was she trying to elude him?

Stephen was beginning to grow impatient with his role as lovelorn suitor. The thought had occurred to him recently that he should abandon this tiresome courtship and simply take from Athena what he wanted.

She was no trembling virgin to be treated with velvet gloves. She was a vibrant woman who would doubtless welcome the attention of a virile man like himself—especially since her Scottish lover had been gone for so many months. Why not give her what he knew she truly wanted rather than pretend that he was even remotely interested in marrying her?

"I'll be sure tae gie her yer best wishes, Master Kensington."

Stephen looked up into Tykie Downs's narrowed black eyes and felt a warning stab in the pit of his stomach. Was it possible that this oafish fool could read his mind? Of any obstacles that might stand in his way, his fear of the enormous Highlander was the greatest. There was an unacknowledged rivalry being waged between them, for Stephen was just as determined to make Athena his as Tykie Downs was to protect her.

It would have been relatively easy for Stephen to use his wealth and position in the colony to see that Tykie was dealt with discreetly. Yet he knew how much Athena adored the hulking giant, and he wasn't about to let anything distract her from his courtship. On the other hand, he was just as determined not to let a half-witted servant get the better of him, and his smile was decidedly cold as he conceded Tykie victory for the time being.

"Please tell Miss Athena that I'll call on her tomorrow."

Tykie's weathered face was almost angelic in its innocence.

" 'Twould be better if she sent word tae ye first, sir. She may no be recovered by then."

Stephen's cheeks flushed. No servant had the right to speak so insolently to a member of the ruling class. For a moment he contemplated cuffing the disrespectful fellow, but he thought better of it when Tykie folded his massive arms across his chest and stared down at him expectantly.

"Very well," he muttered. "I'll wait until your mistress feels well enough to send for me." Turning heel, he called irritably for his mare.

"Now for Miss Athena hersel'," Tykie murmured smugly, striding toward the house.

How best to cheer her? he wondered, opening the back door and stepping into the whitewashed kitchen with its oak cabinets and polished cookware. Prudence was in the root cellar collecting the makings for dinner, which was just as well, for an altercation would surely have arisen at the sight of Tykie's filthy boots on her clean stone floors.

"Where be Miss Athena?" Tykie asked Nan, who was busy at the pump with a kettle of steaming washwater.

"In the parlor serving tea to the mistress." Nan's youthful face was a thundercloud of outrage. "If I didn't care for Miss Athena so much I vow I'd give notice on the spot! 'Twas bad enough when we were ordered about like animals, but now the old woman's got it into her head that only Miss Athena can care for her while she's bedridden! 'Tisn't fair, and I don't see how Miss Athena can—"

Nan broke off as the back door opened, while Tykie, expecting to see Prudence's ominous form, guiltily began to polish the toes of his boots on the back of his trouser legs. But it was only Wills, stamping with the cold and rubbing his hands together.

"Good thing molasses don't freeze," he remarked, shedding his greatcoat and hat, "or we'd have two busted barrels on the back of the sleigh."

"Been tae town?" Tykie inquired interestedly.

The footman nodded. "Hardly anyone about, and those who were did naught but complain of the weather. 'Twill be a late spring, they're predicting, and I'm inclined to agree with them. Where is Miss Athena?"

"I' the parlor wi' Mistress Bower," Tykie replied while Nan shook her head and compressed her lips, determined to say nothing more.

"I've a letter for her," Wills went on, drawing a small leather packet from his vest. His normally dour expression was softened with a smile. "I believe it may be from Master Fletcher."

Tykie's delighted whoop all but shook the raftered ceiling and brought Athena on the run, certain that something terrible had happened in the kitchen. She stopped short in the doorway, her woolen skirts swirling about her, and gazed in bewilderment at the three expectant faces turned her way.

"Whatever is going on here?" she demanded, sweeping inside, hands propped on her slim hips. "Where is Mr. Kensington, Tykie?"

The big man burst into laughter at her suspicious tone. "I threw him doon the well!" To everyone's amazement he began to caper about the room, causing the pots on the walls to rattle ominously. "Ye've a letter frae Fletcher, lass! Will ye no read it an' tell us how he's farin'?"

Athena stared at the thick packet the grinning Wills was holding out to her, Stephen already forgotten. " 'Tis from Fletcher?" she repeated, collapsing weakly into a chair.

"Yes, miss. John Burke gave it to me when I was over at the post. It came last night."

Her fingers trembled as she broke the seal and pulled the contents from the packet. There were four letters, all of them quite lengthy, dated from November through the end of March. Athena read the last one first, a feeling of nervous anticipation filling her heart.

Tykie and Wills busied themselves carrying in the supplies while Nan returned to her dishes, yet their eyes strayed constantly to Athena's bent head, their expectancy difficult to conceal. No one dared to break the silence that fell when Athena finally finished reading and carefully returned the worn pages to their leather case. It was impossible to tell from her expression whether the news was good or bad.

"Master Fletcher be well?" Tykie inquired at last, clearing his throat to hide his nervousness.

Athena gazed at the dear faces above her, and a triumphant smile lit her tired features. It was as if the numbness that had held her in its grip since Jeremy's departure had been replaced by heady elation. All of a sudden the blinding uncertainty of her existence was gone and she knew what she must do.

"Fletcher was injured when Louisbourg fell," she informed the anxious servants. "An Indian tomahawk caught him on the back of the head and gave him a minor fracture."

"Lord have mercy!" Prudence gasped, dropping her heavy basket of supplies as she stepped inside in time to catch Athena's words.

"He assured me in his last letter that he's quite recovered," Athena added. "Luckily another soldier shot the Indian before he could take Fletcher's scalp."

Prudence groaned again while Nan shuddered at the horror that had nearly befallen Courtland Grace's master.

"Where is he now, Miss Athena?" Wills inquired anxiously. Mystified by his mistress's faraway expression, he exchanged a worried glance with Tykie.

"Northeast of Fort Niagara. He spent several months recovering from his injury and says he plans to rejoin his regiment in time for the assault on Quebec."

"They should've sent him home," Prudence fumed, her round face flushed with anger. "Who knows what sort of care he got from militia doctors?"

"If they even have any," Wills snorted.

"What be yer thoughts, lass?" Tykie asked, made suspicious by Athena's silence. He didn't care too much for the determined tilt to her chin, for 'twas a sure sign that she had made up her mind to do something not entirely acceptable.

"My thoughts are yours exactly," Athena stated blandly. "They should have sent Fletcher home. And since they didn't, I'm going to go find him."

A chorus of startled protests accompanied her words, but Athena shook her head to silence them.

"I don't care if the weather makes traveling dangerous, and I don't intend to let army regulations prevent me from seeing him." The tiny frown line between her eyes deepened as her determination increased. "I've spent the winter hiding like a recluse, allowing others to control my life and make decisions for me. 'Tisn't going to happen again. I'm leaving for Fort Shuyler first thing tomorrow, and from there I'll be better able to track Fletcher down. His last letter was barely a fortnight old. Surely he hasn't gone very far since then."

"Wait, lass!"

Tykie had her by the arm as she swept past him, but Athena shook free of his hold, her hair flying wildly about her face.

"Don't try to stop me," she warned, "because my mind's made up. I have to make sure he was telling me the truth, that his injuries were minor and that he's completely recovered."

"Aye, Miss Athena, I ken," Tykie informed her softly. His ruddy face was filled with understanding as he gazed down at her. " 'Tis why I willna try tae talk ye oot o' going. 'Tis why I plan tae gae wi' ye."

Athena's eyes were wide as she searched the twinkling black depths of his own. "You're going with me?" she repeated.

A wide grin accompanied the Highlander's vigorous nodding. "Ye'll need protection on the road. Who be a better choice than braw Tykie Downs, eh?"

Athena's dark eyes began to glow with anticipation. "My dear Tykie, I couldn't possibly imagine!"

As expected, Aunt Amelia fainted dead away when she was informed of Athena's intentions. After being revived with the hartshorn she carried in a silver vial around her neck, she began to wring her hands and loudly bewail the fate that could very well befall her young niece in the wilderness.

" 'Tis about time she thought of someone besides herself," Mercy remarked to her mother as the two of them listened shamelessly at the door.

"Go on, child, she don't care a whit for Miss Athena's safety. She's wonderin' who'll be fetchin' and readin' to her once she's alone." Prudence shook her head disgustedly.

"I don't understand why Miss Athena doesn't do anything about it," Mercy agreed. 'Twas totally unlike her mistress to meekly submit to her aunt's incessant demands!

"One thing be certain," Prudence added, following her daughter back into the kitchen. "I'm glad Miss Athena's decided to go. The poor child was beginnin' to worry me the way she haunted this house like a wraith all winter. 'Tis good to see the spirit back in her eyes."

Hefting her bulk onto the pine stool before the table, she cut herself a piece of pie and topped it with a liberal helping of clotted cream. "Broken hearts do mend, I daresay," she sighed, and licked her fingertip in satisfaction.

Athena groaned as she opened her eyes, aware that her blanket and clothes were damp. The canvas Tykie had erected over her head last night hadn't been as watertight as he'd imagined, and a pool of rainwater had collected at her feet. Sitting up, Athena pushed the hair from her face and wondered if she would ever know the luxury of a hot bath again. Stretching her stiff limbs, she grinned weakly at Tykie, who was sitting before the smoking fire, jaws working rhythmically as he helped himself to the flour cakes in his pack.

"Slept like an angel, did ye?" he inquired amiably. "Not missin' yer ain bed back hame, eh?"

Athena's delicate brows rose archly. "I slept very well, thank you, and I'm not going to go home simply because we've been riding through rain the past ten days."

Tykie chuckled, well aware that 'twould take more than dampness, hunger, and a hard bedroll to deter Miss Athena. He had tried to talk her into going back when the weather turned bad, but she had refused, and his protests were now little more than a joke between them.

Watching her eat, he felt a protective tenderness come over him. The wee lass was pale, and there were dark circles beneath her eyes despite the fact that she kept insisting she wasn't tired. Her golden curls hadn't seen brush nor comb for days, and Athena kept them carefully concealed beneath the cap she always wore. 'Twas part of her outfit, the worn leather cap, as well as a vest, breeches, and sturdy boots, which gave her the appearance of a proper young lad. The idea of dressing like that had been hers, and at first Tykie had been scandalized, refusing to accompany his mistress anywhere when she looked little better than a stablehand.

"I can't very well ride sidesaddle for two weeks on end," Athena had pointed out in that obstinate tone he knew far too well. "Furthermore, 'twill rouse less suspicions if we travel together as companions, not as a lady and her escort."

Tykie had to admit that Athena was in far less danger of being improperly handled by the ruffians they would doubtless encounter if she didn't reveal to them the beautiful woman she was. And 'twould be easier to make discreet inquiries as to Master Fletcher's whereabouts without a dazzling lady to arouse unwanted attention.

"I still dinna like it," he grumbled to himself, shaking his head sadly at the sight of Miss Athena perched on a log beside him, her shoes caked with mud, a ragged tear in one of her stockings.

Her smile was cheerful, her eyes bright despite the weariness etched into her young face. "We haven't much further to go, Tykie. We mustn't get discouraged now."

She rose, dusting the crumbs from her lap, and scanned the little clearing in which they had made camp late last night. They were three days out of the last settlement with naught but mountains and rolling valleys ahead of them. Despite the blanketing mist and the forlorn pall of winter that still lingered in the air, the scenery was magnificent. They had ridden past waterfalls and cascades of breathtaking splendor, and Tykie had caught trout in crystal brooks swollen with melting snow. Wildlife in abundance had fled before them as their horses plodded northward past the last outlying farms, leaving civilization behind.

Athena knew that Tykie was worried about Indians, yet they had encountered no one save Provincial foot patrols during the past week, all of them young soldiers eager to give directions and share their meager rations. Athena had asked them numerous questions and, listening carefully to the answers, felt that she had gleaned a better idea of the current military situation than she had ever gotten from the Provincial commanders back home in West York.

Though she now knew the whereabouts of the Rangers, whose ranks Colm had joined several months ago, no one had been able to tell her a thing about the Highland Regiments. The Seventh Company had spent most of the winter in Albany, Athena knew, and had been reassigned several months ago, yet none of the soldiers she questioned had any idea where they had been sent.

She didn't really care, either, Athena told herself scornfully, stuffing her bedroll back into the saddlebag. Lochiel Blackmoor could be captured by renegade Algonquins for all he mattered to her!

Tykie gave her a leg up into the saddle, and Athena patted the chestnut gelding's damp neck. She had intentionally left Ballycor behind, knowing he would have been ruined for the racing season if he had been forced to negotiate the rocky trails and muddy fields they had encountered thus far.

They rode that morning in silence, Athena with her head bowed while rainwater collected on the brim of her cap and dripped down the back of her shirt. She was cold and uncomfortable, yet she refused to admit to herself how tired and discouraged she had grown. It was obvious to her now that finding Fletcher wasn't going to be as easy as she had thought. Suppose he'd already been reassigned by the time they reached Niagara? How much longer would Tykie agree to chase across the mountains in search of her brother? Impulsive she might be, yet Athena knew she couldn't go on by herself, no matter how determined she was.

"Take a look, lass," Tykie's soft voice interrupted her from her gloomy thoughts.

Athena drew rein beside him and caught her breath at the beauty spread out before her. They were standing on the rim of a mist-shrouded valley through which a river wound its placid way before vanishing in a band of silver into the faraway hills. The air was crisp and cool, and a freshening wind brought with it the scent of springtime and change.

"I'll warrant Fort Shuyler be i' the clearin' below." Tykie's blunt forefinger was aimed at a break in the dense stands of pine and deciduous trees. "And I'll wager Lake Ontario lies beyond them mountains wi' Frenchies teemin' along the shores."

His expression was grave as he turned to regard her. "Will ye no stay behind, lass? 'Tisna games we be playin' the noo. That be enemy territory oot there."

Athena shook her head. There was a spirited gleam in her eyes as she replied calmly, "I'm not afraid of the French, Tykie, and if Fletcher is down there, then 'tis all the more reason we find him."

"I was afraid ye'd say that," Tykie grumbled dourly as the two horses began their descent to the valley floor. He had the uneasy feeling that trouble was heading their way and that Miss Athena was going to be in the thick of it. At least he was here to look after her, he reflected, taking comfort from the feel of the cold knifeblade strapped against his belly. There were two more knives in his saddle bag and a Brown Bess tied across his pack, where he could reach it instantly should the need arise.

"Nay, I'll let no ane harm the wee lassie," Tykie swore to himself, casting a protective glance at the slight figure in the rain-soaked woolen sweater who rode at his side, while the outer ramparts of Fort Shuyler rose amid the barren trees before them.

Nine

The few scattered buildings that made up the settlement surrounding Fort Shuyler were veiled in icy drizzle. The narrow cart trail that led to the fort was a quagmire of knee-deep puddles. Maple trees flanked the roadway, their branches covered with soft red buds, yet this first sign of spring was lost upon the small band of soldiers marching disconsolately through the mire. Their gear was sodden, and none of them spoke, although their spirits, by right, should have been high. 'Twas almost May, and the great assault on Quebec was about to begin.

Lochiel Blackmoor, watching the straggling line of men wade through the muck from astride his horse, couldn't help thinking that they made a sorry sight indeed. Little touched him more than a wet, cold soldier in need of a bed, and 'twas obvious that this division of Provincials had come a long way. Weariness was etched into the unshaven faces, and no one spared him a glance as the mud-spattered line marched onward to the fort.

"A few nights' sleep and some good hot broth'll hae them lookin' like soldiers soon enough," Andy Durning remarked, drawing his mount to a halt at Lochiel's side. He chuckled. "Thot an' a visit to our blanket girls."

Lochiel's eyes were mere slits beneath the brim of his tricorn. Troops had been moving in and out of Fort Shuyler for the past fortnight as General Amherst began to mobilize his armies. Most of them remained a mere night or two before marching on, but from what Lochiel had seen there was little strength or spirit left in the ragtag band of Provincials. The Regulars, too, seemed to have weathered the winter poorly, and he found himself wondering what would happen when his own men were called upon to give their utmost in that last, daring campaign.

"Especially wee Liza," the sergeant-major continued, smacking his lips for emphasis. "Now there's a lassie what can boost any man's morale. Even yours," he added, gazing expectantly at the silent man beside him.

But Lochiel wasn't listening. His attention had been caught by a soldier who was bringing up the rear of the straggling line, his braided blue coat, though worn and unclean, showing that he had achieved the rank of lieutenant. His face, half hidden beneath a sodden hat, was deathly pale, and as the weary band of men marched past, he began to stagger drunkenly and sank without warning to his knees in the mud. Helping hands were extended to pull him upright, but he waved them away, propping himself on the stock of his musket as he came unsteadily to his feet.

"The mon's ill," Andy stated worriedly. A low whistle passed his lips as the lieutenant swayed a second time and fell forward in a faint.

"Can we help?" Lochiel asked, spurring his horse toward the small group of soldiers clustered about him.

The youthful faces that looked up at him were filled with relief.

"Oh yes, sir!"

"Is the lieutenant ill?" Lochiel inquired.

"No, sir," a young spokesman replied, respectfully pushing back his cap. "He was wounded last winter. Sometimes he gets spells like these."

"We're all tired and hungry, mind you, sir," another youth added, not wishing his commander to seem weak in the eyes of this broad-shouldered Highlander who towered above them on his horse. " 'Tis enough to bring on spells in anyone."

"You've got a three-mile march to Fort Shuyler," Lochiel informed them, concerned because the lieutenant, who was being supported under the arms by two of his men, had yet to regain consciousness. "I suggest you permit me to take him on my horse to that farmhouse there in the clearing. The settlers who reside there are well practiced in medicine."

The group of soldiers exchanged uncertain glances. None of them was older than nineteen, and all were totally unaccustomed to making decisions. Yet the Highlander's cool authority had impressed them, as had the fact that he had made them an offer of assistance, not given them orders.

"Mayhap 'twould be best," one of them said at last. "The lieutenant's health matters most."

The others nodded agreement, and Lochiel helped them swing the unconscious man over the cantle of his saddle. "Why don't two of you come with me and the rest go on to the fort?" he suggested to the youth who had been acting as spokesman. His tone was kind, his manner putting them all at ease.

"Evan and I will stay with the lieutenant," the lad responded promptly. "The rest of you can go on to the fort and report to Major Eure. I'm Robbie Pritchard," he added as he followed Lochiel's mount across the rain-soaked field. "We're all New York militiamen, though we've been serving in Pennsylvania the last few months."

"When was the lieutenant wounded?" Lochiel asked.

"Earlier this winter, sir. He was supposed to be discharged and sent home, but he wouldn't go. Said there wasn't anything wrong with him, and usually there isn't except when he gets these fainting spells."

"How often be that?" Andy Durning asked gruffly. The young lieutenant's injuries seemed more serious than Robbie Pritchard realized.

"This is only the third one since the accident happened. Begging your pardon, sir," he went on, glancing up into Lochiel's impassive face, "where is it you're taking him? Who owns this place?" He gestured toward the small cabin made of notched logs that stood near the end of the clearing ahead of them.

"A couple by the name of Bruce and Elizabeth McKenzie," Lochiel explained obligingly. It was obvious that Private Robert Pritchard was still uncertain about the decision he had made. "They're settlers from Perth, in Scotland, and I can assure you that they'll give your lieutenant far better care than anyone at the fort."

Indeed, both the McKenzies were quick to size up the situation when Lochiel's horse halted in the barnyard with its limp burden. Hurrying from the barn where he had been mending harnesses, brawny Bruce McKenzie lifted the unconscious man into his arms and carried him inside. His wife was there to meet him, quickly turning down the rough blankets on the bed while her questioning eyes sought Lochiel's face.

Lochiel wasted no time in explaining what had happened, and Elizabeth's expression cleared as he finished speaking.

"Doubtless 'tis little more than exhaustion," she announced in the same soft burr of the Scottish Lowlands that had drawn Lochiel's attention the first time they had chanced to meet in the tiny outpost that was the settlement's only store. "He should be dried off and allowed to sleep as long as he wishes."

As she spoke she bustled to the crude chest of drawers standing beneath the window and pulled out a long cotton nightshirt belonging to her husband.

"I'll do that, ma'am," Robbie Pritchard offered as she began to tug off the lieutenant's sodden jacket. His cheeks were scarlet at the thought of what she intended to do.

"Ye'll go over by the fire and warm yourself," she commanded, her brown eyes snapping, "and eat a wee bit o' stew." She indicated a caldron hanging in the stone fireplace, from which the tantalizing aroma of cooked meat and potatoes assailed them. "Ye'll stay, too, Major Blackmoor," she added firmly. "Ye be wet to the bone, ye an' the sergeant-major."

"Very well," Lochiel replied, his lips twitching. Though she was small and seemingly meek, Elizabeth McKenzie possessed the iron will of her people and never seemed happier than when she had someone to fuss over. Both he and Andy had been occasional guests in her home and had never come away without feeling that she had adopted them.

"I'll take care of the lieutenant," Lochiel added, taking the nightshirt out of her hands. " 'Twill relieve Mr. Pritchard's embarrassment and leave you free to look after them." His eyes twinkled as he looked down into her lined face, well aware that it annoyed her to take orders from him. Yet it was the famished expression on the faces of the young soldiers that eventually softened Elizabeth's heart, and she clucked softly as she herded them to the fireplace to distribute steaming bowls of stew.

Both Lochiel and Andrew were experienced at tending wounded, and the unconscious man was stripped in no time, his muddy uniform quickly thrown in the washtub by the hovering Elizabeth. Lochiel was relieved to note that his color had improved by the time he was dried off and covered, and that his sleep seemed deep and restful.

"I think we've done everything for him we can, Andy," he said, straightening, his dark head nearly touching the low-raftered ceiling of the one-room farmhouse.

"Och, wait, lad," Andy remarked as they turned away from the bed. "What's this?" Stooping, he picked up an object that had caught his eye, and turned it over in his gnarled hand. Lochiel saw that it was a locket of solid silver hanging on the end of a braided chain.

"Must've fallen off when we undressed him," the sergeant-major remarked. "I'll gie it to ane o' them lads."

" 'Twould be better if we turned it over to Major Eure for safekeeping," Lochiel suggested. "That way there's no chance of it getting lost."

"Aye, you're right," Andy agreed. "Looks valuable. Here, put it i' your pocket, will you? I've na wish to be responsible for it."

"Will ye stay an' eat wi' us?" Bruce McKenzie asked as the two Highlanders drew closer to the fire.

"Na this time, thanks," Andy demurred, though the stew did smell temptingly good and he knew from past experience that conversation with the soft-spoken settler would be enjoyable. "We've been gone lang enough."

"You lads rest awhile," Lochiel suggested as both Evan and Robbie sprang dutifully to their feet. "I'll inform the major that you'll be along shortly."

The two young soldiers cast grateful glances in his direction as he reached for his tricorn and turned to bid farewell to Elizabeth. A moment later he and Andy were riding back toward the fort, the rain falling relentlessly upon them.

"A pox on this foul weather," Andy grumbled, turning his ruddy face to the overcast sky. "Mayhap it rains too much back hame as well, but spring always did ken when to come. Och"—he sighed deeply—"I've such a hankerin' for me ain wee glen. What aboot yersel', Lochiel, lad? Will ye retairn hame when the campaign's over?"

Andy's simple question filled Lochiel with sudden, unexplained anger. All winter long he had immersed himself in his work, allowing nothing to fill his thoughts save his reports, his men, and his duty. There had been no letters from home, which had made it easier for him to forget that he had another life beyond soldiering, that soon the decision of what to do with his future would be staring him in the face.

"I've grown tired o' the war," Andy added softly as their horses passed through the tall wooden gate of the fort, "but I think you be more tired still. 'Tisn't meant to be, Lochiel, a lifetime career for you i' the King's Army. There's talk frae new recruits i' the barracks that folk be gang back to the Highlands, to rebuild what was lost after Cumberland's slaughter. 'Tis a challenge I ken ye'd thirst to accept, especially if you've a bonnie wife to provide for."

"You're quite an imaginative dreamer, sergeant-major," Lochiel grated. His face was expressionless as he drew his mount to a halt before the small stable at the far end of the grounds.

Andy fell silent immediately, warned by the tone of his voice. The two of them had served together so long that he often forgot that Lochiel outranked him. Yet the cold utterance of that "sergeant-major" had been the younger man's way of informing Andy that he was pursuing a dangerous topic best left alone.

Andy sighed disconsolately. The mud sucked at his boots as he waded back to his quarters. Though Lochiel Blackmoor was a good friend, there were times when he could erect a wall about him that intimidated everyone, even people he had grown close to over the course of his life.

'Twas easy for a soldier to become bitter, even callous, Andy knew, and Lochiel Blackmoor had been dealt more than his share of sorrows. A lass with a warm, loving heart could make him forget the pain he bore, yet Lochiel had never shown any interest in women in that respect.

"De'il take the obstinate lad," Andy muttered to himself. He was near thirty years of age. When was he going to forget the horrors of Culloden and permit himself to live again?

The afternoon was spent in a wearisome round of inspections, paperwork, and interviews with Major Eure, the tireless fort commander. Though Lochiel was normally patient with the dull routine of army life, he found himself growing more irritable as the hours wore on. Apparently his men weren't the only ones who were beginning to suffer the consequences of the long, inactive winter.

"We'll start drilling in earnest tomorrow, Andy," he informed the sergeant-major as the two of them separated after dinner that night. "I'm going to send a dispatch to Albany and request reassignment."

The dour sergeant-major rubbed his hands together. "Let's hope they send us north, laddie. I'm more than ready to take on Montcalm and his Frenchies!"

The small room that served as office and living quarters was dark when Lochiel stepped inside. The lamp glowing feebly on the cluttered desk did little to dispel the gloom, and rain continued to tap mournfully on the single pane. Barrett had leave, and Lochiel guessed that he and several of the men in the barracks had taken themselves off to camp for a night of drinking and carousing.

No harm in that, Lochiel thought to himself, stripping off his damp jacket and tossing it onto a chair. Once he, too, had thought nothing of enjoying the charms of the willing girls who resided in their canvas tents, and one in particular had proven herself quite adept at easing the fierce needs that had always governed him.

Yet Lochiel hadn't set foot in camp since the summer had ended, a turn of events that had mystified his men, who had never bothered to conceal their amusement at and admiration for their commanding officer's virility. What had changed? Why his sudden reluctance to partake of the pleasures of the flesh? Surely he hadn't lost his taste for women!

Unexpectedly a memory rose to Lochiel's mind, a memory of silken white skin and flowing gold hair, of soft, persuasive lips that had clung innocently to his. He could feel the ache in his loins as he imagined Athena lying beneath him, her long limbs entwined with his, her fragrance surrounding him as he kissed her deeply. She had stretched like a sleek lioness beneath his seeking hands, her eyes shining like stars, and the pleasure of possessing her had been unlike anything he had ever experienced.

Lochiel uttered a savage curse beneath his breath, aware that he was dwelling on a memory that in truth meant nothing to him. Athena Courtland was no different from the blanket girls who made themselves available to lonely soldiers, no different from the Lovely Nans who waited in the foreign ports Lochiel had visited often in his years of service in the King's Army.

She had given herself to him only because her lover had been late in coming to her, not because she had desired him. Any other man would have served just as well, and Lochiel's eyes were as cold as steel as he reached determinedly for his discarded coat. No, Athena Courtland was no different from Liza Hampton, the skillful, full-lipped enchantress who had always managed to please him in the past. 'Twas time to prove that he had been dwelling on a memory that didn't exist, a foolish obsession that Liza would quickly dispel with her honeyed kisses and experienced hands.

"You should have gone to her long before this," Lochiel berated himself, shrugging the coat over his wide shoulders. There was a grim urgency about him, and he growled irritably as he felt something fall out of his coat pocket and roll beneath the cot.

Stooping, he searched impatiently, but his annoyance faded as his fingers closed over the object, and he realized at once that it was the Provincial lieutenant's locket, which Andy had given him earlier that morning. He'd been so busy all day that he had forgotten to turn it over to Major Eure. Holding it in his palm, he examined it carefully and was relieved that it appeared unharmed.

As his fingers strayed over the delicate engravings, the locket sprang open and Lochiel found himself looking at a pair of miniatures, one of them an older woman of arresting beauty, her unpowdered hair arranged in what had been the current fashion at least a decade ago. She was wearing a gown of dark, vivid blue with a richly embroidered neckline, but Lochiel's attention was caught by the classic perfection of her features and the winsome smile on her soft, red lips. 'Twas obvious that she was a woman of great character as well as beauty, and he found the willful tilt of her square jaw an intriguing contrast to the mischievous sparkle of her eyes.

His gaze traveled to the portrait of the little girl beside her, and at first he thought it must be a younger version of the same woman until he realized that there were subtle differences between them, most notably in their coloring. Yet she was an enchanting child indeed, and as Lochiel continued to gaze at her he felt his breath catch in astonishment. Where in the name of God had he seen her before? Some elusive memory stirred him as he stared down into the pretty little face with its straight nose and great, dark eyes.

He had seen her before, he knew, and the maddening thing about it was that he couldn't remember where. Yet he knew with unswerving certainty that he had once gazed into this same child's face, seen the remarkable blue of those enormous eyes, and been recipient of that delightfully innocent smile—a smile he had never forgotten.

"By God, of course!" he exclaimed, unaware that he had spoken aloud. 'Twas as if the years had suddenly fallen away from him and he was once again a young lad marching to Glenfinnan with the members of his clan to raise the standard for Bonnie Prince Charles. They had been cheered along the route by eager villagers and singing children, and Lochiel could suddenly remember quite vividly the little girl who had broken free of her mother's hold and had run to him with arms outstretched.

Lochiel had been startled by her impulsiveness and by the innocent perfection of her childish features. With blue eyes dancing she had stretched out her hand and he had taken the bannock, the little oat cake, she had been holding in her chubby fingers.

" 'Twill keep your belly full on the march," she had told him, her pink cheeks dimpling. "I made it myself."

Before he could thank her she had fled back to her mother, golden curls tumbling untidily down her back, but Lochiel had never forgotten her gift or the sweet, glowing smile on her five-year-old face. He could well remember even now the determination that had filled him to liberate Scotland from English tyranny and thereby free the likes of the little girl who had trusted an unknown soldier so completely.

"What an ignorant young fool I was," Lochiel thought with the ghost of a bitter smile as he shut the locket with a snap. Yet he was relieved that the memory had come back to him after all these years, relieved because he could finally understand why Athena Courtland had seemed to hold such a mystical sway over him. How often had he puzzled over the shock that had fled through him when he had first gazed down into her face on the moon-drenched parade grounds of Albany fort. She had stirred him as no woman before, yet 'twas only because she had touched with her resemblance to a distant, long-forgotten memory of a little girl with golden hair and soft blue eyes.

No, there was nothing mystical about Athena Courtland and never had been, Lochiel reflected. Nor was she any more real to him than the lovely yet remote little girl whose face he had seen in the locket. 'Twas a relief to realize that he hadn't allowed himself to become besotted, as he'd originally feared, by a faithless woman not worth a second thought.

And yet the burning need that had consumed him not ten minutes ago was suddenly gone, and Lochiel hung his coat away with a shake of his dark head. The last thing he wanted at the moment was to take Liza Hampton to bed. He might as well start on his dispatches so that Barrett could send them off come morning. As for the locket, he reflected, turning it thoughtfully over in his hand, tomorrow he'd ride over to the McKenzies' and give it back to the lieutenant himself.

Morning brought continued rain and a gloomy Piers Barrett with hot tea and copies of the daily reports.

"There's mail from Albany, too, sir," the young adjunct added, speaking softly so as not to make the throbbing in his head any worse.

"Too much whiskey last night, Barrett?" Lochiel inquired amicably.

Piers blinked. He hadn't seen the major in this pleasant a frame of mind for some time now. Peering into the sharply chiseled features, he saw that the harsh lines of tension about the major's mouth and forehead had been smoothed away almost overnight. Was it possible to hope that one could dare breathe around him again without fear of having one's head snapped off?

"Never mind, lad," Lochiel added, drawing on his gloves. As usual he had been up and dressed for several hours despite the fact that the reveille drums had shattered the morning stillness only a short time ago. "I've an errand to run over at the McKenzie place. Try not to work too hard while I'm gone." In the doorway he added over one broad shoulder, "And drink that tea. 'Twill settle your stomach."

"Aye, sir," Barrett said weakly, utterly amazed at this transformation.

Lochiel's spirits were high as he turned his horse through the main gate of the fort. Despite the chill and relentlessly falling rain, he couldn't remember when he'd felt better. Spring was undeniably in the air, a time of renewal and the opportunity to turn one's back on the past, to forget what had been and think only of the future.

He chuckled to himself, amused by the fact that he was waxing philosophical merely because he had managed to thrust Athena Courtland once and for all from his mind. Aye, she'd been a comely piece and he'd enjoyed having her, but the episode was over and 'twas high time he began looking for new diversions. Mayhap he'd ride over to camp after his visit to the McKenzies' and see what caught his eye down there.

A cheery blaze crackled in the stone hearth and the smell of baking bread wafted through the open door as Elizabeth McKenzie let him in. Her plain features lit at the sight of him, for Lochiel Blackmoor had a damnable way of winning the heart of every woman he encountered, regardless of her age.

"I've come to see about your patient," Lochiel informed her, shedding his wet coat as he stepped inside.

Wordlessly Elizabeth gestured to the chair behind the door where, to her immense satisfaction, her "patient" had just downed the last bite of an enormous breakfast. Seeing the Highland officer in the doorway, the lieutenant set down the tray and rose quickly to his feet.

"He wanted tae leave as soon as he awoke this mornin'," Elizabeth said disapprovingly. "Withoot a bite tae eat!"

"Mistress McKenzie convinced me to stay by offering me the most tantalizing meal I've had in weeks," the lieutenant said, smiling warmly at his hostess. His voice was deep and pleasant, and Lochiel was quick to note that he appeared completely recovered from his fainting spell yesterday. They were of roughly the same height, although the Provincial officer was thinner, his uniform, cleaned and pressed by Elizabeth last night, hanging from his lean frame.

Dark hazel eyes regarded Lochiel intently, and he recognized in them the faraway expression of a dreamer. Yet there was strength in the pleasant features and in the hands that hung loosely at his sides. Lochiel judged that little more than a year or two separated them in age.

"Sit down an' hae a bite yersel', Major Blackmoor," Elizabeth suggested, waving both men into their seats. "I've butter fresh churned and eggs collected frae the barn not half an hour ago. Bruce be gone tae his nephews today an' willna be back until late."

"So you are Major Blackmoor," the lieutenant remarked, seating himself and studying Lochiel with open interest. "Mistress McKenzie told me you were responsible for bringing me here after I collapsed on the road yesterday."

"Your men were far too exhausted to take you to the fort," Lochiel explained, propping himself against the wall, his arms folded across his chest while Elizabeth scurried about preparing something for him to eat. " 'Twas far easier to bring you here."

"I imagine I'm quite a disappointment in Major Eure's eyes," the lieutenant remarked with a rueful smile. For a brief moment he found himself wondering if perhaps he was unfit for command after all.

"Major Eure was quite understanding when I explained the situation," Lochiel said.

"And my men?"

"Och, ye needn't worry aboot them!" Elizabeth McKenzie chided, appearing before them with heavily laden plates. Her cheeks were flushed from the heat of the fire, and her graying hair had worked its way loose from beneath her mobcap. "Eat afore ye talk, lads, or 'twill get cold."

Grinning, Lochiel accepted the plate from her, then fumbled in his pocket for the locket he had brought with him. "Let me give this to you now," he said to the lieutenant, who was already attacking his second helping with famished ferocity. "Mistress McKenzie's cooking has a way of making you forget everything else."

An incredulous look passed across the pleasant features as the lieutenant saw the braided silver chain dangling from Lochiel's hand. "Thank God!" he exclaimed, reaching quickly to accept it. "When I discovered it gone this morning, I thought 'twas lost forever!"

" 'Tis beautiful," Elizabeth murmured admiringly, drawing closer as he turned it over in his palm.

"And priceless," he informed her softly, "for it contains a portrait of my mother, who died a great number of years ago."

"She was a bonnie woman," Elizabeth observed, studying the face that was held out for her inspection. "And the wee ane beside her?"

A twinkle appeared in the tired hazel eyes. "That is a picture of a certain Mistress Athena Courtland, the prettiest lass in all the colonies, when she was but six years old."

Both of them looked up in astonishment as Lochiel's plate crashed to the floor, exploding in great shards of earthenware mixed with egg, buttered bread, and jam.

"The devil take you!" Lochiel burst out, his big hands reaching for the startled lieutenant's throat. "Don't tell me you're her lover, too!"

Though both men should have been equally matched in terms of strength, Lieutenant Fletcher Courtland was still recovering from the head wound that had felled him last autumn, and at the moment he found it impossible to disengage himself from the other man's strangling grip. Looking into those glittering silver eyes, he decided that the major had taken total leave of his senses. And what was this about Athena having lovers? Surely they weren't talking about the same woman!

"Athena, sir," he said coldly, "happens to be my sister."

It took a moment for his words to sink in, and even then it was obvious that the irate Highlander didn't want to believe them. Feeling the hands finally loosen from about his neck, Fletcher added curtly, "Perhaps I should have introduced myself sooner. I am Lieutenant Fletcher Courtland of the New York Militia. My sister, Athena, resides in the town of West York some ninety miles east of here. Do you claim to know her?"

Lochiel struggled to regain control of his emotions. He had almost attacked Athena's own brother, he realized disbelievingly, launching himself like a taproom brawler on a man who was obviously still suffering the ill effects of a war injury. What sort of callous brute had he become?

"You intimated that my sister has lovers, sir," Fletcher went on, and now his voice was low and dangerous, causing Elizabeth McKenzie to retreat a step, nervously searching about for a weapon should the need for one arise. "Athena is all of eighteen years old and was raised in a sheltered household. Do you still claim to be discussing the same woman?"

A memory of the laughing blue eyes of the Ranger who had spent the night at Fort Shuyler several weeks ago rose unbidden to Lochiel's mind. His lean jaw tightened recalling the twin brother who had caressed Athena's bare shoulder so intimately the morning he had appeared in the stable door behind her at Courtland Grace.

"I would never dream of besmirching the honor of a lady," Lochiel replied, and the look on his face caused Elizabeth McKenzie's breath to catch in her throat. "And yet I can assure you, Lieutenant Courtland, that we are speaking of the very same woman."

He turned heel and strode out, knowing what would happen if he stayed, knowing he'd never forgive himself if he were forced to lift a hand against Athena's brother. Though he might have proved a worthy adversary if he were well, he was in poor health at present, and Lochiel had no wish to harm him.

"A pox on the Courtlands," he growled to himself, vaulting onto his horse's back and kicking him savagely into a canter. Mud splattered his breeches, although he scarcely noticed. What a sorry day in hell it had been when he'd first heard that cursed name!

Paperwork and an inspection with the sergeant-major awaited him, yet Lochiel had no intention of returning to the fort. Instead he turned his mount down the muck-filled trail leading to camp, his expression savage.

The camp consisted of little more than a dozen tents, all of them drooping beneath the weight of dripping canvas. Several smoky fires burned beneath the barren trees, and the people gathered around them spared little more than a glance for the dark-headed officer who rode into their midst.

Dismounting, Lochiel wrapped the reins about a post and slogged his way toward a tent standing somewhat apart from the others, wondering if Liza would be there. She probably wasn't used to receiving visitors during the day, he thought with a grim smile playing on his lips, but she wasn't going to deny him. Not this time.

"Give me that, damn you! 'Tis mine!"

The high, angry voice came from the interior of a littered tent, and as Lochiel turned to take a curious look he was nearly run down by an ill-kempt boy of sixteen who dashed past him, a leather satchel in his hands.

"Come back here with that, you bloody swine!"

This time Lochiel didn't move fast enough, and the small figure that hurled from the interior of the tent barreled directly into him.

"Oof!" He felt the air rush from his lungs and was just barely able to keep his balance. His youthful attacker was less fortunate, for running unprepared into the Highlander's broad form was no different from hitting a tree, and with a startled exclamation he went over backward, sitting down heavily in the mud.

Lochiel couldn't suppress a laugh at the comical expression on the little face staring up at him accusingly from beneath the brim of a battered cap.

"Here, lad, let me help you up," he said with a grin, reaching down to lend assistance.

"I need no help from you, Lochiel Blackmoor," an angry voice informed him and his extended hand was slapped away.

"What in—" He took a second look at the flushed features before him and a disbelieving oath fell from his lips. Reaching down, he seized the front of the lad's woolen sweater and jerked him to his feet. "You! What in hell are you doing here?"

Athena pressed her lips together, her blue eyes burning into his. She was not going to let him see how shaken she was at seeing him. Furthermore she had to retrieve her satchel, which that oafish boy had stolen from her when she wasn't looking!

"Answer me, girl," Lochiel grated, shaking her back and forth so that the mud flew in wet droplets from her clothes and filthied his uniform. Spectators had gathered around them, although they kept their distance, well familiar with Major Blackmoor's temper.

"Let me go!" Athena cried, struggling desperately, unnerved by the heat of his nearness and the anger, nay the contempt for her she saw in those narrowed silver eyes. "That bloody little beggar stole my things! I've got to have them back!"

"Not until you tell me what in the name of God you're doing here." Lochiel's deep voice was carefully under control now, for he wanted no one, least of all Athena, to see how much her appearance had shocked him. It had been easy enough to recognize her even though her feminine curves and golden curls were well concealed by the faded homespun she wore. After all, how many times had he seen her dressed like this?

Tears of frustration welled in Athena's eyes. She couldn't bear the menace in his voice any more than the knowledge that something frightening was happening to her as he clutched her so tightly against his lean body. Odd tremors were beginning to flee through her, and she was reminded despite herself of longings she had thought forgotten.

"My satchel—" she repeated, her lower lip clenched between her teeth. "Damn you, Lochiel, let me go!"

He saw now that she was crying, though she was trying to hide it from him by turning her head away. Instantly his temper vanished and the grip about her throat was loosened.

"Tell me what you're doing here," he said less harshly, "and I'll see to it your—"

An irate bellow cut through the misty air, causing the gathered spectators to scatter in terror. Lochiel, recognizing the war cry of Tykie Downs, turned with a long-suffering sigh to assure him that Athena was in no immediate danger, but never even got the chance to speak. Tykie, certain that his beloved mistress was being accosted by a dark-headed stranger, packed him firmly by the collar and prepared to throw him bodily into the air. To his utter astonishment the material merely ripped in his hands and he was left gaping, for this was the first time in his life he had been unable to wrestle his adversary down.

Small wonder, he decided with something like amazement, regarding the lean frame before him. This man was too strong to be tossed about and the way he was standing there with his arms folded calmly across his chest made Tykie think of a young oak impossible to uproot.

"Why, 'tis Major Blackmoor!" he exclaimed, his gaze coming to rest on the sharply chiseled features of the other man's face. Bewildered, he began to tug on the gold ring in his ear and shuffle his big feet in embarrassment. "I-I didna recognize ye, sir."

"Never fear, I'm quite unharmed," Lochiel assured him, "though I believe I can't say the same for my uniform."

"I'll pay for your bloody shirt," came Athena's sullen voice from behind him.

He turned slowly to regard her, his expression once more inscrutable now that he had recovered completely from the shock of seeing her. She was gazing up at him contemptuously, her golden brows arching, the beauty of her features not at all diminished by the smudges of dirt on her cheeks.

"Aye, you will," he agreed. "You're also going to answer my questions, every last one of them."

"Not until I get my satchel back."

Mutinous blue eyes held the narrowed silver ones for a long, charged moment. Lochiel was hard put to grapple with his temper, aching to turn her over his knee, yet he forgot his dire intentions when his gaze fell to the area of her body in question and he saw how snugly the buckskin breeches hugged the firm curves of her buttocks.

Wordlessly he turned to one of the curious onlookers and indicated with a curt gesture that Athena's belongings were to be returned by the young thief who had made off with them. Athena watched him suspiciously, hating herself for noticing how tall he was and how arrestingly handsome his hawkish features appeared beneath his tricorn hat. His dark hair was tied in a queue, and she recalled that the only time she had ever seen him wear a wig was at the de Vrieses' formal ball.

Why think about that? she asked herself furiously. Why remember things about Lochiel Blackmoor that were best forgotten? 'Twas true, she had been shocked to find him here, but he would serve no other purpose for her than to tell her where Fletcher's regiment had gone.

"Your things will be returned to you in a moment," Lochiel informed her coldly. "Now, suppose you tell me what in hell is going on?"

" 'Twas my fault," Tykie said promptly, not caring for the harsh tone of the major's voice whenever he addressed Miss Athena. Accustomed to finding his mistress the object of every man's admiration, he could not understand why Major Blackmoor, whom he couldn't help but respect, seemed to consider her little more than an annoyance. "I left Miss Athena here at camp while I went tae see the fort commander."

"You thought 'twould be safer for Miss Courtland here?" Lochiel inquired disbelievingly. God's blood, didn't either of them know what sort of camp this was? Athena had been lucky to get away with little worse than a stolen satchel. 'Twas fortunate she had been dressed like a lad and not a helpless lady! Lucky for her, too, was the fact that she was taller than most and that the dagger at her side was more than a wee bit intimidating. Knowing her as he did, Lochiel had no doubt that she'd not hesitate to use it.

But he was still furious with both of them, Tykie for leaving her here while he rode on to the fort and Athena for having accompanied him through the wilderness to begin with.

" 'Twas your idea, I imagine," he remarked, scowling down into her face, unmindful of the drizzle which continued to fall upon them. "I very much doubt Master Downs would have agreed to bring you this far if you hadn't bullied him into it."

Athena lifted her chin. " 'Tis no business of yours, Lochiel Blackmoor, and I'll thank you to let us go unhindered. You may be accustomed to ordering your men about, but we are neither soldiers nor your personal property. Tykie and I came here for a reason that has naught to do with you."

Her heart jumped nervously when she saw the black look that crossed his hawkish face. 'Twas obvious she had said the wrong thing, and now his tiresome temper had been rekindled. She could not know that Lochiel was wondering whether it was Fletcher Courtland's presence that had brought them here or a quest for her twin lovers, one of whom he had watched march out of the fort gates not two short weeks ago.

"Lass, wait," Tykie cautioned belatedly. He hadn't had the chance to tell her yet that Major Eure had been too busy to receive him and that they might very well have to turn to Major Blackmoor for help. But Athena seemed to have alienated the major already, for Tykie could see the angry tightening of the younger man's mouth. He shifted uneasily, not caring for the tension in the air.

"Major Blackmoor?"

A redheaded girl of some fifteen years came swaggering into their midst, Athena's satchel slung over one arm. Her threadbare cape was drawn back to reveal the tightly corseted tops of her small breasts. Athena's eyes widened, sensing at once what sort of woman this was, and disgust coursed through her at the seductive gleam in the seemingly innocent brown eyes that were fastened on Major Blackmoor's face.

"M'brother Joe stole it," the girl said matter-of-factly. "Said 'e wouldn't've if he'd known he were a friend of yours." She jerked her head in Athena's direction, her tone indicating that this was the least the dandily attired lad had deserved.

Athena bristled but Lochiel, sensing as much, stepped calmly between them. "My thanks, Ailie."

She preened before him and, giggling, made her way back across the muddy field to the fire smoking in the clearing.

No sooner was she gone than Athena gave Lochiel a contemptuous look. "Thank you for getting back my things," she said, half choking on the words. "Are you ready to go, Tykie?"

Lochiel folded his arms across his wide chest. " 'Twould be in your best interest to wait a moment, Athena Courtland."

She looked about nervously, but the last of the spectators had drifted away and the three of them were alone before the sagging tent where Athena had first been invited to await Tykie's return from the fort. No one had overheard the name he uttered, and she said archly, "We want naught from you, major."

He raised a mocking brow, amazed at the depth of the disdain she could put into those few simple words. "Not even the whereabouts of your brother?" he inquired, feeling certain now that Fletcher was the one they were searching for.

The breathless hope that passed across the mud-streaked face stirred his conscience, for he realized now that he had been treating her more than a little unkindly. He sensed the question trembling on her lips, yet she would not bring herself to utter it.

"Fletcher's here, Athena," Lochiel told her curtly. He could no sooner toy with her about something this important than to torment a wounded animal—and he was not a total ogre, despite what she might think.

"Is he—is he all right?"

"He's been ill," he replied, not wanting to lie to her, "but I think you'll find him on the mend."

She looked away, blinking rapidly, and he handed her his handkerchief, hoping to smooth over the awkward moment.

"You could have told us sooner, curse you!" she flared by way of thanks, then blew her nose loudly and fixed him with such a haughty look that he was tempted to laugh. It pleased him that Athena Courtland's seductive powers held no sway over him anymore. In fact, he found himself thinking not of the tantalizing pleasure of having made love to her, but that she was still the same spoiled brat she'd been when first they'd met.

"I'll take you to him," he offered, determined to reunite her with her brother and have done with her as quickly as possible.

Their fingers inadvertently touched as he handed her the satchel, and Lochiel was startled by the heat that seemed to flare between them in that brief moment of contact. Athena, he saw, had felt it, too, for she jerked her hand away and lowered her head to hide the crimson color that spread across her cheeks.

"I haven't got all day," he growled, leading them back to their horses while inwardly denying the emotions that made a mockery of his previous thoughts.

"Then we certainly won't impose on you any longer than we have to," Athena snapped.

They glared at one another in silent fury while Tykie coughed uncomfortably and looked the other way. If things went like this, he decided, the two of 'em would come to blows, and he wasn't rightly sure in that case who'd need protection from whom.

"Lord, let's hope we find Master Fletcher soon enough," he muttered beneath his breath and sent his eyes heavenward in silent appeal.

Ten

" 'Tisn't fair, I tell you! 'Tisn't fair at all!"

Fletcher Courtland's expression was troubled as he gazed into his sister's tearful face. It wasn't often that Athena shed tears, and the knowledge that he was responsible for them pained him deeply.

"I'm thinking of you, my love. Your safety is more important to me than anything else."

Bitter words trembled on Athena's lips, but she forced herself not to utter them. Turning her back on him, she stared out of the window and tried to regain her composure. Bright sunshine bathed the tiny parade grounds of the fort and birds twittered in the budding trees, yet Athena was oblivious to everything but the ache in her heart.

"Your company won't be marching for five more days," she said at last, her eyes filled with mute appeal as she turned back to him. "We could easily spend that time together, Fletcher, and yet you insist on sending me home tomorrow!"

" 'Tis an unjust world at times," Fletcher agreed, giving her a teasing little smile that reminded her a great deal of their father. "Were you hoping I'd agree to come back to Courtland Grace with you, Athena?" he asked gently.

She lowered her eyes to the silver inkwell and quill on the desk before him. "Yes."

"Surely you know I can't."

Athena sighed heavily. "I suppose I've known it all along. 'Tis just so unfair that Tykie and I traveled all this way only to spend less than three days with you." She clenched her hands into fists. "Not only that, but now you tell me you've made arrangements to send us back with Major Blackmoor's regiment! Why, Fletcher? I thought you disliked him."

A frown creased Fletcher's brow. "I've no choice but to trust him, Athena. I can't allow you to travel back to West York alone."

Since yesterday morning reports had begun trickling into the fort concerning the great number of Christian Iroquois who were making their way north toward Fort Oswego. Fletcher felt certain, and Major Eure agreed with him, that Montcalm was beginning to assemble his troops now that winter was loosening its grip and the threat of English attack seemed imminent.

That same day new orders had arrived at the fort sending Fletcher's regiment north toward Lake Champlain while the Highlanders had been recalled to Albany. Fearing for his sister's safety in the wilderness, Fletcher had reluctantly decided to send her home under Major Blackmoor's protection. He had felt certain Athena wouldn't be too happy when he told her this, and her belligerent behavior had been everything he'd expected.

"We've had two days together, love," he told her now, smiling at the rebellious vision she made standing before him in breeches and a leather vest, Jeremy's dirk tucked into her belt, her eyes blazing with lingering mutiny. "I wish it could have been more, but war has a nasty way of ignoring personal desires."

Athena bit her lip. She should be grateful for the fact that she had been able to find him at all and that she herself had been the one to nurse him back onto his feet—with Elizabeth McKenzie's help, of course. Bless the dear woman, for she had not only opened her home to Fletcher in his need, but had insisted that Athena stay with them once she learned of the girl's true identity.

Fletcher rose and prowled restlessly to the window. Now that his strength had returned, he was eager to meet Montcalm in what he prayed would be the final confrontation of a long and ugly war. " 'Tis true I don't care overly for Lochiel Blackmoor despite Tykie's words to the contrary," he admitted, "yet I couldn't think of a better escort for you than seventy ferocious Highland warriors."

Athena was glad his back was turned so that he couldn't see the expression on her face. She didn't want him to guess what she couldn't even admit to herself—that it frightened her to think of spending a fortnight in Lochiel Blackmoor's company, to be entirely dependent on him for protection. She knew that he disliked her and that whatever had happened between them had been of fleeting duration only, yet how to explain the flutter of her heart that rainy morning two days ago when she had seen his handsome, laughing face above hers?

"Please do it for me, love."

Athena looked up to find Fletcher regarding her with that special smile he had always reserved just for her. Pale and thin as he might have grown, he was still so much like his father that she felt her heart ache with love for him. "You know I've never been able to say you nay when you ask me like that," she complained with a resigned shake of her head.

Slipping her arms about his neck, she let him pull her close, burying her nose in the familiar warmth of his shirtfront.

Her innocence and the fragility of the slim body Fletcher held in his arms filled him with brotherly tenderness. Again he was reminded of the things Lochiel Blackmoor had said about her when he had shown Mistress McKenzie the miniatures in his locket. The subject had never arisen between them again, yet Fletcher was determined to see that the arrogant Highlander paid for intimating such monstrous untruths about her.

"Why don't you go tell Tykie what's been decided?" he suggested, untangling himself from her embrace. "I've some work to catch up on, but we can meet later for dinner."

"Mistress McKenzie says you're to take it with us," Athena reminded him.

He nodded by way of reply, already immersed in the ledgers before him. Stepping into the sunshine, Athena pulled her cap low over her brow and unhitched her horse from the post. Several soldiers were lounging nearby, engaged in a game of cards, and they spared her little more than a glance as she rode by.

Men certainly did have it easier than women, Athena decided, cantering through the open gates. No one had paid the slightest bit of attention to her since she had taken to disguising herself as a boy. On the other hand, if she had emerged from Fletcher's office in a ruffled gown instead of breeches, there would have been numerous hoots and catcalls and interested eyes following her every move.

"Mayhap Katrine de Vries relishes such attention," Athena murmured with a derisive sniff, "but 'tis far more pleasant to be treated like this!"

Dusk fell early that evening, and at Elizabeth's request Athena lit the tapers in the McKenzies' cabin while Elizabeth, face flushed from the heat, sampled the contents of the kettle in the fireplace.

" 'Tis tasty indeed," the older woman announced, smacking her lips in satisfaction. " 'Twill put some weight back on that brother o' yers, lass."

Athena smiled at this and thought to herself how kind the McKenzies had been to share what little they had with perfect strangers. She had grown fond of them during her stay here, and she hated the thought of bidding them farewell tomorrow morning.

The sound of hoofbeats came to them from outside, and both of them looked up from their work.

"I'll see who it is," Athena volunteered. "Fletcher might have arrived early."

"Or 'tis Bruce retairnin' frae the fields," Elizabeth cautioned, but Athena had already dashed out into the twilight, eager to intercept her brother before he stepped inside.

Yet it was Lochiel Blackmoor who had turned his mount into the McKenzies' yard, and a startled look crossed his face when he saw Athena running toward him from the doorway. For a daft moment he thought she was glad to see him, but then she drew up short, a scowl darkening her brow, and her behavior reminded him of the way she had stiffened in his arms the night she had mistaken him for her Ranger lover. She had looked at him in the same way, coldly and without compassion, although at the time he had been too consumed with lust to care.

Now he was in no mood to tolerate her sullen antics, and his own expression was grim as he dismounted and came toward her.

"I'm not staying for dinner, so you needn't look so angry."

Athena tilted her head to meet his gaze unflinchingly. "I'm sorry, but I thought you were my brother."

He laughed shortly. "You always seem to be mistaking me for someone else, aren't you?"

She flushed and looked away, and the stiff little shoulders turned toward him unaccountably annoyed him. His hand closed tightly about her upper arm, and he saw her wince as he jerked her around to face him. She wasn't wearing her cap this evening, and her fair hair was swept away from her face so that Lochiel was able to gaze fully at the delicate perfection of her features. Golden curls lay against her smooth white temples, and her sculpted cheekbones were stained a wanton rose. Yet her eyes were as hard and cold as diamonds, and his hold on her arm tightened brutally in response.

"While I have you out here alone, perhaps I ought to make a few points clear about our journey to Albany, Miss Courtland."

"You have my attention, major," she responded coolly. "You needn't break my bones."

He obligingly released her, yet she felt a shiver flee down her spine at the intimidating light that continued to burn in his eyes. As always his nearness unnerved her, and she deliberately forced herself to look away from his compelling gaze.

"What is it you wish to say to me?" she asked in a tone that suggested she couldn't care less.

"Your brother has seen fit to place you under my protection, and I do not intend to be remiss in my duties," he informed her coldly, nettled by the fact that 'twould probably do little good to strangle her. "However, I am not about to burden myself, and hinder the progress of my men, by catering to a helpless woman."

Athena's temper flared. How dare he insinuate that she would slow him down or cause trouble! Opening her mouth to protest, she thought better of it, for he appeared in no mood to argue with her. There was a grim sense of purpose about him, and she didn't like the ruthless set of his hawkish features one bit. Oh, why had Fletcher entrusted her to him?

"I've decided that the safest thing to do is have you travel with the camp followers," Lochiel went on, his tone brooking no argument or interruption. "You will maintain your disguise, for I cannot be watching over you every moment, and as a lad you'll be safer than any woman could be."

"I'll have Tykie to look after me," Athena reminded him.

Lochiel's tone was filled with impatience. "You've proved to me often enough that no single person on earth can look after you properly, not even your faithful Tykie. In addition there are all manner of unsavory men living in camp who recognize no law other than their own. Were you to reveal yourself as the woman you are, I seriously doubt even Tykie could sufficiently protect you from all of them."

He had come closer as he spoke, and now he stood looking down at her with coldly glittering eyes. "Do you understand my meaning, Miss Courtland?"

Athena felt the heat creep to her cheeks. "Surely my brother wouldn't allow such—"

"Your brother believes that I intend to act as your personal chaperon," Lochiel interrupted curtly, "and though I'll do my best to uphold my agreement to see you safely back to West York, I cannot extend you any privileges."

"You mean you won't," Athena said bitterly. 'Twas obvious to her now that he didn't care either way what happened to her and that she and Tykie would probably end up fending completely for themselves.

"I'll see to it that you're accorded respect from those in the camp, but I will not tempt fate by revealing to anyone your true identity. You're going to have to take care of yourself, Athena, and if you don't like it, then I suggest you speak to your brother about it."

He knew bloody well she wouldn't, Athena reflected, gazing with hatred into the coldly handsome face above hers. There was no one else Fletcher could send her home with, and she knew that he would never permit her to travel back through the wilderness alone, not with the risk of an Indian attack increasing every day. No, she would have to abide by Lochiel's demands, no matter how odious he was being about it.

"Thank you for your words of caution," Athena said with icy dignity. "I'm certain Tykie and I can manage well enough as camp followers."

"That remains to be seen," he responded curtly.

She ached to slap his face but could think of no good reason for doing so. How could she ever have talked herself into feeling fascination for this impossibly arrogant man?

"If you'll excuse me," she added rudely, "I believe I'll meet Tykie and Mr. McKenzie now."

She strode off without waiting for his reply, climbing nimbly over the gate to join the two men who were heading toward them across the freshly plowed field. Lochiel watched her go, unmoved by the impudent sway of her buttocks in the tight-fitting breeches she wore, yet there was a savage tightness about his mouth that boded trouble. He'd come back later to talk with Bruce McKenzie, preferably when Athena was already in bed. Right now he didn't think he'd be able to maintain a grip on his temper if he were forced to encounter that haughty little bitch again.

The Highlanders were scheduled to march at dawn, and a faint thread of silver light shone on the horizon as Athena and Tykie started off for the fort. Frost lay thick on the trail, and Athena turned up the collar of her coat, wishing she were back in her warm bed of straw in the McKenzies' loft. She had bid them a fond farewell and had accepted with tears the groaning sack of provisions Elizabeth handed to her, well aware that the middle-aged couple would probably go hungry for the next few days because of their generosity.

"Take it, lass," Elizabeth said sternly when Athena at first refused it. "Ye'll be needin' yer strength, both o' ye, an' ye'll be heartily sick of camp cookin' soon enough."

At the door she had embraced the slim girl and peered for a long moment into the clear blue eyes. What advice could she give this motherless child who had a way of winning one's heart after so short a time? She didn't like the idea that Athena was going to be traveling such a long distance with soldiers and camp followers for company, but she reminded herself that Major Blackmoor would be there to look after her, and if anyone was a proper gentleman who'd do right by a lady—even if she did look like a strapping young lad—then he was the one.

Athena would have laughed bitterly at Elizabeth McKenzie's thoughts, for she had no confidence at all in Lochiel Blackmoor, especially not after what he had said to her last night. Thank goodness neither Tykie nor Fletcher had been present during that encounter, she thought grimly and lowered her head as a blast of chilly dawn wind ripped through the budding branches and threatened to send her cap hurling into the sky.

The Scots were just beginning to line up on the parade ground for inspection when the two of them arrived and Athena heard Tykie sigh happily as the skirl of bagpipes filled the air.

" 'Twill be grand tae spend a wee bit o' time wi' my ain folk," he remarked, his dark eyes gleaming at the impressive sight before them.

Though they were heading into the wilderness, the Highlanders had donned full military dress for their final inspection by fort commander Major Henry Eure. Though Athena had seen them in their military plaids before, she could not help admiring each soldier's arrogant bearing and the obvious pride with which he carried his broadsword and targe. Sergeant-Major Andrew Durning, whom she had met at the de Vrieses' last fall, bore an impressive Lochaber ax as he accompanied Major Eure on inspection, and for the first time Athena began to see why the Highland regiments were so highly thought of.

Tykie had already told her that only Highland-born clan members could be recruited into the elite ranks of the Royal Scots and that each soldier must be at least six feet tall in order to qualify. Most of them were wellborn or had been members of the nobility before King George's reprisals after the Stuart uprising had stripped them of their ranks. They certainly made an impressive sight standing proud and tall in their scarlet coats and plaids, looking every bit like the warriors who had joined Bonnie Prince Charlie in his quest for the British throne.

A shiver fled down her spine as she drew her mount to a halt in the darkness beneath the fort's inner ramparts. It unnerved her suddenly to realize that she would be spending the next two weeks in the care of these brawny, ferocious men. Even Tykie seemed different to her somehow, for there was a look on his bearded face she'd never seen before as he listened intently to the mournful wailing of the pipes. It made her feel lonely, somehow, and curiously abandoned.

She stiffened as she saw Lochiel Blackmoor emerge from the barracks with Fletcher, and it struck her for the first time how similar in height and build they were, although Lochiel, thanks to his training and excellent health, all but overshadowed her brother. It annoyed her that his gold-piped uniform only served to enhance his masculinity and that the well-tailored coat clearly revealed the breadth of his muscular shoulders.

"They'll be marching in a moment, lass," she heard Tykie say. "Best bid farewell tae yer brother."

Athena swallowed hard. She knew she was going to cry, and it angered her that Lochiel Blackmoor would be present to witness her childish behavior.

Yet in the end she and Tykie were almost swept away in the chaos of the march, and there was scarcely time to embrace Fletcher and wish him the best. Lochiel was nowhere to be seen, for which Athena was grateful. Tears were streaming freely down her cheeks, and she was forced to sniffle into her hankie while Tykie guided her mount to the rear of the line, where the wagons and pack mules belonging to the camp were struggling to fall in. The confusion and noise were unbelievable, and Athena wondered how the soldiers marching in orderly columns ahead of them to the accompaniment of the pipers could possibly tolerate it.

" 'Tis a' part o' army life, lass," Tykie chuckled, noticing the bewildered expression on her tear-stained face. "Come on, we'll ride to the front o' the train an' I'll introduce ye tae Mother Hicks."

"Mother Hicks?" Athena echoed.

"She be sort of the camp leader, unofficially o' course," Tykie informed her. His black eyes were averted, but Athena thought she detected a knowing twinkle within them.

"Tykie," she said suspiciously, not bothering to lower her voice since the din was deafening, "how did you chance to meet this Mother Hicks? And am I to assume that her title means she is in charge of—of the girls who—"

"Now, Miss Athena, 'tisna richt tae be askin' sich unladylike questions. Mother Hicks be wham she be an' ye'd best be satisfied with thot. She has a heart o' gold, an' she'll look oot for ye if ye mind wha' she says."

"I believe the introductions can wait," Athena assured him with a shake of her head. How like Tykie to make the acquaintance of the military equivalent of a brothel mistress! Small wonder he had vanished so often during her stay with the McKenzies!

"And remember that my name is Malcolm," she added, thinking that she was going to have a hard enough time remembering that herself.

Tykie tugged unhappily at his earlobe. "I dinna ken wha' Master Fletcher would say if he kenned ye were gang tae continue yer dress-up games, lass. Ye were supposed tae be Miss Athena on the trip hame, not Master Colm. Master Fletcher was countin' on Major Blackmoor tae gie ye the special treatment befittin' a lady."

"Like my own tent and a personal bodyguard?" Athena asked with a curt laugh. "Not Major Blackmoor, I assure you! And 'tisn't a game, Tykie," she added, sobering as she recalled Lochiel's warning about the unsavory men who were part of the camp population. She had seen some of them riding in the wagons while others followed on foot, big, unclean men with scars on their faces and weapons tucked in their belts.

Lochiel had been right, she thought to herself, sitting straighter in the saddle and tossing her head like any lad eager for adventure. 'Twould be in her best interest to continue with the charade, for even Tykie might not prove a match for a dozen armed and lustful criminals.

The air grew warmer as the sun began to spiral into the cloudless blue sky. Several days of uninterrupted good weather had dried the trail that led east across the mountains, and the ox-drawn wagons belonging to Mother Hicks and the rest of the camp population made excellent time.

Athena found herself enjoying the ride regardless of the lingering sadness of her separation from Fletcher and the fears Lochiel Blackmoor had instilled in her the night before. They spent the morning traveling through the length of a fertile valley crisscrossed with clear-running streams. The mountains surrounding them wore a mantle of shimmering spring green, and the air was seductively crisp and new. They saw wildlife in abundance in the forests, and once or twice a doe with a spindle-legged fawn at her side leaped through the trees to escape them. Athena's mount was eager to run after three days of confinement in Bruce McKenzie's barn, and she relented at last to his insistent prancing and head tossing.

Riding past the head of the train, she nodded briefly to the redheaded woman sitting in the first wagon with a chicken, of all things, sleeping on her voluminous lap. Her greeting was returned with a toothy grin and a wink, and Athena, certain that Mother Hicks was flirting with her, blushed furiously and kicked her horse into a gallop.

" 'Twould be best if Tykie makes that woman aware of who I really am," she muttered to herself, lowering her head over the gelding's crested neck as he thundered off across the grass. She didn't know what she'd do if, disguised as Malcolm Courtland, she began to capture the interest of the overweight prostitute or one of her younger charges!

A mile or so ahead of the wagons marched the Highlanders, their kilts swinging, accoutrements gleaming in the sun. Athena slowed her horse to a trot, a scowl on her face as she surveyed the tightly knit ranks. She had no trouble recognizing Lochiel, who rode a bay charger at the rear of the procession. He was bareheaded, as usual, and his black locks glinted whenever the breeze ruffled them. His military seat was superb, and Athena felt a stab of resentment in her heart.

Always in command, always so calm and capable, that was Major Lochiel Blackmoor, and Athena was beginning to resent him heartily. How dearly she would like to take that arrogant devil down a peg or two!

She saw him turn his head and say something to the sergeant-major who rode at his side. His countenance was relaxed, his hawkish features softened with enjoyment at being on the move again, and the resentment in Athena's heart changed to a dull, indefinable ache. Despite herself she was reminded of how those carnal lips had captured hers, how he had lain above her and touched her intimately, in a way no man ever had before, how he had become a part of her and transported her beyond all imagining.

A low moan fell from Athena's lips as hungry longing came over her unexpectedly, the same ache she had tried so hard to deny during those lonely winter nights when she had tossed, sleepless, in her bed. She did not want Lochiel Blackmoor, she told herself savagely, denying the fierce need that tugged at her heart. She had responded to his lovemaking that night in Courtland Grace's garden because she had been ignorant and without experience, not because she had been swayed by his masculinity.

"I hate him!" she whispered fiercely to herself. Shouldn't hatred be enough to subdue the curse of womanly weakness he had inflicted upon her? Wheeling her horse around, she galloped back to Tykie's side, vowing to keep her distance from Lochiel Blackmoor until the journey was over.

Camp was made that night in a small clearing in the thick of a fragrant forest. Ferns grew in abundance in the rich earth, and tiny snowbells thrust their heads through the layer of pine needles carpeting the forest floor. Fires were permitted, and no sooner had the wagons and mules been drawn to a halt than wood smoke began to curl up into the trees to mingle with the smell of cooking stew.

Though she was exhausted, Athena fed and watered her horse before collapsing before the tent that Tykie had erected on the outskirts of camp. It was Fletcher who made certain that they were given one, appalled by the fact that his sister had slept beneath the open sky on the journey to Fort Shuyler. Though it was barely large enough for their bedrolls, it would afford them privacy, an invaluable asset in terms of Athena's safety.

Neither of them spoke as they consumed the hearty meal produced from Elizabeth McKenzie's pack. Athena sat on the ground with her slim legs crossed and studied the activity around her as she ate. She had learned the names of most of her fellow travelers throughout the course of the day and had been surprised at how kindhearted and friendly they had turned out to be.

'Twas common for enlisted men's wives to accompany their menfolk from campaign to campaign, and camp followers had been an accepted facet of army life for thousands of years. Athena knew that few of the Highlanders of the Seventh Company had brought their wives with them from Scotland and that the women and girls of this particular camp were little better than prostitutes, or blanket girls, as she'd heard them called. They served no other purpose than to bring pleasure to lonely soldiers' lives, yet none of them had fitted Athena's image of what whores should look like. For the most part they were young and kept themselves clean and well dressed and some of them could even be labeled pretty.

Athena couldn't help smiling to herself wondering what Aunt Amelia would say if she knew that her niece was at this very moment living in an army camp populated mainly by whores and men of dubious honor whose very existence depended on the generosity of the regiments they followed.

"Aunt Amelia would have naught to say," Athena murmured with a laugh. "She'd simply die of heart failure."

" 'Tis a blessin' she canna see ye the noo," Tykie agreed, overhearing enough of her words to guess what she was thinking. He himself hated to see his beloved mistress reduced to wearing breeches and mingling with lowborn riffraff, yet their success in finding Master Fletcher made all of that well worth it. He only hoped Miss Athena would be content to give up her wild ways for good once they returned home.

"Tykie, isn't that the boy who stole my satchel the day we arrived?"

He looked up at the sharp-featured youth who was filling his plate from a caldron bubbling over the main campfire. "Aye, thot be Joe Madison. Ye'll be rememberin' his sister Ailie?"

Athena's expression was distasteful, recalling the plain little redhead who had simpered so brazenly at Lochiel when she had brought the stolen satchel back to him.

"They were orphans until Mother Hicks took both of 'em in," Tykie continued. "The lad keeps himsel' busy tendin' horses an' runnin' errands for the soldiers."

"And stealing when there's no better work to be had," Athena added darkly.

"I've been told he's a wild one," Tykie agreed. "Best stay clear o' him, Miss Athena—Malcolm," he amended hastily when she scowled.

"And what about that girl there, Tykie?" Athena went on, her attention centered on the small group gathered before the fire. "Is she another of Mother Hicks's protégées? I don't recall having seen her before."

Tykie coughed uncomfortably, unable to accustom himself to the bluntness with which genteel Miss Athena brought up the subject of prostitutes. She was gesturing boldly at a young woman in a dress of ivory muslin that appeared to be a little better made than those worn by the others. Her hair glinted a fiery midnight as she bent close to the flames for warmth, the air having grown chilly with the setting of the sun.

Athena saw her laugh in response to something that was said, throwing back her dark head to reveal a long column of smooth white throat. The fullness of her breasts was clearly revealed against the clinging material of her gown, inadvertently reminding Athena of her own discomfort, for she had been forced to wear constricting clothes to hide the roundness of her own body.

An aura of sultry seductiveness emanated from this black-haired woman, and Athena felt dislike and an odd defensiveness creep through her as she stared into the flushed and undeniably beautiful features. Why she should feel threatened by this unknown woman was a mystery to her, for she had always dismissed the members of her own sex as beneath her notice.

"That be Liza Hampton, and ye'd best na tangle wi' her," Tykie warned. "She be a shrew frae wha' I've heard, an' no enemy ye'd like to make."

"She doesn't scare me in the least," Athena retorted with a toss of her head, her uneasiness fading. "You forget I spent a year at school in Edinburgh, where I learned to handle creatures who could eat Miss Hampton for supper."

Tykie was forced to grin at this. He'd forgotten that Miss Athena had spent her fourteenth year in England, fulfilling what had been one of Fiona's dying wishes by attending a very proper finishing school for young ladies. It certainly hadn't polished the chit up a bit, as everyone well knew, but Athena had enjoyed her stay in the Scottish Lowlands despite her fierce homesickness for Courtland Grace.

Fiona, Scottish-born herself, had taken her daughter home with her on several occasions before her death. Foster had rarely accompanied them, feeling no pull to the land he had left behind, nor could his sons be persuaded to leave New York even for a little while for what they termed the stuffy confinement of the Old World. Athena, on the other hand, had enjoyed her visits to Fiona's colorful aunt in Aberstrath and had mentioned often to the delighted Tykie how moving she had found the rugged beauty of the Scottish mountains.

"I hear Liza Hampton be a great favorite among the officers," Tykie went on conversationally. " 'Tis said Major Blackmoor himself took quite a fancy to her."

"Is that so?" Athena inquired casually.

Tykie glanced at her keenly, alerted by some undefinable change in her tone, but it had grown darker and he could no longer clearly see her face. He grinned sheepishly, aware that he'd been gossiping like a cursed woman. Rising stiffly to his feet, joints creaking, he stretched his arms high over his head.

"I'll be takin' me a wee walk afore I turn in, lass. Ye'll hae a care while I'm gang awa'?"

"I won't move from the spot," Athena promised.

He had expected her to tease him, for surely she must know that he intended to take a stroll past Mother Hicks's tent, and he was a little surprised when she chose to say nothing.

"I willna stay too long," he promised, reluctant to leave her yet unable to stop thinking about the tempting redhead and her talents.

"I can take care of myself, Tykie," Athena reminded him sternly, "and I can always scream if anyone dares accost me. Besides," she added with a self-deprecating laugh, "who would want to pay the least bit of attention to a skinny lad in hand-me-downs without a farthing to his name?"

Forced to agree with the wisdom of this, Tykie took himself off, and

Athena listened to the sound of his happy whistle fading into the darkness before snatching up her tin bowl. Dashing it with all her might against a nearby tree, she found the hollow clang it made unleashing her pent-up fury.

So Major Blackmoor had taken a fancy to the alluring Liza Hampton, had he? Had her midnight beauty appealed to him better than her own fair looks? The rutting stag! How many women had he bedded since he'd seduced her last autumn? One? Two? Half a dozen? How many women did it take to satisfy the bloody swine?

Square jaw tightly clenched, Athena set about cleaning up the remains of their dinner. Now and then she would pause to feed the fire Tykie had lit, snapping branches in two and tossing them onto the flames, wishing it were Lochiel Blackmoor's bloody neck she was breaking with her bare hands.

"Damn the pox-ridden swine," she muttered to herself, turning away from the fire with a murderous expression only to barrel directly into the wide chest of a man who had come up unnoticed behind her.

"Oh!" she gasped, but her fear changed to outrage when the flickering firelight revealed to her the sharply etched features of Lochiel Blackmoor. How dare he steal up behind her this way, especially when she was so furious with him?

"This may only be an army followers' camp, major," Athena informed him coldly, "but that still doesn't give you the right to startle a lady."

The irony of her words was almost laughable, for she could not have looked less like a lady than she did at the moment, with her worn buckskin breeches and thick woolen sweater. Tangled curls had worked themselves loose from beneath her cap, and the hostility in her young face was not a typical expression for a female of genteel upbringing.

"My apologies, Miss Courtland," Lochiel said stiffly. "Next time I'll send my valet ahead with a calling card."

Athena turned her back on him, shaking with silent rage as she rinsed off the last of the supper dishes. "Did you wish to see me about anything in particular, sir?"

Lochiel forced himself to remain patient, though her insolence made him want to shake her until her teeth rattled. "I've come to take you and Tykie back to camp where my orderly can look after you properly. You shouldn't have to wash dishes or wear those clothes any longer."

"I have my own tent here, thank you," Athena reminded him, hiding her surprise at his words. "As for these clothes, they're all I have, and didn't you warn me yourself of the consequences of revealing my identity to your lecherous followers?"

Lochiel gritted his teeth. He had no desire to explain to her that he had exaggerated the chances of her being attacked merely because she had annoyed him last night at the McKenzies' with her sharp tongue and flashing eyes. He had never really intended for her to assume the role of a camp follower and had been somewhat surprised when she had accepted his orders without running to her brother to protest.

Didn't she realize that a single word from him would be enough to afford her protection from the men of this camp? And didn't she know that her brother had made arrangements for her to travel in comfort with Piers Barrett to provide for her and a tent of her own for utmost privacy?

He had banished her to camp only because she had made him lose his temper last night. A few hours of hard work and drudgery should have left her quite eager to agree to come with him, and it annoyed him that she continued to balk. Was she being difficult merely to punish him?

"I said you weren't supposed to be doing that," he grated, stooping down to pry a dirty dish from her hands.

"And who do you suggest should be doing it for me?" she challenged. "One of your blanket girls?"

She had turned her head as she spoke, only to find her cheek nearly touching his broad shoulder. Though the evening was cool, he had not bothered to don his tunic and was wearing nothing but breeches and a woven long-john shirt that hugged his muscular torso. The buttons at the throat had been left undone, and as Athena turned toward him the wind caught a silky strand of her hair and brushed it against the pulse beating so strongly there.

Scarlet-faced, Athena jerked away, but the intimate moment had been enough to rekindle the longing for him she had never been able to deny. "Go away," she commanded, retreating to the far side of the crackling fire. There was a catch in her voice, for she knew now that the danger for her here lay not in the unscrupulous thoughts of the men of the camp but in the helpless attraction she felt for Lochiel Blackmoor. "I'm not going back with you," she added determinedly. "Tykie and I are staying here with the camp followers until we get home to West York."

In the flickering light her face had taken on a wild, pagan beauty, the dancing flames deepening the sultry darkness of her eyes. Lochiel was powerless to control the primitive desire for her that arose within him, unleashed by the subtle fragrance that had surrounded him when her silky hair had brushed his bare skin. She was pure seductive beauty despite the bulky wool sweater, despite the battered cap and dusty leather shoes. Golden firelight danced against the white column of her throat, and he ached to plant his lips there, to feel the heat of her flesh and the tremor of her body as she yielded to his touch.

Athena swallowed hard as she saw the desire spring into those glittering silver eyes. A hot need coursed through her in response, and she knew that she'd be lost if he touched her.

"I'm not one of your blanket girls, Lochiel Blackmoor," she said, her voice trembling dangerously as he came slowly toward her, "nor did my brother intend for me to become your personal concubine. Is this how you plan to keep your word to him to look after me?"

There was a moment of tense silence while Lochiel fought with his temper, aware that she spoke the truth.

"If you insist on remaining here, Miss Courtland, I'll not attempt to dissuade you," he said at last, his expression sinister. "Mayhap a few days of primitive living will teach you that childish tantrums can be costly."

Turning heel, he vanished into the darkness, leaving her shaken by the violence of their encounter. Crawling into the tent, she opened her bedroll with a furious kick and threw herself down upon it. Damn him to hell! How could someone she loathed so thoroughly upset her like this?

"I do hate him, I do," she whispered petulantly to herself. He was cruel and despicable, and she hadn't mistaken the lust she'd seen in his eyes when he'd stared at her across the fire.

Closing her eyes, she tried to sleep, but it seemed as if Lochiel Blackmoor had robbed her of the ability to rest. All she could remember was how close they had come to touching when he had knelt down beside her to take the supper dishes from her hand. She had found her gaze drawn to the lean, bronzed cheek only inches from hers, mesmerized by the play of firelight upon hard bone before the wind had blown her hair against his chest and she had felt the shudder of his lean body in response. Or had she been the one who had trembled with the intimacy of the moment and the heat that had flared at his nearness?

Athena couldn't remember, and she moaned low in her throat as she tossed fretfully upon her narrow bedroll. She was not a wanton, she was not in love with Lochiel Blackmoor. Why then had her limbs turned to water when he had stared at her with such bold intent across the fire?

"Damn him to hell," she whispered again, squeezing her eyes against the tears that threatened to fall.

Wind sighed in the trees overhead and mingled with the muted sounds of laughter coming from the other tents in the darkness. Athena lay, dry-eyed, on her back, arms propped beneath her head, and tried to sleep despite the terrible gnawing ache within her heart. She couldn't remember when she had ever felt so alone.

Eleven

The hush of twilight hung over the hills, and the primal forest floor was cool and damp. The sun, setting in amber splendor behind the rugged granite peaks, tinted the budding branches of the elm trees with gold. Far across the fields an English settler and his dogs were rounding up cattle for the night, their plaintive lows echoing in the gathering gloom.

" 'Tis a sunset meant for dreamin'," Andrew Durning murmured, inhaling a deep lungful of crisp mountain air as he surveyed the darkening valley below him. "All the more precious because the Frenchies could storm this place any time an' lift the scalp off yon hardy soul down there."

A faint smile curved the slashing mouth of the tall man standing on the bluff of the hill beside him. "I've a feeling the settlers in this valley won't let a few roving bands of Indians or Frenchmen defeat them."

"Aye, New York colonials be a hardy lot," Andy conceded. "Tough as leather an' afraid o' naught."

Despite himself Lochiel was forced to think of a certain young colonial woman with a will of iron who did not shrink from sleeping in the wilderness or spending endless days in the saddle riding astride like a man.

"It takes a special sort to survive here," he agreed softly, his gaze sweeping the vista before him. The herdsman and cattle were gone by now, and darkness was beginning to steal like a hazy purple mantle across the hills. 'Twas a beautiful land, this colony of New York, yet Lochiel found his thoughts turning homeward, to the rugged mountains of northwestern Scotland. 'Twould be a challenge to build a life there as well, he reflected, to take what had been destroyed by English hands and return it to its former glory.

"I imagine the lads have finished setting up camp," he remarked to Andy, abruptly deciding he'd been daydreaming long enough. Unexpected weariness was etched into his face as he turned away from the magnificent view, and he found himself wondering where his thirst for military life had gone of late.

Because no French or Indian patrols had been spotted since the Highlanders had left Fort Shuyler, fires were again permitted that night. Several of them had already been lit by the time the two officers returned, their cheerful orange glow dispersing the gathering gloom. Sergeant-Major Durning sniffed appreciatively at the scent of roasting game hovering in the chilly air.

"When I think back on some of our marches I'm grateful for nights like these," he remarked, hunger causing him to increase his stride.

Lochiel nodded in agreement, recalling times when they had camped in freezing rain or blizzards, their equipment soaked, their paths blocked by mountainous drifts or deep, sucking mud. After the terrible loss of Fort William Henry last year, they had been forced to retreat in total darkness, marching for hours on end with no rest and little more to eat than a handful of grain. Perhaps the nights were still bitterly cold this early May of 1759, but Lochiel, having endured far worse, found their present lot more than acceptable.

Most of the men seemed to share his sentiments, for they were in high spirits as they relaxed around the fire washing down their meal of roasted venison with icy water from a nearby spring.

"We're layin' wagers on our new assignment, major," Davie Skelley called to Lochiel as the tall officer stepped out of the darkness.

"What seems to be the popular opinion?" Lochiel inquired curiously, bending to slice a piece of succulent meat from the spit with his dirk. Seating himself on the ground, he stretched his long legs before him and began to eat.

"Most of us say 'twill be Quebec after a wee bit o' drillin' in Albany," Corporal Martin said. In the flickering light his bearded features wore a contented look, for there were few things he loved more than sitting before the fire after a hard day's march.

"All the better for me," young Iain MacLachlan remarked with a grin, rubbing his hands together. "I'm the only one says General Amherst'll send the Seventh west to join Prideaux's troops for the assault on Fort Niagara."

"Ye're daft, mon!" Davie snorted, licking his fingers before helping himself to another piece of meat.

"An' a guinea says I ain't," Iain retorted.

"A guinea? Where've ye fools come by such wealth?" the sergeant-major demanded, joining them in time to catch Iain's boastful words.

"Wagerin' wi' the Provincials back at the fort." Davie Skelley chuckled. "Those poor lads haven't much i' the way o' common sense, an wagerin' wi' them was easier'n stealin' scones frae a blind mon. Lord," he added, shaking his sandy head, "if I were a Provincial colonel I'd tear out me hair havin' tae mother such a sorry excuse for soldiers!"

Spoken with all the wisdom of his twenty years, Lochiel decided, his thoughtful gaze studying the familiar faces around him. Yet Davie and the other youths of the company were experienced fighters who had seen a lot of action. They wielded their heavy claymores along with the best of them and could launch themselves without a moment's hesitation against a deadly line of rifle-carrying French Regulars.

All of them were fearless, these brawny Highland warriors, even Skelley and MacLachlan, the youngest of them all. Yet many of the familiar faces were gone now, and Lochiel still felt the pain whenever he thought of the friends and comrades they'd been forced to bury in the hard ground below the bastions of Fort William Henry and Duquesne.

No sense in dwelling on the past, he decided grimly, finishing his dinner and rising to his feet. He had enough to worry about at present, and one of his thorniest problems was waiting for him not a half-mile away. 'Twas time to deal with it, too, before the situation got entirely out of hand.

"Gie bonnie Liza my best, laddie," a voice called after him as he untethered his horse.

That was Andy, of course, and Lochiel's harsh visage softened with amusement. Let them think what they wanted, even though he wasn't planning a call on Liza Hampton. His eyes narrowed to slits. No, nothing as pleasant as that lay before him. He was on his way to confront the rebellious Athena Courtland and see if she'd had enough of pretending to be something she wasn't. Surely the number of miles they had covered today had left her soft derrière quite sore and her appetite for adventure severely shaken. The prospect brought a rather pleased smile to his lips, and he uttered a curt laugh as he kicked Glenrobbie into a trot.

A cold wind had picked up with the coming of night, and the pine trees quivered beneath its onslaught. Stars shone brightly from the blue-black canopy of sky, and the winter constellations were visible over the mountain peaks. An enormous fire had been lit before the uneven circle of tents and most of the camp followers had gathered there to take advantage of its warmth.

Mother Hicks sat holding court at one end of the blaze, busily picking fleas out of her blanket as she chatted with those around her. She was a heavyset woman of some forty years whose sagging features still bore the remnants of what had once been surprising beauty. Friendly brown eyes regarded the world without censure, and her infectious laugh had a way of making even the most miserable creatures feel welcome.

It pleased Mother Hicks that Tykie Downs had finally managed to talk his shy young companion Malcolm into joining the others that night, for some of the camp folk were beginning to wonder why the two of them kept so to themselves. A pretty little lad, Sarah Hicks had decided critically when they were introduced, and certainly old enough to take his pleasure with any one of her girls.

But Tykie wasn't about to permit any of that, she saw, for he wouldn't let Malcolm out of his sight, and his fierce scowl was enough to intimidate even the boldest of her charges. She'd have to talk to him about that, the former taproom wench decided with firmly compressed lips. A big, strapping lad like Malcolm Courtland didn't need mothering at his age!

"Don't yer remember what it was like when yer was a beardless boy, dearie?" she whispered into Tykie's ear, leaning forward so that her enormous breasts brushed against his coat.

"Nay, woman," Tykie replied promptly, his black eyes gleaming, for he had already consumed quite a bit of the whiskey that was making the rounds that night. "Did ye no ken that Tykie Downs was birthed full grown frae his mither's loins?"

"Then where came yer by such a pulin' name?" the big woman inquired suspiciously. She'd heard tales about the pagan practices that went on in the remote glens of Scotland, of magic and witchcraft and enchanted creatures who cast spells on unsuspecting men. Mayhap what Tykie said was true!

"He was such a little tyke when he was born that his mother didn't believe he'd live," Athena answered for him, interrupting what she knew would be a long-winded ramble, for whiskey had a way of loosening Tykie's boastful tongue. Athena, who had been surprised to discover that she actually liked Sarah Hicks, didn't want to see her teased, for it was obvious that the kindhearted old soul was rather superstitious and might be inclined to believe anything Tykie said.

"Well, 'e ain't no little tyke no more, m'boy," Mother Hicks replied, her amused voice filled with double meaning. "Don't yer agree, Tykie me love?"

But Tykie wasn't so far gone in his cups that he had forgotten how inappropriate such talk was for a gentlewoman's ears. Mumbling beneath his breath, he glanced at Athena with his woolly head bowed, wishing he hadn't given in to Sarah's prodding to bring Miss Athena into their midst.

"Why, I believe he's being modest, Mother," Athena responded with a gentle smile, hoping to ease his embarrassment. Poor Tykie, 'twasn't his fault that he had been thrust into the role of protecting her from the crudeness of camp life!

Scarlet-faced, Tykie rose unsteadily and stumbled off into the darkness, thinking that a few gulps of cold night air might help clear his head. He shouldn't have let that copper-haired hussy get him so drunk, not with Miss Athena to be looked after!

"Let 'im go, dearie," Sarah Hicks said as Athena rose worriedly to follow him. " 'Tis the call o' nature 'e be answerin'. 'E'll be back by the by."

Reluctantly Athena returned to the fire. Bending to refill her tin mug with coffee from the hissing black kettle, she felt something strike her hard from behind, sending her toppling toward the crackling flames. Rolling to one side, she just managed to keep from being burned, and her shocked expression gave way to anger when she scrambled upright to find Joe Madison laughing down at her.

"Couldn't resist when I saw the seat o' yer pants just askin' for a good, swift kick," he told her, grinning broadly.

"I could have been badly hurt!" Athena accused, pale with lingering fright.

"You gonna do something about it?" Joe inquired softly, folding his arms before his thin chest. There was an ugly look on his sharp features Athena didn't like, and she swallowed hard, aware that he was deliberately challenging her. Had he been carrying some sort of grudge against her since Lochiel forced him to return her stolen satchel days ago?

Looking around at the sober faces revealed in the firelight, Athena was certain of it. Though she detected an inkling of sympathy in many of the eyes turned her way, she sensed that no one would try to help her. She had already learned that interfering in another's personal matters was against the unwritten laws that governed the camp.

Knowing she would have to handle the bully alone, Athena lifted her chin, her tone imperious to hide the quiver of fear she felt within. "You certainly found an opportune time, didn't you? How long have you been waiting for Tykie to disappear?"

The haughtily arched brows and the dignity with which she confronted him caused the older boy's gaze to falter for an instant. There was something about Malcolm Courtland that had annoyed him from the first, and Joe Madison refused to admit to himself that it was envy—envy for the fine horse the younger boy rode, for the gentrified air about him, for the fact that Major Blackmoor had seen fit to take him under his personal protection.

"I been waitin' for yer to come out from behind Tykie's skirts," Joe admitted, recovering his composure. From the corner of his eye he could see his sister Ailie's approving expression, and it helped to bolster his resolve. "Yer can't hide behind 'em forever, yer little runt, or is it more than that?" His smile grew ugly at the sudden thought. "Do the two of yer have some kind o' . . . special relationship, eh?"

Athena gasped as she realized what he was hinting at. It enraged her that this ill-bred churl would dare slander Tykie when he wasn't around to defend himself. 'Twas an act of utter cowardice, and she had been raised in a household where cowards were considered beneath contempt.

"You foul-mouthed swine!" she cried, launching herself at him so unexpectedly that even Joe was taken by surprise.

Balling her hand into a fist, Athena struck him full in the face. She had allowed Colm and Jeremy to lure her into boxing matches often enough as a little girl and understood the sport sufficiently to throw a punch without injuring herself. Though the blow she aimed at his jaw lacked any real strength, the unexpectedness of the attack worked to her advantage, causing the unsuspecting Joe to lose his balance and crash over backward.

Spectators scattered, laughing openly as the startled boy landed heavily on his rump. Shaking his head to clear it, he scrambled to his feet, his expression murderous. Athena whirled to escape him, her heart thumping with sudden fright. For her this was no battle of supremacy between rival adolescents, no sideshow to amuse the bored and weary camp followers. She was no match for Joe Madison, and it was too late to reveal to any of them why.

With the fury of wounded pride, Joe hurled himself upon her, but Athena managed to turn her head aside so that the blow he aimed at her chin glanced off her cheek without much force. Yet it was still enough to send her sprawling, and with a yell of delight Joe came after her again.

A cry of mingled pain and surprise fell from his lips as his wrists were unexpectedly trapped from behind in an iron grip that halted him in his tracks.

"That's enough," a harsh voice grated, and Joe's eyes widened in alarm as he stared up at the shadowed features above his.

Silence had fallen over the noisy spectators, and Athena, coming dizzily to her feet, stared about her in astonishment. What had happened? Nursing her throbbing cheek, she turned back to Joe and her eyes widened much as his had done when she saw him being held none too gently by the towering form of Lochiel Blackmoor.

"Are you hurt?" No change came over the savage countenance, and in fact he didn't even look at her. Athena could only shake her head by way of reply.

"Then go to your tent."

Lochiel experienced a moment of bitter amusement as she vanished wordlessly into the darkness, for this was only the second time in her life Athena had ever obeyed him. Releasing his grip on Joe Madison's wrists, he watched without an inkling of sympathy as the boy began to rub them vigorously, wincing as the blood returned to his numbed fingers.

"Malcolm Courtland may be as tall as you are," Lochiel said at last, "but he's half your weight and certainly wasn't raised to be a fighter.

Would you like to see what it feels like to be attacked under similar odds?"

Joe's face drained of color, leaving it looking like a bleached skull against the contrasting blackness of the night. There was no doubt in his mind what the Highlander was suggesting, and he felt his mouth grow dry as he stared up into those ominous silver eyes. The unspoken menace radiating from that broad-shouldered form terrified him, and he couldn't take his eyes off the heavily muscled forearms the major revealed as he casually rolled back the sleeves of his shirt.

"Well, Joe?"

"N-no sir," he stammered, not caring that his voice had risen to a fearful pitch. Sweat stood out on his brow and his mouth worked nervously.

"You'll leave the lad alone, then?"

"Yes, s-sir, I promise, sir."

Lochiel's coldly arrogant gaze surveyed the rest of the camp, his unpleasant expression causing even the most hardened among the menfolk to look away uneasily. Even Mother Hicks, who was rarely at loss for words, sensed that it would be wisest not to speak. She'd send Liza over to the major's tent later, she decided, bending discreetly over her blanket. He was a wild one, the major was, but not at all immune to Liza's charms, and no doubt the girl'd be able to coax him out of this fine temper.

Looking from one uneasy face to another, Lochiel knew that nothing more needed to be said to ensure Athena's safety for the remainder of the journey. He was nonetheless enraged that he hadn't anticipated something like this, knowing how suspicious the camp followers were of newcomers. His admittedly cruel decision to throw Athena to the wolves had resulted in her confrontation with Joe Madison, and he alone was to blame for it. In a foul mood, he strode off in the direction of her tent to see how badly she'd been hurt.

Athena, sitting on her bedroll with her face in her hands, scrambled to her feet as he thrust the canvas flaps aside.

"Stay where you are," he growled, pushing her back. It did his temper little good to notice the tears glittering in her eyes. "Let me see your face."

She refused to obey his command, and he took her chin in his hand, deliberately turning her so that he could see the angry red welt on her cheek.

"Can't you be left alone for a day without resorting to brawling like a street urchin?" he demanded, although his touch was gentle as he probed the injured area.

Athena was stung by what she thought was his contempt. "By God, Blackmoor, I wasn't—"

"Don't say another word," he warned, disturbed by the puffiness of the skin over her cheek. He had poured icy spring water on his handkerchief before coming inside, and now he touched it carefully to the side of her face. " 'Twill be a pretty bruise," he remarked, kneeling down beside her. "I hope you weren't deserving of it."

"No, I was not!" Athena cried, jerking out of his grasp. Tears filled her eyes anew as she gazed at him accusingly. "That pox-ridden creature was saying terrible things about Tykie . . . and . . . and me."

"And so you had to defend your honor," Lochiel agreed, hiding his concern behind mockery.

Athena's head bowed. She felt too dazed and in pain to trade words with him. "Go away," she whispered.

She felt his hands on her shoulders, strong but surprisingly gentle, turning her around so that his lean face was close to hers.

"I'm sorry, Athena," he said in a voice made rough with remorse. "I want to comfort you, not hurt you. I suppose my bedside manner is better suited for soldiers needing a boost in morale than a woman in need of some reassurance."

He pulled her closer as he spoke so that her head fell against his chest where she could feel the strong, steady beat of his heart. The throbbing in her cheek was beginning to subside beneath the cold, soothing compress he held. With a sigh she closed her eyes and let the pain and fear of the last few minutes slip away into the warmth and security of the strong arms that held her.

She was still for so long that Lochiel thought she might have drifted off to sleep. Reluctantly lifting his chin from the golden head upon which it had been resting, he began to ease Athena out of his arms in order to lay her down amid the blankets. She gave a murmur of protest and turned her face to his, her blue eyes for once soft and compelling, not hostile or rebellious. No man, least of all Lochiel, could remain impervious to her unconscious appeal.

Taking the compress away, Lochiel allowed his hand to stray hesitantly over the already darkening bruise. "I would have done anything not to be responsible for marring your beautiful face," he confessed thickly. His strong fingers slid down to cup her chin and Athena trembled at his touch.

"I was wrong to try to punish you for being proud," he went on hoarsely, "especially because I, too, am guilty of that sin. But then, I believe that's why I cannot help but desire you, Athena, because you are equally arrogant as I. In you," he added, his lips caressing her bruised cheek tenderly, "I think I have found a worthy match."

Athena's head fell back and she whispered his name, her husky voice kindling his passion. He laid her upon the bedroll as though she were made of the most fragile porcelain, releasing the pins in her hair so that the glorious mass sprang free in his hands. His eyes, shadowed in the dim light, shimmered silver as he bent over her, his lean body deliciously heavy upon hers.

Pressing his mouth against hers, Lochiel found her lips parted in anticipation of his kiss. Heady with the scent of her and the softness of her body beneath him, he kissed her deeply until she moaned, passion flaring after the long months of denial.

"I want to make love to you, Athena," Lochiel murmured, knowing in his heart that he had wanted none other since he had first tasted her sweetness in the moonlit gardens of Courtland Grace. "And I think you want me, too."

She moved her warm body languidly beneath his by way of reply, her eyes sultry in the darkness. Slipping her arms about his neck, she allowed her fingers to stray through his hair, reveling in the instinctive knowledge that he had taken his pleasure with no one else since he had loved her that first, glorious time.

She closed her eyes in anticipation of another kiss, her face raised eagerly to his, and a startled exclamation fell from her lips as she felt his weight abruptly lift away from her. Puzzled, she sat up to find him standing with his back to her, his breathing harsh as he leaned against the tent pole.

"What is it?" she asked in alarm.

He uttered a curt laugh, his countenance set in a rigid mask. "Though I am tempted beyond belief to enjoy your offered charms, my dear Athena, I'm afraid I cannot."

Total bewilderment was mirrored in her wide blue eyes. "Why not? What have I done?"

He looked away again, for it was madness to gaze at her when he knew he must not have her. God's blood, why had reason returned to him now while he ached to possess her? What had made him think of duty and honor rather than the sweetness of her willing surrender when he had gazed into her passion-darkened eyes? He wasn't the first to have loved her! What in God's name was he afraid of?

"You haven't done anything," he told her harshly. "I've my conscience to blame, though I never would have confessed before this night to owning one. I have my word to consider, Athena, the word I gave your brother. That and the fact that an incensed Tykie Downs should be storming in here at any moment has given me pause to reconsider our impetuous actions."

Athena stared at him with growing dismay. How well she remembered the way he had spurned her last time, and how she had shamelessly wept and pleaded with him not to desert her. Well, she wasn't going to play the stricken female this time or ever again. She was not some object Lochiel Blackmoor could pick up and discard at his whim!

"I'm certain my brother would be very pleased if he knew of your gentlemanly inclinations," she said stiffly. "Obviously he is a better judge of character than I shall ever be." Hiding her hurt pride behind a dignified show of anger, she added coldly, "And should your baser instincts still be troubling you, then perchance Liza Hampton can provide willing relief."

"Perhaps you are right," Lochiel agreed. "I'd quite forgotten that Miss Hampton's skills are far superior to your own. I cannot imagine why I didn't seek her out to begin with."

Dry leaves crunched beneath his boots as he vanished into the darkness, not sparing her another glance. With a wounded cry Athena threw herself face down on her bedroll, oblivious to the throbbing pain of her bruised cheek. Bitter tears fell from her eyes as she tried to make sense of the confusion in her heart.

If Lochiel had truly desired her, he would never have allowed his promise to Fletcher to stand in the way of having her. Though he was a man of his word, Athena knew without question that he was also a man accustomed to taking what he wanted. And she had given him no reason to doubt that she had desired him, too. Why, then, had he turned away? Did he truly care more about his promise to Fletcher or what Tykie might think?

"He doesn't care for you, Athena," she whispered to herself, choking back a sob at the thought of Lochiel hurrying to the waiting arms of Liza Hampton. "He never has and you were a fool to hope otherwise!"

She could not control the tears that coursed down her cheeks, for her young girl's heart was all but broken. In the face of Lochiel's cruel rejection Athena had been forced to confront her true feelings and admit to herself that she had fallen in love with him the moment his lips had met hers in the velvet darkness of a long-ago October night.

Yet now the dreams she had acknowledged only in her innermost thoughts had been crushed beneath the contemptuous words of the one man who had the power to wound her. Athena felt nothing but hatred for him now, hatred for the man who had made a mockery of her innocent love.

When a frantic Tykie burst into the tent a short time later he found

Athena fallen into an exhausted slumber, tears mingling with lines of suffering on her defenseless young face.

"Excuse me, sir." Piers Barrett shuffled his feet nervously as he met Major Blackmoor's intimidating gaze. "There's a fellow outside who insists on seeing you."

"A fellow?" Lochiel repeated unpleasantly. Laying down his quill, he gave his adjunct an impatient glance. "You know damned well I'm not to be interrupted while I'm working on my reports. What fellow are you bloody talking about?"

"This one, major," came a low growl from outside, and the tent flaps were thrust aside to reveal the towering form of Tykie Downs.

It was barely dawn, and only a faint glimmer of color above the eastern mountain peaks hinted at the coming of the sun. In half an hour the regiment would be roused and camp would be broken for another day's march, yet at the moment all was still. A night bird called mournfully in the thickets, and a chilly breeze blew across the valley floor.

Without taking his eyes off the bearded man before him, Lochiel jerked his head at his adjunct by way of dismissal. Leaning back in the small camp chair, he crossed his arms before his chest. He had been up all night brooding over paperwork, and his mood was not the best.

"What is it you want?" he inquired curtly.

" 'Tis aboot Miss Athena, as I'm sure ye ken." Tykie's florid features were filled with menace, and his big hands clenched and unclenched as he spoke.

"I see. What about her?"

"Blood an' fury, mon, did ye no see her face?" the irate Tykie burst out. " 'Twas there when I came i' last night, though I didna notice until first light this mornin'!"

"Are you referring to her bruise?"

"Aye, her bruise! I'll hae ye ken, major, thot no mon ever laid a hand on Miss Athena afore! She ain't deserving o' violence!"

Privately Lochiel thought that several vigorous spankings during her formative years might have done Athena Courtland a world of good, but Tykie was right in claiming that she shouldn't have been exposed to the violence of her confrontation with Joe Madison last night.

" 'Tis hard enough for anyone tae look after Miss Athena properly," Tykie went on, rage and remorse mingling in his voice, "an' I'll be the first tae admit I failed her, but by God, mon, ye were tae keep her here among yer Hieland troops who ken how tae treat a lady! Instead ye let the riffraff wha' calls itself yer followers go on thinkin' she's a lad. Surely ye kenned there'd be trouble!"

His deep love for his mistress was evident in his voice, and the accusing words only served to echo Lochiel's own feelings of guilt. He should never have permitted Athena to continue her charade, never have left a defenseless young girl vulnerable prey to the unpredictable characters who populated the camp. Nor, Lochiel reminded himself bitterly, should he have allowed himself to succumb once again to the lure of her seductive beauty.

"You're right, Tykie, I'm entirely to blame for what happened last night." Lochiel rose and began to prowl about the tiny tent, oblivious to the look of astonishment on the older man's face. "I can understand your anger at being unable to protect Athena from being hurt, but you were right in admitting that 'tis nearly impossible for one man to look after her even without the added danger of a military march to consider."

"If ye could just see her face, mon," Tykie growled for lack of anything better to say. He had ridden here expecting a confrontation, not agreement and even understanding from the enigmatic Major Blackmoor.

"I've seen it," Lochiel answered softly, and for a moment a hard line drew his brows together. 'Twas entirely likely that seeing Athena's lovely face so terribly injured had been responsible for softening his resolve never to succumb to her wanton charms again. Thank God cold reason had returned to him in time to prevent him from making the mistake of his life.

"I assure you it won't happen again," he added briskly, bitterly aware of the ironic double meaning of his words. "Miss Courtland will be placed under the watchful eye of my R.S.M., who will see to it that no further mishaps occur. Sergeant-Major Durning, by the way, has four daughters of his own and can be trusted to keep his sanity where Miss Courtland is concerned."

Tykie grinned broadly, for this was exactly what he had wanted to hear. Oh, to have help at last in keeping his beloved mistress safe from harm! "I'll be tellin' Miss Athena when she wakes up," he said eagerly. "The poor mite fell asleep wi' her breeks on last night, so tired was she, an' I willna—"

Both men exchanged startled glances as the dawn air was suddenly rent by the unmistakable crackling of musket fire.

"What the de'il?" Tykie burst out in astonishment while Lochiel pushed past him into the slate-gray morning light. With experienced eyes he probed the darkened valley below him and then called sharply for his orderly, a grim urgency settling over his hawkish features.

Piers was panting heavily when he appeared, and his boyish face was deathly pale. "The sentries've just reported in, sir," he called out as he approached. " 'Twould seem a band of Indians stumbled on us in the darkness, and from the direction of the gunshots McKetcham's fair sure they've attacked the followers' camp!"

A fierce gleam sprang into Lochiel Blackmoor's eyes, and with a ruthless sense of urgency he began to bark orders at the men scrambling, half dressed, from their bedrolls. Seconds later he was astride his horse, lips curled in predatory fashion as he sent the long-legged beast hurling down the slope, his regulation rifle across one knee, his dirk unsheathed in his hand.

Through the graying light he could see the scattered tents below and the sporadic flaring of discharging muskets. Savagely he dug his spurs into the horse's heaving flanks and hoped that Athena had had enough sense to keep out of the line of fire.

Unmindful of the danger, he galloped at full speed down the rock-strewn trail, reaching the valley floor in time to see four men emerge from a dense stand of trees ahead of him. Dropping the reins, Lochiel lifted the rifle smoothly to his shoulder, only to lower it again as he recognized the familiar green hunting shirts and buckskin breeches of Rangers. Brows raised questioningly, he kicked his mount forward.

It was a middle-aged man with dark, greasy hair tied in a queue who saw him first. Propping his musket casually in the crook of his arm, he waited for Lochiel to draw rein beside him.

"Lieutenant Dartlin Smith of Rogers's Rangers," he announced in an easy New England drawl.

"Major Blackmoor, His Majesty's Regulars, Seventh Highland Company." Lochiel's manner was cool and alert as he acknowledged himself. "What's going on here, lieutenant?"

A grin split the deeply lined face. "Just a bit of hit 'n run, nothing to get excited about. We was marching west, been newly reassigned from Trent Town in New Jersey, when we ran across a band of redskins heading north. I think we surprised them just as much as they surprised us. Some of my boys took some potshots at 'em and they scattered like a bunch of hares. Stumbled right into that camp of yours, and that must've scared the daylights outta them completely. Never seen so much confusion."

He scratched the growth of gray stubble on his chin. "My fellows'll have 'em rounded up in a minute. No need for yours to get involved." His eyes twinkled amiably. "Don't call it boasting, major, but I'll tell you that six of my boys can round up a band of redskins easier than your entire Seventh Company. We ain't been sittin' on our arses all winter, that's for sure."

Lochiel took no offense at the mildly uttered words, well aware that the Rangers, despite their filthy habits and lack of discipline, were the fittest soldiers in the colonial army. Unlike Regular troops, which didn't believe in fighting during the winter months, the Rangers had been on constant maneuvers, scouting and marching and keeping in excellent physical shape. Lochiel himself had never condoned the European habit of sitting out the winter months to resume fighting in the spring, but that was something no single man could change. At least one could take comfort in the fact that the Marquis de Montcalm, a Frenchman himself, subscribed to similar habits.

At the moment, however, Lochiel wasn't interested in the condition of Lieutenant Smith's Rangers or the roundup of surviving Indians. His concern lay with the camp followers and the haunting possibility that there might have been casualties among them.

"Major Blackmoor!"

He glanced up to see Hugh Martin hurrying toward him on foot with several Highlanders behind him. All of them were armed with claymores and dirks.

"We made an inspection o' the camp, sir," Hugh announced, coming to a halt before the major's leggy gelding. The rest of the Highlanders gathered around him, comparing askance their own scarlet regimentals with the untidy uniforms of the colonial scouts under Lieutenant Smith's command.

"Your report, corporal?" Lochiel asked quietly.

"Two Indians be dead and the rest taken into custody. One of the Rangers got tomahawked, but 'tis likely he'll recover."

"That was Givhans," Lieutenant Smith put in with a sorrowful shake of his head. "Kinda new to the game, so I guess he can't be blamed for makin' a mistake."

"He'll've learned his lesson now, eh, lieutenant?" one of his men said with a laugh, aiming a stream of tobacco juice at a nearby tree stump.

"What about the camp, corporal?" Lochiel persisted. The air of controlled impatience about him caused Hugh's bushy brows to rise.

"We dinna ken just yet, sir. 'Twould seem a lot of damage was done when the Indians retreated right into the middle o' things. There was a lot o' panic to be sure an' some injuries, but I dinna think any were serious."

Lochiel's lips thinned. "I suggest you leave conjecture out of this, Corporal Martin. I want to know the exact extent of the damage and," he added grimly, "the names of those who were injured."

"Aye, sir."

Lieutenant Smith turned to his men as the Highlanders retreated. "Might as well lend 'em a hand, boys."

"Sure thing, lieutenant," one of the gaunt Rangers agreed with a grin. "No tellin' what kind of trouble them girls'll get into."

The others laughed heartily at this, for undeniably masculine and powerful as the Highlanders appeared to be, none of the Rangers could get used to the fact that their regulation uniforms consisted of gold-piped tunics and kilts. Joking among themselves, they disappeared amid the trees, muskets slung over their broad backs in unsoldierly fashion.

"Hope you don't mind my boys referrin' to yours as girls," Lieutenant Smith drawled, gazing with twinkling eyes up at the Scottish major. "We just ain't used to men wearin' skirts."

"Nor we to soldiers who don't wear uniforms," Lochiel countered, studying the green buckskin breeches and stained shirt of the older man before him. The grimness about his mouth softened into a smile as the lieutenant burst into amused laughter.

"The Frenchies got a word for that, major. *Touché!*" He scratched himself industriously. "Guess we oughta see what's goin' on back at that camp o' yourn."

The sun had risen above the mountains by the time Lochiel's mount trotted into the middle of a cluster of sagging tents. Golden rays of light touched the crowns of the towering trees, and the air was soft and warm, giving promise to a beautiful spring morning.

While Lieutenant Smith went off to take a look at the captured Indians, Lochiel was approached by his sergeant-major.

"Not much damage done," Andy informed him in his customary growl. " 'Twould seem the savages were runnin' retreat when they stumbled into camp. A few o' the lasses panicked an' were hurt runnin' into trees when they escaped frae their tents." His expression was grimly amused as he indicated the pale, shaken girls who were being ministered to by a sympathetically clucking Mother Hicks. " 'Twas lucky the savages came on 'em by surprise. They'd no hae survived a proper attack."

"Camp followers travel at their own risk," Lochiel reminded him. His voice was curt. "The British army has never guaranteed their safety or for that matter even acknowledged their existence. If they wish to protect themselves in the future, they're going to have to start posting guards of their own. I don't intend to make our company responsible for them."

"That won't be necessary, major," came an insolent voice from behind him. "We can look after ourselves."

Nothing could have prepared Lochiel for the shock of being confronted by Athena Courtland with a colonial issue Brown Bess in her hands, booted legs planted firmly apart as she glared up at him with fearless intent. She had seized her musket and crawled outside as soon as the first grisly cries of the approaching Indians had echoed through the sleeping camp, certain that Tykie had already rushed out to defend her.

Wanting to help him, she found instead that a handful of Rangers had already subdued the savages. Searching fruitlessly for Tykie, she had stumbled across Lochiel in time to overhear his callous words. Raising her chin, she met his silver-eyed gaze unflinchingly. There was nothing but animosity in her heart for the man who had hurt her so cruelly the night before. "You've already made it clear to some of us how little we matter to you," she added coldly, "so you needn't quote regulations to justify your lack of interference."

"God's blood!" The oath emerged through tightly clenched teeth as Lochiel responded to her contemptuous words. Not only was the chit playing games with her life, he thought in disbelief, but she was fast turning into a barbarian bearing no resemblance at all to the young socialite he had first met at Egon de Vries's months before. Was this what happened when willful Athena Courtland was permitted to run wild? Lochiel was not about to be responsible for her transformation into a buckskin-clad savage. 'Twas time someone took her firmly in hand, and in his present frame of mind he dearly relished the chance of imposing a bit of discipline himself.

"You bloody little fool," he snarled, dismounting and jerking the musket out of her hands. She paled but stood her ground, unlike Andy Durning, who gasped in amazement at the major's unexpected outburst.

"What do you think you're playing at?" Lochiel continued savagely. "Do you consider this a game like barking squirrels off trees? You do know how to do that, don't you? I understand 'tis a skill every colonial lad in short pants learns at some time or another."

She bit her lip and glared at him defiantly, but he didn't allow her to speak. The sight of the bruise that still darkened her cheek enraged him further, serving to remind him that he, a veteran of countless army campaigns, had been unable to successfully look after a mere eighteen-year-old girl.

"I've had enough of your insolence and disobedience, Athena Courtland," he grated, his voice so low that Andy couldn't hear. "You've been naught but a thorn in my side since I first laid eyes on you, and I'm going to put a stop to your wanton ways this instant."

Athena's lips trembled, but she refused to look away from the eyes burning into hers. Never had such white-hot anger been directed toward her, and she could feel her heart hammering fearfully in her breast. The tightness around Lochiel's mouth and the rigid control he was exerting upon himself warned her that he was close to turning violent.

"You're coming back to camp with me," Lochiel continued, satisfied by the fact that she flinched at his words, a sign that he had finally gotten through to her, "and you're going to obey every last command I give you.

You are not to cause me one single moment of frustration for the duration of the march."

She lowered her eyes, but not before he saw the light of mutiny that sprang into them. Uttering a savage curse, he seized her roughly, his hands biting into her flesh until she winced.

"What will it take to rid you of your rebellious nature, Athena? Am I going to have to beat you or clap you in irons? By God, I vow I'll do either without regret."

Looking up into those ruthless features, as cold and predatory as a hawk's, Athena knew he was speaking the truth. They were enemies now, and he was just the sort of man who would hold good to his word regardless of the fact that she was not a prisoner of war but a woman who had been placed trustingly under his protection.

"You needn't resort to such extremes, major," she told him, her voice shaking, tears of accusation glistening in her dark blue eyes. "I'll stay in your bloody camp with you."

"Good. And do you promise to behave yourself in a manner befitting your station?" he demanded, thinking at the same time how absurd such a question was, for when had Athena ever behaved that way before?

When she didn't answer, he gave her a cruel little shake, only to find her gone rigid in his grasp, her eyes wide as she stared past him.

"What now?" he snapped ill-temperedly. "Is this another of your tricks?"

"Oh, Lochiel, something's happened to Tykie!" she cried, ignoring his question.

Lochiel turned to see a mule-drawn cart trundling down the hill, a solemn Liza Hampton leading the animal by its bridle. Sarah Hicks and Tykie were reclining in the back, Tykie's grizzled head lying on the big woman's voluminous lap. He looked pale and haggard but was grinning contentedly at the attention he was receiving. His left foot, swathed in thick bandages, was propped on a grain sack in front of him.

Lochiel might have found amusement at the sight if it hadn't been for the anxious expression on Athena's face. As she ran forward to intercept the curious procession, it occurred to him that he might have treated her a bit more kindly.

The grin faded from Tykie's lips when he caught sight of Athena hurrying toward him, her little face pale with fright beneath her cap. Signaling the cart to a halt, he struggled out of Sarah's arms and gave his young mistress a sheepish look.

"No need tae worry, bairn," he assured her. "Mother Hicks be lookin' after me proper an' I ken I'll mend a'richt."

"Oh, Tykie, what happened?" Athena cried, clutching the side of the cart with white-knuckled hands.

Tykie coughed uncomfortably. "Just a wee accident, laddie. Na reason tae fuss o'er me."

"Broke 'is foot, the barmy scoundrel," Mother Hicks interrupted with a cackle. "I thort it'd be best if I went to fetch 'im myself. Shouldn't be puttin' no weight on't fer a while. Not to worry, dearie. It'll mend in no time."

But Athena was not at all mollified to hear this. Never in her life had she seen Tykie lying flat on his back, and the shock of it, coupled with her recent encounter with Lochiel Blackmoor, left her completely shaken. She bit her lip, afraid that she was going to burst into helpless tears and shame herself in the eyes of Mother Hicks and the haughty Liza Hampton, both of whom thought her a lad too old to cry.

"How did it happen, Tykie?"

Lochiel's deep voice was calm, and Athena felt absurdly grateful for the big hand that settled firmly on her shoulder. Though she would cheerfully have driven a dirk through his heart not a minute ago, she found his presence oddly soothing now.

"You were right behind me when I left camp," the major added, aware of Tykie's embarrassment.

"And so I was," Tykie admitted, unable to meet the silver eyes squarely.

"Well?" Lochiel prompted when the injured Scotsman coughed and fell silent. Aware of Athena's clenched jaw, he tightened his hold on her shoulder, thinking it would serve appearances better if she didn't succumb to a fit of womanly weeping.

"Me brawny lad wuz gonna be a 'ero," Mother Hicks responded proudly. Her brown eyes were soft as she peered into Tykie's bearded face, and Lochiel made the startling discovery that this buxom old prostitute seemed genuinely fond of him.

"I heard wha' yer orderly said aboot the gunshots comin' frae camp, major," Tykie explained, "an' it sounded tae me like an Indian attack." His eyes were on Athena's face, telling her that his worry had been for her alone.

"So's 'e jumped on a 'orse," Mother Hicks continued eagerly, "an' wuz ready ter gallop down ter save us all when the 'orse throwed 'im neat as day inter a thicket o' thorns."

"When I grabbed his reins he stepped on my foot, an' thot be how I broke it," Tykie finished, red-faced with shame. "I dinna ken wha' Master Fletcher will think o' me the noo," he added mournfully, beginning to feel very sorry for himself.

It was fortunate that his head was bowed so he couldn't see the relieved smile Athena hid behind her hand or the twinkle that appeared in Major Blackmoor's eyes.

"Never yer worry, me brave duckie," Mother Hicks crooned, patting his hairy hand in maternal fashion. "I'll looks after yer til yer back on both feet. Yer can ride i' my wagon wi' me an' I'll fetch an' cook fer yer when we make camp at night."

Tykie shook his head stubbornly although the prospect was extremely tempting. "I'll be needin' tae look after Malcolm here."

"No need for that, Tykie," Lochiel assured him. A mocking light sprang into the silver eyes and his expression was impossible to fathom as he gazed at Athena's bowed head. "He's coming back to camp with me. I'll see to it that he's kept out of trouble."

"Be that true, lad?" Tykie asked, gazing hopefully into Athena's averted face.

She gave him the brightest smile she could muster and assured him with forced cheerfulness that this was indeed the case.

"Then I'll na worry nae more," Tykie announced with a contented sigh and leaned back gratefully in Sarah Hicks's arms.

The cart took off with the creaking of wood, and it suddenly dawned on Athena that Liza Hampton's dark eyes hadn't left Lochiel Blackmoor's face for a moment. The invitation in her saucy smile was so blatant as the wagon began to pull away that Athena felt the color rise to her cheeks. Shaking herself free of the major's hand, she waited until they were alone before glaring up at him defiantly.

"I may have no choice but to stay in camp with you," she conceded, breathless with hurt anger, "but that doesn't mean I'm going to let you make a fool out of me in front of people like that!"

Lochiel's brows rose in mock amazement. "My dear Athena, whatever are you talking about?"

She stared with hostility into his handsome face, wondering miserably if he had spent last night in Liza Hampton's arms. "I'm not going to let you reveal who I really am," she said thickly, "not after everything that's happened to me! No one suspects I'm not Malcolm Courtland and I'd rather they were never enlightened."

She was outraged when Lochiel threw back his head and burst into hearty laughter. For a moment he couldn't speak at all, and she had to grit her teeth to keep from bashing in his wretched skull with the stock of the heavy Brown Bess.

At last Lochiel sobered and looked down at her, an amused smile playing on his sensual lips. "So you do have a reputation you worry about," he remarked softly. "I never would have thought as much, judging from the trouble you've gotten yourself into in the past. Why this sudden change of heart, my dear?"

Athena looked away, not really knowing what to tell him. It wasn't because of Liza Hampton, she told herself furiously. Why should she care what that brazen slut thought of her?

"Never mind," Lochiel said after a long pause, oddly disappointed that she refused to confide in him. "I'll give the matter some thought, though I will admit 'tis likely the tale of your masquerade as an army camp follower will reach the ears of the good people of Albany. And that, I'm afraid," he added, gravely, "would do your reputation little good."

"Thank you for your understanding," Athena said with icy dignity before striding away.

Lochiel watched her go with narrowed eyes, feeling a resurgence of the anger that had consumed him earlier. This time, however, it was directed toward himself, for if he had permitted Athena to travel with his camp from the onset of the journey, no one would ever have suspected that she and the lad known as Malcolm Courtland were one and the same. It was too late now not to set idle tongues wagging, and the fact that he was to blame for it did little to improve his mood.

"A fine hole you've dug for yourself, Major Blackmoor," he muttered as the slim figure in buckskins vanished amid the tents below. How on earth was he going to survive the next ten days having to look after a troublesome wench he'd just as soon make love to as turn over his knee?

Twelve

A fire had been lit in the center of a small clearing, the flames crackling high into the night. With the impenetrable darkness and chill mountain air held at bay, the two men huddled before it ate their meal with relish, content for a time to rest their tired limbs, for they had been traveling through the wilderness at a furious pace.

From somewhere in the darkness a bobcat gave a sudden scream, and the two men exchanged uneasy glances, the savory stew abruptly forgotten.

"Makes the hair on your neck stand on end, don't it?" one of them asked in a whisper.

"Never could listen to that without thinkin' 'twas a woman shriekin'," his companion confessed.

The unnervingly humanlike scream came again, but it was farther away this time, and the two men began to relax.

"Glad we don't have to listen to that every night," the oldest remarked. With a big, unclean hand he massaged the back of his neck and grimaced. "I'm startin' to wonder if the money we're getting is worth all this." Tossing another branch onto the fire, he added dourly, "No tellin' if the next scream we hear's gonna be a wildcat or an Indian ready to lift our scalps."

"That's why we got these," his companion reminded him with a grin, patting the glinting barrel of the musket that rested across his knees. Born and raised in the Adirondack Mountains, Asa Brewster feared nothing that might lie in wait in the dense forests beyond the firelight. The grisly raids made by roving Mohawks and Algonquins on colonial settlers over the past few years disturbed him not at all, for he knew their ways, was well versed in their tongues, and could lift a scalp as easily as the best of their warriors. Furthermore he was not obsessed with doubts like Toddman Tyner because he knew that their quest would end in the payment of a handsome reward.

But Tyner could not be so sure. 'Twas true they'd been given enough gold to whet their appetites before they left West York, but how to guarantee there'd be more when they returned?

"Think we'll find the girl?" he asked now, setting his empty plate aside and belching loudly.

"You tell me," Asa Brewster replied with a snort. "You're supposed to be the one knows what he's doing. I'm just the scout."

Toddman Tyner shrugged his thick shoulders. It had been easy enough to follow their quarry's obvious trail, but he hadn't suspected that it would take them across the most barren mountain ranges he had ever encountered. Some of the peaks had still been under snow, and he had shivered throughout the journey, asking himself if the money they'd been promised was really worth the price of freezing half to death.

But he was good at his craft, and some said there wasn't a person on earth who could escape when Toddman Tyner came after him. Mostly he specialized in locating bonded servants who ran away from cruel landowners before their indentureship was up. Once or twice he had recovered runaway brides for exorbitant fees, but most of that took place in cities he was familiar with like Philadelphia and New York.

Chasing a missing heiress across hills and valleys in wintertime was not something he was accustomed to, and he was grateful for the company of the small but crafty man noisily sucking his soup beside him. Brewster was something of a halfwit, but he knew the terrain and was experienced at backwoods survival. For this reason Tyner had insisted he be sent along when he'd first been hired for the job.

They made an unusual team, the big, unclean Philadelphian and the dull but loyal Asa Brewster. Bound by greed, they sought to win the sizable reward that had been offered for the immediate return of one Athena Courtland, who had vanished from her home over a fortnight ago.

"You think the girl's a real heiress?" Toddman inquired curiously, pulling a yellowed clay pipe from his coat pocket.

Asa looked uncomfortable. That was a detail his employer had foolishly let slip during their last meeting in a tavern along the Albany riverfront. Kensington had been extremely drunk, and Asa was sure he hadn't meant to mention it, but alcohol had a way of making it hard for a man to curb his tongue.

"The Courtlands got money of their own," he admitted reluctantly. "Don't know nothin' about the daughter bein' an heiress. There's three brothers to share the family fortune, and most everything went to the oldest when Foster Courtland died."

He didn't care for the calculating gleam in Toddman Tyner's reddened eyes. The man was forever scheming, and Asa wasn't sure just how far he could trust him. He'd heard rumors about the sort of man he was when he'd first made inquiries in Stephen Kensington's behalf. Tyner could be counted on to deliver his goods provided he was well paid, but he was supposedly brutal in his methods, and there had even been talk about the murder of a wealthy landsman down in Virginia last year for whom Tyner had been working at the time.

"Master Kensington's been courtin' the girl all winter," he went on carefully. "Didn't like it too much when she disappeared the way she did."

"From what I hear, if she does have money, he's better off findin' her fast," Tyner agreed, bending to light the end of a stick in the fire. Bringing the glowing end to his lips, he sucked energetically at his pipe, then leaned back and exhaled, his swarthy features half hidden by smoke.

Stephen Kensington had promised plenty for the prompt return of Miss Athena Courtland. Lovesick young men were always prepared to pay the highest fees, and Tyner had heard enough gossip about the two of them to expect that Kensington could be persuaded to pay a whole lot more when the time came.

Far in the distance the howl of the hunting bobcat came again, but this time Toddman Tyner paid no attention. His eyes were mere slits as he leaned back against a fallen log and dreamed contentedly of his pending wealth.

It was truly a night meant for keeping close to the fire. The air was bitterly cold, and the spring sun, once vanished behind the mountain peaks, could not extend its lingering warmth to the earth, which had lain in the frigid grip of winter for so many months. While the two rather unscrupulous men huddled close to the welcoming heat, another blaze was burning brightly not many miles to the south, the mood of the men surrounding it far more festive.

Blending with the melodious skirl of a bagpipe, the masculine voices were boisterous as the spectators stamped their feet in accompaniment to four kilted dancers performing an energetic Highland fling in the flickering orange light. There was a wildness to their movements, and in the enthusiastic whooping of the watching men that seemed to dispel the bone-chilling cold and push back the ever-increasing darkness.

Athena Courtland's features were all but hidden by the thick wool plaid she had wrapped about herself, yet there was a wistful smile playing on her lips as she watched the dancers perform. She would never have suspected that such tall, broad-shouldered men could move so gracefully or that they, who had seemed so serious when she had first met them, could abandon themselves so totally to the exuberance of the dance.

Davie Skelley and Iain MacLachlan, the youngest of Lochiel's men, were the lightest on their feet, but Athena was particularly impressed by the prowess of the burly corporal Hugh Martin, whose athletic leaps were astonishing given his size. He was a man who rarely spoke, Athena had learned, and, like her brother Fletcher, was something of a dreamer, which was surprising, considering that he was one of the most ferocious-looking of the Highland warriors.

Athena's gaze wandered among the gathered men, picking out weathered faces and linking them to the names she had learned earlier that morning. It hadn't surprised her that these towering soldiers had welcomed her so readily into their midst. Clannish and suspicious as Highlanders were, Athena knew that they would not hesitate to risk their lives for one of their own kind.

Her smile deepened. She had Tykie to thank for that, who had insisted on accompanying her to camp when she had moved in with the soldiers that morning. To her bemusement he had hobbled over to the fire where the company was gathered before muster and addressed every man jack of them in Gaelic, warning them that Malcolm Courtland was to be given the courtesy accorded any fellow Scotsman. It was Athena who had decided the night before to take matters into her own hands and not wait for Lochiel to make up his mind to protect her true identity. She wasn't sure she could trust him and had decided, with Tykie's reluctant blessings, to introduce herself to the men of the Seventh as Malcolm Courtland before Lochiel had the chance to inform them otherwise. To justify her appearance she had decided to take over Joe Madison's responsibilities of tending the army horses—a task the sullen boy had relinquished readily after a few brief words from Tykie himself.

Taking over the role of company groom would offer her the best means of remaining unobtrusive, she had decided, and thanks to Tykie's colorful introduction, none of the Highlanders had questioned her presence. Indeed, they had welcomed her so enthusiastically that there had remained no other obstacles for Athena to contend with save informing Major Blackmoor of her new place among his ranks. That rather daunting prospect had been delayed by the fact that he had not been present for Tykie's speech, and Athena had seen nothing of him until the march began. Even then she had been unable to speak with him, for he had kept to the front of the line, where he remained deep in conversation with the sergeant-major.

Not until a brief midday rest had Athena finally been able to approach him, and she shivered now, recalling how totally unpleasant that encounter had been.

"Will ye no try yer hand at the dancin', lad?"

Startled from her thoughts, Athena shook her head as she made room on the log for Sergeant-Major Andrew Durning. She found the blustery officer a far cry from the strict military R.S.M.'s she had met in the past, for he behaved more like a foot soldier than a company commander. Athena suspected that his approachability was what appealed to his men and made him so popular among the recruits. The fact that he had taken time out to speak to her showed exactly how conscientious he could be.

Andy Durning, in fact, had taken an instant liking to the young boy who had appeared in camp just after dawn in the company of Tykie Downs, a man Andy had come to know and like extremely well. It wasn't simply the fact that Malcolm's mother had been Scots herself as Tykie, leaning on a crudely made crutch, had informed the amused men who had assembled to hear him speak. No, what Andy liked about the lad was the way he had introduced himself to the unsuspecting Major Blackmoor earlier that day as the Seventh Company's new groom.

Though there were grooms, cooks, orderlies, and messengers aplenty among the Highland companies stationed in Albany, none but the foot soldiers and officers themselves had made the long march to Fort Shuyler that winter. It had been the sergeant-major's wish to travel light, and he had been able to find enough willing workers among the camp followers to replace those left behind.

Andy hadn't particularly cared for Joe Madison, the surly sixteen-year-old who had been looking after the horses since the regiment's departure. The boy was heavy-handed on the reins and provided the loyal animals with a bare minimum of care. Malcolm Courtland, on the other hand, had ridden into camp on a blood gelding in excellent condition, and his enviable seat had attested to long years in the saddle.

Andy chuckled now, recalling the expression on Lochiel Blackmoor's face when Malcolm had marched boldly into his presence, interrupting a midmorning meeting to announce himself Madison's replacement. It was the first time in his life that Andy had ever seen Lochiel at a loss for words, and his amusement increased recalling the startled, nay, stunned look on that hawkish face at Malcolm Courtland's defiant disclosure.

'Twas almost as if the lad had been daring Lochiel to contradict him, Andy thought to himself; the result being that Lochiel had worked himself into a fine fettle from which he had yet to recover. Not only had he brooded all afternoon long, but the mention of wee Malcolm's name had earned Andy an ill-tempered setdown when camp had been made for the night. Since supper Lochiel had remained sequestered in his tent, and even the gay skirling of the pipes hadn't managed to lure him out.

"Yer mother didna teach ye the auld Hieland dances?" Andy asked now, smiling at the youthful features half hidden amid the folds of the dark green plaid.

Athena shook her head again, wondering a trifle uneasily why the gruff sergeant-major seemed to find such amusement at her presence here. Did he perhaps suspect who she was? But no, he couldn't. She was Malcolm Courtland to the men of the Seventh, and as yet Lochiel Blackmoor hadn't chosen to inform them otherwise.

Athena licked her dry lips, recalling how furious Lochiel had been with her. She had seen as much in the ruthless tightening of his lean jaw, and she could well remember how her heart had hammered in her breast, certain that he would expose her. Yet much to her astonishment he hadn't, and she should have been relieved by that, but Athena had already learned that there was no escaping a reckoning where Lochiel Blackmoor was concerned.

" 'Tis a shame Tykie broke his foot," she remarked now, thrusting this unpleasant thought from her mind. "I've seen him dance before and I wager there's none among your men who could beat him at the Ghillie Callum."

"There be a challenge I'd dearly like to accept," Andy sighed wistfully, "for MacLachlan claims the Ghillie Callum be his finest piece o' work." He sighed again, thinking of the money that might have been won on a bet like that.

The dancing ended at that moment amid a flurry of applause and a high, keening wail from the pipes. Exchanging good-natured insults, the gathered men dispersed into the darkness.

"Where are they going?" Athena asked curiously as Andy lifted a hand to acknowledge Iain's and Davie's departure.

"To visit the lassies."

"Oh." She colored deeply at this casual disclosure, but the fire had died sufficiently to cast her face in shadows. Tracing a pattern in the dust with her boot heel, she asked diffidently, "Does—does Major Blackmoor ever join them?"

Andy chuckled, seeming to find nothing odd about her question. "Aye, lad, aye! Couldn't keep the rutting stag away frae ane o' the lasses i' particular," he informed the suddenly silent Athena and slapped his knee as he remembered virile Lochiel's infatuation with the beautiful Liza Hampton. It didn't occur to him to mention that his ardor for Liza had cooled of late and that she had been turned away from Lochiel's tent only last night. He must have been harsh with her indeed, given the expression Andy had seen on her face when the dark-haired beauty had stormed away.

"Have ye never had yer pleasure wi' her, lad?" he inquired, giving Athena an affable dig in the ribs.

Her mumbled answer and averted profile alerted the ever-watchful

Andy to the obvious fact that the lad had never bedded a woman before. 'Twas as he'd expected, and he felt a sense of protectiveness rise within him. There was something vulnerable about Malcolm Courtland that touched Andy Durning's gruff old heart. Perhaps it was the innocence in those dark blue eyes or the slightness of the lad's tall frame, but whatever it might be, he resolved to give the motherless boy the kind treatment Tykie Downs had so vehemently requested earlier that day.

" 'Tis never wise to rush into things ye're na ready for," he remarked now in what he hoped was a paternal enough manner. After having raised four daughters, he wasn't exactly sure how to speak to a boy standing on the brink of manhood, but he could still remember the words his own father had said to him at that age.

"I'm certain Malcolm won't be found guilty of indulging in the sins of the flesh with any of our blanket girls," came a mocking voice from behind them.

Andy could feel the slim form beside him stiffen and he cast a warning glance at Lochiel, who had stepped from the shadows in time to catch his words. There was a look in the narrowed silver eyes Andy didn't like and a brutal grimness about the sensual mouth that indicated to him that the major was in a less than charitable mood.

"Come an' join me for a dram," Andy invited, hoping to divert the younger man's hostility away from the hapless head of the lad sitting beside him.

But Athena was not about to back away from her inevitable confrontation with the scowling major. His temper would only grow worse the more Sergeant-Major Durning tried to shield her, and though she was grateful to the grizzly officer for his help, she knew she couldn't rely on his protection indefinitely.

Despite her determination to be brave, her limbs were shaky as she rose and faced the towering form of Lochiel Blackmoor. "Do you wish to speak with me, major?"

Lochiel's lips thinned. Though she was striving to sound respectful, he found contrition, however genuine, an unlikely facet of her normally rebellious character. The discovery that Athena's tiresome spirit appealed to him more than her attempts to be cooperative only served to fan his anger even more.

"Aye," he acknowledged curtly. "Privately, if you don't mind."

She followed him from the circle of light, aware of Andy Durning's sympathetic eyes upon her. Lochiel's tent had been erected a good distance from the others, and she felt a sense of dread build within her as he held the flap aside to permit her to enter. The youthful aide whose name,

Athena recalled, was Barrett, exited wordlessly after taking one look at the intimidating expression on the officer's face.

Unlike the tiny shelter in which she and Tykie had been sleeping, Lochiel's gray canvas tent was large and roomy. A lamp hung suspended from the center pole, and a cot covered with a rough woolen blanket took up one corner. Athena was at once aware of the masculine presence of its owner and of the very size of the man who entered behind her, his lean shadow hovering threateningly above her.

"You can stop pretending you're at attention," he snapped, his broad back turned to her as he busied himself with a stack of papers on the makeshift desk. "You've reminded me often enough that you're not one of my soldiers. More's the pity," he added malevolently, "for yours is a disciplinary problem I would love to solve using tried and true military methods."

Such as torture and coercion? Athena wondered. Her mouth went dry. Surely she hadn't goaded him enough to tempt him to violence?

"And lower that obstinate chin of yours. I'm in no mood for a clash of wills tonight."

She could feel her pulse pounding uncomfortably in her temples. Lochiel's expression when he finally turned around made her swallow nervously. Save for a night bird calling eerily from the hills, the night was deathly silent, adding to her sense of foreboding.

"I didn't confront you sooner," he told her, speaking coldly across the few feet that separated them, "for I was genuinely afraid that I might kill you with my bare hands. Damn you, Athena, what in hell did you think you were doing? Do you believe all the world is as safe as Courtland Grace? Do you think you can romp around as you will and play games with my men without risking the repercussions that may very well follow?"

Athena said nothing, her eyes wide as she stared up into that ruthless face, which had once held so much fascination for her.

"You seem to consider all of this a game to be played at your whim, that my men and I, even Tykie and your brother, are players to be manipulated as you see fit. The Seventh Highland Company was not sent here from Great Britain for Athena Courtland's amusement. I needn't remind you, I hope, that we are at war and that your presence here is tolerated only because I gave my word to Fletcher." The silver eyes seemed to bore into her. "After all, I do not normally make a habit of bending regulations by providing escort service for civilians."

Athena's voice was subdued. "I suppose 'twas presumptuous of me to take Joe Madison's place without—"

"Presumptuous?" He came out of the shadows, and she had to steel herself not to back away.

"Presumptuous?" he repeated disbelievingly. Looking down into those gold-fringed eyes, he experienced a moment of helpless frustration. How was he going to convince Athena that the dangers she faced were brutally real? He, who had seen enough innocent women slaughtered at the hands of enemy soldiers, could he allow the same to happen to her? Worse still was the thought of someday seeing her bright golden hair dangling like a prize from the waist of some bloodthirsty Algonquin.

"I gave you my word that I would consider your request for anonymity, Athena," Lochiel went on harshly. "Surely you must have realized I'd do what was best for you, and yet you had to take matters into your own hands."

She was staring at the pulse beating so strongly in his tanned throat, his aggressive maleness throwing her into confusion. "I-I can take care of myself," she told the rigid expanse of chest before her.

"Can you?"

Sinewy forearms reached out and closed about her, and she uttered a frightened gasp in response.

"If I were to forget my promise to your brother, my sense of duty, and take you against your will right here and now, would you still be able to take care of yourself?"

She could feel the tautness in the rippling muscles that imprisoned her and hear the controlled violence in Lochiel's deep voice. Fear coursed through her veins as she tried to ease herself out of his grip, only to find herself unable to move.

"Answer me, Athena. What makes you so certain you could protect yourself from me?"

She made no reply, and he gave her a slight shake. "You cannot even defend yourself against a man who has given his word to protect you. How, then, do you propose to save yourself from Indians or Frenchmen or any other manner of person intent upon harming you?"

He could see her lips tremble, their rosebud curves only inches from his own. The silvered depths of her eyes were reflected in the lantern light as she gazed up at him obstinately, determined not to reveal her fear.

"I have no reason to defend myself against you, Lochiel Blackmoor. You wouldn't dare r-rape me."

"No, never rape, Athena," he contradicted unpleasantly, "but there are other ways of taking what I want from you. Surely you've had enough men in the past to realize that you cannot deny the sort of woman you are."

One powerful arm shot out to capture the small hand that flew up to slap him. In a moment he had subdued the frantically struggling girl by crushing her against the whipcord length of his body. Lowering his dark head, he let his lips capture hers in a bruising kiss.

Athena moaned and tried to turn her head, but Lochiel had seized the back of her neck in one big hand, his thumb pressing the wildly beating vein beneath her jaw. His manhood rose hard against her breeches, and she squirmed away, seared by the heat of its touch. Deep within her the fear began to give way to desire, a yearning too powerful to resist.

"No," she panted, her lips still crushed beneath his, yet already the familiar ache between her thighs was making a mockery of her denials.

Lochiel's hands explored the softness of her skin beneath the leather jerkin she wore, impatiently thrusting aside the material that bound Athena's breasts so that their ripe fullness sprang free. His strong fingers slid over her shoulders and delicate collarbones, unbuttoning as they went until the thrusting pink nipples were pressed against his palms.

Caressing them boldly, Lochiel continued to kiss her, his man's scent assailing her senses, filling her with delicious need. Shuddering, Athena fell against him, her parted lips softening beneath his insistent onslaught, and he did not have to look into her dusky eyes to know that her passion equaled his.

"By God, Athena, I've been near mad with want of you," Lochiel whispered hoarsely. The deep voice with its North Highland burr was rough with emotion. "Instead of wanting to punish you, I find I want only to make love to you."

Her lips clung to his, and she slipped her arms about his neck, drawing him closer against the enchanting curves of her body. He groaned and slid his hand across her buttocks so that they were intimately pressed together, hips moving in an ancient rhythm.

Athena gave a gentle sob of relief as Lochiel lifted her into his arms, unable to deny that she wanted him, that she had been born to let him love her. Laying her onto the rough blankets, Lochiel let his lips and tongue trace a searing path from her mouth to the curve of her jaw and the hollow of her throat. Tremors ran through her, centering in the ready openness of her womanhood.

"Lochiel," she whispered, her eyes sultry with need.

Kneeling beside the cot, the lantern light flickering across his darkly handsome face, Lochiel lifted her against him, his mouth fastening onto hers as she began to work impatiently at the buttons of his shirt.

"Lochiel! Ye've no harmed the lad, have ye?"

The worried voice of Andrew Durning came from just beyond the tent flaps, startling the would-be lovers apart. Athena's hand went to her lips to cover her gasp of dismay while Lochiel pressed her face to his shoulder. She must not cry out now or Andy would come storming in, convinced that unnecessary evil had befallen Malcolm Courtland.

"Lochiel? Are ye there?"

For a moment Lochiel leaned his head against Athena's and closed his eyes. Drawing a ragged breath, he tried not to notice the warm body pressed so intimately against his or the parted lips that hovered so dangerously close. He should be thankful that no shadows within the lighted tent had revealed to Andy's eyes what had been transpiring within, yet all he could think of was the throbbing unfulfillment of his body and the nearness of the one woman he yearned to possess.

"Naught's amiss, Andy," he said almost wearily, opening the flaps to address the darkness. Athena watched him with wide, frightened eyes and tried to blink back her tears.

After a moment Lochiel stepped back inside and stood regarding her without speaking. His black hair was rumpled and his shirt was opened to reveal the bronzed expanse of his chest. Athena could feel a betraying tremor flee through her in response to the memory of its warm strength beneath her palms.

"Get dressed," he said at last, ignoring the spasm of pain that darted across her oval face.

Wordlessly she fastened her jerkin and repinned the curls that had tumbled loose in the roughness of his embrace. In the meantime Lochiel leaned against the desk, his broad back to her, massaging the nape of his neck.

"Do you want me to leave now?" she asked in a small voice.

He turned to find her standing before him looking achingly beautiful in her breeches and leather vest, her piquant little face once again half hidden by the battered cap.

"No, I want you to stay right here," he said, the words coming out far more harshly than he'd intended. She flinched in response but he would not relent. "I'm going out for a time and I don't want you getting into trouble. You'll sleep here tonight until I can decide what's to be done with you."

"Here?" Athena's cheeks flamed as her eyes went to the narrow cot before them.

Lochiel's brow darkened. "I'll sleep on the floor."

The pink stain spread further across her cheekbones. "Oh."

"I expect you to obey me," he warned, the intimacy between them shattered.

"Lochiel, wait." Her hand was on his sleeve as he brushed past her and he looked down at her impatiently, her slim legs almost trapped between his booted ones.

"What is it?" he demanded.

"Wh-where are you going?"

An unpleasant smile curved the lips that had teased hers so devastatingly only minutes ago. "My dear Athena, just because we shall be spending the night together, albeit quite platonically, doesn't mean that you have the right to delve into my personal affairs."

The hated name of Liza Hampton trembled accusingly on her lips, but Athena could not bring herself to utter it. She would not humiliate herself so thoroughly before him. Instead she turned away without speaking, slim back stiff with iron self-control, and did not see the look of utter frustration that passed across the hawkish features before Lochiel strode angrily into the night.

Only when the sound of his footsteps had lost itself in the tentative chirping of the crickets did Athena fling herself down onto his cot. Burying her slim nose in the pillow, she tried to ignore the scent of him that seemed to taunt her cruelly.

"I hate him!" she whispered to herself, tears of despair trickling down her cheeks to dampen the bedclothes.

She did not know how long she lay crying brokenly before drifting off into a fitful sleep. Only once did she awaken to find the moon beginning to set in the frozen heavens, its pale light falling softly onto the floor of the tent. The bedroll she had laid out for Lochiel earlier was still empty, and Athena shut her eyes quickly against the unwanted truth.

When Athena awoke again it was to find a pearl-gray light stealing across the horizon. Turning her head, she gasped softly when she saw Lochiel's long body stretched out on the bedroll in the far corner of the tent. So he hadn't spent the night with Liza after all!

Her heart constricted oddly as she studied his profile, her eyes caressing the firm line of his jaw and the hard, masculine mouth above it. Even in sleep his features remained harshly uncompromising, yet Athena took secret delight in its perfection, openly admiring the retroussé nose, which gave his countenance such a hawkish appearance. Crisp black hair lay rumpled across his brow, and she denied with a painful intake of breath the desire to run her fingers through it. Lying back against the pillow, she realized that there could be no more rest for her, not with Lochiel's deep, even breathing reminding her constantly of his presence.

Reaching for her vest and shoes, she crept silently outside, using all the skills of stealth she had learned from her brothers, who had taught her from an early age how to ghost noiselessly through the forests and fields. A sigh of relief escaped her when she was finally free of the confinement of Lochiel's tent and the danger of his nearness.

Though the air was chilly and mist clung to the treetops, the freshness of a spring morning hovered across the darkened mountains as Athena made her way silently past the circle of tents and the sleeping forms of the soldiers wrapped snugly in their plaids. Some of them were snoring, others slept as though dead, and she found no one awake save Angus McCutcheon, who had drawn guard duty for the night.

"The horses willna need tendin' til reveille," he told her as he recognized her, thinking she had risen early to begin her duties. "Might as well gae back to bed."

Athena answered his smile with one of her own. He was a craggy-faced individual with a scar running down one cheek, the result of an injury sustained two years ago during the fall of Oswego to Louis de Montcalm and his troops. Not long afterward the fall of Fort William Henry had cost him the life of his younger brother, a tragedy that had embittered him greatly. Despite the air of sadness about him, he was a gentle and friendly man, and Athena's innocent smile touched a soft spot in his heart.

"Back tae bed wi' ye, lad," he repeated, propping his musket across his knees. "Ye dinna have tae prove ye'll be a better worker than bloody Madison. Ye've an honest air about ye wha' speaks as much as actions."

Athena dimpled, liking him at once. In fact, she had found all of Lochiel Blackmoor's men to be kind and open with her regardless of the diversity of their personalities. Her smile faltered suddenly as she thought of him.

"I couldn't sleep," she confessed to the weathered soldier sitting on a tree stump before her. From the nearby hillside one of the hobbled horses whickered as it grazed and Angus chuckled, seeing the restless look that leaped unawares into the blue eyes in response.

"Why don't ye have yersel' a ride, then?" he suggested. "Just remember ye'll be workin' hard when ye retairn, so dinna tire yersel' oot."

"I think I'd better save myself for the day's march," Athena told him, rubbing her derrière to illustrate her point. She spent enough time in the saddle as it was. "Perhaps I'll take a walk," she added as the Highlander's amused laughter died away. Surely Lochiel would be up and about by the time she returned, and she could busy herself with readying the horses for the march. There would be no need for them to confront each other again until nightfall.

"Ye'll be careful?" Angus asked.

Grinning, Athena showed him the dirk tucked into the belt of her breeches before starting down the hill. She had always felt at home in the forest, and the serenity of coming dawn soothed the nerves that had been stretched so taut since her encounter with Lochiel the night before.

It was difficult to believe on a morning like this that her country was at war with another and that vicious Indian ambushes had taken the lives of many brave settlers since the conflict had begun. Nor could Athena imagine that a man the likes of Lochiel Blackmoor could have brought so much confusion into her well-ordered life. Why did he frustrate and anger her so when she was accustomed to holding herself aloof from men who were as annoying as he was—like Stephen Kensington?

"Egad, now you've got both bloody fools on your mind!" she mocked herself aloud. Better to enjoy the sunlight and scenery and not let her thoughts stray too far from her walk!

Songbirds were twittering amid the pine boughs as Athena wandered through the dew-soaked grass. Following the stream that meandered away from camp, she emerged eventually from the canopy of trees onto the banks of a small lake. Mist rose from its placid surface, and the first rays of sunlight coming over the mountains touched the colorful array of pebbles scattered along the bottom.

Slipping off her shoes, Athena splashed through the sandy shallows, shivering deliciously in the chilly air. On impulse she cast a look about her, and, finding herself quite alone save for a solitary loon, she stripped off her breeches and shirt, tossing them without ceremony onto a nearby rock. Pausing long enough to shake her hair free, Athena dove neatly into the water.

The shock of it left her gasping, and she swam with bold, sure strokes until the tingling in her limbs disappeared. Rolling over onto her back, she tread water and sighed contentedly, wondering why she hadn't thought to indulge herself like this sooner.

Swimming back to shore, she scrubbed herself with handfuls of sand until her skin glowed pink. It wasn't as effective as a scented soap bath, she thought with a giggle, but she felt wonderfully clean and invigorated. Rising to her feet in the ankle-deep water, she stretched her arms high overhead and lifted her face to the warmth of the sun that had emerged, amid washes of gold, into the morning sky.

"Athena!"

She whirled about, her hair flying wetly about her hips, drops of water running down her slim calves. Lochiel Blackmoor was standing on the shore, booted feet propped against the boulder where her discarded clothes lay, and she gasped aloud as she saw the fury of his countenance.

Yet even as her blue eyes locked with his silver ones, she saw his anger give way to something else and she grew very still, her arms falling to her sides. So quietly had Lochiel come upon her that even the loon had not taken flight but continued to paddle contentedly on the far side of the lake. The forest was silent, so silent in fact that Lochiel could hear the sound of Athena's breathing.

She stood before him like a graceful doe poised for flight. Sunlight touched her naked body, and his eyes caressed the hollows where it did not dare intrude, a hunger too long denied rising hot within him. Slowly he splashed into the water, not caring about the expensive leather boots he wore, willing her with the compelling power of his eyes not to bolt away from him. She stood her ground, her square chin raised so that she could look into his face, and he noticed that she was trembling. Slowly, afraid to startle her, he reached out his hand to touch her, and a sense of wonder filled him as the blue eyes softened in response. There was a tremulous catch in her voice as she murmured his name. Lifting her into his arms, Lochiel carried her back to shore and laid her gently onto the warm sand.

Through eyes half-lidded with starry anticipation Athena saw him shed his clothes above her. Bronzed muscles rippled across his torso as he tossed aside his shirt and breeches. His hungry gaze never left her upturned face, and then he was beside her, taking her into his arms and pressing her against a body much larger and stronger than her own. Her chilled flesh began to warm in his rough embrace, and her head fell back against his arm as his lips found the hollow at the base of her throat.

Neither of them spoke, and the dreamlike stillness of the forest surrounded them. Lochiel's mouth was upon hers then, demanding and tasting, and her lips parted beneath his as a moan escaped her. Sensations overwhelmed her, the rough sand against her skin, the warmth of the rising sun on her face, the heady fragrance of the forest, and always, always there was Lochiel, whose burning kisses commanded everything.

Athena felt herself growing alive beneath his seeking hands as they explored the curves of her hips and traveled ever lower. His lips were upon her breasts, sucking gently so that the nipples came erect, a swollen fullness that left her aching with need, and she whispered his name against the heated width of his chest.

"I thought you'd run away, Athena," he murmured, speaking for the first time, his voice hoarse with lingering fear. "I thought I'd driven you away at last with my constant unkindness." His hands slid up her thighs, taking possession of her silken flesh, and she trembled with the force of the desires which shook her.

"Last night," she murmured against his mouth, "you were not . . . unkind. Oh, Lochiel, I wanted—"

"Aye," he whispered, his lean body sliding down the heated length of hers. "I know what you wanted."

It was as if they could wait no longer. Since their first rapturous encounter at Courtland Grace they had hungered for one another with a passion vehemently denied by bitter pride. Each was a flame that fed of the other, and Athena, golden hair spilling into the sand, like some tawny lioness, pulled him down upon her, heart bursting with the knowledge that only Lochiel Blackmoor had the means to quench the fire within her.

She felt his swollen shaft against her, and her slim thighs opened to offer herself completely to the one man who had the power to enslave her. Lochiel's arms were about her hips, raising her toward him, and she arched herself upward to meet him.

His lips continued to hold hers, and she found herself whirling adrift beneath the burning passion of his kisses. His intimate touch against her womanhood enflamed her, and she pulled him even closer, aching for the sweetness of becoming a part of him.

Slowly, he filled her, and Athena's hips rose to take all of him deep within the essence of her being. Her love for him shone in her eyes as he glided in and then out again, touching her in a way that left her gasping. Her very bones seemed to melt and become a part of his body, and she could feel herself being carried higher and higher on a tide of sensation as Lochiel worked his magic upon her.

Tightening his hold about her slender hips, he drove even deeper, filling her completely and building a momentum that caused a moan to fall from her parted lips. His tongue plundered the soft recesses of her mouth, moving to the same intoxicating rhythm until both of them were on the brink of what must have been oblivion.

Certain that she could endure no more, Athena gasped aloud as wrenching ecstasy carried her to its stabbing climax, and the firmament itself seemed swept away in the triumph of fulfillment. In wild abandon she clung to Lochiel, felt him surge against her as his ultimate possession took her far beyond anything either of them could have imagined. And like the waves that lapped about their joined bodies it gentled them back to earth in a slowly receding tide of golden wonder.

Thirteen

Teeth clenched, Athena lifted the heavy military saddle and laid it across Glenrobbie's broad back. Crawling beneath his belly, she buckled the girth and pulled the stirrups neatly from their leather straps. With a cloth taken from the back pocket of her breeches, she lovingly dusted the gleaming saddle and spent a few minutes more fussing with the black gelding's carefully plaited mane.

Hearing voices behind her, she whirled about, and her heart leaped wildly as she saw Lochiel Blackmoor and Sergeant-Major Durning coming toward her from the direction of the camp. Both men were dressed for the day's march, Lochiel with his black hair in a neat queue beneath his tricorn, fawn-colored breeches hugging his muscular thighs. He was smiling in response to something Andy had said, his gray eyes crinkling at the corners so that he looked irresistibly young and carefree to Athena's yearning gaze.

The two of them had parted not an hour ago from the shore of the sun-drenched lake, Lochiel watching her slip on her breeches and shirt as he lounged against a rock, the look in his eyes making her blush.

"You'd better go back without me," he had told her, rising in one easy motion, a smile touching the corners of the mouth that had claimed hers so ravenously. "We don't want to set tongues awagging, and I can only hope no one saw us here."

He reached out a long finger and traced the line of her jaw. "I'm not sure how I'd go about explaining the fact that I just made love to Malcolm Courtland, my groom."

Mischief sparkled in the compelling eyes, and Athena felt a spasm of longing flee through her. He had pulled on his breeches after their impassioned encounter, but naught else, and she was sorely tempted to run her hands across the wide expanse of his naked chest.

As though anticipating her thoughts, Lochiel reached out and captured her slim fingers in his, and she gloried in the warmth of his strong male pulse. "The drums have probably beaten reveille by now," he told her huskily, for he, too, found it difficult to turn away from the enchantment that surrounded them.

She had left him reluctantly, breathless with the kiss he had bestowed upon her after pulling her roughly against his muscular torso. Like a flower she had opened herself to him, desires rekindled by the mere touching of their lips, and she could not know the discipline he had been forced to call upon in order to let her go.

Back at camp the company was already stirring, and Athena had hurriedly fed and watered the horses. She had groomed and saddled each of them with care, saving Glenrobbie for last. The magnificent black gelding was Lochiel's, and she had turned his handling into a labor of love, patiently brushing him and plaiting the long mane and tail so that the big animal gleamed in the sunlight.

"By God, take a look at your horse, Lochiel!" the sergeant-major cried, catching sight of the glossy animal. "Malcolm's got him lookin' fit for a dress parade!"

Despite the fact that he hadn't seen Glenrobbie so well groomed in months, it galled Lochiel to realize how hard Athena had worked. Reaching out, he took the polishing rag from her hands. "You needn't go to so much trouble, lad," he told her, keeping his tone casual.

Athena quickly lowered her eyes, not wanting to arouse suspicions by blushing idiotically every time Major Blackmoor so much as looked at her. But, oh, how hard it was to remain unaffected by the sight of him, magnificent in his dark blue coat, his lean cheek close as he bent over her. His nearness and the clean male scent of him reminded her of their lovemaking, and she felt a familiar ache fill her heart and flow through her being.

"What about my mare, lad?"

Andy Durning's gruff voice was like a glaring intrusion jolting Athena back to reality and reminding her that their impassioned interlude had been just that: a precious moment stolen from the harshness of military life.

The surprise on the sergeant-major's ruddy face was genuine as the mare was brought to him, and he saw her carefully oiled tack and glossy coat. "By God, lad, you're a rare ane indeed," he enthused, giving her a clap on the back that nearly sent her sprawling.

Lochiel had to agree with Andy's observation, thinking to himself that there never had been and never would be again a woman quite like this spirited wanton in woolen vest and homespun. Taking Glenrobbie's reins from her, he could not ignore the warmth of her fingers as they brushed against his.

"Will you be riding with the supplies?" he asked. He had intended for

Andy's benefit to speak to her curtly, but looking down into the shyly smiling eyes in that upturned little face, he felt a damning tenderness wash over him. "You're welcome to take your place with the sergeant-major and me."

"I thought I'd spend the day with the camp followers." Athena had to swallow before she could speak, unable to tear her gaze away from that slashing mouth. "I want to see how Tykie's faring."

Andy chuckled as he and Lochiel swung themselves effortlessly into the saddle. "I've a feelin' ye'll find him cooing contentedly at Mother Hicks's thoughtful ministrations."

Guiding the prancing Glenrobbie to Athena's side, Lochiel reached down and casually took her chin in his long fingers. "Promise me you won't get into any more boxing matches with Madison and his friends," he warned, silver eyes looking deeply into hers and belying the lightheartedness of his tone.

He was gone before she could reply, cantering Glenrobbie to the head of the procession that was forming as soldiers and horses fell into line. A bagpipe began to skirl a rousing tune, and Athena's heart skipped a beat as the regiment started off, kilts swinging in response to the Highlanders' loose-limbed strides. Sunlight reflected their shining accoutrements and glinted on Lochiel Blackmoor's black hair as he sat tall in the saddle, his broad shoulders proudly thrown back.

Tears welled in Athena's eyes, and she dashed them away with a swipe of her sleeve before anyone could notice. She could not forget the gentleness with which he had spoken to her before riding away, and her bruised lips and aching body were a constant reminder of the wild abandon of their lovemaking.

"I love him," she whispered to herself, wrapping the delicious knowledge close to her heart.

"Malcolm! Do ye want to be left behind? Stop that daft daydreamin' an' mount up, ye pox-ridden imp!"

Heart singing, she responded to Andy Durning's sour cry with self-conscious laughter and threw her leg over her gelding's back. A minute later she was galloping across the dewy grass toward the procession of camp followers, resisting the urge to thumb her nose at Liza Hampton, who perched on the seat of the lead wagon.

What did it matter that she was a raven-haired beauty of unparalleled skill? Lochiel had not chosen her, Athena thought exultantly, and her eyes were shining as she drew rein beside the lumbering wagon, from which she could hear Tykie's robust voice raised in song.

Athena spent most of the day in his company, coaxing him out into the sunshine when the interior of the covered wagon grew too warm. With his bandaged foot propped comfortably on Sarah Hicks's knees, Tykie traded insults with the redheaded woman and listened wonderingly to Athena's chatter. Surely the lass had never seemed so happy or, for that matter, looked so beautiful with a bloom of color across her cheeks and the laughter of a child in her voice.

"Ye're gettin' eager to be hame, eh, Malcolm?" he inquired at last, pleased with himself for remembering not to call her Miss Athena.

A shadow dimmed Athena's bright eyes, but Tykie, taking a long swallow from the canteen on his lap, didn't notice.

"We'll be puttin' thot stallion o' yers back into trainin'," he added, giving her no time to answer. "I've a feelin' wi' Amherst's campaigns aboot tae begin, the good people of West York will be i' the mood for diversion."

Sarah pulled affectionately at his beard. "Yer sure to be a rich man if that 'orse be as fast as yer say. Will yer forget me when yer gets wealthy, yer big, 'airy creature?"

Tempted to nuzzle her enormous breasts, Tykie resisted, aware of Miss Athena's presence. "Ye be a hard woman tae forget," he told her instead, his black eyes gleaming meaningfully.

Camp was made that night along the banks of the Mohawk River, and Athena rationed out oats for the exhausted horses with the rumbling of whitewater in her ears. Melting snow from the mountains had swollen the river beyond its grassy banks, and the few bateaux she had seen navigating the waterway before darkness fell had been moving at an alarming rate.

The sturdy bateaux, laden with supplies bound for Schenectady, had been Athena's first indication that they were leaving the wilderness behind. She felt no elation at the knowledge that their journey, unimpeded by snowfall, had taken them much less than the predicted fortnight to complete. By tomorrow evening they would be in Schenectady, where she and Tykie would travel across the hills to West York, while the Seventh Company would follow the banks of the Hudson into Albany.

There, Athena already knew, Lochiel was scheduled to meet with General Amherst and the colonels who commanded the British Regulars to decide whether the Highland regiments would be sent to Lake George to assist Brigadier General Prideaux in his attack on Oswego or accompany Amherst himself to Ticonderoga, Crown Point, and Montreal as the thrust to open the southern route into Canada was finally launched.

No matter where the Seventh would be sent, it seemed to Athena as if Lochiel would never be safe. Once she couldn't have cared less what happened to him and had even searched cheerfully for ways to rid the earth of the arrogant blackguard herself, yet now the thought of losing him brought a wrenching pain to her soul. Oh, how bitter was her love for him, and if only Albany and the realities of war lay far, far in the distance!

Apparently the Highlanders did not share her sentiments, for there was a great deal of boisterous activity going on in camp when Athena returned, her work finished for the night. Some of the men were again demonstrating their prowess at sword dancing while others gambled, their fearsome dirks and broadswords lying at their feet as they occupied themselves with a worn deck of cards.

At first Athena turned down Hugh Martin's invitation to join them, but when he persisted she sat down to the game, a bowl of venison stew balanced in her lap. Fletcher had taught her to play cards long ago, and she was skillful enough to bring frustrated curses from the burly Highlanders who fell victim to her winning hands.

"You've the bloody luck o' the draw," Angus McCutcheon grumbled as Athena's small pile of silver coins began to grow. Clamping his pipe firmly between his yellowed teeth, he growled, "Deal again."

"Nay, 'tis a' for me," Hugh Martin protested, tossing in his hand.

"Aye," Davie Skelley agreed as his last few shillings were added to Athena's hoard. Scratching his coarse beard, he regarded her suspiciously. "Where did ye learn to play, lad?"

"Obviously not from the same person who taught you," she retorted cheekily, for the arrogant Davie had lost badly that night.

Both Hugh and Angus laughed heartily at this while the others slapped Davie consolingly on the back.

"Ye've a pulin' tongue, Malcolm," Davie growled, though he couldn't help liking the boy. "What do ye make o' Master Courtland, major?" he added, addressing the tall form that stepped into their midst. "Robbed me of a week's pay, he did."

Keeping her head down, Athena took her time scooping up the coins and depositing them in the pockets of her breeches. She didn't want anyone to see the flush that had spread across her cheeks at Lochiel's appearance.

Lochiel didn't reply for a moment. The sight of Athena sitting lost between the hulking bodies of Hugh Martin and Angus McCutcheon had startled him almost as much as the silver she was trying to fit into her already bulging pockets. Not only had these foul-tongued, suspicious old warriors invited her to play cards with them, but she seemed to have beaten them neatly. What was he to make of her, this impetuous creature who didn't seem to possess any of the characteristics one expected of a gentlewoman?

"What'll you do with your winnings, lad?" Davie asked before Lochiel could speak.

"I ken a lass at the other camp wha' could be persuaded to do plenty wi' that kind o' money," Angus supplied helpfully.

" 'Tis where I ought to be instead o' losin' me savings to a beardless boy," Davie Skelley agreed promptly. Rising to his feet, he grinned at his companions. "Who'll join me i' payin' a visit to our willin' beauties? Major?"

Head still bowed, Athena caught her breath, pain squeezing her heart as she recalled Andy Durning's remarks about Lochiel's infatuation with the lovely Liza Hampton.

The pause that followed seemed like an eternity to her until she heard Lochiel say amiably, "I'm afraid you'll have to go on without me tonight, lads."

"Wha' about ye, Malcolm?" Hugh Martin asked unexpectedly.

Athena's head came up, eyes wide with astonishment. "Me?"

"Aye! Dinna tell me ye've never tasted the pleasures o' the flesh?" Angus McCutcheon demanded. "Surely ye canna plead yer age! Took my first chambermaid at thirteen, I did."

"And hasna come up for air since," Hugh Martin added to the merriment of the others.

"Well, what'll it be, lad?" Angus prodded, ignoring him.

"I-I—" she stammered and glanced helplessly at Lochiel.

"I believe Miss Hampton's tastes run to slightly older . . . er . . . men," he said, looking very serious.

"Aye, ye ought to ken, major!" someone called with a laugh.

Athena scrambled to her feet, cheeks flaming. She didn't want to hear any more of their ribald jests about Lochiel and the prostitute he seemed to have taken such a fancy to.

"Malcolm, stay here."

Lochiel's tone was a command, halting her in her tracks. For a moment she was tempted to disobey, but she didn't exactly relish the scene that would doubtless follow, not with the grinning Highlanders as witnesses. Fortunately most of them seemed eager to follow Davie Skelley's lead and were soon sauntering toward the other camp.

"Athena!" Lochiel said sharply, striding toward her.

She raised her eyes from the polished boots to the lean face above hers. "Yes, sir?"

He had meant to remark on her rebelliousness but forgot everything as he gazed at the curve of her mouth and the gold-dusted lashes veiling her dark blue eyes. She was exquisite, even clad in rags, and he found himself remembering how those soft lips had parted beneath the firm pressure of his own when he had made love to her on the sandy shore of a hidden lake.

"Did you want something from me?" Athena asked a trifle breathlessly, for her heart had begun to beat very fast.

Lochiel's lips twitched, for only Athena could phrase an innocent question so suggestively. "You've played right into my hands," he murmured, a gleam in his eyes, "for indeed there is something I want from you, Athena Courtland."

He saw the indigo depths of her irises widen as she caught her breath. "You w-want—?"

"A kiss," he responded evenly. " 'Tis simple enough payment for rescuing you from the unwitting harassment of my men."

"Rescue?" Athena echoed indignantly, regarding him with cocked brows. "You all but made sport of the situation, knowing that I was quite helpless to defend mysel—"

The rest of her words were lost against Lochiel's mouth as he took her into his arms and kissed her deeply. Her slim arms wound themselves about his neck, and she unashamedly insinuated herself closer against his lean frame. Fires only recently quenched were rekindled instantly, bringing the heat to Lochiel's loins and a trembling to Athena's slender form.

"Have I demanded a price too high?" Lochiel inquired, releasing her at last. He smiled down into her upturned face.

"Oh no, truly not," Athena sighed. Her arms were still wrapped about his neck, and her shining eyes held a measure of shyness that delighted him.

"Then I wouldn't seem forward were I to ask for another?" he went on huskily.

Athena's lips parted. "One could never consider you forward, major."

"Lochiel," he said against her cheek. "Call me by my name, Athena."

"Lochiel," she murmured, but it was little more than a sigh lost in the swirling sensations of his hungry kiss.

The sound of footsteps crackling through the underbrush drove them apart. Reaching for the dirk at his side, Lochiel quickly placed Athena behind him. No longer the tender lover, he stood menacingly tall against the firelight, his eyes searching the darkness.

"What's amiss, MacLachlan?" he rapped out before Athena could even recognize the man who stumbled into the clearing.

"Algonquins, sir! They've just made a raid on a settlement south of here! One o' the survivors made it to camp. Mother Hicks be seein' to his wounds."

Lochiel's eyes narrowed. Indian raids were common in the colonies, although most of them took place in more remote settlements where there were no blockade houses or forts to seek protection in. The fact that a raiding party had ventured this far east could only mean that the Iroquois nation was girding for warfare—and that the French were responsible for this increase in activity.

"Did they take prisoners?" he demanded curtly.

"No, sir, but they did quite a bit o' damage."

Lochiel's lips thinned. "Have Corporal Martin round up all available men. We'll see what we can do to help."

"Aye, sir."

He had almost forgotten Athena, his thoughts occupied with what lay before him. There would doubtless be fires to put out, wounded to be cared for, and cattle to be driven back into their barns—not exactly military duties and certainly disappointing tasks for his men, who would prefer to hunt the redskins down themselves. Yet there was no sense in that, Lochiel knew, for the Algonquins would be long gone, melting into the forest as swiftly and silently as they had come.

"Red bastards," Andy Durning muttered as he appeared with Glenrobbie in tow. Already astride his mare, the big Scotsman was fingering his pistol with murderous intent. "I've got the lads mounted up an' waitin' on yer word."

Lochiel swung his leg over Glenrobbie's broad back and prepared to kick him into a canter. An insistent tug on his sleeve caused him to look down. His brow darkened when he found himself gazing into Athena's pale face.

"Permission to go with you, sir," she said formally, aware that the sergeant-major was listening.

"Permission denied." Lochiel's tone was cold.

"But, sir—"

"Permission denied, lad. There may still be Indians about."

Athena's face was stark, his words confirming her worst fears. Algonquins were a treacherous lot who often lay in wait to ambush their hapless victims. What did a Scottish-born major know of their ways? "Lochiel, please."

A savage light entered the silver eyes. "Stay here, Malcolm," he ordered in a voice that brooked no argument. "You'll only be in the way." He had to relent when he saw the stricken expression that crossed her features. "Promise me you'll stay here," he added less harshly.

Athena felt powerless to fight the compelling intensity of the eyes that locked with hers. "I promise," she heard herself whisper.

"Good lad."

Her cheek was patted in what looked to the watching Andy like a fondly paternal gesture, but Athena could feel the tenderness in the fingertips that lightly caressed the tendrils of hair curling at the nape of her neck. Then he was riding away, Glenrobbie's powerful hindquarters churning, and Athena was left with the memory of how warm and alive his touch had been.

She didn't know how long she paced about the now-deserted fire, abstractedly answering the questions of the men who had been awakened by the commotion. Many of them rushed off upon hearing what had transpired, battle cries echoing fiercely through the night air. Too many of them had lived through enemy raids themselves, for the Highland clans had been feuding since time immemorial, and they were determined to help hunt down the savages who had dared attack a sleeping English settlement.

Athena watched them go with tears in her eyes. She had promised Lochiel she'd stay here, and he had trusted her not to break her word. "I mustn't betray his trust in me," she whispered, trying to convince herself that it must be so. Yet all she could think of was the fear for him that painfully clogged her throat.

Impulsively she ran across the deserted grounds to the cluster of tents standing beneath the stars. Rummaging through Lochiel's footlocker, she withdrew one of the silver-appointed officer's pistols she had seen him wearing in the past. Inspecting it to make certain it was primed, she tucked it into her belt and dashed off to the riverbank, where her horse had been hobbled for the night. She would have preferred to take the Brown Bess with her, for the musket was a weapon she was more familiar with, yet there wasn't time to go after it. Furthermore, Tykie would never permit her to leave once he found out what she had in mind.

The gelding came to her willingly, though he snorted uneasily as he sensed her fear. Athena spoke to him soothingly, her fingers fumbling with the buckles of his bridle. Slinging her foot over his bare back, she was completely caught off guard when he threw up his head and reared, the whites of his eyes showing in terror.

"Hold still, you bloody fool!" Athena cried through clenched teeth, trying to recapture the reins that had been jerked out of her grasp. The gelding reared again, refusing to allow her to mount.

"Whatever is the matter with you?" Athena demanded, never having known him to behave so skittishly. Reaching up a hand to soothe him, she suddenly felt a prickle of instinctive warning flee down her spine. Whirling about, she gasped, eyes wide with alarm, but by then it was far too late and the big hand that clamped itself over her mouth effectively cut off her scream for help.

It was dawn when Lochiel and his small party of Highlanders rode back into camp, his uniform smelling of smoke, weariness etched into the normally proud features. Turning Glenrobbie over to one of the waiting men, he retired to his tent, shoulders bowed with exhaustion. At Andy's suggestion he had ordered a two-hour delay before reveille was to be sounded, and the thought of catching some sleep caused his stride to quicken.

Would he be able to find rest, he wondered, pushing the flaps of his tent aside, or would he be haunted by images of blackened houses and barns? Instead of peaceful dreams, would he see before him the bodies of the settlers who had been tomahawked by the Algonquins and left for dead on the single dirt street of Deerfield Towne?

A soft smile touched the corners of Lochiel's mouth as he became aware of the woman sleeping soundly on his cot. How long had Athena waited for him before retiring? He didn't know, yet he was suddenly profoundly grateful for her presence. Surely rest would not elude him when he held her soft body near, her warmth helping him to forget the horrors of the past night.

Stripping off his coat, he bent over her still form and reached out his hand to caress the tousled curls that spilled onto the blanket. His gentle expression hardened when he saw that they were not the warm gold he had expected but an ill-kempt black and coarse to the touch.

"What the devil?" he demanded, ripping the blankets aside.

Liza Hampton blinked sleepily as she sat up, rounded breasts almost spilling from the bodice she had loosened before slipping into his bed. Rubbing her eyes, she smiled up at him seductively, not noticing that the light of expectancy had faded from his face.

"I got tired waiting for you," she confessed huskily, running a hand through her midnight tresses. "I hope you don't mind that I lay down for a bit."

"I mind very much," Lochiel informed her, a dangerous glint in his eyes. "Who let you in here? Barrett?"

Liza's pretty mouth pulled in a petulant frown. She had expected to be awakened by an ardent kiss and the feel of her lover's muscular body against hers. "I crept in when no one was looking. No one knows I'm here." She tossed her head, her liquid brown eyes regarding him suspiciously. "What's happened to you, Lochiel? You used to enjoy it very much when I joined you for the night."

An unmistakable note of pleading had crept into her voice, and hearing it, she quickly fell silent. Lochiel Blackmoor was not a patient man, and she had warned herself earlier to play her cards carefully if she wanted to recapture his affections. For lost them she had, she knew that now. When he had first cooled to her last autumn, Liza had thought perhaps the pressures of the campaign had temporarily curbed his voracious male appetite, but she knew better now, and her almond-shaped eyes hardened with frustration. Oh, if only she'd not been so blind!

"I'm very tired, Liza," Lochiel told her curtly, turning his back on her and stripping off his shirt. "I'd like to get a few hours of sleep, if you don't mind."

She was too preoccupied admiring the rippling bronze muscles of his upper torso to hear the impatience in his deep voice. A longing ache began to throb between her legs, and she could not deny how fiercely she wanted him. She, who had taken so many men to her bed, had become a captive slave of this sinew-lean Highlander, her demon lover, as she called him in her thoughts. She knew she couldn't live if she lost him.

"Can't I stay with you?" she asked in a tone that had never failed to bring him into her arms, those haunting silver eyes glinting with passion.

Pouring water from a ewer, Lochiel scrubbed his grimy hands and fought with his temper. "I think not," he said at last, his voice even, his gaze indifferent as he turned to look at her.

Reclining suggestively on his cot, long white legs exposed beneath rumpled skirts, Liza could ignite any man's hot blood. Once she had done the same for him, but now he found her rounded fullness and scarlet, pouting lips almost vulgar, his taste for midnight-haired wenches replaced by an almost insatiable desire for the warm, golden beauty of one particular, impetuous woman.

"But Lochiel—"

" 'Tis time for you to go, Liza."

In one swift movement he bent down and seized her wrist in an iron grip. Jerking her to her feet, he gazed down at her for a moment without speaking, and she quailed at the impatience she saw in those unnerving eyes. Biting back the bitter words on her lips, she tried not to succumb to the heat of his nearness, yet her hungry gaze feasted on the muscular expanse of his chest and his narrow, masculine hips.

"Please, Lochiel," she entreated, her eyes traveling lower to where she knew the object of her longing waited only for a touch from her to spring to throbbing life. She insinuated herself closer, her breasts brushing against his naked chest. "Please—"

"I said you'd better go," Lochiel grated, thrusting her aside so that she stumbled and nearly fell. There was no passion or lust in his voice, only a weary indifference that was all the more galling because she sensed instinctively that no amount of physical manipulation on her part would arouse him.

Shaking with suppressed rage, Liza draped her discarded shawl about her shoulders. What did she care that Lochiel Blackmoor didn't want her? There were plenty of men who would give a month's pay to taste of her charms! Just wait until he came crawling back to her once he discovered that she was the only one who—

"Wait a moment, Liza."

She whirled about, longing and suspicion mingling on her beautiful face. Had he changed his mind? Didn't he realize how foolish he was being?

His casual words effectively quenched the last of her hopes.

"You didn't happen to see Malcolm Courtland when you came in?"

Liza could have screamed with frustration. Ooh, how she longed to claw his handsome face to shreds! 'Twas bad enough that he was casting her out while her body burned for him, but this, this was the ultimate humiliation!

"Yes, I did," she responded helpfully, her bitterness hidden behind a guileless smile. "He was just leaving for the other camp when I got here. I heard him tell Piers that he was on his way to Mother Hicks's to spend the night with Tykie Downs." Liza waited for him to react to this, but he merely turned away, her presence already forgotten.

Slipping into the darkness, she gave a low, angry laugh. "Mayhap I've lost him," she whispered spitefully to herself, "but at least I've seen to it that Malcolm Courtland can't have him, either!"

Jealousy burned in Liza's heart as she thought of the mysterious girl who was the object of Lochiel's current affections, yet soothed herself with the knowledge that this unknown creature was no longer at camp. Mayhap in time Lochiel would forget her, and Liza intended to use every skill at her command to draw him back under her own spell.

She laughed again, delighted to have become privy to the secret that only Lochiel and Tykie Downs had known about. It didn't matter to her at all what had become of the girl who had called herself Malcolm, nor was she the least bit curious as to why Lochiel had forced her to masquerade as a boy and thereby hide her identity from the rest of the camp. No, none of that mattered to Liza at all, for soon, she promised herself eagerly, soon her demon lover would be hers once again.

Fourteen

Lochiel Blackmoor slowed his lathering mount to a trot, his eyes narrowing in disbelief. Over a rise in the road he could see the imposing facade of Courtland Grace, and it seemed to him as if every room were ablaze with lights. Knowing how frugal Amelia Bower had been with her tapers, he could not fathom this odd turn of events. What in bloody hell was going on? Was it possible that Athena was here?

For two days Lochiel had been pushing Glenrobbie at a killing pace, barely pausing to rest as he crossed the deep valleys between Schenectady and West York. Few of his men would have recognized him as their fastidiously attired regimental commander, for his breeches were stained and a dark stubble covered his unshaven jaw. Weariness and a grim sense of purpose had made his ruthless expression almost frightening to behold.

Four long days had passed since Athena had vanished from camp, and Lochiel cursed the time wasted searching for her amid the smoldering ruins of Deerfield Towne. How sure he had been when he had learned of her disappearance that she had followed him there despite his orders to the contrary! Even now he could easily recall the fear that had haunted him as he imagined Athena a prisoner of the bloodthirsty Algonquins, a fate that the hand-wringing Tykie had been convinced had befallen her.

Lochiel had turned Deerfield and the surrounding countryside upside down, his men falling in willingly to help, although they were puzzled by his driving need to locate the missing Malcolm. All of them had grown fond of the lad and were disturbed by his disappearance, but they were at a loss to understand Major Blackmoor's obsession.

Not until the search in Deerfield was abandoned and Lochiel turned to questioning the camp followers did the Highlanders learn the startling reason behind his dogged quest. Faced with the wrathful inquisition of a desperate man, Liza Hampton had broken down and admitted to seeing Malcolm Courtland ride off in the company of two strange men the night of the Algonquin raid.

"Only 'twasn't Malcolm," she had choked, bitter with the realization that she had lost Lochiel forever. " 'Twas a girl, for I saw her take off her cap and show them her hair." Her tears flowed faster as she recalled how envious she had been of the beautiful tresses that had spilled like newly minted gold down the girl's slim back. 'Twas obvious that Lochiel was in love with her, for never in her life had Liza seen him so pale and distraught, behaving like a man possessed. And he had been so cruel when he questioned her, the angry heat in his eyes convincing her that he could easily turn violent if she didn't tell him the truth.

The news of her confession had spread like wildfire throughout both camps. Even as Lochiel and Tykie extracted a thorough description of the two men from the weeping Liza, soldiers and followers alike were wondering among themselves who this mysterious woman might be and why she seemed to mean so much to Major Blackmoor.

"Sure she be his lover," Hugh Martin reasoned excitedly. "Never seen the major so out o' sorts o'er a woman before!"

But his companions were forced to disagree, aware that Major Blackmoor was behaving more like a man incensed over the loss of his property than one who had suffered a bereavement of the heart. The relentless air about him when he had ridden off in pursuit of the two unknown men made it obvious that he was thirsting for vengeance, something the seasoned Highland warriors could well understand.

During the long ride to West York, Lochiel's torment had grown. Neither he nor Tykie had been able to link names to the men Liza had described, and Lochiel was still unwilling to accept her word that Athena had accompanied them without a struggle. His anger at Athena had reached towering proportions as well. Impulsiveness and troublesome behavior were characteristics he expected from her, but not foolhardiness. Why hadn't she waited for him to return before vanishing into the wilderness with strangers? And why in bloody hell hadn't she left word as to where she was bound?

The possibility that he might not even find her in West York haunted him. She could be anywhere at the moment, and Lochiel's expression was savage as Glenrobbie clattered into Courtland Grace's stableyard. Noticing the number of carriages assembled before the whitewashed stone building, he forgot his dire musings. The Courtlands were having a party, he realized in astonishment, yet surely Amelia Bower had no reason to be entertaining on such a grand scale while living alone! Or had she? His lips tightened ominously. Was Athena here after all? Had she blithely planned this gala event while he was driving his prized horse into the ground in an effort to find her?

"Good evening, sir." It was Hale, Courtland Grace's young stablehand, who had been lured outside by the sound of hoofbeats on stone. Acting as head groom in Tykie's absence, Hale was resplendently attired in satin hose and knee breeches, a snowy white stock spilling over the front of his vest.

"Why, 'tis Major Blackmoor!" he exclaimed, recognizing the newcomer in the lights from the stable behind him. "Welcome back to Courtland Grace, sir!" His enthusiasm was genuine, for Hale had greatly admired the Scottish officer ever since Major Blackmoor had rescued Miss Athena from the clutches of the soldiers dispatched to steal Ballycor last autumn.

"Thank you, Hale." Lochiel's manner was curt as he drew off his gloves and handed his whip to the boy who had scurried out at Hale's heels to take Glenrobbie from him.

"Have you come for the celebration, then?"

Lochiel's brows drew together. "Celebration?"

Hale's grin widened. "Yes, sir. Set most of the valley on its ear, it did, but there's no one wouldn't want to wish Miss Athena the best."

The dark head came up attentively. "Miss Courtland is here, then?" Lochiel inquired softly.

"Of course, sir. She's been back since Mistress Bower's—" Hale broke off when the major turned heel and strode away without another word. Gentry! he thought to himself. Never did like to listen to gossip, did they? "Get that horse cooled and watered," he ordered his assistant crisply, "and mind you have a care with him. That's prize horseflesh, in case you're too stupid to notice."

Crossing the darkened lawn, Lochiel could hear the strains of a lively gavotte floating to him on the calm night air. Through the French doors opening onto the terrace he could see the dancing couples twirling past and his annoyance increased. By God, Athena had bloody well better provide him with some answers or he'd wring her pretty neck!

His sharp rap on the front door was answered by a lanky servant in satin knee breeches and embroidered burgundy coat. It was Wills wearing a carefully powdered wig, his expression as aloof as any discriminating London majordomo.

"Good evening, sir. You wish?"

"I am Major Blackmoor of His Majesty's Regulars," Lochiel replied curtly. "I'm here to see Miss Courtland."

Instantly Wills's haughty manner vanished. Though he had never met Lochiel Blackmoor face to face, he was quite familiar with the name. "Please come in, sir," he invited, retreating from the doorway.

Lochiel had never set foot in the house before, and he forgot his anger when he stepped into the entrance hall. Unlike the overwhelming opulence of the stately homes he had visited in Europe, Courtland Grace did not boast its owners' wealth with countless antiques and priceless works of art. There was, contradictions aside, an almost cozy elegance in the few engravings that hung on the pale yellow walls and a charming simplicity in the inlaid cherry sideboard gracing the area beneath the winding stairwell. Rather than hothouse orchids, the arrangement upon it consisted of wildflowers that had been gathered from the fields earlier that morning.

The patterned rugs that covered the pegged oak floor were worn but still beautiful, and Lochiel could see that their pleasing color schemes of burgundy, cream, and blue were continued into the parlor and sitting room further down the corridor. The house reminded him too disturbingly well of Tor Blackmoor, his ancestral home, which had been burned to the ground by the vengeful English so many years ago. There, too, one had felt welcome the moment one stepped inside surrounded by furnishings, lovingly cared for over the years, that gave the house a sense of purpose and function, not the austere atmosphere of a showcase.

Lochiel could well imagine Athena growing up within these cozy rooms. He could almost hear her childish laughter and see her roughhousing with her brother in pantaloons and short skirts, her golden curls tied with colorful ribbons.

Aware of the foolishness of his thoughts, he forced himself to remember why he was here. The sight of the lavishly attired guests conversing together in the drawing room at the end of the corridor made it clear to him that his concern for Athena had been utterly misplaced. Obviously she had been in haste to get home so that she wouldn't miss her aunt's party.

"I'll tell Miss Athena you're here, major. Would you be kind enough to wait for her in the parlor, please?"

Wills hoped fervently that Major Blackmoor would take no offense at being relegated to a back room. There was no delicate way of informing him, after all, that his attire was utterly inappropriate for making an appearance at a gathering as formal as the one taking place in the withdrawing room.

In fact, Wills thought disapprovingly to himself, the major looked as if he had just returned from a long and exhaustive campaign. His breeches were travel-stained, his coat was badly wrinkled, and the shadow on his jaw suggested that he hadn't made use of a razor in the past several days. Furthermore he didn't care too much for the unnerving glitter in those oddly colored eyes. Wills had heard plenty from both Tykie and Hale concerning Major Blackmoor's admirable assets, yet he was inclined to form a less favorable opinion of his own, for the major seemed like a man possessed, restless, malevolent, and intimidating.

"Miss Athena will join you shortly," he added politely, showing Lochiel into a pleasant room decorated in shades of blue and rose chintz.

"I've all the patience in the world," the tall Highlander assured him, but there was a gleam in his eyes that contradicted his words and left Wills with a decidedly uneasy feeling.

Prowling to the window, Lochiel drew back the heavy drapes and peered into the darkened gardens. Polite applause from the drawing room drifted to him and alerted him that the dance had ended. Turning, he folded his arms before his chest and waited with narrowed eyes for Athena to appear in the doorway.

In the drawing room, meanwhile, the musicians had struck up a stately minuet at the request of Ambrose Kensington, who was red-faced with the exertion of leading Athena through the lively steps of the preceding gavotte. Mopping his brow with a handkerchief, he smiled in relief as his son appeared at his elbow and politely requested his partner's hand.

"Take her, take her, m'boy," he panted, "I'd better sit this one out. Not as young as I used to be."

"My father has been monopolizing you far too long," Stephen murmured intimately into Athena's ear. "Now 'tis my turn."

She gave him a smile by way of reply; the same fixed smile that had been playing on her lovely lips all evening. Seeing Wills gesture discreetly to her from the far corner of the room, she raised her head and tried to slip her hand free of Stephen's possessive grip.

"What is it?" he demanded, refusing to let her go.

"Wills is trying to get my attention."

Stephen shrugged, not even sparing the footman a glance. "Whatever he wants can wait," he said, leading her onto the floor with a hand resting intimately in the small of her back. "This dance is mine."

He was well aware of the fact that they were the most attractive couple on the floor tonight. In a cutaway coat of puce and gold, his wrists and collar flowing with fine Mecklenburg lace, Stephen considered himself a perfect foil for the ivory-clad beauty beside him.

Indeed, Athena had never looked lovelier. Her ivory silk gown shimmered as she moved, drawing all eyes to the flowing lines of her graceful body. Black velvet ribands trimmed the sleeves and bodice, and the full skirts were caught up in the front to reveal the rustling black petticoats beneath. Her slender feet were encased in white Moroccan kid slippers, and black silk stockings clad the slim line of her ankles.

She wore no jewelry save a teardrop-shaped sapphire at the end of a delicate silver chain. Her hair was unpowdered, the color of warm, sun-ripened wheat as it reflected the glittering candlelight, and a spray of tiny diamonds and pearls in the shape of a flower had been tucked behind one small ear. Her cheeks were flushed and her blue eyes seemed to sparkle as

Stephen twirled her across the polished floor. No one who saw them could fail to remark on how eminently suited they were.

At the conclusion of the dance Athena sank into a deep curtsy before her partner, one gloved hand holding her skirts aside, the other gripping the ivory handle of her fan. Smiling up into his eyes for the benefit of anyone who might be watching, she knew that she must escape him soon or go mad with the effort of pretending to be so happy. Her jaw ached from smiling so much, and she didn't know how much longer she could tolerate the envious looks of people like Katrine de Vries who hated her for having stolen Stephen from them. Dear God, if they only knew—

A shrill scream from the corner of the crowded room brought Athena to her feet. "What's happened?" she demanded of Stephen, who stood tall enough to see over the crush of couples on the dance floor.

" 'Twould seem Mrs. Axminster has fainted," he replied, referring to the minister's wife.

"Oh dear! I hope 'tis nothing serious!"

Stephen laughed. "You know quite well that she faints every time she squeezes herself into one of those impossibly tight corsets. I don't believe —my God, it can't be!"

Craning her neck, Athena could see nothing except the backs of the guests who had gathered around the fallen woman. "What is it, Stephen?" she asked, aware of the awkward silence that abruptly fell over the room.

Even as she spoke, the crowd parted before her and Athena caught her breath, the fan falling unnoticed from her grasp as she found herself staring into the hawkish face of Lochiel Blackmoor. Catching sight of her at the same time, he strode toward her, scandalized whispers following his progress across the dance floor.

"He looks as though he hasn't changed his clothes in a week!" Katrine commented excitedly to her mother. "And did you see the expression on his face? Small wonder Mistress Axminster fainted dead away!"

"He might at least have taken time to shave." Marianne sniffed disapprovingly.

"How dare he!" Stephen choked, growing red-faced with outrage. "Athena, did you invite him? Athena!"

Athena made no reply, although he had shaken her arm quite cruelly. The joy that had leaped into her eyes went unnoticed by everyone except Lochiel, who halted before her amid the curious murmurs of the gathered throng.

He had come, Athena thought exultantly to herself, exactly as she had prayed he would, and it didn't matter to her at all that his unkempt appearance had startled her guests and caused poor Mrs. Axminster to faint. He had come, and nothing else mattered.

"May I ask the meaning of this, Major Blackmoor?" Stephen asked coldly into the silence. "I do not recall your having been issued an invitation, and 'tis highly insulting of you to appear thus attired."

The assembly pressed closer, not wanting to miss a word of their exchange.

"My apologies, Mr. Kensington," Lochiel responded evenly. "I came to speak with Miss Courtland, not to disrupt your gathering. I felt I'd been kept waiting in the parlor long enough, and I beg forgiveness if I insulted anyone with my untimely appearance."

There was a mocking gleam in his silver eyes and an arrogance in his manner that caused the gathered menfolk to bridle and the younger women to blush excitedly behind their fans. Even in worn buckskin breeches and sweat-stained shirt, smelling of horseflesh and the outdoors rather than pomade, Lochiel Blackmoor seemed to dominate the room. There was something dangerously attractive in his raw masculinity that caused the ladies' fans to flutter, although all of them could see that he had eyes for no one but Athena.

She herself felt breathless at his nearness, her nerve ends alive with awareness of him, and there was a soft, persuasive light in her eyes as she looked up into his beloved face. His ill-concealed anger didn't frighten her, for she knew that it couldn't be directed at her. Oh no, how could it, when he had obviously come for her?

"Lochiel—"

The softly uttered name was drowned out by Stephen's icy words. "You will address Athena as Miss Courtland no longer, sir. As of today she is my wife, and you'd do well to remember it."

The silence that followed seemed to hammer in Athena's ears. Lochiel, she noticed, had grown pale beneath his tan, and a muscle began to twitch in his lean jaw. Instinctively her hands reached out to him, but the look in his eyes caused them to fall unnoticed to her sides, where her fingers twined themselves convulsively in the folds of her skirts.

With the same mocking smile playing on his lips, Lochiel sketched an insultingly brief bow in Stephen's direction. "My apologies," he said dispassionately. "I wasn't aware of Miss Courtland's intentions when she disappeared from my camp four nights ago. I only hope, sir, that you find no cause for disappointment when you lead your 'virgin bride' to her marriage bed."

Turning heel, he vanished through the drawing room door, oblivious to the uproar he left in his wake.

He was halfway down the road leading into West York, Glenrobbie galloping at a furious pace, when he heard a voice calling his name behind him. He knew at once that it was Athena and cursed savagely as he drew his exhausted mount to a halt. What the devil did she want from him now? Hadn't she made it plain that she needed him no longer? He saw her materialize in the moonlight, her white gown shimmering like gossamer, the billowing skirts blending eerily with Ballycor's ghostly color.

Lochiel drew in his breath, hating her for looking so beautiful with her golden hair tumbling unpinned to her hips, her eyes mysterious and black in the moonlight. Drawing the nervously stamping stallion to a halt beside him, Athena's silken skirts brushed against his booted leg, the material rustling softly.

"Did you come alone or is your husband somewhere behind you?"

She swallowed hard, stung by the lash of his voice. "I managed to slip out in the confusion. Oh, Lochiel, don't you know he'll call you out for saying what you did?"

He gave a curt laugh, unable to look at her. "Am I to fear the vengeance of an insulted groom? The art of fighting duels is not unknown to me, my dear."

Athena blinked back the tears that welled in her eyes. How could she reach through the impenetrable wall he had erected about him? What could she say to erase the terrible anger and the crushing contempt for her she heard in his deep voice? She must explain to him what had happened so that he could help her instead of being so angry!

She never had the chance to speak, for Lochiel reached out suddenly, causing Ballycor to throw up his head in alarm, and had her fast by the shoulders, his grip bruisingly painful.

"Why, Athena?" he grated, his breath hot against her brow. "Why did you wed him without a word to me?"

She lifted her eyes to the glittering ones only inches from hers, and for the first time in her life her courage failed her and she had to look away. "I didn't marry him, Lochiel, at least not in the way you think." She drew a deep breath, aware of his mounting impatience. There was so much to explain to him. How was she ever going to get him to listen?

"The two men who came to camp to fetch me told me there'd been a death in my family," she continued in a small voice, her confidence seriously shaken. " 'Tis why I had to leave so abruptly. Didn't Piers Barrett give you the message I left?"

"There was no message." Lochiel's grip tightened on her slim shoulders, refusing to acknowledge the softening of his heart as he gazed into her ravaged features. Her nearness and the bareness of her flesh beneath his hands was wreaking havoc upon his senses. Yet he would not allow this deceiving wench to fool him ever again.

Athena's eyes were filled with confusion. "Toddman Tyner, one of the men who came for me, said he'd leave word with Piers. I don't understand why he—"

"What difference does it make?" Lochiel interrupted, wanting to hear no more. " 'Tis obviously a lie, for you returned here to marry Kensington, not to attend some fabricated relative's burial!"

" 'Tis the truth!" Athena protested, her voice nearly breaking. " 'Twas my aunt Amelia who died, and when I returned home I discovered she had consented to a proxy marriage between Stephen and myself. She signed the papers only a day before her death. I didn't know anything about it, and Stephen said he went through the ceremony without my knowledge only because he knew there was no one left to look after me anymore."

"Do you honestly expect me to believe that, Athena?" Lochiel's voice chilled her. "You're far too clever to come up with such a ridiculous tale. Why didn't you simply tell me that you were pledged to wed Kensington all along?" His fingers tightened, biting into the soft flesh of her shoulders so that she winced and tried to squirm away.

"Perhaps it doesn't matter," he added thoughtfully, gazing coldly at her averted face, unmoved by the tears that were trickling down her pale cheeks. "I'd forgotten how much you enjoyed seducing unsuspecting soldiers. Were your Ranger lovers and I sufficient diversion for a bored and restless bride?" His laugh was harsh and filled with self-loathing. "By God, I wonder if Kensington knows what sort of woman he's shackled himself to?"

"Please let me go," Athena whispered. "Y-you're hurting me."

He did as she requested, pushing her away from him as though unable to bear her nearness. Ballycor, startled by the sudden shifting in weight of the rider on his back, sidestepped nervously, causing Athena to lose her balance. Sliding from the saddle, she landed with a painful thump on the roadside, where she buried her face in the soft grass and burst into tears.

Instantly she felt gentle hands upon her and heard Lochiel's gruff voice as he lifted her against him. "My God, did I hurt you, Athena? I swear 'twas not my intent!"

"Go away!" she sobbed.

"Athena, for God's sake, let me—"

"Don't touch me! Don't ever touch me again!" It was the way she shrank from him, like a wounded animal fearing a beating, that startled him more than her bitter cries. Tightening his hold about her, Lochiel stared down at her with concern. She had stopped her useless struggles and lay with her face against his coat, her eyes closed as though trying to shut herself away from him.

"Athena, look at me."

There was no reply, although the tears continued to roll unchecked down her cheeks. His hand shook as he reached to brush them away.

"Don't touch me," she repeated, jerking away from him as though burned by his touch.

"Athena! Athena, where are you?"

The dark and the golden head, both bent so close together, lifted in unison at the cry that came through the darkness. Pushing herself away from the wide chest against which she had been lying, Athena struggled painfully to her feet. Her beautiful gown was smeared with grass stains and scratches mingled with the tear tracks upon her grimy face. Pressing a hand to her lips, she watched the approaching rider while Lochiel came to his feet, oblivious to the fact that his stance was aggressively protective as he hovered over her.

"Athena!"

She uttered a soft cry as she recognized that voice, realizing for the first time that it was not Stephen who had come after her but Fletcher, her beloved brother.

"Here I am!" she cried, running forward, skirts held aloft, her hair tumbling untidily down her back.

Moments later she was in her brother's arms, and the comfort and warmth she felt as he clasped her to him was a bitter reminder of how much she had hungered for the same protective gestures from the silent man behind her.

"Oh, my love," Fletcher groaned, feeling her hot tears splash his vest. "I came as soon as I heard! You're not hurt, are you?"

She tried to tell him that she was fine now that he was here, but the words were little more than unintelligible sobs. Fletcher lifted his head, his eyes mere slits as he regarded the lean Highlander who was watching Athena weep in stony silence.

"My regiment was recalled to Albany by Colonel Baker," Fletcher informed him coldly. "As soon as we received the orders I started after your company, thinking to intercept it and escort Athena home myself. You can imagine my surprise when I found Tykie alone at camp spouting incoherent tales of Athena's kidnapping by hostile frontier trappers. My bewilderment grew when I arrived at Courtland Grace just now to find the place in an uproar, every man jack in the drawing room arming himself to avenge Athena's insulted honor."

"Oh, Fletcher, that can't be true!" Athena breathed.

"Indeed it is," he responded grimly. "I had quite a difficult task persuading them to calm themselves. I've no idea what you said to them, Blackmoor, but I can assure you—"

"How did you find me?" Athena interrupted quickly, hoping to prevent further words between her brother and Lochiel. She didn't think she'd be able to bear it if the confrontation between them turned violent.

"Kensington told me he thought you'd withdrawn to your rooms," Fletcher replied, reaching into his pocket for a handkerchief and tenderly drying her eyes. " 'Tis fortunate Mercy informed me otherwise, because this way I can confront you alone. I didn't have time to talk to Stephen about any of this, and I'd really rather discuss it with you first." His voice grew rough as he gazed into Athena's tear-stained face. "You didn't really agree to marry him, did you?"

"I doubt, lieutenant, that you care to have an outsider take part in this discussion."

Athena stiffened at the cold finality in Lochiel's tone. If only she could explain to him what had happened, but the hostility in both men's expressions warned her that they would never allow her the chance. Turning in Fletcher's arms, she gasped as she saw Lochiel reaching for Glenrobbie's reins. Was he simply going to ride out of her life without another word?

"Lochiel, please . . ."

The broad back stiffened at her whispered plea, and for a moment she thought the dark head would turn in her direction. Then he stirred and abruptly swung himself into the saddle. Seconds later horse and rider had vanished from sight behind a moon-drenched rise in the road.

"Let's go back to the house, Thena," Fletcher suggested, his heart constricting as he gazed into her haunted eyes. Though his anger and bewilderment were great, he spoke to her gently, sensing her suffering without really understanding its cause. He did not want her to see how shaken he was to discover that she had suddenly become Stephen Kensington's wife, for he had never trusted the arrogant fellow and could scarcely believe that Athena had consented to marry him.

Not having been informed of his aunt's death as yet, Fletcher had to assume that his sister had married the man by choice, and his arms tightened briefly about her before he helped her mount the waiting Ballycor. How she had changed, his willful baby sister, and he wondered sadly if her irrational decision had been prompted by the fact that she had endured so many hardships since their father's death. Would things have been different for her if he and the twins hadn't abandoned her? 'Twas a painful question to ask and one he wasn't sure he could answer.

Reaching up, he placed a comforting hand on the cold little fingers that clutched the reins so tightly. "We'll work everything out, Thena, I promise."

She tried to smile, but her lips trembled dangerously. How could she explain to him that her heart was broken, that nothing could be done to mend the rift between herself and the man she so desperately loved? "Oh, Fletcher, I d-don't think anything can be done to—"

The loud report of a musket exploded the tranquil night air, interrupting her choked words and sending a pair of sleeping guinea hens squawking into the sky. Their raucous cries were drowned out by the shriek that fell from Athena's lips as she watched her brother spin about beneath the impact of the lead ball that plowed into his body. Even before he went sprawling into the dust she was beside him, trying to lift him as warm, sticky blood spilled onto the pristine white bodice of her gown.

"No!" she screamed hysterically. "Oh, Fletcher, no! Someone, help me, please!"

Fifteen

Lochiel Blackmoor's handsome face was expressionless as he followed General Amherst's secretary into the second-floor study of the elegant home the general occupied in a quiet section of Albany bordering the riverfront. He spared no glance for the priceless antiques and superb pieces of furniture gracing the entrance hall, his thoughts preoccupied with other matters.

Accustomed to receiving summonses from Amherst at odd hours, Lochiel was not surprised to find the commander of the British forces reclining behind his desk in a silk dressing robe, his unpowdered brown hair tied back in a queue. Though he respected the general for his military genius and personally liked the man despite his more than cautious nature, Lochiel could return his warm greeting with only a curt one of his own. Fortunately the general, busy with parchment and quill, appeared not to notice.

"Sit down, major," he invited and waved his secretary from the room. "I understand the Seventh Company arrived in Albany yesterday morning."

Lochiel acknowledged this, although he refrained from adding that he himself had returned almost two days earlier. 'Twas not for the general or anyone else to know that he had spent the time since leaving West York getting unpleasantly drunk and waking up this morning in a flea-ridden bed in a waterfront pub. Fortunately he'd found himself quite alone, and the fleshy-jowled proprietor had been quick to assure him that he hadn't taken his drunken pleasure with any of the simpering barmaids. Lochiel had been relieved to hear it, though he had to admit to himself that he wouldn't have remembered even if he had seduced one of them.

He thrust the unpleasant thought away with a frown. At the moment he wanted nothing to remind him of the bitterness of Athena's betrayal, which had driven him to the filthy tavern to begin with. The general, he realized at the same moment, had finished writing and was leaning back in his armchair, fingers steepled thoughtfully before him.

"I imagine you're wondering why I sent for you at this hour," he began with the ghost of one of his famous smiles.

Lochiel's brows arched in amiable response. "To discuss strategy, of course. You've told me often enough that you plan your greatest campaigns after the rest of the world has long since gone to bed."

General Amherst was forced to laugh heartily at the young officer's canny accuracy. "Well, then, I expect we should get right down to it," he agreed. "As you know, major, our meeting with Franklin and his colonial assembly is scheduled for eight o'clock tomorrow morning. Colonel Wallace Baker has also been invited to sit in, as has Brigadier General Wolfe. I thought 'twould be advantageous if the two of us talked first. I would like to hear your opinion on French troop movement along the Ontario shore."

The general tapped the side of his head for emphasis. " 'Tis always best if I have a clear picture here before turning myself loose upon the colonials."

Lochiel nodded, familiar with the careful planning that went into every phase of General Amherst's campaigns and the constant questioning he was forced to endure from both the colonial commanders and civilian leaders. Normally he didn't mind helping the general map out his strategy, yet at the moment he was distracted by a name that had been mentioned. "Colonel Baker of the New York Militia will be joining us tomorrow?" he asked.

Amherst nodded. "He'll be a valuable asset in detailing the area north of Crown Point. Champlain's his territory, and with the division of Rangers I've inherited I think we'll have all the scouts we need to map out our route. Care for a drink?" he added, rising and taking a cut-crystal decanter from the inlaid rosewood cabinet behind him.

Lochiel declined, but the act of pouring brandy had turned the general talkative. "I was speaking to Baker earlier today," he remarked, returning to his seat, "and he mentioned to me that he'd lost one of his best officers in a tragic mishap two days ago. Young lieutenant by the name of Fletcher Courtland, and I couldn't help wondering why that sounded so familiar to me. We were both in West York last autumn, major. Wasn't there a family residing there by that name?"

Lochiel's restlessly tapping boot had suddenly grown still. "There was," he acknowledged with seeming indifference. "Miss Courtland herself was presented to you at the de Vries ball."

General Amherst's face cleared. "Ah, yes, I remember now. Quite a beauty, though a bit forward for my tastes. Asked questions about the campaign a woman shouldn't be troubling herself over." He shook his head and sipped the contents of his balloon-shaped glass. "A pity about her brother."

"What happened to him?" Lochiel inquired, feigning indifference, though a keen observer might have noticed the unnatural stillness about him and the tension in the lean body that reclined so casually in the leather armchair.

" 'Tis odd, actually," General Amherst replied. " 'Twould seem young Fletcher returned home to celebrate his sister's marriage and instead found the wedding party being disbanded, the menfolk ranting about forming a lynching party to catch some fellow who'd dared insult the new bride's honor."

He leaned forward, smiling rather sheepishly. "I have all of this on Baker's word, mind you, and he isn't the sort to listen to gossip. No telling the details involved or even if the story's true."

"But something did happen to Miss Courtland's brother," Lochiel prompted, striving hard to conceal his impatience.

General Amherst had warmed to the tale now that he found himself with a seemingly interested audience. "As Baker tells it, and he heard it from one of his adjuncts who was actually present that evening, the bride herself had slipped from the house for some unknown reason, and Lieutenant Courtland had ridden after her. He was shot by one of Miss Courtland's vengeful admirers, who mistook him in the darkness for the scoundrel who had supposedly insulted her to begin with." The general shook his head in disbelief. " 'Od's blood, I'd dearly like to know what was said to her! Stirred up one hell of a hornets' nest, I vow!"

Lochiel said nothing.

General Amherst twirled his glass in one long-fingered hand. "A pity," he repeated, "especially because I do remember the young lady in question. I must admit, however, that I'm not altogether surprised that something like this could happen. Hers was the sort of beauty that could easily stir men to violence."

"And her brother is dead," Lochiel said harshly, his expression so bitter that the older man's brows rose in astonishment.

"Heavens, did I say that?"

"Then he isn't?" Lochiel demanded, leaning forward in his chair.

General Amherst sighed. "Might as well be, judging from the injuries he sustained. Colonel Baker implied 'twould be a mere matter of time before—where in bloody hell are you going, lad?"

Lochiel turned in the doorway long enough to sketch a curt bow. "My apologies, sir. I've just remembered something extremely urgent I need to take care of."

He took the stairs two at a time, ignoring Amherst's startled calls. The streets were deserted at that time of night, and he was able to put Glenrobbie to a canter. Without even glancing at the imposing fort that sat high on the hill above town, Lochiel turned north along the Hudson. There was an acid taste in his mouth, and his eyes blazed with an urgency that had never possessed him before.

It was fortunate that Glenrobbie was as fit as his master, for no other mount could have sustained the killing pace that Lochiel set that night. Sleeping settlements and dairy cattle grazing in the darkness behind stone fences passed in a blur as the muscular gelding pounded along the winding road leading out of town. When the moon rose to cast its silvery light on the slumbering hills, the way was sufficiently lit for Lochiel to coax the gelding into a gallop. Hoofbeats echoed hollowly on packed earth, and only the creatures of the night that foraged in the rustling thickets witnessed their whirlwind passage.

It was nearly dawn by the time Lochiel clattered the spent animal into Courtland Grace's deserted stableyard. A warm wind was blowing, and already the stars were beginning to fade from the onyx canopy of the heavens. A single light was burning in the small shuttered window of the tack room, and as Lochiel dismounted the door burst open, revealing a hulking frame on the threshold.

"Who be't?" a familiar voice demanded.

" 'Tis Lochiel, Tykie."

The figure hesitated a moment before approaching, and Lochiel's brows rose as he noticed the long-barreled musket held firmly in the big, hairy hands. Wordlessly he turned to loosen the girth of Glenrobbie's saddle so that the winded gelding could blow easier.

"He needs a thorough rubdown and water once he's cooled," Lochiel said over one shoulder. "Where's Hale?"

"I've orders na tae let ye onto Courtland land, Major Blackmoor." Tykie's voice was gruff with regret and embarrassment.

Lochiel's dark eyes narrowed in mock astonishment as his gaze came to rest on the wretched man's face. "Oh?"

Tykie's expression was that of a faithful hound who'd been beaten for some little-understood transgression. " 'Twas Mr. Kensington wha' gave the orders," he confessed.

"I imagine as Athena's husband he had the right to." The steely edge of Lochiel's voice caused the other man to wince. "Well, Tykie, shoot me if you must, but tell me first how Fletcher is faring." The silver eyes were hard, as though the soul of the man they belonged to had turned completely to stone. "Tell me, too, how well Athena is holding up under all of this, and I'll go contented to my grave."

Tykie did not hear the heavy sarcasm in the harshly condemning voice.

To him the major's mockery was real, and suddenly he tossed the musket to the ground and turned his back, his enormous shoulders shaking with what could very well have been sobs.

Lochiel was taken aback by this, and it dawned on him that Fletcher must have died. Why else would this big bear of a man be weeping? His stony countenance softened perceptively, but before he could speak Tykie had whirled around to face him, his reddened eyes reflecting the pain of a simple man who had been plunged into a world where things no longer made sense.

"I dinna ken where tae turn na more, major!" he burst out, his deep bass voice wavering. "When Master Fletcher brought me hame wi' him after lookin' for Miss Athena at camp, I thought tae mysel' 'twould a' be well the noo!" His bearded jaw worked. "But 'tisna well! Naught be well na more! Why, Mistress Bower wasna even cold i' her grave when we retairned, an' yet thot bastard Kensington be throwin' a weddin' party for our wee lass he claims he married by poxy! I tell ye—" He broke off, his breathing labored.

"A poxy?" Lochiel echoed in bemusement. "God's blood, Tykie, you don't mean a proxy marriage, do you?" he demanded, a stunned look on his face. "You're telling me Kensington married Athena by proxy *after* the death of her aunt?"

"Aye, aye, or some sich nonsense! Dinna ask me tae explain, for I dinna understand!"

"Tykie," Lochiel said curtly, "is Master Fletcher still alive?"

Tykie blinked, the major's stern voice restoring a measure of his sanity. What had he been babbling about? he asked himself, shaking his grizzled head in an effort to clear it. Blood and fury, he'd almost started greeting like a bairn, right there before Major Blackmoor's eyes!

"Master Fletcher?" he echoed uncertainly.

Lochiel gritted his teeth, sensing the other man's confusion. Poor Tykie had been through enough shocks, and it was obvious from the circles under his eyes that he was exhausted to the point of delirium. No telling how much that broken foot was still paining him, too. "Is he still alive?" Lochiel repeated softly.

Tykie's head bowed and his big hands curled into fists. "Aye, though no ane kens for how much longer."

"And Miss Athena, is she here with him or—" He was enraged at himself for being unable to complete the question, but Tykie seemed to understand.

"She wouldna go wi' Master Stephen tae live, na wi' her brother sae puirly."

Lochiel's eyes traveled to the imposing manor house, where a single light glowed from an upper-story window.

"Aye, she be there wi' him," Tykie acknowledged. "Hasna left his room since they carried him there. Major, wait," he called as Lochiel started up the drive.

Sensing the impatience in that lean frame, he struggled to find the proper words. "I heard wha' ye said aboot Miss Athena i' the drawin' room that night. Half the colony kens, too. 'Tisna my place tae question yer reasons or ask why ye hurt the lassie so, but—" He broke off and gazed helplessly into the harshly chiseled visage before him. "If I let ye upstairs tae see her, ye'll not hurt her again?" he blurted at last.

A vision of the tear-stained little face that had stared up at him in mute appeal two nights ago rose unbidden to Lochiel's mind. He could see the smudges of dirt on the pale cheeks and the agony in the blue eyes that had always held his with such spirited arrogance.

"No, Tykie," Lochiel said softly. "I'll not hurt her again."

A hopeful smile lit Tykie's weary face. Mayhap the future's outlook was not as bleak as he'd imagined. "Wait here an' I'll fetch the key."

The interior of the house was dark, and Tykie cursed as he fumbled to light the tapers in the entrance hall. Handing one to Lochiel, he indicated the staircase before them.

"They put him i' the master bedroom. 'Twas to hae been Miss Athena's bridal chamber." He coughed uncomfortably and eyed the silent officer questioningly. "Shall I tell her ye be here, or will ye gae up yersel'?"

"What the devil is that fellow doing in this house?"

Tykie blinked at Wills's curt demand, never having heard the middle-aged footman use such a tone before. Wills was standing in the doorway leading from the salon, his normally neatly powdered hair disheveled, worn leather slippers on his feet. It was obvious that he had been napping on the sofa, but he would not permit his appearance to put him at a disadvantage. Indeed, he might have been wearing silk hose and tails, given the dignity of his demeanor as he bore down on the two men standing in the hall.

"Major Blackmoor is no longer welcome here," he declared, dour face filled with hostility. " 'Tis fortunate I chose to sleep downstairs, where I could hear Miss Athena call, because without my interference you would obviously have given him free run of the house. Are you mad, Tykie?"

"I dinna—I wasna—" Tykie's stammering faded into silence and he began to shuffle his big feet indecisively. No matter what Wills or anyone else in the household thought of him, he knew the sort of man Lochiel Blackmoor was. Stephen Kensington's orders be damned, the major had a right to see Miss Athena if he wanted to!

"I've come to see how Lieutenant Courtland is faring, Wills." Lochiel spoke calmly, taking no offense at the servant's words.

"Haven't you done enough?" Wills blurted. Concern for his mistress and the gravely injured master gave him the courage to address the Highland officer so rudely. Glaring at the grizzled Tykie, he added, "Kindly show him out, or shall I fetch Master Foster's pistols and do the job myself?"

A glint of steel appeared in Lochiel's eyes. "I'm afraid that I cannot be persuaded, with weapons or otherwise, to leave these premises until I've spoken with Miss Courtland." Folding his powerful arms before his chest, he gave the flustered Wills a mocking smile that dared him to make good his threat.

" 'Tis Mrs. Kensington, now, Lochiel, and I pray you will remember it."

All three men turned at the soft voice that came from the landing above them. It was Athena, her wrapper of midnight-blue silk trailing behind her as she started down the stairs. Her golden hair was carelessly confined by a velvet ribbon, and wayward curls had escaped to fall untidily down her back. To any casual observer she appeared hopelessly wanton, her dishevelment enhancing her unconscious sensuality, but Lochiel was quick to notice the hollows in her pale cheeks and the weary slump of her slim shoulders. Though the proud tilt of her square chin was still there, the spirit seemed to have vanished from her blue eyes, leaving them shadowed and sad.

"I let him in, Miss Athena," Tykie confessed miserably, having secretly hoped that she'd run into the major's arms to greet him.

Lochiel, who had perhaps been expecting the same thing, allowed none of his feelings to show in the carefully arranged mask on his face. "I came as soon as I heard the news, Mrs. Kensington," he said politely. "I had no idea I was breaking rules when I set foot on your property."

Athena's expression did not change in response to his tone. In fact, she seemed as remote to Lochiel as she had on the night he had first spoken to her in Egon de Vries's study, when her aloofness had convinced him she was a woman without feeling.

"We can speak privately in the salon," she told him quietly. "Wills, please bring some brandy for the major." Only when her gaze fell upon Tykie's unhappy countenance did her expression soften somewhat. " 'Tis good that you let him in, Tykie. Major Blackmoor and I have a great deal to discuss."

While Wills withdrew to fetch the brandy, Athena led Lochiel into the salon, where she set her lamp down on an octagonal table. He watched wordlessly while she bent to light another, the flaring flame illuminating her delicate profile and the length of her white throat. Straightening, she tossed her head so that the golden curls fell sinuously down her back and adjusted the silk wrapper, which had fallen open to reveal the creamy tops of her breasts above the sheer batiste nightrail.

"I haven't much time," she informed him in the same distant tone, "as I dislike leaving Fletcher alone for so long."

"Damn it, Athena," Lochiel ground out. "What game are you playing at?"

She cocked a tawny brow. "Game? 'Tis no game, Lochiel. I am married to Stephen Kensington and I intend to remain so."

He gazed at her in growing disbelief. She seemed to mean what she said, and the arrogant tilt of her golden head reminded him all too annoyingly of his own stubborn self. Unconsciously his eyes went to her hands, which were folded demurely together, and his brow darkened ominously when he saw the gold band winking accusingly on her slim finger.

Sensing his growing anger, Athena said quietly, "I'd like to explain to you what happened, if you're willing to listen to me now."

He was tempted to slap her, not only because he was certain she was mocking him, but because he could think of no other way to break through the icy reserve that surrounded her. What in bloody hell was the matter with her?

"I don't blame you for refusing to listen to an explanation before," she added with such a guileless look on her beautiful face that he had to believe her. "Tykie told me you never got the message I left with Piers Barrett when I rode out of camp and that both of you were certain I'd fallen into the hands of some unscrupulous trappers." She smiled sadly. " 'Twas never my intent to cause either of you so much worry."

Lochiel said nothing, still pained by the memory of those harrowing days when he had feared she had fallen victim to a band of bloodthirsty Algonquins. Perhaps a measure of his thoughts showed in his face, for Athena abruptly moved to the window and drew back the heavy drapes. Unaware of the effect her silk-clad form and unbound hair were having upon the silent man behind her, she gazed out into the darkness for several long minutes.

"On the night of the Algonquin raid two men came into camp looking for me," she began at last, her back still turned toward him. "Of course they were looking for Athena Courtland, and they treated me rather roughly at first, thinking I was a boy. You can imagine their surprise when they discovered who I really was. I suppose they hadn't expected to find me so easily."

"Who sent them, Kensington?" Lochiel demanded.

Athena nodded, her face still averted. "My aunt had died unexpectedly, you see, and he was hoping to fetch me home in time for the funeral."

"How kind of him," Lochiel remarked sardonically.

Though Athena had always bridled whenever he had used a similar tone with her in the past, she merely turned her head to give him a vague smile. Softly she added, "When I first decided to leave West York to find Fletcher, my aunt did her best to prevent me from going. By defying her I must have unwittingly convinced her that she had lost control of me completely. According to Mercy, my maid, she was quite beside herself the day I left, and Dr. Nolan seems to believe that the shock might have been too much of a strain on her heart."

Guilt and sadness mingled on her beautiful face. "Can you imagine how relieved she must have felt when Stephen arrived the next morning, quite oblivious to my absence, to offer for my hand? 'Twas her idea to draw up a marriage contract to assure herself that someone with authority, meaning Stephen, of course, would look after me once I returned."

"Yet Kensington, not satisfied with a contract, suggested the proxy papers instead," Lochiel said pointedly. "That way he could have you whether you consented to marry him or not."

Athena's eyes flashed. " 'Tis true the proxy marriage was his idea, but he never intended to make use of it. 'Twas only after Aunt Amelia died unexpectedly several days later that he realized 'twould be in my best interest to exercise his rights. After all, I'd been left without a guardian and couldn't be expected to live here alone until my brothers returned from the war!"

"How noble of Kensington," Lochiel grated. "I'd no idea you were so enamored of him."

"Damn you, Lochiel!" Athena burst out bitterly. Why did he have to insist on making this difficult for her? " 'Twas you who convinced me that marriage to Stephen was not the worst thing that could ever happen to me. What you said to me the night you came here, the way you—you—" She broke off, afraid that the protective shell about her heart was far too brittle after all. "And then when Fletcher w-was shot—" She tried again, but her voice broke and she had to turn away, biting her lips to keep the tears from trickling down her cheeks.

Lochiel clenched his fists in helpless frustration. She would shatter if he touched her, he knew, and her pride would never allow her to forgive him. "How is Fletcher?" he asked instead.

The slim shoulders lifted in a shrug. "He's been unconscious since Stephen and Wills brought him home. Dr. Nolan's come twice to bleed him, but it didn't do any good."

"Do you have any idea who was responsible?"

She turned to face him, a sad smile playing on her lips. "You had them so up in arms that night, Lochiel! It could have been anyone."

"Athena—"

Alarmed by the softening she thought she heard in his tone, she retreated a step and was relieved when Wills appeared in the doorway with a serving tray containing the brandy decanter and a crystal snifter.

"Will that be all, miss?" he asked, sending a meaningful glance in Lochiel's direction.

Athena nodded firmly. She could take care of herself. During the lonely hours she had tended Fletcher, not knowing if he would live or die, she had managed to convince herself that her love for Lochiel Blackmoor was gone. Thinking of how quickly he had doubted her, how he had ridden away while Fletcher lay bleeding in her arms, she had come to the conclusion that little else was left for her than to turn to Stephen Kensington for help.

She had been astonished and grateful at Stephen's leadership the night Fletcher had been shot. Alerted by her screams, he had arrived on the scene and quickly taken command of the situation. After organizing litter bearers and sending the remaining volunteers off into the darkness to search for the person responsible for shooting Fletcher, he had taken Athena into his arms and lovingly comforted her.

Throughout the next few days he had remained discreetly in the background, always there when Athena needed him, yet never forcing himself upon her. He himself had volunteered to return to his parents' house to stay until Fletcher had recovered, thus taking the normal pressures of a newly wedded bride from Athena's beleaguered shoulders.

The aversion and despair she had felt upon returning to Courtland Grace to find herself married to him had gradually begun to disappear. Having suffered too much heartbreak even for a woman of her iron will, Athena found herself turning to the one man she had vowed never to love, and turning her back forever on the man she did love.

"I'll be close by if you need anything else," Wills was saying, casting another dour glance in Lochiel's direction.

"Thank you, Wills," Athena replied solemnly, though a sparkle of amusement had crept into her eyes at the thought of the thin, middle-aged footman trying to physically expel the muscular Highlander from her house.

"I cannot believe you would willingly consent to remain married to a swine like Kensington."

Athena turned to find Lochiel towering over her, the brandy snifter in one long-fingered hand. A flash of anger shot through her, born of the undeniable awareness that his nearness could still affect her so strongly.

"Stephen is willing to help me start a new life," she flared at him, eyes blazing into the hostile silver ones so close to hers. " 'Tis more than you could ever offer me, Lochiel Blackmoor! Stephen knows about us—he knows you and I were—" Color flooded her face, but she forced herself to continue. "He was willing to make me his wife even though no respectable man would tolerate what I've done. By forgiving me, he has seen to it that naught will ever damage the Courtland name, despite what you said before the entire assembly at my wedding reception!"

The tinkle of glass caused her eyes to fall from his, and she saw that the snifter had shattered in Lochiel's hand. Tossing the shards into the fireplace, he seized her by the arms and shook her cruelly.

"Damn you, Athena! You speak as though what happened between us was vile, an odious tarnish on your name." His hot breath was on her brow, his slashing mouth almost touching hers. "Tell me you really believe that and I'll leave here this moment, never to return."

She opened her mouth to say so, but he never gave her the chance. With a savage oath he pulled her against him, his lips covering hers with brutal need. Athena struggled to turn her head away, but Lochiel was relentless, his kiss growing deeper until it seemed that her very soul was being drawn from her body. She moaned low in her throat, and despite herself her lips parted beneath the onslaught of his. Slim arms entwined themselves about his powerful neck, and she pressed herself closer, feeling the taut muscles of his body through the sheerness of her wrapper. Athena felt herself drowning in the swirling sensations aroused by Lochiel's kiss, while an undeniable longing rose within her for this one man she had sworn to hate.

"Tell me, Athena." Lochiel's deep voice rang in her ear, his lips leaving a trail of fire along her burning throat. "Tell me that Kensington can kiss you like this. Tell me you'd rather let him make love to you and that he knows how to give you pleasure better than I do."

Athena's breathless sigh was lost as his lips found hers again, causing the fire to travel through every fiber of her being and centering at last in the secret recesses of her womanhood. Through the silk wrapper she could feel Lochiel's manhood rise taut against her, and she sobbed deep in her throat, wanting him yet knowing it would be utter madness to succumb to his raw desire.

"No!" she cried, wrenching herself away, though the denial was little more than a moan of despair. Loathing herself for having responded to his kiss, hating him for having shattered her carefully nurtured composure, Athena slapped the lean face above hers, the sound cracking accusingly in the silent room.

"You may be able to sway me still with your practiced kisses," she confessed in a voice that shook dangerously, "but you'll never own my mind or my heart, Lochiel Blackmoor! I've made my choice, and 'tis Stephen who will have them. Since first I laid eyes on you I've suffered naught but humiliation and abuse at your hands. Stephen has never said an unkind word to me in his life. How can I possibly compare the two of you when you will never be the sort of man he is?"

Lochiel's visage had darkened as he stared down into the flashing blue eyes. For a mad moment he was tempted to seize Athena in his arms and tear the wrapper from her body, to drive deep inside her and prove that her accusations were nothing more than lies. It was he, not Kensington, who knew how to caress her, where to touch her perfect body so that her eyes darkened with yearning for him alone.

In his rage he very nearly lost control of himself, but even as he reached for her he stopped, arms falling uselessly to his sides. A grim smile began to play on his sensual mouth and his eyes were like steel as he gazed down into her flushed, angry face.

"Very well, Mrs. Kensington," he said softly. "I wish you happiness in your married life."

With cold finality he turned away and was gone, and Athena, left alone in the salon, felt a chill settle over her soul. She had made the right decision, she told herself angrily while hot tears began to roll down her cheeks. Lochiel had never said he loved her! 'Twas obvious that he had merely used her to sate his male needs. If she had succumbed to his passions tonight, she would have been throwing away the last chance she had of maintaining the respectability of the Courtlands and her own fierce integrity.

She was Stephen's wife, regardless of the fact that she had been an unwitting pawn in Aunt Amelia's game. Lochiel Blackmoor was a Scottish soldier, and once his tour of duty was finished he would return to his Highlands without her, perhaps even leaving her with a bastard child in her belly. No, she had done right to make the choice she had!

Hearing the faint sound of voices from outside, she ran to the window and drew back the heavy drapes. Pressing her nose to the glass, she saw Lochiel emerge from the stables astride Glenrobbie, his dark hair blowing in the wind. Tykie was speaking to him, but it was obvious that Lochiel wasn't listening.

As Athena watched he brought the whip down mercilessly on the black gelding's flanks, and the startled beast leaped away at a gallop. Moments later horse and rider had vanished into the night, and Athena turned resignedly away, the last vestiges of hope dimming from her tear-filled eyes.

Sixteen

"I say, Stephen, are you certain you want to build a house this size? Surely sixty rooms is rather extravagant for the two of you!"

Stephen Kensington's dark eyes narrowed irritably as he gazed into his father's fleshy face. The two men were alone in Ambrose's study, where they had withdrawn after supper so that Stephen could ask his father's opinion of the house he planned to build for his beautiful new bride. Not having expected to find himself the object of the older man's subtle criticism, he was forced to struggle with his temper.

"Athena will provide me with sons soon enough, but that is beside the point." His head came up arrogantly. "I want our house and everything in it to remind the citizens of New York that Kensington is a name to be respected."

"A fine ambition," Ambrose agreed, staring down at the blueprints spread on the desk before him. "But the cost, my boy, think of the cost! Your mother and I have already given you the land as a gift, and we'll do what we can to help with the financing, but . . ." He coughed delicately into a lace handkerchief and let his words trail away.

A smile tinged with contempt touched Stephen's lips. "You needn't worry about the cost, Father. 'Tis all been taken care of."

Ambrose's jowls quivered with silent laughter. "Your little bride must have brought a finer dowry than any of us suspected, eh? 'Sblood, I'd no idea the Courtlands were so rich!" Pride began to glow in his reddened eyes. "Ye did right to marry her when she ran away, lad. Took your mother and me by surprise, I'll confess, but there was no other way to clip that restless little pigeon's wings, I vow!"

"No, there was not," Stephen agreed with an answering gleam in his own eyes.

"I thought for sure we'd hear some criticism about it, given how well liked the Courtlands be in these parts," Ambrose added, refilling his glass from the decanter at his elbow. "So far the consensus seems to be that you did right by the girl. Only way to tame that spirited filly, egad!"

"I do not like to think that I won Athena's hand through trickery," Stephen remarked with sudden frostiness.

"Now, now, 'tisn't a soul in this colony what thinks that," Ambrose hastily assured his son. Settling his bulk into the leather armchair behind his desk, he pulled his wig from his head and began to comb it with vigor. "The girl's proven often enough that she's not one to be led about like a docile lamb. Always thought her behavior most unladylike," he added, head bowed, the lamplight reflecting the sheen of sweat on his shaven pate. "But that's what you like about her, eh?"

Stephen thought of Athena's wanton beauty and the sweet mysteries of her body he had yet to sample. "Indeed," he answered simply, raising his glass to his lips.

Anbrose's belly shook with mirth beneath the elaborately embroidered vest he wore. "And if she hadn't wanted you in turn, don't ye think she would've kicked up the devil's own hell by now? Egad, son, she seems quite content to abide by the arrangement, so surely there's not a soul in this colony thinks you deceived her into marryin' you!"

His father was right, of course, Stephen thought to himself as he began to roll up the collection of blueprints. Athena had seemed surprisingly willing to accept him as her husband, her acquiescence saving him the tiresome confrontation he had been expecting. Now only Fletcher stood in their way, and as soon as the poor devil made up his mind whether to live or die, Athena would have no more excuses in denying him the basic rights of a bridegroom.

Stephen's dark eyes narrowed to slits as he emptied the contents of his glass. By God, he prayed Fletcher Courtland would—

"Excuse me, sir."

A manservant stood in the doorway, expression solemn beneath his carefully tended wig.

"What's to do, Hunt?" Ambrose Kensington demanded happily. Setting his own wig back onto his head, he hauled himself to his feet, immensely pleased with the information he had managed to glean from his son tonight. If his new daughter-in-law was indeed as wealthy as Stephen intimated, his own financial woes would soon be ended. Of course, he'd have to go about this in a most discreet manner, but if—

"A visitor to see you, sir," Hunt was saying, turning to Stephen. "He did not give a name, and I'm afraid I've no idea who he is." The distasteful look on his face indicated that he did not think too highly of the caller.

"Did you show him in?"

Hunt drew himself up, affronted by the question. "I left him on the doorstep, sir."

"Ha, then he's surely no acquaintance of mine!" Ambrose chuckled.

"Your friends, Stephen, be the sort one always leaves on doorsteps! Go on, boy, see who 'tis. I'll finish the last of the port without ye."

Striving hard to conceal his annoyance, Stephen tucked the blueprints beneath his arm and strode out. How he disliked his fat, foolish father and how happy he would be once he and Athena were ensconced in the magnificent estate house he intended to build them on the tract of land they'd been presented upriver. A pox take the red-faced, drunken fool! By fall the house should be finished, and he'd not have to listen to his father's painfully boring conversations ever again!

The night air was refreshingly cool, but Stephen had eyes only for the hulking form of the man that waited for him in the shadows of the nearby hedgerow.

"What in hell are you doing here?" Stephen demanded, coming close enough to recognize the swarthy features of Toddman Tyner. "You gave me your word you'd return to Philadelphia once you'd been paid!"

"That be the problem, sir," Toddman pointed out politely. "I ain't been paid of yet."

Stephen could have groaned aloud, recalling that this was true. How much had he promised the man during their meeting in Albany? He'd had too much to drink, and it seemed to him that he'd been overly generous with his offer. Good Lord, he'd been desperate to find Athena, though! And it was true that Tyner had delivered her intact, exactly as he'd promised.

"How much is it I owe you?" he inquired coldly.

" 'Twould seem to me three guineas'd settle the debt."

Stephen was glad that the darkness hid his start of surprise. Three guineas! More than most men of Tyner's caliber earned in a year of honest work! Had he really promised this unsavory fellow so much?

"Brewster claims you're a gentleman o' yer word." Toddman Tyner's voice remained polite, but his tone warned Stephen that he was not about to be pacified with a few shillings pressed into his palm.

"Of course he's right," Stephen said haughtily, annoyed that a lowborn cur like Toddman Tyner would dare speak so rudely to a member of the gentry. "I apologize for the delay in settling our affairs, Mr. Tyner. Tomorrow I shall have my banker in Albany draw up a draft in your name and—"

A blunt finger came out of the darkness to tap him softly on the chest. "No drafts, Mr. Kensington. Gold. 'Tis what we agreed on and what I'll take from you now."

Stephen struggled to control his temper. He had no intention of paying out a sum that large and wondered what arrangements could be made by tomorrow to convince the surly fellow that he should be grateful for whatever he got.

"Very well. Until tomorrow, then, Mr. Tyner," was all he said, inclining his head curtly and striding back into the house.

In the hallway he was intercepted by his mother, a plump, nervous woman who was wont to prattle excessively and bore both her family and long-suffering staff to distraction.

"Oh, Stephen, whatever shall I do?" she quavered, tears glistening in her kohl-rimmed eyes.

"Is aught amiss, Mother?" Stephen asked politely, striving to conceal the lingering annoyance he felt at Toddman Tyner's audacity.

"That horrid girl your father insisted we hire to help in the kitchen dropped the roast Belle has been curing for the past three days! The dogs were upon it before it could be rescued!" Tears welled and began to trickle down her powdered cheeks.

"What a pity," Stephen remarked indifferently. "Is there aught you expect me to do about it?"

Leda Kensington twisted her plump, bejeweled fingers together. "You know perfectly well 'twas to be served to our guests tomorrow! I've no idea what to offer them now, and Marianne de Vries will surely spread the news throughout the entire colony if I dare substitute something as base as—as fowl!"

Stephen could barely maintain his sympathetic smile. Bloody hell, he'd forgotten all about the intimate little dinner party his mother had planned for tomorrow to celebrate his marriage. A large-scale celebration would have been tasteless in view of Amelia Bower's recent death and the fact that only five days had passed since Fletcher Courtland's shooting.

The thought of enduring an evening of mindless chatter set Stephen's teeth on edge, but he had agreed to it mainly to keep his mother happy. To his surprise she had even managed to persuade Athena to leave her brother's sickroom long enough to attend. Perhaps that in itself would make the evening tolerable and also offer him an excuse for stalling on Toddman Tyner's payment while he considered how to get rid of the persistent fellow.

"Stephen, are you listening to me?" His mother was all but wailing by now. "Whatever shall I do?"

"Zounds, woman!" came the impatient voice of Ambrose Kensington from the nearby salon. "How can a man find peace with ye babblin' about tomorrow's meals? Didn't Belle tell you there was a side o' pork left down in the smokehouse?"

Leda's tears flowed faster. "Pork! Oh, Mr. Kensington, we couldn't possibly serve pork!"

"I'm sure you'll find something appropriate," Stephen said placatingly, patting his mother's hand. "You always do." Unable to tolerate any more, he rang for his coat and headed down to the stables, thinking that a drink or two with friends in town might help improve his mood.

Waiting for his horse to be saddled, he found himself thinking of the things his father had said to him earlier that evening. Was it true that most people considered his proxy marriage to Athena Courtland a blessing? Did they really admire him for daring to discipline an untamed woman few would have wished to battle themselves?

His lips curved into a satisfied smile. If that were indeed the case, then everything had turned out far better than he had ever imagined.

Bright fingers of light escaped through a parting in the heavy drapes covering the windows in the Kensingtons' formal dining room. Through the glazed glass one could hear the clink of cutlery on china and the boisterous laughter of the assembled guests. Now and then a shadow fell upon the rich velvet hangings as a footman hurried to refill a wineglass or clear a plate for the next course. It was obvious from the brisk conversation and the amount of empty wine bottles that were carried from the room that Leda Kensington's party was an enormous success.

In the stone stable beyond the house a yawning groom settled himself on a stool near the doorway, content to savor the cool night air until it was time to lead out the carriages for the dispersing guests. Stars twinkled above the darkened mountains, and the breeze that blew from the river was fresh with the smells of spring. Scratching himself and yawning again, the groom leaned his head against the wall and contentedly closed his eyes. A moment later he had fallen into a deep slumber, his soft snores masking an odd rustling in the hedges across the pebbled courtyard.

Kensington Manor, with its imposing facade and numerous wings, had been landscaped by an Italian architect hired years ago by the ever-appearance-conscious Leda. Boxwoods, lilacs, and countless other varieties of perennial shrubs had been planted in geometric patterns about the property in an effort to re-create the rolling parks of a typical English country estate. Over the years the plantings had grown extremely large, and many of them now prevented a clear view of the gardens from the lower-story windows of the house itself. In fact, most of them had grown broad enough to offer ample concealment to anyone who wished to approach without being seen.

Toddman Tyner, crouching amid the boxwoods beneath the lighted windows, was grateful for the opportunity to stand undetected beneath the dining room itself, where he could easily overhear the conversations within. Having spent most of the day in West York waiting fruitlessly for

Stephen Kensington's summons, he had knocked on the imposing oak door, only to be informed by a hostile footman that Mr. Kensington was busily preparing for his wedding celebration and could not be had at the moment.

It was obvious to Toddman Tyner that Stephen Kensington had no intention of paying the money owed him, an oversight the unsavory Philadelphian was about to remedy. He wasn't exactly sure what he was going to do, but he was not daunted by the number of foppishly attired guests visible through the slit in the curtains. Once he chose to strike, he would do so swiftly and no one would be the wiser, least of all these overweight dandies with their dissipated expressions and too-loud laughs.

"I've already told you, Stephen, I've left Fletcher long enough! I really must go home!"

Toddman's curious gaze swung from the windows above his head to the stone terrace, which was separated from the dining room by a row of tall French windows. His interest quickened when he saw Stephen Kensington step through them, his hand wrapped restrainingly about the arm of a young woman whose dark green gown shimmered like a gemstone in the muted light. Moving stealthily from one shrub to another, he was able to position himself directly below the young couple, his presence further concealed by the high stone wall of the terrace.

"Surely you can stay a little longer," Stephen coaxed, a hopeful smile on his lips.

"I'm sorry, I can't. Your mother promised me I'd only have to make a brief appearance, and I've been gone too long as it is."

Toddman Tyner had to admire the determination in the soft voice as well as the arrogant tilt of the proud beauty's head. A small waist and womanly breasts encased in emerald silk gave evidence that she was a creature of delectable charms, and he found pleasure in the bold manner in which she shook herself free of Kensington's grip.

" 'Twould be kind of you if you'd have someone fetch my horse," she added more gently, aware that she had been speaking rather harshly to him.

She turned her head as she spoke so that the man watching from the ground below saw the long, slim length of her neck and the distinctive beauty of her features. By God, 'twas the Courtland wench, Toddman Tyner thought in astonishment. Who would've thought that the bedraggled little whelp he'd brought back to West York was in truth such a tempting morsel of womanflesh?

"I should've had 'er just for the sport," he grumbled to himself, for he had often taken his pleasure with the women he'd been paid to find. Toddman derived a great deal of enjoyment defiling someone else's property, particularly when they screamed and raked him with their nails, especially the virgins. As far as he knew, none of them had ever raised an accusing finger against him—he'd seen to that with his dire threats and cruel blows—and if they had, he was usually too far away by then to suffer retribution.

Athena Courtland hadn't appealed to him at all with her breeches and boots and seemingly flat, boyish breasts. Looking at her now, Tyner realized she must have kept them bound and that she had deliberately concealed her seductive golden locks beneath a battered cap. At the time he had been none too impressed with her square jaw and almost mannish appearance, yet he saw now that those same undesirable attributes were stunningly unique when enhanced by silken finery.

Aye, she was a rare one a'right, the heavyset man with the cruel, possessive eyes thought to himself, but he was not one to mourn a lost opportunity. His purpose in coming here was to collect his three guineas, not to avail himself of Kensington's new bride. Besides, from what he'd heard about her in the few days he'd been hanging about waiting to be paid, she was dangerous fire to be playing with. Hadn't half the menfolk in West York ridden after the man who'd insulted her at the wedding, all of them hellbent on revenge?

" 'Tisn't no kettle ye'll be burnin' yer fingers on, me fine fellow," Toddman Tyner muttered to himself. "Ripe piece o' womanhood she be, but ye'll only end up shot through the back like that brother o' her'n if you try anything."

Stephen, in the meantime, had resigned himself to the determination burning coolly in Athena's dark eyes. Annoyance overwhelmed him when he realized that he would have to curb his desires yet another night, to grapple once again with his rising lust while Athena played nursemaid to her dying brother. Damn the wench, couldn't she spare him one brief hour? Didn't a wife owe that much to her husband regardless of the tragic circumstances surrounding their marriage?

"Are you certain you can't entrust Fletcher to Mercy's care?" he asked huskily. "Just for tonight?"

Even Toddman could hear the longing in Stephen's tone, and a cruel smile curved his fleshy lips. So the rutting young bridegroom hadn't possessed the lovely lady yet, eh? An interesting discovery. How could he use it to his best advantage?

"Oh, Stephen, as soon as Fletcher's out of danger we'll have plenty of time to ourselves," Athena said soothingly, feeling genuinely guilty. Hadn't she sworn to herself that she would be a proper wife to him and deny him naught? Yet how could he expect her to concern herself with anything but Fletcher's health? His fever was growing worse by the day, and even now she was overcome with a fierce need to return to Courtland Grace and assure herself that he was still alive.

For a moment there was silence between them, and the unnoticed spectator amid the shrubbery below was careful not to give himself away with even the slightest rustling of branches.

"Very well," Stephen said at last. "I'll have the carriage readied."

Athena's brows drew together. "But I rode over on Ballycor!"

Stephen took her hands in his. "And scandalized Mama into a fit of the vapors by doing so! Thank goodness no one else saw you arriving astride that enormous beast. Can't you travel in a proper conveyance like other well-bred young ladies?"

" 'Tis half the distance across the fields, and Ballycor can clear any fence between our property and yours. I would have lost another half-hour if I'd taken the road," Athena pointed out.

Stephen laughed indulgently, though inwardly he was determined to put an end to his wife's unseemly ways as soon as possible. "Very well, you may ride home if you wish, but I insist on accompanying you. 'Tis late and quite unsafe for you to be about alone."

He was gone before she could reply, leaving her to pace restlessly to and fro, oblivious to the eyes watching her interestedly from the darkness. Oh, if only Stephen would hurry! She should never have agreed to come tonight, never have left Fletcher at all. Why, even in the space of an hour his condition could take a turn for the worst and—

"Stop it!" she whispered to herself, hands clenched into small fists. Fletcher was going to live no matter how grave his injuries. Courtland blood flowed in his veins, after all, and any day now Jeremy and Colm should be arriving in response to her summons. Surely their presence alone would be enough to strengthen him once he regained consciousness!

Toddman Tyner's eyes had narrowed speculatively as he watched the distraught young woman pace about the darkened balcony. Forgotten were the laughing guests in the nearby dining room; forgotten, too, was the plan he had originally formulated for entering the house undetected and confronting Stephen Kensington alone in some secluded parlor. This silk-clad beauty was all he needed to assure prompt payment of the three guineas owed him, and if he had his fun with her before returning her to her distraught bridegroom, then all the greater his reward.

'Twould be best just to abduct her into the darkness, Toddman decided, licking his lips as the plan took shape in his mind. Grab her before she could alert the revelers with her screams and take her down to Albany where he knew a dozen places to safely hide her.

Actually, why bother overpowering her at all? He'd been respectful enough to her on the way back to West York, thanks to Asa Brewster's whining insistence that Kensington wouldn't tolerate any abuse of his coveted prize. The lovely Athena Courtland would surely remember him and readily agree to walk with him for a moment in the garden while he discussed something urgent with her.

The thought of possessing that pale ivory body caused the saliva to flow in Toddman Tyner's mouth. Moving cautiously from his hiding place, he was about to call to her when the sound of a sharp voice in the garden brought him to a standstill.

"A pox on your posturings, Kensington! Have out with it, man, before I lose my patience!"

The irately uttered words caused Toddman to scurry back into his hiding place while Athena, standing in the darkness on the terrace, froze in surprise. Who could possibly be speaking to Stephen in such a rude tone of voice?

"By my troth, sir, hold your tongue! They'll overhear us!"

Athena gave a start as she recognized Ambrose Kensington's hushed plea. From her vantage point on the terrace she could see her pudgy father-in-law pause beneath a trellis of climbing roses not far from the house. The man with him had his back turned to her, and she had no idea who he might be.

"The lot of 'em are half besotted," this unidentified stranger announced with a contemptuous air. "There's a pleasant roaring in their ears, I wager, and they'll hear naught of our conversation."

Suddenly aware that she was eavesdropping on a private matter, Athena caught her breath and pressed herself against the ivy-covered wall of the house. She had no desire to announce her presence to the obviously angry men below her, and she prayed that she was not about to become privy to some unpleasant secret about either of them.

Likewise aware that he had stumbled onto a clandestine meeting not intended for the ears of outsiders, Toddman Tyner held himself very still. Sometimes extremely useful information could be garnered from chance encounters such as these, and he thrust Athena and the fate of his three guineas into the background for the time being.

"Out with it, Ambrose," the broad back with its lavishly embroidered coat commanded. "Why insist on this meeting? You know everything was arranged days ago."

Athena watched as Ambrose dabbed the sweat from his brow with a white handkerchief. His wig looked sadly wilted, and his expression was fearful in the dim light that fell from the house.

"Those arrangements be the trouble, sir," he blurted at last. "I'll not do it any longer!"

His companion threw back his head and uttered a bark of derisive laughter. It was then that Athena recognized him as Thomas Painsley, a merchant from Albany who had been sitting across the board from her at dinner tonight. Her father had done business with him from time to time, and it was said that he had made a fortune investing in the abundant commodities the colony of New York shipped across the Atlantic to England.

He was a tall and neatly groomed individual with a roving eye for pretty women. Though he was well respected in New York, there were many who wondered at his enormous success in sea trade, and Foster Courtland had broken relations with him several years before his death because of the unscrupulous business ties Painsley was suspected to possess.

Athena had never really liked him, for he had piercing eyes that made her feel unaccountably cold whenever he looked at her. Jeremy had told her once that he had approached their father over her hand and that the consequent friction between the two men had helped to dissolve their relationship. Thomas Painsley was, after all, twenty years older than Athena and was rumored to have left a wife and child back home in England. He never spoke of them or acknowledged himself as married, which deepened the mystery around him, but few women could resist his dark good looks or men his business acumen.

"You want out, Ambrose?" Thomas Painsley was saying now, the derisive laughter still evident in his tone. " 'Tis rather late for that, wouldn't you say? Think what would happen if you were to lose this . . . ah . . . convenient source of income before your debts were settled. Have you developed a sudden yearning for debtors' prison?"

"I've found another means of handling my finances," Ambrose retorted coolly, seeming to have collected himself. "I've done enough for you, Painsley, and now I wish to end our relationship."

There was a long pause, and Athena didn't care too much for the Albany merchant's sudden stillness. Suppose he was about to turn violent?

"Very well, Ambrose." Thomas Painsley's voice was low and dangerous. "You can get out if you wish, but not before this last exchange. The goods have been paid for, and you know what will happen should we fail to deliver."

Ambrose's pale face glistened in the dim light. "You can have it your way this time, Painsley. Just leave me be in the future."

Thomas sketched a mocking bow, and his soft laughter floated to Athena on the terrace. "If peace is your goal, my friend, I certainly hope you find it."

Turning heel, he vanished into the shadows, pausing long enough to add over one shoulder, "On the Sabbath at midnight, as agreed."

"My lads'll be waiting by the mill," Ambrose responded miserably.

For a moment he stood dejectedly beneath the roses, then kicked savagely at a clod of grass with one silver-buckled shoe. There was open rebellion in his fleshy face, but both Athena and Toddman Tyner saw fear as well, and each wondered what to do with the information he or she had unwittingly gleaned.

Athena promptly forgot about it when Stephen brought Ballycor to her and the two of them galloped off into the night. Worry over Fletcher's health drove all else from her mind, and she responded distractedly to Stephen's lighthearted conversation. At Courtland Grace she bade him a brief farewell, without bothering to invite him in, and Wills was the only one who saw the expression on Stephen's face as Athena hurried upstairs to the sickroom, her bridegroom already forgotten.

"Your mistress has a great deal on her mind these days," Stephen commented with an attempted smile as he met the footman's curious gaze. It annoyed him that he had been so transparent, but, by God, Athena could have at least bidden him a tender good night instead of dashing away without another word!

"Your patience is a great help to her during this troubled time, sir," Wills responded.

Stephen scowled. Was the fellow making fun of him? Tykie Downs's insolence was bad enough. He'd not tolerate it from another of Athena's servants. Just wait until she was his acknowledged property!

Without even asking after his brother-in-law, Stephen left the house and rode briskly away. He'd give Athena a few more days, he decided, but then 'twas over with her coddling and nursing. He'd make her see that her duty lay with her new husband and the life they would have together.

"If you'll only do me the favor of dying soon, my dear Fletcher," Stephen said aloud. " 'Twould make everything so much more simple."

For Athena the next several days continued much as they had since Fletcher's accident. She slept little, and then only in brief stretches on the sofa near her brother's bed. Meals were taken from a tray that Prudence sent up, while Mercy sat beside her and did her best to coax her mistress to eat.

Fletcher's fever continued to ravage his weakened body, leaving his skin transparent and waxy, his limbs wracked with spasms. Athena sponged him constantly in an effort to cool him and patiently tended the ugly hole the musketball had plowed through his shoulder right above his heart. For her it was a cruel irony that the wound was healing well while fever continued to sap Fletcher of his precious strength.

"I'm fearin' for the lass as well as the master," Tykie admitted in a troubled whisper to Prudence in the kitchen one warm spring morning not long after the Kensingtons' dinner party.

Swallows dived amid the apple trees beyond the windows, and the lowing of the cows in the fields came to them on the sweetly scented breeze. Prudence was bent over the big oak table kneading pastry dough with her capable hands. Pausing to push a strand of unruly hair from her brow, she regarded the bearded Highlander with a frown of her own.

"Pale and thin she be," she agreed with pursed lips. "Won't eat though I sends up her favorite things every night. She'll be makin' herself ill, too, if this be goin' on much longer!"

"If only Master Colm or Jeremy would retairn," Tykie added mournfully, not even interested in stealing a spoonful of the fragrant pie filling bubbling over the fire. "I canna believe they couldna get leave wi' Master Fletcher sae ill!"

"There's more for the army to worry about at the moment than the fate of a single man," Prudence observed, though her tone indicated that Fletcher's health should have taken precedence over the entire war effort itself. 'Twas a pity no one really knew where the Courtland twins were, for she and Tykie would have left home long before this to fetch them back. They were the only ones, she knew, who could persuade Miss Athena to get some much-needed rest.

"I warrant Major Blackmoor could find 'em," Tykie remarked, the thought bringing a sudden brightening to his unhappy countenance.

"I'll thank ye not to mention that name in my kitchen!" Prudence snapped. "You'll be rememberin', I hope, that what he said about Miss Athena was the cause of Master Fletcher's injuries to begin with!"

Tykie nodded placatingly, unwilling to do verbal battle with the formidable Prudence Goodson. Inwardly, however, he was mulling the possibility over in his mind. Regardless of what everyone else thought of Lochiel Blackmoor, he had never lost his respect for him or the conviction that, outside of Miss Athena's brothers, no one else had ever handled her so well. Hadn't he seen as much during the long journey back from Fort Shuyler? Why, once or twice he'd almost been sure Major Blackmoor intended to turn Miss Athena over his knee! Mayhap Miss Athena had suspected the same thing, for she'd instantly become docile and obedient—an almost unheard-of turn of events.

"I'll be lookin' i' on the beasties," Tykie said now, lumbering to his feet, still mindful of his broken foot. "Ballycor be needin' a wee bit o' work if he plans tae win this season's races," he added innocently, well aware that

Prudence was clever enough to guess what he had in mind if he were to suddenly take the stallion on a lengthy ride without an explanation.

'Twas true that a good long ride would limber the stallion up a bit, Tykie thought blandly to himself. Surely Miss Athena would agree that he hadn't had much exercise in the past few months and wouldn't object to the suggestion that he be taken on an outing—perhaps to Albany and back?

"Prudence! Tykie!"

Both of them exchanged startled looks at the breathless cry that came from the hallway, each one's unspoken fear mirrored in the eyes of the other.

" 'Tis Miss Athena," Prudence murmured, hastily wiping her hands on a linen dish towel. "God have mercy, what—"

She was interrupted by her mistress, who burst like a whirlwind through the kitchen door, disheveled golden hair flying about her shoulders. Weariness was etched into her small face, but her eyes were glowing like stars.

"Fletcher's fever has broken!" she cried, hands clasped together like a delighted child's. "Tykie, fetch Dr. Nolan as quickly as you can! I think he's going to live!"

"Och, bairn, bairn, if it be true!" Tykie stammered while tears coursed unashamed down his leathery cheeks.

"He's going to get better," Athena assured him, straightening her stooped shoulders with a conviction that neither of them could ignore. "Just wait and see."

Dr. Nolan was more cautious in his optimism, but his words were encouragement enough for the small group that gathered in the sitting room of the bridal suite to await his verdict. It amused and touched the elderly gentleman to see how protectively the servants gathered around their mistress as she rose at his appearance following the examination.

The fact that her husband was not in attendance did not even occur to him. He had known Athena since childhood, and she would always be a Courtland to him, not a Kensington. It had been difficult for him to believe that this spirited woman, who had always delighted him with her precocious ways as a child, could have consented to marry an arrogant boor like Stephen Kensington, whom Dr. Nolan secretly despised.

Forgetting his musings and suspicions, he smiled encouragingly into the worried faces that were turned his way.

"How is he, doctor?" Athena asked hoarsely. With Tykie's muscular arm placed protectively about her shoulders, she appeared helplessly young and fragile.

"Not out of danger yet, I'm afraid," the gray-haired physician responded truthfully, "but I consider his lowered temperature a good sign. A very good sign indeed."

"Will he live?" Tykie demanded bluntly, voicing the question that was foremost in their minds.

The half smile on Dr. Nolan's lips broadened. "I would hazard a guess that his chances are good."

"The good Lord be thanked," Prudence and Mercy breathed together while Wills and Tykie beamed.

Athena herself, aware that this was an excellent prognosis from someone as conservative as Dr. Nolan, could scarcely keep the tears of joy from her eyes. Fletcher was going to live! Suddenly it was as if her legs could no longer bear her weight, and if Tykie hadn't been holding her she might have collapsed.

"You're going to get ill yourself if you don't rest, Miss Athena," she heard Dr. Nolan say from what seemed like a very great distance. Smiling up into his stern features, she murmured unintelligibly as Tykie lifted her into his arms and carried her to her room. She was asleep before Mercy and Prudence had even undressed her, yet the smile continued to linger on her lips, giving her exhausted face the undeniable sweetness of repose.

"Do you know, Miss Athena," Mercy said to her the following evening as she joined her mistress in the parlor, " 'tis a miracle how quickly Master Fletcher's recovering now that his fever's gone."

Athena nodded happily as she bent over the breeches she was mending. Fletcher's clothes were in appalling condition, and with Mercy's help she was trying to put some semblance of order into his wardrobe since he would soon be up and about.

"Mistress Kensington was asking after you at worship today," Mercy added, biting the thread with her small white teeth. "I told her Master Fletcher was ever so much better but that you didn't want to leave him so soon."

Athena was forced to grin. "I vow she considers my soul eternally damned since I've missed so many church services."

Her breath caught in her throat as she recalled that today was the Sabbath, the realization bringing to mind the mysterious exchange she had witnessed between Ambrose Kensington and Thomas Painsley in the garden of Kensington Manor several nights ago. Something unusual was going to happen at the mill at midnight, Athena remembered, something Ambrose Kensington was reluctantly involved in and which Thomas Painsley considered a rendezvous of great significance.

Though she had forgotten all about their encounter until today, Athena was suddenly determined to see for herself what odd activities occupied her father-in-law's nocturnal hours. The mill Ambrose had referred to stood near the river some four miles beyond the village common. She could easily cover the distance on horseback, Athena knew, for Ballycor was familiar enough with the countryside to negotiate anything in the darkness. Mercy could look after Fletcher while she was gone, which would leave her free long enough to discover what sort of unscrupulous business Ambrose was involved in.

Athena said nothing of her plans to anyone, especially Tykie, who would have forbidden her to go. Though it had occurred to her that it might prove dangerous to spy on Thomas Painsley's men, Athena had no intention of changing her mind. No sooner had the clock downstairs struck half past eleven that night than she quietly left the house after assuring herself that Fletcher was resting comfortably and that Mercy was somewhere nearby.

She was dressed once again in the same buckskin breeches and heavy wool vest she had worn during her journey to Fort Shuyler and back. Surveying herself in the looking glass in her room, she had berated herself fiercely for the pang that had swept through her as she saw before her the slim, blue-eyed lad who had been befriended by Lochiel Blackmoor's savage Highlanders.

Unbidden, memories had rushed to her mind, and it was almost as if she could feel Lochiel's presence, recapture the joy and pain of accompanying his small army of men through the wilderness. Yet that part of her life was over now, she reminded herself, turning away from the image that gazed back at her in the glass. She was Stephen Kensington's wife and not some lovestruck young girl yearning after the likes of one Lochiel Blackmoor.

Soft lips pulled into a stern line, Athena had thrust Lochiel from her mind and strode across the grounds to the stables. The sound of Tykie's sonorous snoring came to her from the tiny room above the loft, and Athena had to smother a laugh upon hearing it. Tykie never failed to sleep soundly on a full stomach, and Prudence's bountiful Sabbath supper was to thank for the grizzled Highlander's lack of vigilance tonight.

No longer afraid that she'd be caught, Athena led Ballycor from his stall and saddled him quickly, taking care not to let the stirrups clang together. The big animal must have sensed her urgency, for he began to whicker when she bent to buckle the girth.

"If you aren't quiet, Tykie will hear us after all," she whispered, leading him to the mounting block and slinging her leg over his back. A full yellow moon hung over the treetops, and once the darkened house had fallen from view, Athena was able to kick Ballycor into a gallop. Leaning low over his gleaming white neck, she urged him across the deserted fields, her heart filled with nervous anticipation.

West York's only grist mill stood on a bend in the shallow, rock-strewn river a full half-mile away from the tidy cottage belonging to Joshua Brinston, the miller. Athena was familiar with the layout of the mill, for she had accompanied Tykie there often enough as a child to watch Courtland Grace's grain being ground into flour for use in Prudence's kitchen.

Though she hadn't been here in many years, she could well remember which fork in the path led down to the mill and which one meandered onward to Joshua's home. Knowing that the bright moonlight would make it difficult to conceal Ballycor's white coat, Athena dismounted when the mill came into view and left the stallion tied to a tree near the river's edge. The big stallion, accustomed to his mistress's odd habits, made no fuss at being abandoned. Lowering his head, he began to crop grass.

Moving silently amid the trees, Athena soon emerged downriver from the mill. In the moonlight she could easily make out the big, creaking waterwheel and the ghostly outline of the two-story building. Though the hour of midnight had already come and gone, there was nothing save the gurgling of the water to indicate that Athena was not alone. She found herself wondering if she had been mistaken about the meeting place Ambrose had mentioned. Had he been referring to another mill in some other town?

Athena's breath caught in her throat as a thin, flickering light appeared without warning amid the beams of the open shed that adjoined the mill. Moments later another light flared briefly in the darkness, this one farther upriver where a covered bridge traversed the foaming water. Slowly the two lights began to move toward one another until they finally met on a grassy knoll not far from the riverbed. Athena's eyes widened seeing that they were lanterns hung from the wooden slats of a pair of mule-drawn carts.

Though it was too dark to make out the number of men moving about in the shadows, Athena could see that they were transferring a load of long wooden crates from one of the carts to the other. It was obvious to her that some sort of exchange was being made, but what were the goods and who were the parties involved? A clandestine rendezvous at this time of night in an area as remote as Joshua Brinston's mill could only mean some illegal activity!

Silently, Athena crept closer. She was not afraid, for she was quite at home in the forest and could move as silently as an Indian amid the trees. As a precaution she had traded her heavy leather shoes for a pair of deerskin moccasins, which enabled her to tread noiselessly across the leaf-strewn ground.

Crouching behind a weathered barrel that leaned against the outer wall of the mill, Athena strained her eyes to see what was happening on the knoll above her. It was impossible to recognize the features of any of the men transferring the crates, and the few words they uttered were so low that she couldn't make them out.

Athena bit her lip indecisively. If something unlawful was transpiring before her eyes, shouldn't she ride into town to fetch help? Yet what good would that do? By the time she returned, the mule carts and the goods they had carried would be long gone.

"Halt in the name of the king!"

The shouted command that came out of the darkness took everyone by surprise. For a moment there was stunned silence among the men gathered about the carts, then all of them dropped their heavy burdens and began to run. Pistol shots cracked through the night, leaving chaos in their wake, and Athena gasped as over half a dozen horsemen galloped into the clearing behind her.

"Sergeant, I want every last one of them! Shoot any who try to resist!"

Athena's heart thundered in her breast, and she crouched even lower behind the barrel as the mounted leader's horse cantered past, churning dust into her face. She saw him come to a halt on a patch of hard earth near the enormous waterwheel, the moonlight falling full on his dark head and harshly chiseled features.

"Lochiel!"

The name fell in a shocked whisper from her lips.

He was wearing the uniform of a Highland officer, but the men who had accompanied him were not British Regulars. That they were trained in hand-to-hand combat was obvious, however, and Athena watched, open-mouthed, as they effortlessly subdued the struggling rowdies.

"I think that's all of 'em, Major Blackmoor," someone called at last.

"Line them up, sergeant," Lochiel replied. Still astride his horse, he gazed ruthlessly at the straggling line of captives that were being herded into the clearing before him. Dismounting at last, he handed the reins to a young soldier who had hurried to his side. Athena's throat grew tight as she watched him, thinking to herself how magnificent he looked towering over the bedraggled prisoners, his long legs encased in polished leather boots, an officer's sword resting casually against his hip.

"Divide them into groups," Lochiel ordered in the same curt tone Athena had heard him use before. "All colonials in one and Canadians—"

"Just a minute, sir!" a youthful voice interrupted him. "I've found another!"

Athena uttered a startled cry as she felt her collar packed firmly from behind. In the excitement she had forgotten to keep herself concealed, and the moonlight reflecting on the golden curls escaping from beneath her cap had alerted a watchful guard to her presence.

"Found 'im hidin' behind a barrel," her captor said as he dragged Athena into Lochiel's presence. Taking a second look at her, he added thoughtfully, "I warrant he's quite harmless, sir. Seems little older than a boy."

With her arms pinned painfully behind her back, Athena was forced to cease her useless struggles. Raising her head, she stared boldly into Lochiel Blackmoor's intimidating face and saw the startled look that crossed his stern features in response.

"Harmless, Jacobs?" Lochiel inquired coldly. "I wouldn't be so sure."

As he spoke he bent down and made a quick search of Athena's clothing, his mouth tightening grimly as he withdrew a pistol from her belt. Ignoring Jacobs's startled exclamation, he gave Athena a hard glance.

"I always wondered what had happened to this," he remarked coldly, recognizing it as his own. It was a handsomely wrought officer's pistol with silver appointments, a gift from the king himself, the same weapon Athena had taken with her for protection the night she had ridden off with Asa Brewster and Toddman Tyner.

"I was going to return it," Athena said with a scowl, but Lochiel had already turned away and was issuing orders in an even less charitable tone than before. The fact that he was furious was obvious to Athena when Jacobs released her and she found herself confronting him face to face. They were standing alone in the moon-drenched clearing beside the creaking waterwheel, Lochiel's men having withdrawn to carry out their orders.

"Were you simply passing by, Mrs. Kensington, or are you perchance a member of this unsavory group?"

Lochiel had folded his arms across his wide chest as he spoke and was regarding her with icy impatience. Athena found herself growing unnerved by his intimidating anger, and the realization galled her. What did she have to fear from this despicable cad? He meant nothing to her!

"I'm not one of them," she assured him haughtily, meeting his smoldering gaze squarely, "nor do I have the slightest idea who they are. I was hiding there behind that barrel when you arrived because I wanted to find out what—"

"You cursed little fool!" Lochiel rasped, and the contempt she heard in his voice caused the color to drain from her face. Never in all their stormy confrontations had he spoken to her so coldly before, and a pain she had thought long forgotten filled her heart with a steady, throbbing ache.

All at once Athena realized that it wasn't fear that had unnerved her when she had first gazed up into Lochiel's dark face, nor was it hatred that clogged her throat and made her heart hammer in her breast. She was still hopelessly attracted to Lochiel Blackmoor, and she had learned enough about the love between a man and woman to realize that his compelling masculinity, not her fear of him, was causing her to react so bitterly to his unkindness.

"I had to come tonight," she defended herself, hiding behind an icy aloofness that concealed her feelings from him. "I had to know what Ambrose Kensington was doing involved in this—this—" She broke off and regarded him with sudden uncertainty. "I don't even know what any of this is about!"

The childish frustration in her voice unexpectedly defused Lochiel's anger. "Impulsive as ever, aren't you?" he inquired softly. His eyes, a gleaming silver in the moonlight, were suddenly quite close. "Hasn't it ever occurred to you, Athena, that—"

"Major, we've got everything loaded up and ready for transport. Do you want to question the bastards before we lead 'em off?"

Lochiel straightened with an almost weary sigh and turned to the sergeant who had interrupted them. "Did you have any luck with them yourself?"

The burly shoulders lifted in a resigned shrug. "I didn't learn anything new, if that's what you mean, sir. Most of 'em are scared to death, but they won't mention any names besides Ambrose Kensington's." He shook his bewigged head in utter frustration. "Their leader must be a terrifying fellow, whoever he is. To a man jack they refuse to betray him."

"They'll talk once they're in custody," Lochiel responded confidently, then jerked his head in the direction of the waiting carts. "Get them out of here, sergeant. The sooner they're under lock and key the better. Bailey can take care of the crates."

"What about him, sir?" The sergeant gestured with open hostility toward Athena. "Want me to clap him in irons, too?"

The Highlander's lips twitched. "Believe me, sergeant, 'tis a tempting offer. I vow he's a bloodthirsty little devil, but I believe I can handle him myself."

"Yes, sir."

"Tell me what happened here tonight," Athena demanded as soon as the carts moved off with creaking wheels, the captured men, roped together, sitting under heavy guard.

The softness in Lochiel's visage abruptly vanished. "Your meddling is most unbecoming for a married woman, Mrs. Kensington. Instead of risking your pretty neck with foolish escapades, shouldn't you be at home warming your husband's bed?"

Athena gasped. "That isn't fair, Lochiel!"

"No?" He had her by the arms, his grip bruisingly painful. " 'Tis time you learned that your newly married status entails certain responsibilities, among them the adoption of the trappings of a proper lady. Do you think your husband would take kindly to the scandal if your presence here tonight were made known?"

Athena's head was whirling. What exactly would Stephen say? She had no idea, nor was she any wiser concerning the shipment of goods that Lochiel and his men had successfully intercepted. She didn't even know why he had involved himself in a civil matter like this when he was an officer in the British army, and it seemed likely that he wasn't going to give her the chance to find out. Oh, how stupidly she had handled this!

"Did you come alone?" Lochiel asked, and his tone warned her that his patience had all but run out.

She nodded wordlessly, her throat too dry to answer.

"On Ballycor?"

She nodded again. "I left him tethered downriver."

"Then I suggest you get him and ride back home. I'm not going to ask you how you learned about the rendezvous tonight, but I warn you that you may very well be called in for questioning should the men we captured tonight fail to supply us with the information we need."

Athena gasped. Lochiel wouldn't dare force her to stand up at a hearing, would he? "C-couldn't you just let me explain now?" she asked in a small voice.

His expression was so hard that she could scarcely believe he was the same man who had loved her so tenderly on a golden beach in the solitude of a virgin forest. "My dear Mrs. Kensington, we have nothing more to say to one another. You should have considered the consequences of your foolish actions before you left home tonight." His eyes branded her with his sarcasm. "If the thought of an interrogation in Albany distresses you, you might consider turning to your husband for support. Though I promise you"—his fingers tightened their hold about her arms—"should it come to light that Stephen was involved in his father's crimes, I'll personally see that both of them are hung by the neck."

Pushing her away from him, he added harshly, "Get out of here before I change my mind and haul you off to jail as well."

Athena stood rubbing her arms, her eyes dark with pain and accusation as she gazed into the hard face above hers. How could she ever have fancied herself in love with this cruel, dictatorial man?

"I hate you, Lochiel Blackmoor," she whispered.

His lean jaw tensed in the moonlight. "The feeling is quite mutual, madam."

She whirled wordlessly and fled from him while Lochiel continued to stand as though turned to stone, grappling with his anger and the frustrating turmoil this blue-eyed child-woman never failed to arouse within him.

"Corporal Bailey!"

His curt command was answered immediately by a hulking young man who carried a heavy musket effortlessly in his big, callused hands. "Aye, sir?"

"Take one of the horses and follow that lad until he's safely home," Lochiel instructed. "You needn't make your presence known."

"Very well, sir." The simple-minded corporal did not seem at all surprised by Major Blackmoor's odd request.

Dismissing Athena from his mind, Lochiel turned to oversee the reloading of the wooden crates that held, he well knew, dozens of newly forged muskets that had been smuggled out of Albany and were bound for the hands of French-sympathizing Algonquins. If Ambrose Kensington was guilty of treason, as Lochiel indeed suspected, he could very well end up paying for his crimes with his life. A frown marred his brow as he called for his horse, wondering what the consequences would mean for Athena.

As the mounted soldiers and the confiscated mule cart vanished down the winding trail, a heavy stillness descended upon the moon-drenched mill. An owl began to hoot somewhere high in the trees, only to fall silent when the door to the mill creaked slowly open. Looking cautiously about him to make certain he was alone, the man on the threshold stepped quickly outside and carefully slid the bolt behind him. Seconds later he was hurrying through the trees in the direction opposite that which the soldiers had taken.

Toddman Tyner was grinning to himself as he untethered his horse. Though he wasn't exactly sure yet what to do with his information, he knew himself clever enough to come up with something useful. His smug grin widened and he rubbed his hands together, recalling the heated exchange he had observed between Lochiel Blackmoor and Athena Kensington, whom he had recognized immediately in her faded breeches and woolen vest.

"Aye, my fine fellow," he chortled to himself, thinking of the unsuspecting Stephen Kensington, "three gold guineas won't even begin to cover what it'll cost you to learn what your wife's been up to!"

Seventeen

Fair hair spilling in riotous disarray to her hips, Athena leaned over and blew out the bedside lamp. Though the room was now plunged into darkness, the milky white of her lace-embroidered nightrail was clearly visible in the tall mirror that stood in the corner. Moving closer to examine her reflection, Athena saw that her face was pale and that her eyes were luminous in the dim starlight that poured through the row of tall glazed windows behind her.

With a sigh she turned away, the sheer material falling to her small feet, caressing the willowy length of her body. Laying herself across the bed, Athena wondered if Stephen would be pleased with what he saw. Something that sounded suspiciously like a sob tore from her throat, and she pressed her hot face into the plump pillows, slim fingers curled into fists.

The bedroom in which Athena found herself was nothing short of opulent. Mahogany paneling and priceless tapestries covered the nine-foot-high walls. The furniture was sandalwood inlaid with ivory, and the objets d'art scattered across the dresser and table tops had been collected from the finest auction houses of France and Italy. Even the sheets upon which Athena lay were of satin, lightly scented with attar of roses in honor of the bride who had finally come to sleep there.

Rolling over on her back, Athena stared, wide-eyed, at the ceiling. She would have given anything at the moment to be in her own beloved bedroom at Courtland Grace, surrounded by the handmade pine and maple furniture that had been hers since childhood. She didn't care at all for the pretentious possessions of the Kensingtons, and she found the bedchamber that was intended for Stephen and herself utterly oppressive.

Biting her lip, Athena heard the clock on the landing strike ten. Where was Stephen? He had told her that he'd join her shortly, and the lustful gleam in his eyes when he had kissed her hand had made it plain that he was more than eager to consummate their marriage at last.

Oh, why had she ever agreed to come to Kensington Manor to live with him? Athena asked herself forlornly. Why hadn't she insisted that she remain at Courtland Grace because Fletcher needed her still? She sighed, aware that she would only have been delaying the inevitable. Stephen had visited Fletcher only yesterday morning and had seen for himself how well her brother was recovering. There had been no more reasons for Athena not to return home with him, and she had had no other choice than to give in to his demands.

Lying there in the darkness, Athena knew that she dreaded above all the thought of her husband's lovemaking. His animal thrusting and grunting, she felt sure, would leave her forever shamed of the carnal act, and for the sweeping ecstasy she had experienced with Lochiel Blackmoor . . . Tears welled in Athena's eyes, for she knew she would never experience such pleasure again.

She stirred restlessly on the big bed, unaware of the tempting vision she made with the starlight bathing her nearly naked body silver. Two nights had passed since her encounter with Lochiel at Joshua Brinston's mill, and she wondered if seeing him again had been responsible for this sudden aversion to Stephen.

Athena could not deny that her thoughts since then had dwelled constantly on memories of Lochiel's darkly handsome face, of his deep, pleasing voice, and the way her heart had hammered at his nearness. Even though they had parted enemies, she could not forget the compelling pull of his masculinity upon her woman's soul. It angered her that her waking hours were spent in dreamy reverie and that she hadn't even bothered to consider what would happen to Ambrose now that Lochiel had discovered his criminal activities.

Would her father-in-law be arrested? Athena wondered now. What charges would be brought against him for his involvement in the curious goods exchange she had witnessed at the mill? To her surprise she found that she simply didn't care. Her natural inquisitiveness had been replaced by an annoying inclination to dream again of Lochiel's warm body pressed against hers, the memory subtly serving to undermine the feelings of tenderness she had begun to nurture for the man she had married.

Footsteps in the corridor brought Athena's head up with a start. Holding her breath, she waited for Stephen's voice to address her through the darkness. She could scarcely credit the relief that coursed through her when she heard Aramintha and Eliza giggling together as they retired to their own rooms.

This would never do, Athena told herself peevishly, nerves raw with the strain of waiting. Rising from the bed, she drew a wrapper about her shoulders and shook her golden hair free. She would simply have to fetch Stephen herself, she decided, and get this whole bloody affair over with as quickly as possible.

In the study below, meanwhile, a half-drunk Stephen was sitting behind his father's desk staring with hostile eyes at an unwelcome visitor who had arrived several minutes before. The fact that this heavyset man with his ugly, pockmarked face was keeping him from his bridal bed annoyed Stephen to no end. How to get rid of the fellow without causing a scene?

"I imagine you've come for your money," he remarked impatiently, pouring himself another shot of rum without offering a glass to his guest.

Toddman Tyner's eyes narrowed, the slight not having gone unnoticed. "Oh, I've come for more'n that, sir," he announced, his fleshy lips curved into a smile. "I've come to tell ye a thing or two about that new bride o' yourn."

Stephen regarded him coldly, resenting the way the obnoxious fellow was lounging in the leather armchair before him. His cocksure manner was beginning to set Stephen's teeth on edge and he opened his mouth to say as much, though he never got the chance.

"Flighty little creature you've up an' wed," Tyner continued, regarding the grimy palms of his hands with studied indifference. "Though 'tisn't odd, considerin' she's such a rare beauty. Knows how to use her looks to win a man's heart, she do." He cast a meaningful glance at Stephen from beneath the greasy forelock spilling over his brow. "Ain't no surprise, is it, that there be men willin' to risk anything to make an assignation with her?"

Stephen set his glass down. Despite the unpleasant fog that clouded his brain, he sensed perfectly well where Tyner's words were leading. He himself had paid out too many bribes in his life not to realize when he was being set up for blackmail.

"Suppose you tell me what you're talking about," he suggested calmly.

Toddman Tyner needed no further prompting to recount with uncanny accuracy the meeting between Athena and Lochiel at the mill. There could be little doubt from his description that the encounter had indeed taken place, though he took great care not to provide Stephen with any clues that might lead him to guess the identity of the man Athena had met. Nor did he see fit to mention the exchange of goods that had taken place that night or the fact that Kensington's father had been involved, a fact that Stephen appeared ignorant of. Toddman already had other plans for that information, plans that would be set into motion once Ambrose had been arrested. Until then he could well afford to remain patient.

Throughout the brief but detailed narrative Stephen listened with heavy-lidded eyes, his blunt fingers steepled on the desk before him. A slight flush had suffused his cheeks, although nothing else revealed the great rage that shook him at the simple but compelling evidence of

Athena's infidelity. Tyner wasn't lying—Stephen was shrewd enough to realize that. And the fact that Athena had taken a lover once before made it all the more likely to him that she had done so again.

A vein began to throb in Stephen's temple. Faithless bitch, how dare she deceive him now that they were married? How dare she deny him his conjugal rights with the excuse that she had to tend her wounded brother and fly instead into the arms of some rutting boar of a lover?

The tip of his index finger began to trace a pattern on the oiled desktop before him. "And the name of this man, Mr. Tyner?"

The big Philadelphian spread his hands in mock surprise. "Did I forget to mention it? Stupid of me, eh."

Stephen's lips thinned. "I will not play games with the likes of you, Tyner. How much do you want?"

Toddman could scarcely keep the satisfied grin off his face. Despite his best efforts to hide it, Kensington was insanely jealous. Where his golden-haired bride was concerned, he seemed to lose all sense of reason. " 'Twould seem to me ten guineas be a fair enough price," he said promptly. "Three of 'em," he added politely, "be owed from our last agreement, if ye'll remember, sir."

Sweat glazed Stephen's brow, and his face contorted with the force of his rage. Springing to his feet, he gestured savagely toward the door. "Get out! Get out before I put a bullet through that ugly face of yours! Ten guineas is a preposterous sum no sane man would ever agree to pay! You're entitled to naught, you cur, either three guineas or ten, and I'll have you clapped in irons should you show yourself hereabouts again!"

Toddman Tyner came to his feet with surprising swiftness for a man his size. He hadn't expected such a violent reaction and wondered if he had miscalculated Kensington's lust for his blue-eyed bride after all. "Seven guineas for the name of her lover and three for what you already owes me," he tried again, his voice no longer smug, his eyes filled with hostility.

"Get out," Stephen rasped. Jerking open the top drawer of the desk, he removed his father's pistol and aimed it with cold deliberation at the other man's swarthy face.

Toddman Tyner hadn't kept his unsavory skin intact all these years by misconstruing the difference between bluster and murderous intent. Realizing that his first plan had failed, he was not about to linger long enough to think of another. Without taking his eyes off Stephen, he backed out of the room and quickly left the house, slamming the front door behind him.

Alone in the study, Stephen sank back into his chair and pressed the heels of his hands against his eyes. A throbbing red light danced through his brain, and as the pressure mounted so did his anger. As if in a dream he could see Athena lying in the grass below Brinston's mill, moonlight silvering her sleek white limbs. She was laughing with abandon into the face of her unknown lover, who had shed his clothes and was pressing his mouth to hers in a searing kiss.

The red veil swirled before his eyes, and Stephen fancied he could hear his faithless bride moan with passion, her body trembling as strong, dark hands caressed her satin flesh. Golden curls spilled against the damp earth, and her lover buried his face in their scented softness for a moment before allowing his lips to travel to her rosebud breasts. Stephen could see Athena arch in quivering response, opening her slender thighs to take him deep inside her, the two of them becoming one as they surged together in the timeless rhythm of unbridled passion.

Oh, God, he couldn't bear it! With a savage sweep of his arm Stephen sent the contents of the desktop crashing to the floor. Staggering, he came to his feet, his pulses pounding. He had to find Tyner before it was too late, had to learn the name of the man whose image he must vanquish forever from Athena's traitorous heart. By God, he was angry enough to kill the deceitful wench!

Draining his glass and sending it clattering to the floor, Stephen ripped open the study door and strode into the hall. His hair was disheveled, his stock unknotted, and the livid expression on his face thoroughly unnerved the young woman who had frozen at his appearance on the landing above.

Athena realized immediately that Stephen was drunk. For a terrifying moment she thought that he was coming upstairs to ravage her, and her eyes widened in astonishment when she saw him reach for his cloak. Where could he possibly be going at this time of night?

Stephen, in the act of fumbling for his gloves, gave a startled exclamation as a loud knock sounded on the front door. "What the devil?" he demanded, jerking it open. "Is it you, Tyner?"

"I beg your pardon for the untimely intrusion, sir," came a man's voice Athena didn't recognize. "We're here to see Mr. Ambrose Kensington."

"Out of my way," Stephen snapped. "I haven't time for this."

Athena, still watching from the landing, gasped as she saw Stephen being thrust back inside by two men who stepped, uninvited, into the entrance hall. Both of them were tall and broad-shouldered, but it was the one in the scarlet uniform who claimed her attention. A dress sword swung casually at his hip and his kneeboots gleamed with polish. The figure he cut in his gold-braided coat and neatly folded stock was so magnificent that it all but dazzled her. Athena's gaze traveled to the dark face beneath the wig and tricorn, and suddenly her hand flew to her lips. How could she have failed to recognize those harshly chiseled features? Of course, it could be none other than Lochiel!

His deep voice sounded cool and authoritative in the dim elegance of the entrance hall. "I, too, regret the intrusion, Mr. Kensington, yet we have business to discuss with your father, and I'm afraid it cannot wait."

Stephen's head had snapped up at the sound of the Scot's voice, and now his reddened eyes narrowed with recognition. "By God, 'tis you, Blackmoor," he breathed, and abruptly all of the hatred roiling within him was centered on this one man who had possessed Athena's perfect body while he, her husband, had not.

"You swine," he grated, suddenly convinced that this was the man Toddman Tyner had seen with Athena down by the mill. The thought of those silver eyes gazing upon the naked beauty of his wife's smooth body, those brown hands roving her willing flesh, drove him into a frenzy.

Uttering an inhuman sound, he launched himself at the startled Lochiel, intending to strangle the life out of him. Recovering quickly, Lochiel warded off his grasping hands so that Stephen succeeded only in ripping the snowy white stock before he found his arms pinned in an iron grip behind his back.

"The man's obviously drunk!" the watching Lieutenant Wilkes exclaimed in astonishment.

"And ready to tear out my heart with his bare hands," Lochiel added mildly, sounding not at all breathless despite the fact that Stephen was struggling furiously. "Would you care to explain your actions, sir?" he asked politely.

"You're going to die for what you've done, Blackmoor," Stephen panted, sweat pouring down his face. It didn't seem to occur to him that he was hopelessly outmatched by the powerful Highlander. All he could think of was his blinding need for vengeance. "Did the bitch cry out when you took her?" he demanded thickly. "Did she moan with pleasure when you caressed her breasts and touched—"

Lochiel's face went rigid. Cold fury shook his big body as it dawned on him what Stephen was raving about. Though he had no personal quarrel with the drunken fool, he could not allow him to speak thusly about Athena whether he was her husband or not. Thrusting Stephen away from him, he drew his dress sword smoothly from its scabbard.

"Lochiel, no!"

He recognized her voice even before the choked cry had registered in Stephen's brain. Whirling about, he froze as he saw Athena flying down the stairs, gossamer nightrail trailing behind her, riotous curls spilling to her hips, looking more wantonly beautiful than he had ever seen her.

Had she been warming Stephen's bed until he could come to her? Lochiel wondered, finding the thought intolerable. His unreadable gaze traveled from the flushed and drunken Stephen, who was staring like a lost soul at his wife, to Athena, the object of both men's tormented fascination.

"Lochiel, you mustn't," she whispered, her great blue eyes fastened pleadingly on his face. He turned away abruptly, knowing it was madness to gaze into their damning sapphire depths.

"Go back upstairs," Stephen grated, jealousy rising like bile in his throat. "You needn't concern yourself with this."

"Do as he says, Athena," Lochiel said harshly.

" 'Sblood, what be going on down here? Can't a man find rest in his own home?"

The startled faces of all but Lochiel Blackmoor swung up to the landing where an irately scowling Ambrose had appeared. With a tassled nightcap covering his thin, sleep-rumpled hair, he looked no more menacing than the little spaniel that had followed him down the stairs and now cowered at his heels. His wife and daughters stood behind him peering over the billowing folds of his nightshirt, ruffled mobcaps on their heads, their faces smeared with cream.

Despite the seriousness of their encounter, Lochiel had to suppress the urge to laugh aloud. Never had he seen a more absurd collection of creatures than the Kensingtons in nocturnal garb, yet he sobered as his gaze fell on Athena, who stood like a long-limbed goddess in a midnight-blue wrapper beside him, staring, open-mouthed, to the landing above. This was her family now, Lochiel reminded himself, and abruptly his amusement was gone.

"I'd like a word with you in private, sir," he addressed the plump gentleman politely.

Ambrose had gone rigid at the sight of the two soldiers in the hall below him. Vivid purple color rose to his fleshy cheeks when he saw the revealing attire worn by his daughter-in-law, who stood boldly at the tall officer's side, seeming not at all ashamed to find herself in his presence.

"Pulin' lobsterback!" he burst out, all but ignoring the lieutenant, who was wearing the uniform of the New York Militia. His contempt was for Lochiel alone. "How dare ye disturb my household this time of night! And you, Stephen, didn't you have the sense to turn 'em away at the door? I want no pox-ridden Regulars filthying my home!"

"Mr. Kensington!" Leda cried, aghast at her husband's outburst.

"Hold your tongue, woman!" Ambrose bellowed, "and get you back to your rooms! 'Tis enough that he be ogling Stephen's wife! Next he'll be coming after you!"

Aramintha and Eliza squealed in terror at this, their cries fanning Ambrose's temper. "Where's my pistol?" he demanded, stomping down the stairs in his worn kid slippers.

"Just a moment, Mr. Kensington," Lochiel said crisply, determined to put an end to this nonsense. Whom was Ambrose trying to impress? Surely not his cowering wife and daughters, or was his bluster merely designed to hide his own fear because he already suspected what was to come?

"Lieutenant Wilkes and I are here on official business," Lochiel went on in a tone that brooked no more interruptions. Even Athena's pleading blue eyes could no longer sway him from his purpose. "Though I regret the unseemly hours, I am under orders—"

"I want you out of here this instant!" Ambrose commanded, seemingly unimpressed by the tall officer's authoritative stature, though beads of sweat had gathered on his brow. "If the army wants something from me, they'll have to do better than to send a lobsterback—a pulin' Highlander at that!"

Athena saw Lochiel's lean jaw tighten, and her heart ached for him, knowing that his rigid countenance hid the soul of a man deeply proud of his Highland blood.

"Ambrose Kensington," Lochiel said quietly, his words ringing in the sudden stillness, "under orders from Commanding General Jeffrey Amherst and the governor of this colony, I arrest you in the name of His Majesty, King George the Second. You have been charged with treason against the Crown and it is within my—"

The rest of his words were drowned out by a shriek from Leda, who crumpled in a dead faint on the elegant carpet.

"You bloody cur!" Stephen breathed, and Athena cried out in alarm as he launched himself at Lochiel. Was Stephen mad? Didn't he realize that Lochiel could easily snap his neck in two with just the strength of his bare hands?

But Lochiel didn't even give Stephen a second glance. Thrusting him aside like an annoying insect, he pushed his way to the staircase, and only then did Athena notice that her father-in-law had collapsed against the newel post, his face deathly pale as he gasped for air.

"Athena!"

She came at once to Lochiel's side, responding with the blind instinct of a woman who implicitly trusts the man who calls her name. "Oh, Lochiel!" she whispered, shocked by the wheezing that issued from Ambrose's bluish lips.

The eyes that regarded her were fondly fierce, his urgency tempered by tenderness as he assured her softly, "He's going to be all right. Just find me some smelling salts and send someone into town to fetch the doctor."

"Is there anything I can do to help, madam?"

Athena peered up into the worn yet trustworthy visage of the elderly manservant Hunt, who, alerted by the commotion, had hurried downstairs to see if he was needed. "Major Blackmoor has requested smelling salts. Do you know where they are?"

Hunt obligingly held up the small hartshorn vial he had brought with him as a precaution, and Athena took it from him gratefully. In the meantime Lochiel and Lieutenant Wilkes had managed to lower Ambrose's bulk onto the carpet. Removing a dirk from his belt, Lochiel began to cut the tight collar of the fallen man's nightshirt. It was at that moment that Leda Kensington regained consciousness, and seeing the broad-shouldered Highlander bent over her husband's prone form, she let out a blood-curdling shriek.

"Stephen, stop him! He's slitting your father's throat!"

It was an invitation her son was only too happy to oblige. Striking an army officer was normally a punishable offense, but surely no judge in all the colonies would condemn him for attacking a major in the British army in order to prevent his own father from being murdered!

Stephen had been gnashing his teeth as he watched his faithless wife dance attendance on her handsome lover, his anger mounting to blinding proportions. The way the Highland savage had looked at Athena just then, his eyes caressing her as though she belonged to him instead of to her lawful wedded husband, had caused his blood to boil with hatred.

At the sound of his mother's terrified cry, Stephen lunged for the dirk that Lochiel had placed on the floor beside him. Lochiel, who was holding the hartshorn vial beneath Ambrose's nose, was unaware of Stephen's intentions until he heard Athena's sharply indrawn breath. Lifting his head, his countenance hardened as he saw Stephen brandishing the weapon, with a triumphant smile playing on his lips.

Silence fell over the entrance hall as Lochiel rose slowly, towering a full head taller than his opponent. There were nervous whispers from the servants who had gathered in the doorway to watch, and on the landing above, Leda and her daughters stood as if frozen, hands pressed to trembling lips.

"Put the dirk down, Kensington," Lochiel said softly.

"So that you can kill my father with it?" Stephen sneered. Jealousy ate at him as he noticed that Lochiel had deliberately placed his lean body directly between himself and Athena. Did the bloody swine think he was going to harm his own wife?

"You know damned well I was cutting your father's collar so that he could breathe easier," Lochiel responded, his voice soft, although it carried the sting of a whip.

"My father has suffered these attacks before and has always managed to survive without your intervention," Stephen retorted with an indifferent jerk of the head toward the still-unconscious Ambrose. "You're the one, Major Blackmoor, who poses a danger to his health, and I intend to see that you are dealt with before tragedy occurs."

Athena's throat constricted at those ominous words. Never had she seen Stephen so close to losing control. His usually neat hair was disheveled, his expression wild, and the hand that held the dirk shook slightly with the force of his anger.

"Put it down," Lochiel repeated slowly.

Over his scarlet-clad shoulder Stephen caught sight of Athena's pale face, her blue eyes so wide that he could clearly see the indigo rims of her irises. Her lush, kissable lips were parted and trembling, and choking rage rose within him as he realized that her fear was not for him but for his hated rival, this lean, savage Highlander who deserved little better than to die.

With an incoherent cry he pounced, yet he had already made the mistake of letting his attention wander. He gave a startled cry as a hand suddenly clamped about his wrist, the grip strong enough to crush his bones. Looking up, he met a pair of silver eyes in which bloodlust had risen high, and for the first time in his life he knew what it meant to know fear.

Lochiel Blackmoor, Stephen realized in that moment, would kill him without a second thought. All his life he had heard of the savagery of the Scottish Highlander, and in those silver eyes he suddenly saw the civilized veneer stripped away to reveal the barbarian beneath. How could Athena love a man like this? he asked himself, the pain of his captured wrist forgotten. If he had had time for introspection, he might have realized that the fires kindling in his reckless wife burned brightly in the lean Highlander himself. No man but Lochiel Blackmoor could possibly have tamed her.

"I've already asked you twice to drop your weapon, Kensington." Never had Lochiel seemed so large or full of power as he loomed over his adversary. As the iron fingers tightened relentlessly about his wrist, Stephen felt something snap, and the accompanying pain caused him to cry out, the dirk clattering harmlessly to the floor.

Suddenly the heated tension in the air was gone, and movement returned to the witnesses who had been watching the struggle between the two men in frozen silence. Leda hurled herself down the stairs, sobbing openly as she fell to her knees at Ambrose's side, while the servants were directed by an authoritative Hunt to remove their fallen master to the salon sofa. Aramintha and Eliza were weeping hysterically, while poor Lieutenant Wilkes stood uncertainly near the front door, wishing he had been assigned some other duty that night.

Scooping up his dirk and tucking it back into his belt, Lochiel lifted his head and his gaze fell on Athena, who was standing amid the confusion with a curiously bereft expression upon her young face. Though he had always loved her best when she was glaring fiercely into his eyes or laughing in that fresh and impudent way of hers, he felt his heart constrict with tenderness at the lost look of a child she had about her.

Pushing his way to her side, he scanned her upturned features with an unfamiliarly protective tightness in his chest. "Why don't you let me take you home, Athena?" he asked softly. "There's little sense in remaining here. Regardless of Ambrose's condition, I'm still duty-bound to carry out his arrest, and I fear it won't be pleasant."

She lifted her face to gaze up at him, her square jaw set in that stubborn line that had always enchanted him, yet there was no softness in the dark blue eyes that had once sparkled into his with the brilliance of stars. A strong finger came up to touch the point of her chin.

"What is it, lass?"

Athena found herself trembling in response to the intimate gesture, and her eyes went from his lean, beloved face to Stephen, whose back was turned toward her while Hunt did his best to bandage his injured wrist. It was pity, not love, that stirred her heart as she studied her husband's stooped shoulders, and she tried not to think of the humiliation he had suffered at Lochiel's hands. Though she had been shocked by the violence Stephen had exhibited, she could understand what forces had driven him, and as her uncertain gaze returned to Lochiel's watchful one, she resigned herself forever to the fact that she must stand by him no matter how much her heart might ache for another. She must abide by her decision now, when Stephen needed her most, and live with the knowledge that her love for Lochiel had been naught but a futile dream.

Lifting her head, she looked coldly into Lochiel's eyes. "You say you'll take me home? Kensington Manor is my home now, major, not Courtland Grace. As for your persistent meddling—" she gestured with her small hand toward the room where the unconscious Ambrose had been carried—"don't you think you've done enough?"

Tossing her head, she moved with what Lochiel could only think of as feline grace to her husband's side. He saw her place her slim hand on his arm, and speak to him softly, her blue eyes tender with concern. Jealousy, an emotion never before experienced, clawed at his heart, and in that one moment Lochiel knew that he had lost her and realized, too, the staggering extent of his loss. Athena, the woman with the name of a goddess and the golden beauty of an angel, had slipped like quicksilver from his grasp.

Why had she turned her back on him and chosen Stephen Kensington? Surely she must realize that he was not the man for her! No kindred flame burned within them, no aspect of Stephen's petty personality could possibly be suited to the golden-haired beauty whose spirit he would soon crush like the fragile wings of a butterfly.

Lochiel's jaw tightened as he remembered the passion-darkened eyes that had gazed with such poignant longing into his the morning he had made love to her on that sandy beach. Kensington would never be able to love her like that, could never evoke in her the same, quivering response. Damn her to hell, why had she decided that he could?

"Major Blackmoor?"

He glanced sharply at Lieutenant Wilkes, whose youthful face flushed in nervous response to the intimidating expression on that hawkish countenance. "What is it?"

"Dr. Nolan has arrived. Did you wish to speak with him?"

A muscle twitched in Lochiel's cheek. "Aye."

The prognosis was not good. Even the young lieutenant could see as much when he followed Major Blackmoor into the salon and caught sight of Ambrose Kensington's gray face. Lochiel spoke briefly with the physician, his tone too low for Wilkes to catch the words, then gestured curtly for the lieutenant to join him in the hallway.

"There's nothing more we can do tonight," Lochiel told him harshly. "We may as well take a room in West York and return in the morning."

The lieutenant nodded wordlessly, already dreading the prospect of spending the night in some deserted inn, for Major Blackmoor's mood promised poor company indeed. The two men slipped, unnoticed, through the front door, Lochiel pausing long enough to speak to Hunt, who, refusing to forsake his duties, had appeared on the threshold to show them out. The manservant's expression was regretful as he shook his head in response to Lochiel's tersely uttered question.

"Dr. Nolan has given her something to help her sleep. I'm afraid you can't see her at the moment, sir."

Lochiel passed a weary hand across his eyes. What good would it do to offer his sympathies to Leda Kensington anyway? If her husband died, as now seemed likely, she would forever hold him responsible. Seeing him now would only serve to fan the hatred she must be feeling toward him. As for Ambrose, Dr. Nolan had been adamant in his belief that he would not regain consciousness until morning at least—if he ever did. Lochiel was not about to torment the Kensington family by hovering like a vulture over the stricken man. No matter what Athena thought of him, he was not so heartless.

" 'Tis a regrettable situation," Hunt was saying softly, his eyes resting on the closed salon door behind which his employer lay. "Surely Mr. Kensington is not guilty of the charges you bore against him, sir!"

"I'm afraid so." Placing his tricorn upon his head, Lochiel allowed his gaze to sweep the subdued servants standing vigil before the salon. Aramintha and Eliza, he noticed, had vanished upstairs with their mother. Stephen, too, had disappeared, and Lochiel wondered fleetingly if Athena had led him off to their bedchamber to soothe his wounded pride in private.

With a savage tightening of his lips, he strode into the darkness, where Glenrobbie stood tethered to the post at the foot of the steps. Swinging onto the gelding's broad back, Lochiel was about to kick him into a gallop when he felt a detaining hand on his boot heel.

Looking down, he found himself gazing into the swarthy features of a man he had never seen before. In the dim light falling from the house behind him, Lochiel could see a pockmarked face and dark eyes set beneath a protruding brow. Experience told him that this was a man belonging to the cast of unscrupulous characters who made their living preying on the wealthy and the weak in the teeming streets of great cities. Pickpockets, thieves, highwaymen—the names all meant the same thing, and it was obvious to him that this man with the angry, darting eyes belonged to their ilk.

"What the devil do you want?" Lochiel demanded curtly.

"I wish only a word with 'e, sir," the unpleasant fellow rasped in a low voice, a single look into the officer's face having told him he was not the sort to be bargained with.

The silver eyes were cold. "I've no time for the likes of you, my friend, and I suggest you take yourself away from here before I find cause to arrest you."

Toddman Tyner obligingly released his hold on the stirrup leather, yet his determination to avenge himself against Stephen Kensington did not waver. He had watched the dramatic proceedings in the entrance hall of the house through a window and had not missed the tense encounter among Athena Kensington, her husband, and the British major. Tyner understood enough of human nature to realize that love, hatred, and jealousy could destroy a man as easily as a lead ball in the back. What he had witnessed inside the house had convinced him that a few doubts planted in just the right places should take care of his problems quite effectively.

"Mr. Kensington hired me to find the Courtland girl, sir," he said, speaking in a low tone so that the other officer would not hear what was being said. "Told me he'd pay me three guineas to bring 'er back 'cause there'd been a death in her family."

Lochiel's features took on a ruthless cast in the flickering light of the lanterns. "I'm well aware of the details," he remarked curtly. "And I'll have you know that I'm not the least bit interested in the fact that Mr. Kensington paid you an exorbitant sum to return his wife home in time for her aunt's funeral." Tightening his hold on the reins, he jerked Glenrobbie's head about and signaled the waiting Wilkes to accompany him.

"Ye've got it wrong, sir!" Tyner protested urgently. "The old woman wasn't dead yet! She were still alive when Brewster and I set off to find the girl. He didn't have no proxy papers signed at the time, either. Told me so himself the last night we met in Albany. Now why do you suppose Kensington'd tell his bride and everyone else them lies, eh?"

For a moment the broad back remained still, then Lochiel turned his head in a gesture of impatience. "I'm afraid the Kensingtons no longer interest me. If you feel the need to gossip about them, I suggest you find someone who is interested."

Digging his boot heels into the gelding's muscular sides, Lochiel vanished into the darkness, leaving Toddman Tyner to clench his fists in utter frustration. Bloody hell! He'd been so sure the Highlander would take his bait!

No matter, he soothed himself, shrugging his shoulders indifferently. There was still another way to ensure Kensington's downfall and earn him some gold in the bargain. 'Twould entail little more than a brief trip to Albany, and if he left immediately he should be there before morning.

Eighteen

Athena lifted the teacup to her lips, only to find the contents distastefully cold. Setting it aside, she ran a hand through her unruly curls and rose stiffly to her feet. A night without sleep had left her exhausted, with dark circles under her normally bright eyes. The gown she had slipped over her head only an hour ago was already hopelessly wrinkled, yet she paid no attention to her appearance.

Hearing the clock in the salon chime six, she stepped into the hallway, thinking that Hunt should be up by now. Perhaps he might be persuaded to brew another pot of tea. Crossing the marble floor, Athena halted at the sound of a knock on the front door. Smoothing her wrinkled skirts, she opened it to find herself face to face with Lochiel Blackmoor. For a moment they stared at one another in silence; then Lochiel's expression hardened as he took in her exhausted face and untidy curls.

"Athena, what is it?" he demanded, grasping her shoulders.

"Ambrose died a little over an hour ago," she responded wearily.

"My God," Lochiel whispered softly. Staring down into Athena's pale face, he shook her slightly. "You didn't stay up with him all night, did you?"

She nodded. "Dr. Nolan just left. He never regained consciousness, Lochiel."

"And his wife?"

"Dr. Nolan had to give her another dose of laudanum. She was extremely upset. It wasn't very pleasant." A shadow passed across her face as she recalled Leda's hysterical wailing and the horrible things she had said about Lochiel, though he hadn't been at all responsible for her husband's death.

Lochiel's lips tightened grimly, for he could see well enough from Athena's expression what she had endured that night. He cursed himself for not having tried harder to persuade her to go home, then reminded himself savagely that she was no longer his responsibility.

"What'll we do now, major?"

Lochiel had all but forgotten the lieutenant. Releasing his grip on

Athena's shoulders, he addressed her in the precise, formal manner of a military officer addressing a mere civilian. "Where is your husband, Mrs. Kensington?"

"Still asleep upstairs," Athena replied equally coolly, trying not to recall how relieved she had been when Stephen had finally retired to his room last night, leaving her alone with Dr. Nolan downstairs. His anger at Lochiel, the pain of his sprained wrist, and the headache the rum had given him had combined to put him in a foul mood, which Athena had found unbearable.

"I'm afraid someone will have to awaken him," Lochiel remarked apologetically, his countenance made of stone.

Athena's manner had become just as stony. They might have been strangers meeting for the first time; the warmth that had existed between them gone forever. They had begun as antagonists that long-ago night at Albany fort, Athena remembered with a dull ache in her heart, and though she had fallen desperately in love with him, they were antagonists still.

"You said last night that Ambrose was guilty of—of treason," she said now. "What did he do? What was in those crates that were brought to the mill?"

"Muskets," Lochiel informed her curtly, his gaze no longer gentle as he looked at her. "In order to pay off what seem to have been staggering debts, he chose to betray his country by selling arms to French Algonquins."

Athena bit her lip, not certain whether this distressing news or the callous way in which Lochiel was regarding her upset her more. "I'll have Hunt summon Stephen for you," she said quietly.

Oh, Lochiel, she thought to herself, slim back stiff as she left him, if only things could have been different between us! 'Twas hard to believe that only a little over a fortnight had passed since he had taken her into his arms and loved her with the warm, masculine strength of his body.

How well she could remember the bitter reluctance she had experienced at leaving him, not knowing whether he had returned safely from the ravaged town of Deerfield, and how shocked and dismayed she had been upon returning to Courtland Grace to find her aunt dead and Stephen Kensington her husband by proxy.

"I had no choice but to turn to Stephen after you said those terrible things to me that night," Athena whispered to herself, her eyes prickling with tears left stubbornly unshed. It was Stephen who had helped her through the dark days following the shooting of Fletcher, comforting her with his presence and accepting her willingly despite the fact that she had not come to him a virgin bride. Though Lochiel had continued to weave his compelling spell over her heart, Athena had come to the bitter realization that she must remain loyal to Stephen, for there could be no hope of happiness for her with a soldier who had never even professed to love her.

"You might as well go back to Courtland Grace while I'm in Albany," Stephen told her when he came downstairs to speak to Lochiel and oversee the removal of Ambrose's body. " 'Twill probably take several days to straighten out the matter of my father's death, and it won't be pleasant for you here."

Athena's heart leaped at the thought of going home. They were alone in the study, where he had led her for a few private words before his departure, neither of them wanting to come under the scrutiny of the curious servants who still haunted the hallway outside the room where Ambrose lay.

"Your mother may need me," Athena protested, compelled by a sense of duty to her new family. "The burial arrangements—"

"I'll stop by the vicarage and discuss the matter with Reverend Axminster before I leave," Stephen promised.

Feeling an odd tenderness come over her, Athena slipped her arms about his neck and kissed him, not at all repelled by the stale scent of rum that lingered about him or the stubble that shadowed his heavy jaw. " 'Tis kind of you to do so. You won't be gone long, will you?"

Startled by this show of affection, Stephen slung an awkward arm about her shoulders. Though he remembered little of the night before, he hadn't been drunk enough to forget Toddman Tyner's allegations or the murderous certainty he'd felt in his heart that Athena had renewed her tempestuous affair with Major Lochiel Blackmoor.

Looking down into her face with its achingly lovely features, her slim, straight nose and maddeningly clear blue eyes, he found it impossible to believe Tyner's words. Athena couldn't be deceiving him. She wasn't clever enough to bring such a guileless smile to her lips if it weren't genuine!

"I should be home in time for the funeral," he assured her, determined to forget the savage jealousy that had clawed at him the night before. Tightening his arm about her, he bent his head to kiss her, and Athena dutifully raised her lips to his.

"In that case I suggest we make haste, Mr. Kensington. General Amherst is not a patient man where domestic affairs are concerned."

Athena's stricken gaze traveled to the burning one of Lochiel Blackmoor, who had appeared in the doorway in time to witness the seemingly tender exchange between husband and wife. Turning her back on him, she smoothed her skirts and tried to compose herself, unaware of the tempting picture she made to both men in her primrose gown with its dainty waist, her fair hair falling to her hips.

"I'll not be riding with you, Blackmoor," Stephen informed him coldly. "And as for the general, I'm certain he'll be quite interested to learn how a British soldier was instrumental in the death of my father."

Athena went cold inside at his biting tone. There was going to be enough trouble, she sensed, when word of the inquest spread and people began asking themselves why a British officer and not a Provincial had been sent to make the arrest of a highly respected private citizen. If Stephen managed to stir up bitterly suppressed prejudices, no one would stop to take into consideration the fact that Lochiel, as a king's officer, had had every right to investigate a crime against the Crown. She found herself despairing over what that might mean to Lochiel's future—and perhaps even his safety.

"You'll ride under my personal escort, Kensington," Lochiel responded, an edge of steel to his voice that caused the other man to clench his fists in helpless frustration, recalling how effortlessly those long fingers had nearly snapped his wrist the night before.

"Very well, if you insist," he ground out, "but I do so under protest."

"Duly noted," Lochiel responded with an insulting smile curving the corners of his mouth. "Your servant, Mrs. Kensington."

Athena looked around to find Lochiel standing over her, a mocking light in his pale gray eyes. Taking her hand in his, he lifted it to his lips and added arrogantly, "I regret any inconvenience we might have caused you."

She wanted to make a stinging retort, to slap his face, but instead found herself snatching her hand away as the warmth of his flesh sent a current shivering through her. "Just go away," she whispered, golden head bowed, the normally proud shoulders slumping wearily.

Lochiel's mouth tightened grimly, but before he could speak again he was interrupted by Hunt's appearance in the doorway.

"Your horse is ready, sir," Hunt informed Stephen, who had been watching the stiff exchange between his wife and the lean Highlander with narrowed eyes. "I've also taken the liberty of ordering the carriage round for Mrs. Kensington so that she may be taken to Courtland Grace."

Athena's head came up, and only Lochiel, who was standing closest to her, saw the light of relief that entered her tired eyes. "I'd like very much to go home," she said softly. "Thank you, Hunt."

"My pleasure, madam," Hunt replied with a bow, blushing awkwardly beneath her gentle smile.

As the carriage swayed across the familiar road that would take her back to Courtland Grace, Athena leaned her head against the leather seat and tried not to give in to her threatening tears. She was exhausted and upset, last night's terrible events having taken their toll. Once Stephen returned and the investigation against Ambrose was over, she would do her best to put the past forever behind her. Surely the war wouldn't last much longer, and once Lochiel Blackmoor was sent back to England with his company, she need never be reminded again of the hopelessness of having loved him.

When the carriage rumbled to a halt before the front door of Courtland Grace, a smiling Tykie was there to help Athena alight. His grin broadened when he noticed that she was alone.

"Ye've left him then, lass?" he inquired eagerly, speaking with the bluntness of a servant who had long ago forgotten his place where his beloved mistress was concerned.

Athena's expression mirrored her confusion. "Who?"

"Why, young pimple-faced Kensington," Tykie answered jovially, placing his big hands about her waist and swinging her to the ground. "One night i' his house an' ye've already realized ye belong here at hame, eh?"

"What a horrible thing to say, Tykie!" Athena burst out, though she couldn't really blame him for being unaware of the previous night's tragedies. "My husband," she said pointedly, "had to go to Albany unexpectedly and decided I should stay here until he returned."

"Ye be tired, lass," Tykie observed, his amusement vanishing.

"I haven't slept all night," Athena confessed. She leaned gratefully against his muscular arm as they started up the steps, her golden hair spilling against his shirtfront. "You can't imagine what happened." Her eyes were suddenly dark with pain and Tykie was quick to interrupt her.

"Explanations can wait, Miss Athena. 'Tis a nap ye'll be havin' and then summat tae eat frae Prudence's larder."

Athena didn't have the strength to argue with him. "Where is my brother?"

"Still restin' i' his rooms," Tykie replied, "an' ye'll be doin' the same."

"Aye, sir," she murmured, thinking that it would be heaven to slip between the covers of her own bed.

Much to everyone's satisfaction, Athena slept well into the following afternoon. By then, of course, the news of Ambrose Kensington's death and the shocking reasons behind it had already reached Courtland Grace via a traveling tinker. Curious as the household might be, they were not about to disturb their sleeping mistress and allowed her to awaken on her own.

When Athena finally appeared downstairs, she looked well rested and extremely fetching in a russet gown with capped sleeves and pale gold petticoats. Her unruly blond curls had been subdued in lace netting, swept back from her face so that the square line of her jaw and the smoothness of her temples were clearly emphasized. Bright blue eyes sparkled with eager anticipation as she yawned prettily and demanded of a smiling Wills what Prudence might have for her to eat.

"I'm utterly famished," she confessed, sounding exactly to the delighted servant like the Athena of old.

"I'm certain something can be found to satisfy your appetite, miss," Wills responded gravely, though his eyes were twinkling. "May I add how good it is to have you back?"

She had only been away for a single night, and yet she found herself equally content to be home. "Thank you, Wills. Is Fletcher still in his rooms?"

"No, miss, he's out on the balcony enjoying a cup of tea."

Athena brightened. "In that case I'll join him there."

"Very good, miss."

She experienced a pang as she stepped through the long window to find Fletcher sitting in the warm spring sunshine with his back to her. How thin he had grown since his illness, but oh how grateful she was to have him alive! His once-bronzed face was pale and haggard, and the hand that lifted the cup to his lips shook slightly, yet he had made significant strides since the fateful shooting. Time would ease the lines of suffering about his mouth, Athena knew, and the sun would bring back the color to his face while Prudence's delectable meals filled out the once-muscular frame.

"Awake at last, you lazy creature?" Fletcher inquired, feeling a pair of slender arms slide about his neck, the softness of the cheek pressed against his telling him all too well that it was Athena. His approval at her appearance was obvious as he smiled at her.

She regarded him with aloofly cocked brows, thinking to herself that she was never happier than here at Courtland Grace with at least one of her brothers beside her. The smile wavered a bit as she reminded herself that her stay was only temporary and that the gloomy atmosphere of Kensington Manor awaited her upon Stephen's return.

"We've already heard about Ambrose," Fletcher told her softly, having seen the shadow that passed across her face. "It must have been awful. Were you there when it happened, my love?"

She told him everything then, the words spilling over themselves in her relief to be confiding in him at last. She spared him no details, even Stephen's drunken confrontation with Lochiel, though she did not admit, of course, that she had witnessed the actual crime at Brinston's mill the night it had happened. Fletcher would have been infuriated with her recklessness, and she wasn't about to upset him unnecessarily.

" 'Tis tragic indeed," Fletcher remarked regretfully when she finally fell silent. "I had no idea Ambrose's finances were in such deplorable condition. Didn't Stephen know?"

Athena shook her head as she took a dainty bite of the lemon-filled tartlet Prudence had provided for dessert. "Stephen knew nothing at all about his father's activities—or of their financial status. He was quite shocked when Lochiel mentioned it this morning."

"Father always said Ambrose never had a head for figures, and his wife was far too extravagant in her tastes," Fletcher added thoughtfully. "Overspending on luxuries and a few bad business decisions in the hands of an inept manager have a way of creating monstrous debts before long. Still, I never would have suspected such a meek little man of resorting to arms sales to the French to recoup his losses! 'Tis a dangerous business to be involved in, and I can't imagine poor, fat Ambrose dealing with the likes of gun-running Algonquins."

Athena said nothing. She was thinking of Thomas Painsley and realizing that it was he, not Ambrose, who had probably been the driving force behind the arms sales. Doubtless he was only one of many creditors Ambrose had owed money to, and had used his position to draw the poor man ruthlessly into his covert activities. Perhaps he had even resorted to blackmail, Athena thought with a shiver, recalling the ugly scene between the two of them the night of the Kensingtons' party.

She had never told anyone what she had overheard, not even Stephen, certain that Lochiel would be able to learn of Thomas Painsley's involvement from the men he had arrested that night. Athena had no wish to come forward with what she knew, especially now, when it would only bring further scandal to the Kensington name. Oh, how she wished she'd been able to control her cursed curiosity that night and never gotten involved! She hoped Lochiel would prove a gentleman and not drag her name into the entire blasted mess.

Lochiel, a gentleman? She almost snorted aloud. Being arrogant and inconsiderate was as natural to him as the need to breathe!

"And you'll go back with him when he returns, Thena?"

Her tawny brows drew together. "What?"

Fletcher had been watching her closely, her restlessness telling him that she was troubled by something. It annoyed him that he, who knew her so well, had no idea what was going on behind those gold-fringed eyes of hers.

"I asked if you planned to go back to Kensington Manor with Stephen when he gets back from Albany. Surely you must realize the family is in deep trouble. There's no reason on earth for you to burden yourself with a destitute collection of in-laws." Fletcher coughed delicately. This was the first time since his return home that he had openly mentioned his sister's unexpected marriage.

"I imagine Stephen will inherit his father's debts," he continued, his gaze straying from Athena's face to the flower-filled border running along the terrace wall. Bees droned amid the blossoms, and the air was heavy with the scent of spring. In contrast to the cultivated gardens of Kensington Manor, the overgrown flower beds of Courtland Grace were a charming collection of disorderly plantings. Primroses mingled in total disarray with daisies and sweet williams along the uneven brick walks, while black currants, gooseberries, and raspberries grew wild along the low stone fence that separated the supposedly formal gardens from the stableyard.

"I'm also concerned about the scandal," Fletcher added honestly, his restless gaze roving over the tangled greenery without seeing its unstructured beauty. "How do you suppose our friends and neighbors will react to the knowledge that there was a traitor among them? I seriously doubt the Kensingtons will maintain the same social prestige they enjoyed before all of this came to light."

Athena's soft lips tightened into a determined line that reminded Fletcher all too painfully of their mother. How stubborn Fiona had been at times and how convinced in her own mind of what was wrong and right! Fletcher could well remember how the sparks had flown between Foster and his headstrong wife no matter how unswerving the love between them. Athena, he despaired in that moment, had grown far too much like her.

"I am Stephen's wife," Athena said with an imperious tilting of her chin, "and though our marriage may have been forged under very unusual circumstances, I'm not going to hold him responsible for what his father has done. I'll not use this as an excuse to leave him."

"Damn it, Thena!" For the first time in his life Fletcher was truly angry with her. "Aunt Amelia arranged that marriage, not you! You have every right to dissolve it now, in light of what's happened, and no one, least of all your family, will blame you for doing so!"

Blue eyes locked challengingly with hazel. "I have no wish to leave Stephen," Athena informed him at last. " 'Tis true I was as shocked as you were when I returned from Fort Shuyler to discover that he and Aunt Amelia had arranged my future so neatly behind my back. But the idea of marrying Stephen was never new to me, and when you were shot and he was so kind to me, I realized I might have fared a great deal worse."

Fletcher's mouth tightened in grim reminiscence of a displeased Foster Courtland, a sight that had never failed to bring contrition into the rebellious hearts of his wayward sons and, far too often, his only daughter. "Are you sure of that?" he demanded.

Athena's traitorous heart wavered as she thought of Lochiel. "Stephen has already shown me that he will be a kind and attentive husband," she said, bending her head to pour tea, her face all but hidden from him.

"Kind and attentive, bah! You'll never be happy with that sort of life! You'll be bored with your lot in a month. I know you far too well, Athena!"

"Fletcher, please, you mustn't excite yourself so," Athena said worriedly, noticing the agitated color that had risen to his thin cheeks.

"Just tell me that you love him and I won't accuse you ever again of having made a mistake," he demanded relentlessly.

"Excuse me, sir."

Fletcher passed a hand across his eyes, angered by Wills' ill-timed interruption. What on earth was he going to do with his puzzling, unapproachable baby sister? He was too weak still from the shooting and the head wound he had suffered last winter to really think straight let alone take matters into his own hands. If only the twins were here and the bloody war over! Yet what difference would it make? Athena seemed determined to remain Stephen's wife regardless of the fact that she neither loved him nor seemed to have come to terms with the arrangement itself. The Athena of old, bold, reckless, tempestuous, would never have agreed to such manipulation. Damn Amelia Bower for her unjust meddling!

"What is it, Wills?" he asked curtly.

"Mistess de Vries and her daughter are here to see Miss Athena."

Brother and sister groaned aloud, then burst into helpless laughter at their mutual dismay.

"I imagine they've come to offer condolences," Fletcher remarked, his tension replaced with wry amusement.

"Bloody hell they have," Athena responded with spirit. "They've come to sniff out the sordid truth from the source itself."

"Shall I send them away?" Wills inquired innocently, though his tone hinted that he would relish the chance.

"Oh, let them in," Fletcher sighed with a resigned wave of his hand. " 'Twas promising to be a long afternoon anyway." He sobered as his eyes fell on Athena's face. "Unless you don't wish—"

"And ruin their fun?" she inquired dryly. "I wouldn't dream of it." In truth she was far more eager to discuss Ambrose's shocking death with Marianne and Katrine than to continue talking about Stephen with her brother.

Placing her hand beneath Fletcher's arm, she led him inside, her heart filled with grim resolve. No one, least of all her brothers, must ever know of her shameless love for Lochiel Blackmoor or the fact that she could never have accepted another husband than the one she had. Only Stephen had been willing enough to overlook the fact that she wasn't a virgin, and she must convince her brothers that she was happy as his wife. If time should prove the opposite, as Fletcher had so direly predicted, 'twas a burden that she must bear alone—for the remainder of her life, if need be.

Ominous thunderheads had gathered from the west, and lightning seared the darkening sky when Stephen returned to Courtland Grace two days later. Rudely tossing his dripping cloak at Wills when he was admitted into the house, he wordlessly followed the sound of Athena's voice into the salon. Wills glared at the muddy footprints on the gleaming floor, his dislike for Stephen Kensington obvious in his disgusted expression. Couldn't Miss Athena have chosen a more civil man for a husband? he asked himself with uncharacteristic disloyalty. 'Twas common knowledge that Kensington enjoyed gaming and wenching, not to mention the fact that he was a heavy drinker and an ill-tempered lout to boot. And Miss Athena wasn't one of those timid young girls who meekly submitted to the wishes of her elders! Knowing all this, why had Miss Athena agreed to accept the arrangements Mistress Bower had made for her?

"I suppose I'll never understand women," Wills muttered to himself, putting away the wet cloak.

Athena was serving tea to Marianne and Katrine de Vries when Stephen entered the room. Her slim back was turned to him as she performed the time-honored ritual with graceful movements. A lamp glowed softly on the table beside her, catching the gilded glow of the soft curls that lay against the nape of her neck. In a cream-colored gown with burgundy inserts and matching ribands edging the three-quarter-length sleeves, she looked deceptively demure, the picture of girlish innocence.

Stephen paused for a moment, admiring the slim line of her jaw that was revealed by the swept-back hairstyle, and a burning excitement coursed through him. He had waited longer than a man should have to possess Athena Courtland, but she would be in his arms tonight, and naught short of Armageddon would keep him from taking her at last.

Becoming aware of her guests' sudden silence, Athena turned her head to find Stephen standing beside her. His dark hair clung wetly to his wide forehead, and there was an expression on his swarthy features she didn't recognize. Only when she rose, revealing to him the clinging lines of her gown, did she realize what he had been thinking.

"Oh, Stephen, how good it is to have you home at last," she exclaimed warmly, letting none of her aversion show.

Aware of the curious eyes of the de Vries women upon her, Athena hurried forward, her arms outstretched. Stephen bent to kiss her cheek politely, although the gleam in his eyes told her that he was not content to let it end there.

"Good afternoon, Marianne, Katrine." He nodded in turn to each of the women, his arm possessively about his wife's small waist. Having known the de Vrieses all of his life, he spoke with easy familiarity, his rain-dampened mood vastly improved by Athena's warm welcome.

Katrine's eyes had narrowed as she studied the young couple who had been married under such outlandish circumstances. In truth she had been consumed with jealousy by the romance surrounding Athena's proxy marriage, and it galled her not only to have lost Stephen to her most hated rival, but to be forced into the background—a position she loathed—while the entire colony discussed with seemingly endless fascination the adventures of Athena Courtland.

Katrine had been delighted to learn of the unexpected scandal that had struck the Kensington family. At her insistence, she and her mother had been making daily calls on Athena at Courtland Grace, hoping to learn anything new concerning Stephen's summons to Albany. Nothing would have pleased Katrine more than to see Athena Kensington fall flat on her face, but to her annoyance most people to whom she had broached the subject seemed to feel sympathy for the young bride's unfortunate circumstances.

Unfortunate! Katrine could have screamed aloud. Why did Athena always manage to convince everyone of her sweetness and innocence when in truth she was a rebellious wanton not fit for proper company? Why had Stephen decided to marry her when he knew perfectly well that she had formed a liaison with a Scottish soldier months ago?

"I hope your meeting with General Amherst wasn't too unpleasant," Athena remarked innocently. From the corner of her eye she could see Marianne and her daughter lean forward expectantly, and a knowing gleam entered her eyes. So they had come to offer their condolences, had they? Insufferably prying busybodies! She'd love to give them both a good swift kick in their carefully corseted backsides!

"He was extremely cordial," Stephen replied, pouring himself a drink from the elegant sideboard. Settling himself in a striped damask armchair, he crossed his legs comfortably before him and, to the de Vrieses' ill-concealed annoyance, refused to say anything more.

Talk proceeded in a desultory fashion thereafter, and when it became obvious that the subject would not be raised again, Katrine and her mother took their leave. Athena suffered their effusive farewells with a vague smile, then breathed a sigh of relief when Wills shut the door behind them.

"Thank goodness they're gone," Stephen remarked from the salon doorway, where he stood leaning against the wall with a glass in his hand. His eyes rested hungrily on his wife's white throat. "I never thought we'd find ourselves alone."

Athena swallowed hard. Surely he didn't expect her to tumble into bed with him the moment he returned!

"Athena," Stephen murmured, setting his glass onto the floor and coming toward her. Running his hands over her shoulders, he feasted his eyes on the lush softness of her lips.

"So you're back, Stephen! I hope the rain didn't make your trip uncomfortable."

Stephen stifled a groan as Fletcher Courtland appeared on the staircase above them. Was there some sort of conspiracy being carried out here to keep him apart from his wife? His expression was sullen as he shook hands with his brother-in-law, secretly annoyed that Fletcher seemed to be recovering so well. Dressed in faded buckskin breeches and a leather vest, Fletcher looked as though he had just returned from working the fields. Though he carried his upper body stiffly and a bandage still swathed his shoulder and chest, he was not the same man Stephen and his friends had carried, bleeding and near death, into the house several weeks ago.

"The roads were still passable," Stephen growled. "I don't believe Albany has had the same amount of rain as West York." Deliberately turning his back on Fletcher, he took Athena's hand possessively in his own. "Are you ready to go back home with me?"

She was caught off guard by the blunt question. Leave Courtland Grace so soon?

"You can't possibly leave in such weather," Fletcher protested, indicating the rain that lashed the panes relentlessly. "And Prudence has been working in the kitchen all morning. Surely you can stay long enough to dine with us?"

Stephen had no choice but to agree. Fletcher Courtland was not a man he cared to alienate, and now that they were related by marriage 'twould be in his best interest to nurture a sound relationship with all of Athena's brothers. Reluctantly he nodded his head, but his determination to possess his wife was rapidly becoming an obsession.

"Why don't you tell us what happened in Albany?" Athena asked as the three of them returned to the salon.

Accepting a fresh glass from Fletcher, Stephen settled himself into his armchair and gave a bitter laugh. "God, what a bloody waste of time! I've never come across a more inept assemblage of fools than Amherst and his colonels. Not only was I unable to tell them a thing about my father's dealings, but 'twould seem that with his death the true leader of the operation will remain unknown."

"Then your father didn't work alone?" Fletcher asked interestedly.

Stephen snorted. "My father was too much of a coward and an idiot to organize something of that nature. I fear he was little more than a pawn, though I imagine the truth will follow him to his grave."

Athena was shocked by the callous manner in which Stephen spoke of Ambrose. A question Fletcher had asked her only yesterday came back to her unexpectedly: Are you certain, Athena, that you know what sort of man you've married?

A gloating laugh from Stephen brought her thoughts back with a start. "I did find pleasure in one thing, though, and that was seeing how foolish all of this has made Lochiel Blackmoor appear."

Athena's brow furrowed. "What do you mean?"

Stephen laughed again. "Oh, come now, Athena, surely you must realize what an ass he made of himself! Not only did he fail to bring my father to justice, but in killing him with his inadvertent bungling, he also destroyed any chances of learning who his partner had been."

"Major Blackmoor did not kill your father!" Athena burst out hotly. "At least not directly," she added hastily, aware of the scowl that crossed her husband's face.

"And surely other prisoners were taken at the mill the night of the arrest," Fletcher put in to smooth over the awkward silence. "'Tis unlikely they've failed to identify their leader by now."

"Ah, but you're wrong," Stephen replied smugly, rising to refill his glass. "The wretched creatures didn't know a thing. Of course, they were all able to give an accurate description of the man they claimed was in charge, but curiously enough not a single one of them knew his name. Clever fellow to take that sort of precaution, eh? God, but 'twas rich to watch Blackmoor fall flat on his face!"

Athena said nothing, although her hands twisted nervously in her lap. Was it true that Lochiel had been made to look the fool? Had Stephen deliberately helped foster that image in the general's eyes with his hostile remarks?

I know who the other man is, she reminded herself. If I go to Albany to tell the general his name, not only will he be brought to justice, but Lochiel won't be made to look as foolish as Stephen says.

"What does General Amherst intend to do next?" she inquired.

Stephen shrugged. "He's a very busy man. I'm sure there are more important matters on his mind at the moment."

Athena rose casually to her feet, a guileless smile on her lips. "I think

I'll peek into the kitchen and see how dinner preparations are coming along."

"Ever the hungry one," Fletcher teased.

Athena responded to this with a laugh and bent to place a kiss on his brow. No sooner had she left the room than she was racing breathlessly for her bedchamber. Mercy, responding to her mistress's urgent summons, was startled to find Athena seated at her small writing desk, a quill flying across the paper before her. While she wrote, she was busy undressing, flinging stockings and shoes across the room.

"Bring me my habit," she instructed, brow furrowed in concentration.

"You're going riding, miss?" Mercy's freckled nose wrinkled as she peered at the rain-spattered window.

"Tykie and I are going out," Athena responded, golden head bent over the parchment.

Mercy knew better than to persist in her questioning whenever her mistress chose to be evasive. Pulling a midnight-blue velvet habit from the clothespress, she searched about the cluttered trunk for a hat, gloves, and whip.

"There!" Athena exclaimed, satisfied with what she had written. Folding the parchment and laying it aside, she stripped off her gown and petticoats and, with Mercy's help, fitted the habit snugly over her corseted figure.

"Pay attention to what I'm about to tell you," she instructed her maid as she buttoned the trim jacket over her hips. "I've a very important errand to run, and under no circumstances is Stephen to find out."

Mercy's eyes grew round. She was accustomed to being a reluctant accomplice to Miss Athena's shenanigans, but to involve her husband in them? "Oh, miss, I'm not sure I'll be able to deceive him!"

"Don't worry," Athena soothed, her velvet skirts swirling about her ankles as she strode to the mirror. Running her fingers through her untamed curls, she nodded her head in the direction of her desk. "I've written Fletcher a note explaining where I've gone. 'Tis a simple precaution in the event I don't make it back tonight."

"And Mr. Kensington?" Mercy asked nervously, handing her mistress a pair of dainty riding gloves.

"I've asked Fletcher to take care of the situation." Athena couldn't help smiling, albeit ruefully, at the relief on Mercy's face. Apparently she wasn't the only one who was aware that Stephen possessed a difficult temperament. "Don't worry," she repeated. "You're not going to have to lie to him or anything like that. Simply do me the favor of keeping him ignorant of my departure as long as you can. And give Fletcher the note as soon as possible."

"Without Mr. Kensington seeing?" Mercy asked, beginning to understand.

Athena's eyes gleamed as she placed her cocked hat on the mass of curls she had finished pinning to her head. "Exactly."

Taking the back stairway, she left the house via the servants' entrance and hurried across the rain-soaked yard to the stables. She found both Hale and Tykie in the tack room mending harnesses. The big Scotsman's bushy brows rose at the sight of her.

"Be ye gang riding i' this weather, lass?" His tone indicated that she would be daft to do so.

"We both are," Athena responded purposefully. Now that she had made up her mind to see General Amherst, she was not about to let anything detain her. At first she had decided to go alone, then realized that a married woman appearing at the general's door without a proper escort might not be admitted. The general, she had heard, was notoriously conservative.

"It canna wait?" Tykie asked with a groan, recognizing the stubborn set of his mistress's jaw all too well. Despite the fact that the first of June had come and gone, a bone-chilling dampness hung over the valley, and he had been looking forward to a hot meal eaten before the stove in his room.

"No, it cannot." Athena tossed her head and squared her slim shoulders. "Well, are you going to come with me or stay here?"

"I expect I havna choice." Tykie's brow darkened when he caught the glimmer of amusement in Hale's eyes. Reaching down, he cuffed the youth sharply with his enormous paw. " 'Tis humor ye be finding at my expense, lad?"

The blow had been mild, yet Hale and the small stool on which he'd been sitting went over backward. Booted feet dangling in the air, he blinked in bewilderment while Athena covered her lips with her hand, not wanting him to see that she was on the verge of bursting into helpless laughter.

"The lad's thinkin' I'm a poor soul indeed tae be dragged once again into ane o' yer hair-raisin' schemes, Miss Athena," Tykie growled with feigned anger.

Hale shook his head emphatically, although this was exactly what he'd been thinking. At an impatient gesture from Tykie, however, he scrambled to his feet and hurried off to saddle the horses.

"We're going to Albany," Athena explained as soon as they were alone. Anxious to be gone before Stephen became suspicious of her absence, she cast a nervous glance out of the tiny tack room window. "Please don't let

Hale know. He'll only be obliged to tell Stephen the truth, and I don't want him coming after me."

Tykie was both intrigued and delighted by these mysterious words. Pulling the wool over that fop's eyes would be a pleasure, not to mention that Miss Athena hadn't shown so much animation since they'd returned home from Fort Shuyler. She could count on his wholehearted support for whatever it was she had in mind!

Minutes later the two of them were cantering down the road, Tykie with a heavy black cape thrown over his massive shoulders, Athena with her face concealed by the hood of her cloak. Mud splattered her boots as Ballycor splashed through puddles, and she eyed the path ahead with anxious eyes. Although the thunder had ceased to rumble, gray clouds still obscured the sky and rain continued to fall. Stephen had said earlier that the roads to Albany were still passable, but Athena was well aware of how quickly they could become a quagmire of sucking mud.

"I'm not going to turn back," she told herself with grim determination. She had made up her mind to supply General Amherst with Thomas Painsley's name, and nothing short of a flood was going to stop her.

Both man and girl were soaked to the skin by the time the weary horses came to a halt in the yard of a coaching inn on the outskirts of Albany. Leading his mistress into the common room, Tykie shook himself like a wet dog and demanded to see the proprietor, terrifying the serving wench with his dripping beard and demonically dangling earring.

"You certainly know how to charm the lasses," Athena remarked as the young girl scurried away. She had thrown back the hood of her cape and removed her hat, her hair glinting like newly minted gold in the light of the fire before which she stood warming her hands.

" 'Tis a foul hole, this," Tykie responded, though Athena thought it pleasant enough with its soot-stained, raftered ceiling and cheerful collection of stoneware lining the burnished oak walls. "I would hae brought ye elsewhere, but there doesna seem tae be room anywhere else i' town."

Both of them had been astonished by the number of soldiers in evidence. Companies of Regulars and Provincials had passed them by the dozens on the road, all loaded down with full gear, their boots and gaiters splattered with mud. Caught up in her own troubles at home in West York, Athena had been able to forget for a time the assault on Quebec, yet it seemed to her now that the war had never taken on such a frighteningly grim reality.

Fletcher had mentioned to her the day before how sorry he was that he would miss the great march on Canada, yet looking at the youthful faces of the soldiers they passed, Athena felt her heart swell with fierce relief.

She was glad that he was home, glad that he would be spared the terrible slaughter she sensed was to come.

If only she knew the twins' whereabouts, she thought to herself now, her throat constricting with sudden fear. Neither of them had responded to the desperate letters she had sent informing them of Fletcher's accident. Only a brief note from Major Rogers had arrived, explaining to her that he had received her mail while in a bivouac somewhere in New Hampshire. He had promised to forward it to her brothers as soon as possible but had cautioned her not to anticipate an answer. All of his Rangers had been sent into Canada on a scouting mission at Major General Wolfe's request, and Major Rogers doubted that the twins would receive their sister's mail anytime in the near future.

By now the proprietor of the inn had arrived, wiping his grimy hands on his apron, his fleshy jowls quivering as he smiled a greeting at the enormous Highlander. "Good ter see ye agin, Mr. Downs. What'll it be today, eh? A tankard o' my best ale or—"

Tykie gestured toward Athena, who was still standing by the fire. Even with her back turned, it was obvious to the squinting innkeeper that she was a gentlewoman. Trimly tailored velvet skirts fell softly from a small waist, and he could see the hint of a slim, aristocratic jaw illuminated by the flickering firelight.

"I want a private room for Mrs. Kensington," Tykie demanded curtly, "and some o' yer best mead for her tae drink. Be that supper ye be servin', mon?" he added, noisily sniffing the air. "Bring a bit o' that, too."

"There ain't a private room to be had in all of Albany, Mr. Downs!" the proprietor protested. "Why, soldiers be billeted—"

Tykie's big hand reached out to pack the proprietor's vest, a goodly bit of the poor man's flesh ending up twisted in the powerful grip as well. "A private room for Mrs. Kensington," Tykie repeated dangerously, keeping a wary eye on his mistress's back, well aware that she would disapprove of his bullying should she turn around and see him.

"I'll see what I can do," he was promised in a breathless whisper.

Satisfied, Tykie let him go. "Ye be a jewel among men, Tibble."

Rubbing his chest and muttering beneath his breath, the proprietor politely ushered Athena into a small room just off the kitchens. Curtains had been drawn over the single window, and a small table stood beneath it, the linen cloth wrinkled but otherwise clean.

It would do, Tykie decided happily. Not that Miss Athena needed food and rest so direly, but he didn't like the idea of leaving her alone in a place like this. Even with the door closed, he could hear the raucous laughter and the clanking of pewter mugs from the crowded common room. The Crown West Inn was no real place for a lady, but he had been adamant about leaving Miss Athena somewhere warm and dry while he set out to discover General Amherst's whereabouts.

With the number of soldiers in town and the teeming chaos in the streets, he hadn't wanted Miss Athena to accompany him when he rode up to the fort to ask where the general made his headquarters. Though he still had no idea what business she wanted to take up with the commander of the Provincial and British armies, he didn't want her to appear before that most important man looking like a half-drowned waif. Miss Athena, after vehement protests, had finally seen the wisdom of his arguments.

"I'll be back as soon as I've found 'im, miss," he told her now. "Master Tibble be bringin' ye summat tae eat an' drink i' the meantime."

She smiled up at him, her cheeks flushed from the heat of the fire. "Thank you, Tykie."

The warmth that suffused him at her soft words was enough to give him the courage to venture back into the pouring rain. Athena, meanwhile, removed her sodden cloak and hung it on the rack near the door. The tiny room was stuffy but welcomingly private. Pewter flagons were arranged in a cabinet in the corner, and the bleakness of the rainy afternoon was held at bay by the numerous candles that sputtered in their holders along the walls.

Seating herself with a sigh, Athena ran a hand through her damp curls, feeling decidedly glad that she had agreed to Tykie's plan that she remain here. She had no real desire to negotiate those muddy, crowded streets on the nervously prancing Ballycor while inquiries were made as to General Amherst's whereabouts. Besides, Tykie had a way with people that would yield him that information without her interference.

Gaining entrance into the general's doubtlessly well-guarded house was another matter entirely, but Athena didn't expect to encounter any difficulties. Surely the general would remember having met her at Bountiful last October and would be kind enough to grant her a brief audience. It occurred to her suddenly that Lochiel might be with him, and her pulse gave an annoying leap at the thought.

"You mustn't think of any man but Stephen now," she admonished herself severely. Yet somehow the memory of her husband's lust-filled eyes made it difficult for her to recapture the tenderness she had felt for him the night Ambrose died.

"Excuse me, Mrs. Kensington."

Startled from her thoughts, she looked up to find the portly proprietor standing in the doorway. "Yes?"

"There be a gentleman outside requestin' a private room. I told him there wasn't none available, but he said he only wanted to stay for a quick meal. He's been comin' here fairly regular the past few years, and I'd hate ter turn him away. Bad for business, you'll understand."

"And you'd like him to share my room with me?" Athena asked, knowing it was common practice to double up the guests when an inn was full.

He relaxed visibly at the understanding in her soft voice. Sweet young lady she was, he was thinking to himself, not at all a devil terror like that footman of hers! 'Twas fortunate for Mr. Downs that he never failed to spend a week's wages on Tibble's finest ale whenever he was in town, otherwise he'd have found himself out on the street for bullying him around the way he had!

" 'Course I'll be here to act as chaperon," Tibble added hastily, moved by a rare feeling of propriety as he gazed into her dainty features. Now that she had removed her cloak, he saw that she was certainly the lady Tykie had insisted she was, and a lovely one whose reputation could easily be damaged if she were found dining alone in one of his private rooms with a strange man.

Athena's amused smile made him shuffle his feet like an embarrassed schoolboy. "I have no objections to sharing my table, provided the gentleman in question agrees."

"Oh, that he will, miss, that he will."

Tibble hurried away, eagerly adding up in his head the tips he expected to receive for having rented out the same room to two parties. Aye, yer a clever fellow, he murmured to himself.

Having been brought a tankard of mead by a serving girl, Athena was gratefully sipping its sweet contents when she heard the door open behind her.

"Good evening, mistress. Mr. Tibble informs me that you've been kind enough to share your table with me. 'Tis a foul day outside and I appreciate your generosity."

The speaker was a tall, gaunt-featured gentleman in a many-tiered greatcoat. As he spoke, his gaze was drawn like a moth to a flame to Athena's golden hair, which glowed radiantly in the candlelight.

She set the tankard down and smiled up at him, her eyes traveling from his elegant waistcoat of satin to his not unpleasant features. "You're quite welcome," she began, only to have the words die on her lips as their eyes locked across the room. An ominous silence descended, for in that same moment each recognized the other.

Heart hammering in her breast, Athena came to her feet, upsetting her tankard as she did so. Trying to recover her composure, she stammered what she hoped was an innocent enough apology, but by then it was too late.

Crossing the room in two swift strides, the tall gentleman came to a halt before her. A smile that was no longer pleasant played across his lips and in a voice that made her tremble he inquired mockingly, "Is there any reason for you to be disconcerted at seeing me, Miss Courtland?"

Athena took a deep breath and bravely raised her chin. In a voice that faltered only slightly, she responded quietly, "Why, no, not at all. Why should there be . . . Mr. Painsley?"

Nineteen

Toddman Tyner took a long swallow of fiery brandy and sighed contentedly as he propped his stockinged feet on the table before him. Rarely did he get the chance to enjoy such excellent libation, and the thought that he could easily afford another bottle if he chose put a smug expression on his flushed features.

"Will you be wantin' your supper now, sir?"

The owner and proprietor of the Merry Widow Inn was standing in the doorway, the expectant look on her fleshy face never wavering despite the fact that her guest was seated with his rather unclean feet resting on her tablecloth. Dinah Partridge was a fastidious woman, yet cleanliness always managed to lose its importance when a guest with money in his pockets was involved. Mr. Tyner could throw his chicken bones onto the floor and urinate in his pewter flagon for all she cared, provided the coins kept coming. One had to set priorities straight in a business like this, one did!

"Bring me some o' that pork roastin' outside on the spit," Toddman Tyner commanded, "and a bottle o' yer finest wine. 'Tis celebratin' I am."

Dinah flashed him a toothy smile and hastened away to comply. Business hadn't been too good of late, what with all the soldiers in town scaring decent folk away, but this big fellow promised to make up for the slow times, and she intended to see that he was given everything his heart desired.

Pouring the last of the brandy into his glass, Toddman Tyner tossed the empty bottle onto the floor and watched with a satisfied grin as it rolled beneath the table. What could make him happier than his own private room in a quiet inn and a buxom proprietress prepared to give him anything he asked for? Chuckling, he reached a hand into his pocket and shook the heavy leather sack for the hundredth time, enjoying the distinctive melody of gold coins clinking together.

"You done well for yourself, Toddy me boy," he murmured, feeling a pleasant haze envelope him as he drained the contents of his glass. "Easiest fortune ye've ever earned for yerself."

Indeed, it had all been childishly simple. Arriving in Albany the morning of Ambrose Kensington's death, Toddman had encountered no difficulty in locating Thomas Painsley. Everyone in town seemed to know him, and his office had been conveniently located near the river, a part of town with which the unsavory Philadelphian was more than familiar.

He had been forced to wait most of the day before Painsley agreed to see him, but Toddman Tyner could well afford to be patient. His instincts told him that Painsley was the sort of man who could be counted on to close a deal with little fuss. His meeting with the wealthy merchant hadn't disappointed him, either. 'Twas obvious from the first that Painsley viewed the world much as Toddman Tyner himself did, and he hadn't wasted any time in coming directly to the point.

"You realize that this is blackmail," the gaunt-featured merchant had remarked simply when the other man finally finished speaking. His tone was matter-of-fact, and he sat with his long-fingered hands crossed calmly before him on the polished desktop. Muted sounds from the street came to them through the shuttered windows, and beams of late-afternoon sunlight fell through the slits onto the priceless Oriental carpet that covered the oak plank flooring. Toddman Tyner had noticed it when he'd first stepped inside. Its obvious value and the elegant fit of the clothes Painsley wore had convinced him that he was a man who could afford to pay well.

"Call it what you want," he said now, lifting his shoulders in an indifferent shrug. "I likes to think of it as an exchange o' goods. Ten guineas will buy you the name of the other party who overheard you talking to Kensington that night."

Thomas Painsley's dark eyes had narrowed. "And you, Mr. Tyner? Will ten guineas buy your silence?"

Toddman Tyner nodded emphatically. "You can ask around if you likes. There's many hereabouts what knows me."

The long fingers began to drum a soundless rhythm on the desktop. "Suppose you spend those ten guineas and decide you'd like more? I'm not a patient man, Mr. Tyner, and I don't care to find you begging at my door the rest of my life."

Their eyes met across the small space that divided them. Unexpectedly Toddman Tyner felt a prickle flee down his spine, and he wondered if Painsley's gaunt, sallow face and those demonically burning eyes had anything to do with it. He was an odd fellow to be sure, this Painsley gent, but it was his money that Toddman wanted. His unsettling appearance oughtn't affect the outcome one way or the other.

"We'll just have to trust each other," he responded simply.

The dark eyes burned into his. "Yes, I imagine we will."

Thomas Painsley fell silent as he continued to regard the ill-kempt man before him. He knew Tyner's type well enough. Unscrupulous, unsavory, and tending toward violence, this one had been born with just enough intelligence to make him dangerous. There was no doubt in the merchant's mind that he spoke the truth about eavesdropping on his conversation in Kensington's garden, and it was with considerable effort that he managed to maintain his own inscrutable facade while inwardly he smoldered with anger.

Damn Ambrose Kensington! He should never have agreed to talk to the fat fool outside where they had been so easily overheard. Furthermore, the thwarted exchange at Brinston's mill had lost him most of his men and a great deal of money. When he'd first learned of the fiasco, he'd lost control of himself and had gone on a rampage of violence that had left his latest mistress with a broken jaw and his elegant home in shambles.

Since then he'd managed to calm himself. His discretion had paid off in that none of the men who worked for him knew his name, and even if any of them suspected, they would never reveal it. Painsley had made damned sure they were aware of the consequences should one of them dare break their vow of silence.

Only Ambrose had been cowardly enough to be intimidated into revealing Painsley's name. But according to Toddman Tyner, Ambrose Kensington was dead. Ten guineas would buy Tyner's silence, which meant that the only remaining obstacle to be dealt with was this person Tyner had mentioned. Would this unknown individual come forward with his information once he learned of the raid on Brinston's mill and Ambrose's death? Time was running out, and Thomas Painsley wasn't about to sit idle waiting to be indicted.

Unlocking the bottom drawer of his desk, he bent to retrieve a small leather satchel. With eyes unnerving in their coldness he tossed it to Tyner, who caught it deftly. Painsley watched with a contemptuous smile as it was eagerly opened and the contents carefully counted into a grimy palm.

"There be fifteen guineas here," Toddman Tyner stated in astonishment, returning them to the sack.

The humorless smile broadened. "You were fortunate to point that out, my friend. It convinces me of your honesty." The last word was uttered with derisive emphasis, but Toddman was too enraptured to take note of it.

"You're giving me fifteen guineas for the name?"

"And for the assurance that the two of us will never have cause to traffic together again."

This time Toddman did catch the warning in the other's soft tone, and again the same sense of foreboding settled over him. He wasn't exactly sure what it was about Thomas Painsley that unnerved him. In a carefully tended wig and elaborate satin waistcoat, he looked exactly like the wealthy merchant he was heralded to be. Why, then, did that quiet voice and those dark, searching eyes give one the impression that one was staring at the devil himself?

"If our paths cross again, 'twill be an unfortunate act of God," Toddman Tyner assured him hastily.

Painsley seemed to derive amusement from this unconsciously heartfelt remark. For a moment he studied the swarthy face in silence, then said abruptly, "I'm a busy man, Tyner, with no more time for you. The gentleman's name, if you please."

Toddman was just as anxious to be gone. It seemed to him as if the fifteen guineas were burning a hole in his pocket. Already his mouth was beginning to water as he imagined how he was going to spend them.

" 'Tain't no gentleman, Mr. Painsley. 'Twas a lady, and she were out on the terrace the night I came up to the house to see Kensington about—"

"You've already told me the story," Thomas Painsley interrupted him curtly. His thoughts were racing. A woman? Christ's fury, she'd probably told her secret to every last one of her acquaintances by now!

" 'Twas the Kensington wench herself," Toddman responded smugly, delighted for once to be holding the upper hand.

"One of Ambrose's daughters?" That wasn't so bad. Aramintha and Eliza were probably twice as stupid as their simpleton father and would never be able to link the meeting in the garden with what had happened at Brinston's mill.

Tyner was shaking his head emphatically. "Not the daughters. 'Twas that golden-haired wench of Stephen's. Athena Kensington herself."

Sitting in a pleasantly drunken stupor in his private room in the Merry Widow Inn, Toddman Tyner smiled to himself now as he recalled the astonishment that had registered on the cocky gent's gaunt face. Without another word he'd left the elegant office, the fifteen guineas safe in his pocket, feeling immeasurably pleased with himself. Not only had he put his information to good use, he'd also seen to it that Stephen Kensington was going to pay for betraying him.

What did Painsley intend to do to him? Toddman wondered curiously. A sense of unease crept over him recalling those coldly glinting eyes. 'Twouldn't be pleasant, that was for sure. More than likely, too, was the possibility that Athena Kensington would not escape some harm. Toddman felt a pang of regret recalling her innocent beauty, then shrugged philosophically. He'd been well paid for providing Painsley with her name, and his responsibility ended there.

"Here you be, Mr. Tyner."

He sniffed appreciatively at the scent of roast pork, cabbage, and baked apples that accompanied Dinah Partridge into the room. Watching as she set the tray before him, his eyes strayed to her well-rounded bottom. She squealed when he gave it a hard pinch but made no attempt to move away.

"Are ye really a merry widow, my love?" he inquired, encouraged by her smile.

"Depends on what you're willin' to pay, lad," she responded with a wink.

His hearty laugh filled the room, hearing the saucy challenge in her voice. "Why, we'll just have to see, won't we?"

Wordlessly she took his hand in hers, and Tyner, his dinner forgotten, followed her eagerly up the creaking flight of stairs. Leading him into an empty room, Dinah set the lantern down and turned back the covers on the bed. She wasn't particularly beautiful, Tyner thought to himself, watching her, but then he'd heard quite a bit about her prowess. 'Twas said she didn't favor just any man who asked, and he could have rubbed his hands together in glee. By God, fifteen guineas had a way of changing one's life for the better!

"Close the door, dearie," Dinah whispered in a husky voice, unpinning her hair so that the long, reddish mass fell to her shoulders.

He did as she asked, thinking to himself that he'd be a happy man indeed if the coming night never ended.

It was odd that he should experience such sentiments, for Toddman Tyner did not live long enough to witness the coming dawn. Guests of the Merry Widow Inn were shocked to discover the following morning that one of them had been murdered in his sleep the night before, an apparent victim of a brutal robbery.

"Don't surprise me none," one of the guests was overheard to say after the body had been removed and Dinah's staff had resumed serving breakfast with calm efficiency. "Not the way he flashed that bag o' gold 'round the common room last night."

" 'Tis a shame it happened here," his companion added. "Miss Dinah don't usually run a place where guests get stabbed in their beds."

"Oh, she'll weather the storm a'right," came the confident reply. "Too many people knows her for the jewel she be. 'Twere an accident, that's all."

Indeed, the incident seemed quickly forgotten. Around the same time that Athena Kensington was drinking mead at the Crown West Inn, Dinah Partridge's Merry Widow was filling up with revelers while the inimitable proprietress mingled among her guests with the same pleasant smile of old. Not long after the dinner hour had begun, she was summoned to the small room behind the kitchens used as an office, where a visitor waited to see her.

"Full house tonight, I see," the tall, cloaked stranger observed as the proprietress bustled inside.

" 'Twill take more than a simple murder to put me out of business," she responded archly.

"I gather no clues as to the guilty party were found?"

She shook her head. "Naturally not."

"And the sack of gold which was reportedly stolen?"

Sliding the bolt on the door behind her, Dinah stooped to run her hand along the bottom of the table that she used for paperwork. Hooked on a nail conveniently out of sight from probing eyes was Toddman Tyner's sack of coins.

The gaunt-featured man counted it carefully and raised an eyebrow in annoyance. "Didn't waste any time spending it, did he?"

Dinah shrugged.

"I imagine they were all legitimate expenses," he added meaningfully.

She tossed her head defiantly. "Of course they was."

Reaching into the sack, he removed another coin and placed it in her outstretched palm. "Just in case he overlooked anything," he told the grinning woman, then turned and disappeared through the door, his cloak billowing behind him.

The weather was foul. The temperature had dropped steadily as the storm front swept across the surrounding hills. Turning the collar of his cloak against the wind, the gaunt-featured man quickly walked the short distance to the nearby coaching inn. Owned by a garrulous gent by the name of Tibble, it competed directly with the Merry Widow for customers. Though the food was better at Dinah's, Thomas Painsley had decided it would be wiser to dine elsewhere that night. Not that he was particularly hungry, but he had a long trip ahead of him and desired something nourishing before he left Albany.

A private room was his terse request, and Master Tibble, recognizing a man of wealth, had hastily arranged for him to share one with another party rather than to lose him as a paying guest. It annoyed Thomas Painsley that he would be forced to dine with someone else, and he was scowling unpleasantly when he entered the room, though he kept his greeting polite. One could easily imagine the shock that swept through him when his eyes fell on the lovely young woman who was to be his table companion that evening and he recognized her as none other than Athena Kensington.

When she turned at the sound of his voice, he saw her eyes widen, the sapphire depths darkening as she recognized him as well, and a heady feeling of power swept over him. Lady Luck had once again dealt him the winning hand, and when Athena lifted her chin to bravely challenge him, she could not know that her fate was irreversibly sealed.

Tykie Downs paced the floor like a restless animal, a fearsome scowl darkening his brow. Every few minutes he would glance at the clock ticking on the mantel and a growl would sound low in his throat. Where the devil was Miss Athena? Why had she disappeared without leaving word? Blood and fury, the lass was impossible!

"Well?" he demanded impatiently as the door opened behind him to reveal the fidgeting Master Tibble.

"I asked round the taproom, Mr. Downs. No one saw the lady leave."

Tykie ran an exasperated hand through his grizzled hair. "She couldna hae been spirited awa'! This 'gentleman' ye arranged tae share the room wi' her, ye dinna ken wham he be?"

Tibble spread his hands appealingly. "I've already told you three times, Mr. Downs, I've never seen 'im afore." Swallowing nervously, he refrained from adding that he had lied to Mrs. Kensington by telling her the gentleman was a frequent caller at his inn. After all, she probably would have refused his request to dine with a man who was a total stranger to the innkeeper himself. Oh, why the devil had she chosen his establishment to stage such a dramatic disappearance? He didn't deserve to be made the object of Tykie Downs's formidable anger!

"I left 'em alone long enough ter fetch a bottle of wine. When I returned the room was empty."

Tykie resumed his pacing, his expression frightening to behold. What in God's name was he supposed to do now? General Amherst had been in a staff meeting when Tykie had finally found him and wouldn't be available to callers until morning. Ought he to engage some rooms for the night and simply wait here until Miss Athena returned? Yet suppose something terrible had happened to her?

"Bah!" he burst out. " 'Tis a daft thought indeed!"

Who would want to do Miss Athena harm? She must have slipped out on some errand, given the fact that no living soul in the place had seen her go. But what about the gentleman Tibble had described? Did his disappearance have anything to do with Miss Athena's? Blood and fury, why hadn't the lass at least left a message?

"Excuse me, sir."

A young girl of barely thirteen years was standing in the doorway bobbing a timid curtsy, her hands twisted in the folds of her apron. Her face was pale beneath a white scalloped cap, and her eyes flicked nervously from Tykie's bearded face to her employer's.

"What's this?" Master Tibble demanded in a tone that made her cower back against the door. "Forgettin' yer duties again, you lazy wench? Get back in the kitchen afore I—"

His words ended in a startled squeak as an enormous hand clamped itself without warning about his forearm. "Let the lass have her say, Tibble."

" 'Tis about the lady," the girl stammered, gazing as if mesmerized into the coal-black eyes of the towering man before her. His chest alone was broader than the span of an oak tree, and she found herself fascinated and terrified all at once by the gold ring swinging so jauntily from his ear. "I overheard Mr. Tibble askin' Molly about her just a minute ago."

"Do you know where she went, Kitty, or is this another of your foolish games?" her employer asked irritably.

"No, sir, I really did see her," Kitty assured him hastily. Her expression grew dreamy as she remembered how beautiful the lady in question had been. Never had she seen hair so fair in color or a habit of such exquisite cut, the dark blue velvet clinging to a waist that Kitty had envied for its daintiness.

"Well, lass, what happened to her?"

The barely restrained impatience in that deep bass voice startled her from her thoughts.

"She an' some gentleman in a black cape went out through the rear entrance," she said breathlessly. "I was emptyin' slops out back and saw them. Didn't even have her hood up," she went on sorrowfully, "and her pretty hair gettin' all wet in the rain."

Tykie's eyes were blazing. "Did she gae wi' him willingly?"

Kitty stared up at him blankly.

"She wasn't struggling or calling for help?" Tibble put in worriedly. Dear God, he'd be ruined if a lady of quality had been kidnapped from his inn!

Kitty's small face cleared. "Oh, heavens, no! Had his hand under her arm, the gent did, all proper an' polite. 'Twould seem to me they was in a hurry, though."

"Which way did they go?" Tibble demanded.

She shrugged her thin shoulders. "I didn't see."

"Bloody hell!" Tykie burst out, no wiser than before. Helpless frustration overwhelmed him, and Kitty uttered a terrified squeal as he slammed his fist impotently into the palm of his hand.

" 'Twould seem there ain't much we can do," Tibble pointed out timidly, hoping Tykie wasn't about to unleash his anger on himself or his inn. He'd seen the damage the big Scotsman was capable of doing in the course of a single drunken brawl.

A charged silence followed in which Tykie's scowl deepened. What did the fellow mean, there was nothing to be done? Somehow Miss Athena had to be found! But how? Where to begin looking in a town this size? Abruptly, his expression cleared. "Oh aye, there be summat I can do," he said softly.

Tibble and Kitty gazed up at him expectantly, but Tykie did not choose to enlighten them. Instead he poked a blunt finger into the proprietor's chest and growled, "I'll be back within the hour. If Mrs. Kensington retairns, ye'll tell her tae wait."

"Of course, Mr. Downs." It was not a command that Horatio Tibble was about to disobey. He had the uncomfortable feeling that the welfare of his establishment depended on it.

Moments later Tykie was cantering his gelding up the steep, deserted street to the fort. The fact that Ballycor was still in his stall at the inn added to his sense of urgency. 'Twasn't like Miss Athena to leave him, even if she had just gone off somewhere locally with this unknown gent.

Tykie's jaw clamped purposefully as he approached the fort. No matter how angry Miss Athena was going to be, he intended to turn to Major Blackmoor for help. Though he was well familiar with his mistress's unconventional ways, her odd disappearance tonight was not at all like her, a fact that led him to believe that something was terribly wrong. 'Twould be better to turn to someone like Major Blackmoor for help, who was not only far more clever than Tykie himself, but knew Miss Athena well enough to know where to begin looking for her.

The sentry posted at the fort gate recognized the big Highlander at once, for Tykie had questioned him less than an hour ago as to General Amherst's whereabouts. "Still haven't found 'im, eh?" he inquired, aiming a stream of tobacco juice at the puddle in which Tykie's horse had halted.

"It be Major Lochiel Blackmoor I be wantin' the noo," Tykie responded curtly. In the sputtering torchlight his bearded face had a wildness about it that was intimidating to behold.

"Blackmoor?" the sentry repeated, hefting his musket and wondering what this grizzled giant was about. Only a fool would dare venture out twice in weather like this.

"Aye. He be wi' the Seventh Highland Company o' His Majesty's Regulars."

"You'll have to ask at the guardhouse over there," the sentry responded obligingly, deciding not to make it hard for the big fellow, who looked as though he had a lot on his mind.

In the course of the next half-hour a frustrated Tykie found himself being shuttled from one building to another until someone finally directed him to a small office at the end of the barracks where the Highland Regiments were headquartered. Here his foul mood improved substantially as he stepped inside to find himself in the company of fellow countrymen, the two officers seated at the cluttered desk speaking in the low, lilting tones of the ancient Gaelic tongue.

"I believe Major Blackmoor was summoned to General Amherst's this evening for a briefing," one of them replied when Tykie stated his purpose. "The Seventh Company is scheduled to march at dawn."

Tykie stifled a groan, thinking of the long, wet ride back to the elegant townhouse at the opposite end of town where the general had established his residence. Thanking both men, he started glumly for the door, only to have it come close to striking him in the face as it was unexpectedly thrown open from outside.

"Watch yer step!" he snapped, leaping aside just in time.

"Still the same ill-tempered fellow, eh?" a mocking voice inquired.

Tykie's head came up in astonishment as a grinning Lochiel Blackmoor appeared before him, a tiered cloak billowing in the wind behind him. Hands propped on his lean hips, he regarded the bewildered giant with affable humor, although a hint of wariness had crept into the silver eyes. Fond as the major was of Tykie Downs, he always had to remember that Tykie was in Athena's employ—and anything that involved Athena Courtland was dangerous to him.

A smile of pure delight had spread across the Highlander's grizzled features. " 'Tis glad I am tae see ye!" he exclaimed with heartfelt relief. " 'Tis needin' yer help I am, an' time be runnin' short."

Lochiel reached behind him to shut the door and accepted with a nod of thanks the glass one of the officers had poured for him. Propping himself against the desk, he took a leisurely swallow and regarded the grinning Tykie with an indulgent air.

"What is it this time, my friend? Has your mistress been kidnapped by evil French trappers, or worse, left her poor husband for a red-skinned warrior? I warn you, I'm not about to play hero for her again."

Tykie's jaw dropped, thinking for the moment that Lochiel was being serious. When he saw the mocking gleam in the other's eyes, however, he burst out, " 'Tisna warriors or trappers this time, major! Miss Athena be vanished frae the coachin' inn, the Crown West, ye ken, an'—"

Aware of the interested looks on the faces of the others, Lochiel lifted a hand to check the stream of Tykie's anxious words. Ushering him into a tiny anteroom, he closed the door behind him and folded his arms across his chest.

"Now then," he said curtly, "what's this about Athena disappearing? What in hell is she doing in Albany in the first place?"

He listened intently as Tykie hurriedly explained and then was silent for a moment, his expression unreadable. Tykie held his breath, knowing the major wasn't one to be pushed, and relief coursed through him when he saw the purposeful tightening of the officer's lean jaw.

"I suppose we'd better take a look into the matter," he conceded at last.

Tykie's heart leaped. "I kenned ye'd help, sir," he burst out. "I kenned ye'd no forsake Miss Athena!"

Lochiel's expression darkened. "I have no personal interest in Mrs. Kensington's welfare," he said in a voice so cold that Tykie retreated a step, thoroughly taken aback. "I am lending my services simply because I feel obliged to help her after I inadvertently caused her brother's accident several weeks ago."

Tykie nodded to show he understood. Inwardly his newborn hopes were all but dashed.

"I imagine we should begin our search in the Crown West itself," Lochiel remarked when both men were riding off through the rain.

"I've already told ye no ane but the serving wench saw Miss Athena leave," Tykie reminded him glumly.

Lochiel gave a curt laugh. "In that, my friend, you are sorely mistaken. If the inn is as crowded as you say, someone must have observed her departure, and Mrs. Kensington is not a woman one can easily overlook." His voice grew harsh as he spoke, and when Tykie gave him a curious glance from beneath bushy brows, he saw that the carnal lips had tightened grimly and that the rugged countenance had taken on a ruthlessness he had seen only once before—when both men had been certain Athena had been kidnapped by renegade Algonquins.

Horatio Tibble was not at all pleased by the appearance of an army officer in his common room. Stammering a protest, he quickly fell silent when he found himself the unhappy recipient of a warning glance from silver eyes that seemed to peer right through him. Without another word he led both men into the small room where Athena had last been seen.

"I've already told Mr. Downs that the lady left without a word to anyone," he muttered gloomily, hoping the broad-shouldered fellow would take himself off. 'Twas bad for business to have a uniform here on his premises!

"I'm convinced that someone in your taproom saw Mrs. Kensington leave," the Highland officer remarked with arrogant certainty. "Someone who was either in the process of arriving or stepping outside to relieve himself. You'll question every last one of them and report back here to me."

Tibble bridled with indignation. You'd think he'd broken some sort of law and that his inn was filled with common riffraff like the unsavory establishment up the street belonging to Dinah Partridge! His resentment grew, for the Merry Widow was known for its ability to attract disreputable customers. At least here in the Crown West folks didn't get murdered in their beds!

"I'll speak to 'em," he agreed reluctantly, "but they'll not be tellin' me a thing."

Lochiel's half-hooded eyes held a knowing gleam. "Oh aye, they will. Every last one of them is aware of my presence here and will be only too willing to tell you what they know once they learn I'm looking for a woman and not one of them."

"Master Tibble doesna care for ye overly, major," Tykie observed as the door swung shut behind the scowling innkeeper. " 'Tis his pride ye've wounded in suggesting the Crown West attracts dishonest clients."

"I've seen more scrupulous men among the pickings of a navy impressment gang," Lochiel responded dourly, recalling the drunken men he'd seen carousing in Tibble's taproom.

"That uniform o' yours'll loosen their tongues quick enough," Tykie predicted. "I ken the lot of 'em well. Dregs o' society they be, an' ready tae betray each other quick enough for a wee sum."

"I cannot imagine what possessed you to bring Athena here in the first place," Lochiel remarked, peering over his broad shoulder as he began to pace the room.

Tykie's chin thrust defensively. "She were cold an' wet, an' the streets was crowded wi' soldiers. I couldna find room anywhere else, an' I didna think she'd go runnin' off wi' a stranger like this!"

"You still have no idea what she wanted to see General Amherst about?" Lochiel had paused in front of the small table, his brows drawing together over the bridge of his nose, yet he forgot his question when he noticed the pewter flagon before him. The linen cloth upon which it sat was stained, as though the contents had been spilled, and when he raised the lid he saw that only a small amount of liquid remained in the bottom.

Had Athena overturned this? he asked himself curiously. Rude, outspoken, and arrogant she might be, yet she possessed the table manners of a lady—and ladies did not spill their drinks. His eyes narrowed thoughtfully. Was it possible that the flagon had been overturned during a struggle? Had this strange man whose identity no one seemed to know overpowered Athena and forced her away with him? According to the serving girl Kitty, that had not been the case, yet Lochiel found the dark stain on the cloth disturbing.

Damn her! he thought savagely to himself, quelling the urge to slam his fist onto the tabletop. Was this another of her foolish games? When was she going to learn that her impulsive nature always led her into danger—or at least grayed prematurely the hairs of those who cared about her?

"She wouldna tell me why she wanted to see the general," Tykie was saying, oblivious to Lochiel's silence. "I asked her—"

"Major Blackmoor, here's a gent what says he saw the lady leaving my inn!"

The appearance of a breathless Tibble brought an end to the tension that was beginning to build between the two men. Lochiel turned his head to peer searchingly at the perspiring little man in a much-patched vest and breeches standing nervously at the proprietor's side.

The gentleman in question, a timid creature by the name of Franklin Biers, was close to swooning with the shock of being confronted by the demonically scowling army officer. He was a fainthearted man whose only real pleasure in life lay in escaping the acid tongue of his overbearing wife long enough to quaff a few mugs of ale with his acquaintances at the Crown West Inn.

"I never should have come tonight," he mumbled shakily, twisting his plump hands together, his courage having failed him despite the fact that the Highland officer hadn't threatened him or, for that matter, said a single hostile word. Yet it was the impatience burning in those oddly colored eyes that unnerved Franklin Biers completely.

"Mistress Biers warned me 'twould lead to trouble," he lamented. "Oh, I should never have said anything about the young lady either, but 'twas so hard not to feel sorry for her with that brutish man pulling her down the street like a savage!"

"What man?" Lochiel asked sharply.

"I-I don't know who he was," Franklin Biers stammered pitifully. How cold and rigid was that hawklike face! "Tall and rather thin-featured, dressed in a greatcoat, though no one of my acquaintance."

Lochiel groaned inwardly. What good did a vague description do him? "Did you see which direction they took?" he inquired. "Was there a carriage waiting for them outside?"

Franklin Biers shook his head, his heavy wig falling ludicrously over his brow. "They went on foot, sir. I believe he might've taken her over to the Merry Widow. Heard him say something about having left his carriage there."

Lochiel's nostrils flared as he thought of the terrible position in which Athena might very well find herself at this moment. Over an hour had passed since Tykie had summoned him from the fort. Where in hell could she have been taken? Someone at the Merry Widow had to know.

"Major Blackmoor!" Guessing his thoughts, Tykie's hand fell restrainingly on the officer's muscular forearm. " 'Tis best I went tae the Merry Widow alone." Seeing the impatience on the brutal face, he added quickly, "I ken Dinah Partridge, the proprietress. She willna talk tae an army mon. Ye'll get nowhere wi' her, an' time be wastin'. Let me try."

"Very well," Lochiel growled reluctantly, "but I'll come with you."

Tykie shook his grizzled head. " 'Tis best she doesna see you. Trust me," he said, his dark eyes pleading for understanding.

Lochiel's lips tightened. "I always have, you miserable cur. As for Mistress Partridge, I doubt she'll object if I wait for you in the street."

Horatio Tibble and his trembling companion already forgotten, Lochiel strode out, leaving Tykie to follow. Aware that he had caused more than the usual havoc at the Crown West that night, Tykie dug deep into his pocket and pulled out the handful of coins Athena had given him for safekeeping.

"Hope this'll keep us friendly, Tibble," he said engagingly, distributing the reward between the two men.

The innkeeper's eyes gleamed. "Always happy ter oblige a valued customer, Mr. Downs."

Both Tykie and Lochiel were silent as they strode down the street. Unnerved by the sight of the two tall men bearing down on them, pedestrians hastily moved aside and exchanged relieved glances when they remained unaccosted. Rain continued to fall in a steady downpour, filling the gutters to overflowing and dripping unnoticed from the brim of Lochiel's cocked hat.

Raucous laughter and the clanking of pewter against wood came to them through the cut-glass windows of the Merry Widow's taproom. Lochiel's brows were drawn into a frustrated frown as he watched Tykie disappear into the crowded building. Damn Athena Courtland! She was the most exasperating female he had ever known, and he vowed to strangle the life out of her personally if her disappearance tonight was the result of some mere impulsive whim.

Tykie was back a few minutes later, shaking his head as he came through the door. "No much tae be learned here," he grumbled regretfully. "Some poor mate were stabbed i' his bed last night, an' 'tis all the fools inside can talk aboot."

"And this Partridge woman? Did you have the chance to speak to her?"

Tykie nodded glumly. "Aye. She hasna seen anyone fitting Miss Athena's description."

"Damn!" Lochiel cursed softly beneath his breath.

"What'll we do the noo, major?" Tykie asked hopelessly. "We canna take the risk o' waitin' for Miss Athena tae retairn tae the Crown West, can we?"

"Not when there's a chance that she's met with foul play." Lamplight filtered through the grimy glass to illuminate the angular planes of Lochiel's hawkish features. "No telling what's happened to her in the meantime," he added ominously, his lean jaw clenched so that the skin stood out white against his dark uniform.

"Major, look!" Tykie's big hand was on his arm, his voice an urgent whisper as he gestured toward the entrance of the inn. Lochiel turned his head to see a woman on the threshold, her features hidden by the hood of a worn velvet cloak. Stepping out onto the street, she peered furtively over her shoulder before hastening away into the darkness.

" 'Twas the Partridge woman!" Tykie said excitedly.

Lochiel glanced at him sharply.

"Aye," Tykie persisted, "an' frae the look o' things she didna wish tae be followed. Shouldn't we see where she be gang?"

Lochiel glanced up at the inn, his eyes inexplicably drawn to the second-story windows, which were tightly shuttered against the rain. "You go on, Tykie," he said softly. "I believe I'll take advantage of Mistress Partridge's absence by having a look around her venerable establishment."

They parted without another word, each of them silently vowing to find at all costs that which had been taken from them. Lochiel could not explain why he had chosen to remain behind when Dinah Partridge's secretive behavior might very well lead them to Athena's whereabouts. Some sixth sense had stirred him when he gazed up at the darkened rooms of the Merry Widow Inn, and he could not shake the feeling that Athena was there no matter how his more pragmatic side might mock him for it.

Skirting the noisy taproom, Lochiel started for the stairs, which creaked alarmingly beneath his weight. The stairwell was dark and smelled of damp, musty bed linens. All was silent on the landing, and Lochiel's eyes narrowed as he found himself confronted by a long row of doors. Approaching the first one, he was about to knock when the unmistakable sounds of creaking bedsprings and unfettered passion drifted to him through the thin wood.

Lochiel's lips twitched, finding humor in the situation despite his grim purpose. There was no answer when he knocked on the next door and only an irate curse, muffled by sleep, responded at the third.

"What in 'ell do yer want?" the lodger in the fourth room barked, swinging the door wide in answer to Lochiel's summons. His jaw dropped as his eyes traveled up the uniformed chest to the forbidding features of the officer who wore it.

"I'm looking for a young woman who has disappeared from the Crown West Inn." Lochiel was unperturbed by the fact that he had awakened the red-faced man from a sound sleep. Wearing a nightcap and cotton shirt, his skinny legs poking from beneath the hem, the poor fellow was caught at a decided disadvantage and proved only too eager to have done with the interview so that he might hurry back to the warmth of his bed.

"She came in around the same time I did," was the obliging reply after Lochiel had supplied him with a brief description of Athena's appearance. "Had a nasty lookin' bloke with her, and I remember thinkin' to myself that she didn't seem too happy to be with 'im."

"Did they take a room here?" Lochiel asked very quietly.

The tassled nightcap jerked in the direction of the end of the darkened corridor. "Last one on the right. Made enough noise once they got in there, to be sure. Now, do yer mind if I goes back to sleep? A fellow could catch his death standin' in this drafty hall!"

But Lochiel had already turned away, a murderous glint in his eyes. By God, if Athena had been harmed . . .

There was no answer in response to his bold knock on the door in question. Something about the unnatural stillness disturbed him, however, and he knocked again, his pistol drawn.

Sitting in utter darkness on the other side of the door, her hands and legs bound by stiff ropes, Athena Kensington felt her heart hammering painfully in her chest. She dared not make a sound, dared not hope that someone who had come to help her might be standing without. No, 'twas doubtless that horrible woman Dinah Partridge, who had laughed so cruelly when Thomas Painsley had stuffed a foul rag in her mouth and bound her to this hard wooden chair.

Suppose it was Painsley himself? Athena trembled as she recalled how lustfully he had looked at her when he had told her the two of them would be leaving for Acadia in the morning.

"From there we'll take a ship to France," he had added unpleasantly, his fingers trailing through her hair. "Now that you know the truth about me, there's little sense in remaining here. I'd be hanged for what I've done, while in France I'll be given a royal welcome. And you, my dear"—the fingers had tightened possessively about a silky curl—"will be well received as my newest mistress."

Athena had struggled uselessly against the bonds that imprisoned her. Thomas Painsley had watched her futile struggles with seeming enjoyment, then bent lower so that his hot breath fell on her cheek.

"When I return we might as well consummate our relationship," he had intoned in a husky whisper. " 'Tis fortunate for you that I find you so appealing, Athena Kensington. If anyone else had discovered my little secret, he'd have ended up in far less pleasant circumstances." The savage gleam in his eyes left little doubt in Athena's mind as to his meaning.

An amused chuckle fell from the merchant's thin lips at her horrified expression. "I can see from those flashing eyes of yours that you'd prefer death to my amorous attentions. Never fear, you'll find me quite the skilled lover." His hand reached out to cup her breast, and Athena winced as his fingers tightened about the soft mound. "You'll come to beg for the pleasure I can give you, Athena," he murmured with heavy-lidded eyes. "I'm not the inexperienced schoolboy your husband is. I'm a man who knows how to give a woman what she wants."

She had jerked away from his touch, eyes blazing with hatred, but he had merely laughed and sauntered through the door, leaving her alone in the darkness. Time had lost all meaning for Athena after that, and when the first bold knock had sounded on her door, she froze, filled with the dreadful certainty that Thomas had returned.

"Athena, if you're in there answer me!"

A low moan tore from her throat, for she knew then that she was dreaming. Her feverish imagination was playing tricks on her, for it could not be Lochiel out there calling her name in a commanding voice.

"Athena!"

She moaned again, still refusing to believe that her prayers had been answered. Terror filled her heart as the locked door was all but torn from its hinges and the shadow of a broad-shouldered man loomed on the threshold. Footsteps crossed the room, and then a lean cheek was bending close while the strip of cloth that gagged her was snatched away.

"Lochiel, is it really you?" she whispered.

By way of reply she was pulled against a warm, wide chest, and she pressed her face into his neck, feeling the strong pulse beating in his throat.

"Oh, Lochiel!" It was the breathless sigh of a comforted child.

Lochiel held her close, the feel of her warm body easing the fear that had held him in its paralyzing grip since Tykie had first summoned him to the Crown West Inn. Hastily removing his dirk and cutting the ropes that imprisoned her, Lochiel felt her slim arms wind themselves tightly about his neck.

"Did he hurt you, Athena?" he demanded gruffly, his lips brushing her cheek as he bent protectively over her.

Her voice was muffled against the front of his coat. "No, but he threatened to kill me if I tried to run away. He had a pistol hidden in the folds of his cloak where no one else could see it. I had no choice but to go with him." She shuddered convulsively. "When he left me here he said he'd be back and that—that—"

Easing her ever so gently out of his arms, Lochiel lit the taper on the nightstand and then stared down into her ravaged face. Her eyes were dark with fright, the irises almost black, and he didn't have to ask what it was that Athena's captor had threatened to do to her upon his return.

Murderous rage swept through him, although the tender look on his rugged face never changed. "Who did this to you?" he inquired, running a long finger gently down her cheek.

"Thomas Painsley," Athena whispered. Now that the shock was beginning to fade, color was slowly returning to her wan face. " 'Tis why I came to Albany, Lochiel!" she exclaimed, her words gathering strength. "Thomas Painsley is the man who was in charge of the musket exchange at Joshua Brinston's mill! I wanted to tell General Amherst about him because Stephen said none of the men you'd captured that night betrayed his name."

Lochiel wanted to shake her, to berate her for not having confided in him first, yet reminded himself savagely that he had been the one who had erected the final, insurmountable wall between them. Smoothing the tangled curls back from her face, he felt his throat constrict with remorse. "Let me take you back to the Crown West," he suggested. "You'll be safe there, and when Tykie returns we'll come back here to await Master Painsley." His eyes gleamed as he imagined the confrontation to come.

Athena's eyes were wide and her parted lips trembled. "Oh no, Lochiel, you mustn't!" she protested, fear for him making her heart grow cold. "You don't know what sort of man he is! He and that madwoman have already murdered someone because of what happened at the mill, and they did it right here in this very room!"

Lochiel's eyes narrowed. "Are you certain of that? Did Painsley tell you so himself?"

Athena shook her head. "No, I can't be sure, but the man who was murdered here last night was Toddman Tyner."

Seeing Lochiel's blank expression, she added hastily, "He and Asa Brewster were the ones Stephen sent to Fort Shuyler to fetch me when Aunt Amelia died. Though he seemed a rather unscrupulous sort, he treated me well enough. I can't imagine why they would want him dead."

An odd expression had come over Lochiel's face at the mention of Asa Brewster's name, but Athena in her agitation didn't notice.

"Please, Lochiel, will you take me away from here?"

The husky pleading in her voice and the fear that lingered in the dark blue depths of her eyes stirred him like nothing else ever had. Reaching to disengage the slim fingers that had entwined themselves in the front of his coat, Lochiel found her upturned face close to his, her parted lips almost touching his own. He murmured her name, scarcely aware that he had spoken, dazzled by the haunting beauty of her eyes and imprisoned once again by the captivating spell only Athena could weave. What was it about this woman that enchanted him so? How could he find himself so hopelessly drawn to the wife of another?

Athena had responded to his almost caressing whisper of her name with a breathless sigh, surrendering herself to him without even being aware that she did so. Her arms crept about his neck as he pulled her close, and she could feel the steady pounding of his man's heart against her own.

"I prayed you'd come for me, Lochiel," she murmured, raising her face to his so that his mouth grazed hers.

"I've never been able to keep away from you," he confessed, his silver eyes gleaming as he looked down at her. "Athena," he whispered huskily, "close your eyes."

She did as she was told and thrilled to the feel of his mouth on hers. His kiss was tender yet compelling, his lips teasing and tasting, forcing her to respond to the fierce need within him. In that moment all was forgotten: the danger from which Athena had so narrowly escaped, the hatred with which they had last parted, even Athena's husband who by right should have been the only man to kiss her soft, persuasive lips.

Athena's heart trembled with joy, and a shameless desire stole through her yielding body. All the love for Lochiel she had thought destroyed forever poured from her soul, ignited by his kiss so that she was on fire for him, her very blood singing with the glory of being in his arms once again. She sank against him, unaware of the hard floor beneath them.

Athena's hair had come unbound, spilling like a shining torrent of gold into Lochiel's hands. Lifting his mouth from hers, he gazed hungrily into her curl-framed face to find her eyes still closed in anticipation of his kiss, the gold-tipped lashes fanning her smooth cheeks.

She was beautiful, his heart exulted, more beautiful than any woman he had ever seen, and as the full measure of his need for her burst upon him, he pressed his mouth to hers in a kiss that was as timeless as creation itself.

"Goddamn you, Blackmoor, I thought as much!"

Athena uttered a cry of alarm as she peered over Lochiel's broad shoulder and caught sight of her husband in the doorway. Stephen was panting as he leaned against the threshold, his features contorted so that she barely recognized him.

"I've been to every inn in this bloody town. I knew I'd find the two of you at last. A meeting with General Amherst indeed!" he added contemptuously to his wife. "Did you honestly believe I'd swallow such nonsense?"

"Stephen, please—" Athena began, but the words died away in a gasp as Stephen drew a pistol from his cloak, the long barrel aimed directly at Lochiel's wide chest.

Lochiel's expression was menacing as he rose and swiftly pulled Athena to her feet. She gazed beseechingly into his eyes as he pushed her gently aside, but he merely shook his head imperceptibly by way of warning.

"Well, Kensington?" Turning to face Stephen, Lochiel propped his hands on his hips and waited. There was little sense in trying to explain, for Stephen would never believe the truth, and indeed 'twas so far-fetched, Lochiel thought cynically, that he'd be a fool to do so.

"You've always managed to lure her into your bed, haven't you, Blackmoor?" Stephen's voice quivered with fury though the hand that held the pistol never wavered. "I imagine you've been rutting like barnyard animals since the first time you ever laid eyes on her."

" 'Twas your meddling that was responsible for that first time," Lochiel replied arrogantly. "Need I remind you of the letter your man Brewster delivered to my tent last October?"

For a moment Stephen was caught off guard, then an ugly smile curved his lips. "Perhaps that was my doing, Blackmoor, but 'tis of no consequence now. You're not going to leave this room alive, and no judge on earth would condemn me for killing a man who made a cuckold of me."

Lochiel's brow darkened, hearing Athena's frightened gasp behind him. Stephen, he knew, was mad enough to carry through with his threat, and it was Athena's safety he feared for. What punishment would Stephen inflict upon her for her supposed infidelity?

"How can you possibly consider yourself cuckolded," he countered coldly, "when the woman who deceived you is not legally your wife?"

Stephen's features contorted with rage. "What in hell are you talking about?"

"The fact that Amelia Bower was still alive when you sent Brewster and a poor fellow by the name of Toddman Tyner to Fort Shuyler to find Athena. How odd that you would want her to attend the funeral of someone who was not yet dead."

"Perhaps she wasn't dead yet," Stephen conceded with a snarl, "but she still signed those proxy papers before her death, making Athena my legal wife."

"How badly did you threaten her before she agreed to sign them?"

Lochiel asked quietly. "Is it possible that you placed her under such duress that her frail health could not withstand it?"

"Oh, Stephen, no!" Athena cried, hands flying to her lips as she realized what Lochiel was intimating.

"I didn't kill her, if that's what you're getting at!" Stephen burst out. "I just wanted her to sign those papers, but the stubborn bitch wouldn't!"

"And so you threatened her," Lochiel guessed, "until she had no choice but to sign them."

Stephen's jaw worked convulsively. "I swear I never touched her!"

There was no longer any doubt in Lochiel's mind that Stephen had taken advantage of Athena's absence to coerce her aunt into signing the proxy papers. Yet why had he sent two men into the wilderness to look for her before Amelia was even dead—unless he'd intended to murder her all along? It was a chilling thought, and Lochiel was suddenly no longer willing to believe that Stephen was too cowardly to use the weapon he held in his hand.

"Oh, Stephen, why did you do it?" he heard Athena whisper before he had the chance to speak.

"I had no choice!" Stephen said furiously. "With my father's estate on the verge of penury, I had to find another source of revenue, and my only hope was you, Athena. I knew you'd never agree to marry me, no matter how coyly you behaved toward me all winter. But I suppose that doesn't matter now. 'Twas Blackmoor you wanted all along, wasn't it?" He laughed harshly, the laugh of a man on the verge of insanity.

"I could have contested the papers when I returned home, but I didn't," Athena pointed out, hoping to reason with him. "I-I was truly fond of you, Stephen, and I wanted to be your wife."

Stephen's gaze was tortured as he looked into her pleading face. For a moment the pistol wavered, but as he was reminded of the evidence of her faithlessness in the swollen softness of her recently kissed lips and the wanton dishevelment of her attire, he shook his head with cold finality.

"Mayhap you did," he conceded, "but your brother Fletcher would never have permitted us to remain married. I could tell as much when he arrived the night of our wedding celebration. 'Tis why I had no choice but to try to get rid of him. I'm only sorry I didn't finish him off."

"You shot my brother?" Athena whispered in disbelief, her face paling. At his arrogant nod she uttered a strangled sound and flew at him, hands reaching out to attack him.

"Athena, no!"

Lochiel's powerful arms slid about her as she ran past him and he jerked her roughly against his side.

"Let me go!" she cried. "He tried to kill Fletcher!"

Stephen's temper snapped seeing the dark hand that rested so familiarly about his wife's small waist. "Get away from him, Athena," he grated, breath whistling through clenched teeth. Lifting his pistol, he aimed with slow deliberation, and despite the fact that Athena had made no move to obey his order, he coldly squeezed the trigger.

As the weapon discharged with a roar of exploding powder, Athena closed her eyes, reaching blindly for Lochiel and his comforting presence. There was no time for him to thrust her aside, and in that moment, knowing both of them would die, he caught her against him, the full measure of his love for her burning fiercely in his soul.

As the smoke cleared he was more than a little startled to find both of them still alive, Athena clinging to him with all her might, her soft, sweet cheek pressed against his.

"A pitiable waste," came a cold voice from the doorway, "but I'm afraid 'twas inevitable."

Lochiel's head snapped up and his face went rigid as he found himself gazing into the gaunt, grinning features of a man he instinctively knew to be Thomas Painsley. Still holding his discharged weapon in a gloved hand, the merchant gestured indifferently at the body of Stephen Kensington lying at his feet.

"Your husband was a fool, Athena," he remarked contemptuously. "I trust you'll reward me sweetly for getting rid of him for you."

"I'll see you dead first!" Athena cried bravely, though she trembled in Lochiel's arms, her eyes bright with unshed tears.

Cold rage coursed through Lochiel at the suffering he saw on Athena's face, and he moved quickly to grab the unfired pistol that had fallen from Stephen's grasp when he died. Lifting it smoothly, he fired without hesitation, catching the unsuspecting merchant off guard. Thomas Painsley stared in astonishment at the blood spurting from his chest. Reaching out a hand to touch it, he gurgled low in his throat and fell forward, his own weapon slipping from his grasp.

It was then that Tykie Downs's terrified bellowing could be heard from the hall below. Boards creaked alarmingly as he thumped up the staircase like a man possessed.

"Miss Athena, Miss Athena, be ye all right? Oh, God!" The shout became an anguished moan as the sound of the gunshot faded away into silence. "I've come too late!"

Drawing up short in the doorway, a fireplace poker held menacingly in one hand, a struggling Dinah Partridge clutched securely in the other, he blinked in astonishment at the body of Thomas Painsley lying at his feet in a growing pool of blood.

"Dead! He be dead!" he murmured in disbelief, then turned to glower at the woman beside him. "She went tae warn 'im, the bitch did!" he burst out, shaking her like a dog worrying a bone. "I followed 'im like ye told me tae, major, but he slipped away frae me i' the dark. God hae mercy, I thought I were too late!"

Lochiel made no reply. His gaze had fallen on Athena, who had struggled out of his arms and was kneeling at Stephen's side. Reaching to pull her comfortingly against him, he froze when he heard her sobbing words.

"Stephen, oh, Stephen, I'm so sorry," she murmured brokenly, remorse lending her voice a heartbroken catch that the listening Lochiel could only interpret as the pain of losing a dearly loved one.

Growing pale, he turned away unnoticed, his arms falling uselessly to his sides, and only Tykie saw the bitter hopelessness in the once-proud silver eyes.

Twenty

Stephen Kensington was given a Christian burial on a warm afternoon in the middle of June. Songbirds twittered in the trees that shaded the grave, and Reverend Axminster's quiet voice blended softly with the humming of the bees gathering nectar in the fields beyond the churchyard.

Athena stood between her brother Fletcher and the weeping Leda, her face stark beneath the veil that obscured her delicate features. The bright honey-gold of her hair was hidden beneath a black-plumed hat, and the summer breeze stirred the heavy black skirts she wore. She was doing her best to concentrate on the minister's words, knowing he had labored long into the night to write a eulogy that would extol Stephen's virtues and avoid mention of the evidence that proved the sort of man he had truly been.

Fortunately very few of West York's inhabitants knew the truth behind Stephen's violent death. Athena's lips twisted cynically as she surveyed the small crowd gathered around the open grave, feeling certain that most of them had been drawn by curiosity and not respect. The de Vrieses in particular hadn't even attempted to mask their reasons for being there, both Marianne and Katrine staring at her with ill-concealed interest. Katrine had even gone so far as to intimate that Athena deserved little better than to find herself a widow after less than two months of marriage. If Fletcher hadn't placed a restraining hand on her arm as they left the church, Athena would have cheerfully slapped the smug face before her.

No one would ever discover the sort of man Stephen had been, least of all the talkative de Vrieses. Athena herself had decided as much after discussing the matter with Fletcher, and her resolve had only increased after an astonishing disclosure made by a tearful Mercy on the morning after his death. The secret she had confessed to her startled employers had left no doubt in their minds as to the evil of which he had been capable.

" 'Twas a day or two after you left for Fort Shuyler, miss," Mercy had blurted, eyes reddened from crying. "Mr. Kensington came to see you, and he was furious when he found you was gone. No one was at home but Mistress Bower and me, and they had a terrible row in the study."

"A row?" Fletcher had prodded when she fell silent.

Mercy had twisted her sodden handkerchief between her fingers. "Aye, sir. I could hear him yelling all the way to the kitchen. I was frightened, but I didn't dare interfere."

"What happened?" Athena breathed.

"He went away, and Mistress Bower took to her bed. Wouldn't even answer me when I asked if she needed anything. He came back a few days later, and this time he treated her worse than before. They was in the study again, and I heard her cry out for help. That's when I ran to the stables to fetch Hale, but Mr. Kensington stopped me before I got outside and said I'd be in a lot of trouble if I didn't mind my own business."

"Go on, Mercy," Fletcher said kindly when the poor girl fell silent, tears welling afresh in her eyes.

She shrugged her slim shoulders with forced indifference. "There's not much more to tell, sir. After Master Stephen left, I went into the study and found Mistress Bower sitting in a chair looking pale as death. I asked her if she needed me to fetch the doctor, but she said to bring her the smelling salts instead. I helped put her to bed like she asked me, and that's where we found her the next morning."

"According to Dr. Nolan her heart simply gave out while she slept," Athena remembered. She glanced sharply at her brother, whose hazel eyes were dark with rage. Obviously Fletcher agreed with her that Stephen had not only forced Aunt Amelia to sign the proxy papers against her will but had frightened her to the point that her weak heart hadn't been able to withstand the shock.

"This proves that Stephen knew all about his father's pitiful finances," Athena said quietly, "and that's why he was in such a hurry to marry me. I imagine he expected me to come to him with a dowry large enough to save the Kensingtons from disaster." Her soft voice was flat with bitterness. "Small wonder he was so kind to me when I returned! He was counting on making me too happy to contest the arrangement."

"Which you seemed to be," Fletcher reminded her, regarding her curiously, for he had never really come to understand why a woman as rebellious and strong-minded as Athena would commit herself to a lifetime with a man she didn't love.

"I, on the other hand," he continued when his sister remained silent, "would not have accepted the terms of proxy without a thorough investigation. Stephen must have sensed as much, and that's why he tried to get rid of me."

Standing in the churchyard amid the silent mourners on that bright summer afternoon, Athena felt a cold hand wrap itself about her heart as she recalled her brother's casual words. Oh, how she had hated Stephen when he had admitted as much to her! She had wanted to tear his face to shreds for what he'd done, but she had never, never wished him dead!

A shadow passed across her veiled face as she remembered the horror of watching him die at her feet. How she had regretted her own violent feelings toward him in that moment! Yet she mustn't continue to feel guilty, she reminded herself severely. She was not to blame for his death.

A low murmur that swept without warning through the gathered mourners brought her thoughts back with a start. Looking up, Athena saw a man enter the churchyard through the narrow gate, a dark-headed man with broad shoulders wearing the scarlet coat of a Regimental soldier. Athena's breath caught in her throat as she recognized Lochiel. What was he doing here? she wondered frantically. According to Tykie, the Seventh Highland Company had departed for Canada the morning after Stephen's death.

Without sparing anyone a glance, Lochiel took his place at the back of the whispering crowd. Folding his arms before his chest, he gave his attention to the minister, ignoring the stir his arrival had caused. It was plain that none of the mourners gathered here today had forgotten his scandalous words to Stephen Kensington on the night Fletcher Courtland had been shot, and curious glances were sent toward the young widow and her brother. Would there be a confrontation after the service? Katrine de Vries had the gall to giggle openly at the prospect.

Athena was glad for the veil that obscured her face. She was certain that her eyes were glittering unnaturally and that telltale color had risen high in her cheeks. Slipping her gloved hand into the crook of Fletcher's arm, she felt him squeeze it reassuringly, although his expression had grown uncompromisingly harsh. He, too, had noticed Lochiel's arrival.

"May I extend my deepest regrets, Lieutenant Courtland, in the unfortunate loss of your brother-in-law." Lochiel's deep voice was barely civil as he stopped to address the small party of bereaved relatives at the conclusion of the service. His mocking glance turned to Athena, who stood at her brother's side. "And to you, Mrs. Kensington," he added. "I'm aware that you loved your husband deeply."

Athena stared up at him, aghast. How dare he speak like that to her? How could he believe even for a moment that she could possibly love the man who had shot her brother?

"We are honored by your presence, major," Fletcher replied equally politely, the antagonism between the two men obvious from their hostile expressions. Aware of the curious faces pressing closer to listen, he took

Athena's hand in his. "If you'll excuse us, there are others here we must speak to."

Lochiel inclined his dark head, his tricorn riding jauntily over his brow. "I understand." For a moment the silver eyes narrowed as his gaze pierced the heavy veil obscuring Athena's features. "Good day, Mrs. Kensington," was all he said.

She watched him cross the churchyard and untie Glenrobbie from the post. The gold braid of his uniform gleamed in the sunlight, dazzling her with its brightness and reminding her all too painfully that he was a soldier who would shortly find himself facing the impenetrable walls of Quebec and the powerful forces of Louis de Montcalm's army. She couldn't let him go without speaking to him one last time to ask him why he had brushed her aside so indifferently on the eve of Stephen's death.

"Lochiel, wait!"

Ignoring the curious eyes upon her, Athena lifted her heavy skirts and ran from the churchyard. Lochiel had paused at her unexpected cry, yet the impatience on his hawkish face deepened as she drew to a breathless halt before him. Damn her, he thought savagely to himself. Why did Athena always have to look so beautiful, even dressed in black, her singularly magnificent eyes shining like precious sapphires through her veil? A silky curl had escaped the tight chignon that confined her heavy mass of hair, glinting like newly minted gold as it lay against the black shoulder of her gown.

"I was somewhat astonished to hear the minister refer to Stephen's death as a hero's," he remarked when the silence between them had lengthened unbearably.

Athena bridled at his mockery. " 'Twas my idea to let it be known that Stephen lost his life protecting me from Thomas Painsley. What else could I have done? Admit that Stephen had tried to kill Fletcher and that he had followed me to Albany believing I—that you and I—" She broke off and bowed her head, acutely aware of the fact that Stephen's suspicions had so very nearly been justified that night.

"Neither Fletcher nor I felt that Stephen's mother deserved to learn what sort of man he really was, not after losing her husband, too," she finished coldly. "Reverend Axminster alone knows the truth, and he was kind enough to avoid mention of it during the eulogy."

Lochiel ignored the unexpected softening in his heart as he gazed down into Athena's veiled features. 'Twas just like the proud Courtlands to lie in order to spare themselves the humiliation of admitting that Stephen had tried to murder his own brother-in-law. He should have remembered that Athena was shameless enough to resort to any means of protecting her good name and that of the man she loved. Aye, she had loved Stephen

Kensington, Lochiel had seen as much in the broken manner in which she had wept over his fallen body in the Merry Widow Inn.

The silver eyes were suddenly as cold as the winter sun on frozen water. "I'm sorry for the grief you've suffered, Mrs. Kensington. My intention in appearing here today was to lay to rest any rumors concerning your husband's death that the good people of West York might have taken upon themselves to accept. I see now that you and your brother have orchestrated a suitable solution without my interference."

Athena stared at him numbly. It seemed to her as if her heart were being broken into little pieces by the tone of his voice. What had she done to make him hate her so? "Lochiel, please—"

His expression darkened at the utterance of his name. How could she manage to look so innocent, so bloody vulnerable, when her heart was filled with naught but deceit? How dare she look up at him with those damnably lovely eyes of hers glittering with contrived tears? There were others who would comfort her now that Stephen was gone. If all went well and Wolfe took Quebec, her Ranger lovers would doubtless soon return, and this time there would be no Asa Brewster or a jealous, manipulative man like Stephen Kensington to drive them apart.

"You've naught to fear from the future, madam," he said coldly. "Obviously your good name is still intact, and I imagine there are other men willing to comfort you now that you're alone." His lips twisted into a mocking smile. "You might even choose to become a 'merry widow' if you so desire."

Athena recoiled as though he had struck her. Was he implying that she become like Dinah Partridge, willing to take any man to bed for the right price? Thank God that despicable woman was sitting in jail at this very moment!

"Oh, don't look so startled," Lochiel continued, drawing on his gloves. "A widow holds a very fortunate place in society. No one really expects her to follow the laws of convention, and should she wish to take a lover or two, 'tis frowned upon a great deal less than were she an unmarried virgin." He regarded her with a cryptic smile. "You will have to remember to remain discreet, however. 'Tis one of the unwritten rules."

Athena's breath was labored. She could scarcely believe what she was hearing. Lochiel was speaking to her as though she were some sort of whore, a fallen woman to be despised. Swallowing her hurt pride, she looked up with clear, honest eyes into the face of the man she loved.

"Surely, you don't believe me capable of that, Lochiel! You, better than anyone, should realize that there has never been another man besides—"

"Oh, there you are, Athena! Mother and I have been looking everywhere for you!"

Athena stifled a groan as Katrine de Vries hurried into their midst, her avid gaze taking in the silent Highlander and the veiled woman standing at his side.

"We were surprised to see you at the funeral, Major Blackmoor," Katrine continued brightly, lifting her chin to give him a better view of her pale, patrician features. She had almost forgotten how dangerously handsome the Highland officer was, and a tremor of excitement fled through her at his black look. What would it be like to be held by a man like that and to feel those brutal lips kiss yours? Katrine wondered.

"Will you be staying for supper? I understand Athena's mother-in-law has prepared a feast for her guests."

It was in Lochiel's mind to refuse, but then his glance fell on Athena, who was standing as if turned to stone beside him. "I wouldn't miss it for the world," he assured Katrine with a smile that uncannily resembled the predatory snarl of a wolf.

For Athena the afternoon was to prove unbearable. Standing forlornly beside the enormous buffet table that had been set up in the Kensingtons' dining room, she was miserably aware of every coy female glance cast at Lochiel, who mingled with total unconcern among the gathered guests. His polite manner and damnable charm had quickly put an end to the hostile glances that had greeted him when he first strode inside. Even Leda had welcomed him formally, yet her distracted air had led Athena to believe that the poor woman was still suffering from shock and really had no idea who it was she spoke to.

Although Lochiel hadn't spared her a single glance, Athena wasn't deceived by his pleasantries or gallant manner. She sensed inwardly that he was watching her closely, playing a deadly game in which she had become the unfortunate quarry. Over and over again she asked herself why he had chosen to make her his enemy. Why had he bothered to risk his life for her in Albany if he hated her? How could he have kissed her so tenderly, leaving her breathless with love and desire for him, only to turn indifferently away from her once Thomas Painsley lay dead at his feet?

A giggle, quickly smothered in the somber silence that hung over the room, drew Athena's attention to Katrine de Vries. The Dutch girl was standing near the door, wine-brightened eyes glowing coyly into Lochiel Blackmoor's as she responded to some witticism he had obviously whispered into her ear. The amused gleam in his silver eyes tore at Athena's heart. Setting her untouched plate down with a clatter, she quickly fled the room. She had had enough of Lochiel's mockery, of Aramintha and Eliza's weeping, of Leda's uncontrollable sniffling into a soggy handkerchief. She had to get away from the suffocating atmosphere and the funereal faces about her or go utterly mad.

No one but Lochiel saw her leave. His solicitous manner abruptly gone, he excused himself from the startled Katrine and left her to pout at his brusque departure. Striding into the entrance hall, Lochiel caught a brief glimpse of Athena's slim back on the landing above before she disappeared from view. Without hesitation he went after her, taking the steps two at a time.

The west wing of Ambrose Kensington's enormous house was eerily deserted. The servants who were usually hurrying to and fro with mops and brooms, fresh linens and towels, were all belowstairs assisting in the serving of the guests, for Leda had been forced to reduce her staff drastically since her husband's death.

Despite the warm sunshine streaming through the landing windows, a pall seemed to hang over the house, and Lochiel had no trouble finding Athena, for in the stillness the rustle of her skirts gave her away. He found her standing with her back to him in an ornately decorated bedchamber. Crimson wallhangings surrounded the enormous four-poster bed, its embroidered design of cherubs and twining vines continued in the expensive cloth that upholstered the settee and chairs. The plaster ceiling was hand-sculpted to resemble a dome, and the frieze running along the upper wall contained the same elaborate pattern as the bed hangings below.

Lochiel glanced around him with distaste until his attention returned again to Athena. She had removed her small plumed hat, and her normally proud head was bowed. Sunlight streamed upon her blond hair to reflect a radiance that was breathtaking to behold, but for once Lochiel was oblivious to her stirring beauty. As he watched, she moved to the bed, allowing her slim fingers to trail over the embroidered coverlet. The profile that was turned to him was stark, her face pale against the black neckline of her gown, which covered her slender collarbones to end at her chin.

What was she thinking? he wondered. Had this been her and Stephen's bedroom? Was she dreaming of the times they had slept here as man and wife, when Stephen had elicited from her the throbbing responses Lochiel had sworn she'd share with no other man?

Regarding her keenly, he saw a single tear slide unnoticed down her cheek. Its appearance and the trembling of her soft mouth caused Lochiel's temper to snap.

"So," he said coldly from the doorway, "you mourn for him still."

Athena whirled about, eyes growing wide as Lochiel came slowly inside. His anger was palpable, and the heat from his body caused her to retreat uneasily.

"I never realized you cared for him so much," Lochiel added, eyes narrowing in response to her obvious fear. "Was he that good a lover, Athena?"

She found herself pressed against the edge of the bed, her fingers entwined in the coverlet behind her. "What is it you want from me, Lochiel?" she asked, lifting her chin bravely despite the wavering of her voice. "Why do you keep on hurting me like this?"

His expression darkened as he realized that he could not answer her, for he didn't quite know himself. All that was clear to him was the fact that she had played him the fool while it was Kensington, that obnoxious, cowardly drunkard, who had won her love.

"Since the very first you took from me what you wanted, Athena," he said in a low voice. " 'Twas obviously easy for you to do, what with your lovers gone off to war and your husband not yet firmly ensnared in your web. I won't pretend that I didn't enjoy our copulations, but I find my manly pride dealt an unforgivable blow realizing that I was a mere substitute and one so easily duped by your sweet smiles and innocent blue eyes."

He took a menacing step toward her, standing so close now that Athena was forced to tilt back her head in order to look into his face. She trembled at what she saw there. "I-I don't understand what you're saying," she whispered, heart pounding painfully in her chest. Could this cruelly hateful man be the same one she had thought she loved?

Lochiel's lips curved. "Don't you?" he asked unpleasantly. " 'Tis time you learned that not every man enjoys your manipulations, Athena Kensington. All of us are eventually called upon to pay the consequences of our behavior."

As he spoke he reached out, his fingers closing about the neckline of her gown. Athena cried out as it ripped clear to the waist, her corseted breasts spilling into view. It seemed as if his hands were everywhere, tearing and pulling as he pinned her against his powerful body so that she could not struggle free.

Finally he shoved her, naked and panting with fright, onto the crimson coverlet of the bed. Athena scrambled to the far side, hugging her breasts with her arms, her long legs curled beneath her. She saw that he was laughing as he turned to bar the door, then began to shed his clothes on the carpet with deliberate ease.

"Damn you, Lochiel," she breathed, terror coursing through her as his magnificent body was revealed. "Would you r-rape me like some—some filthy animal?"

He tossed aside the last of his garments and flexed his heavily corded arms. His body was lean and bronzed, exactly as powerful and masculine as Athena remembered, but this time the sight of it filled her with panic and revulsion, not hopeless longing. Her eyes flew helplessly to his thickening manhood and she shrank further back against the cushions. Her eyes darted about the room for a weapon. No one in the house would hear her screams, she knew, yet if she could only—

The mattress sagged beneath his weight, and she cried out as his arms came about her. "I've told you once before, Athena," he murmured into her ear, " 'twould never be rape between us."

She felt his hot mouth capture hers and struggled to turn her head away. His arms tightened about her so that her nipples were pressed against his wide chest, her smooth thighs against his muscular ones. She could not escape the searing heat of his kiss, and she moaned low in her throat as his tongue forced its way between her lips.

His impatient fingers pulled the pins from her hair so that the shining mass spilled across the pillows. Pressing her back against them, Lochiel let his lips stray to the curving arch of her bare throat while his hand moved across her flat belly and lower, to the silken junction between her thighs.

"Lochiel, please—" Athena moaned, heart hammering, hating him for the shameless thrill that was beginning to make her ache with longing.

"You cannot accuse me of taking you against your will, Athena." Lochiel's breath was hot against her throat. "Not when you were made for this."

She fought the desire that was fanning hot through her blood, making her limbs weak. On his haunches, Lochiel parted her legs with his hands and Athena gasped, trying to twist away from him, only to find herself moving beneath him instead, yearning for him with every fiber of her being.

"This is all you've ever wanted from me, isn't it, Athena?" he asked her harshly. "No, I wager this is all you've ever wanted from any man, and by God, I intend to see you get it."

His hands continued to caress her boldly, blotting out his hateful words, until she found herself craving him as never before, the magic of his touch, his scent, his hard male body wiping out all else but Lochiel and her fierce, aching love for him.

"Do you still call it rape, Athena?" Lochiel persisted, lifting his lips from hers long enough to peer into her passion-flushed face. His fingers continued to touch and explore, his ready manhood poised to enter her.

"No," she whispered, unable to lie, arching her body upward, resistance forgotten as every inch of her awaited his final possession. "No, Lochiel, I want—"

He laughed triumphantly and Athena gasped as he drove deep inside, his swollen shaft moving within her, the pleasure carrying her far beyond anything she had ever known. Her fingers curled through the dark hair at the nape of his neck, her lips opening to the dominating fierceness of his kiss. How could she have feared him? How could she have felt revulsion when this rippling, wonderful ecstasy went beyond anything she had ever dreamed?

Yet suddenly he was pounding against her in a rhythm that was no longer gentle, riding her swiftly and ruthlessly so that the swirling pleasure became a dull ache, then shattering pain.

"Lochiel, wait," Athena panted, yet he ignored her, continuing the feral pace until she suddenly felt him surge within her. She strained beneath him as an answering ache within her blossomed, yet by then it was too late. His passion spent, Lochiel pulled out so abruptly that she came crashing down to earth as if out of a dream and into the numbing reality of what he had done.

Slowly opening her eyes, her body still throbbing with unfulfilled longing, Athena saw Lochiel standing over her, hands on his hips, an unpleasant smile curving his lips.

"Y-you," she choked, shrinking from him, her eyes dark with pain, "you did that on purpose!"

"How clever of you to realize as much," he responded nonchalantly, his own eyes glittering. Pulling on his clothes, he spared little more than a glance for the figure huddled on the bed, shoulders shaking with suppressed sobs. "Goodbye, Athena," he said coldly. "My thanks for an entertaining afternoon." Unbolting the door, he stepped outside and slammed it shut behind him.

Twenty-one

Landing with a thump on the soft grass where the nervous young colt had thrown her, Athena was aware of Tykie's roar of amused laughter. Scrambling swiftly to her feet, she glared at him as she dusted off her russet-colored habit, the skirts already streaked with grass stains from earlier falls.

"Will ye try again?" Tykie asked in disbelief as she reached for the reins and prepared to swing herself into the saddle. " 'Tis the fourth time he's thrown ye." He eyed her slim body up and down, certain that it was covered with bruises.

"He's got to learn who his master is," Athena responded firmly. Tucking the wayward strands of blond hair beneath her bonnet, she placed her boot in the stirrup and swung herself onto the colt's back. Urging him into a trot, she rode him down the drive and back, keeping light yet steady contact with the bit in the event he chose to buck again.

When he showed no signs of rebelliousness, she eased him into a canter and was pleased when he obeyed, moving with the long-legged grace of his sire before coming to a halt at Tykie's side. The Highlander's eyes gleamed as he assisted his mistress to the ground.

" 'Tis progress ye've made wi' him today, lass. I wager he'll be ready for racin' come fall."

She stroked the black satin neck affectionately. "Ballycor will have himself a son to be proud of. I only wish he'd inherited his sire's color."

Tykie chuckled, sliding the saddle from the colt's sweat-glistening back. "Wi' a dam as black as coal an' a sire like Ballycor, one o' 'em had tae win oot."

"They could have compromised," Athena persisted, drawing off her gloves. "He could have been gray."

"Och, lass, there never be a compromise where male an' female be concerned!"

Athena's expression darkened unexpectedly. "Sometimes I find you too wise for your own good, Tykie Downs."

He glanced at her sharply, but she said nothing more. With the colt between them they walked down to the gate that separated the stableyard from the pasture. Removing the colt's bridle, Tykie gave him a playful slap on the rear, and the young animal leaped away, tail streaming like a banner behind him.

"Oh, Tykie, isn't it a glorious day?" Athena asked, her earlier dourness forgotten. Propping her booted foot against the gate, she lifted her face to the warmth of the late July sun. The baaing of sheep and the fresh tang of pine came to her on the gentle breeze, and she had to quell the urge to roll like a playful pup in the thick grass. Widows of six weeks' standing did not indulge in such childish behavior, she reminded herself with the ghost of a smile.

'Twas easier these days to think of Stephen without feeling a pang of regret or guilt. Fletcher had made a generous offer to Leda Kensington for her arable land, thus enabling the poor woman to keep her house and servants and at the same time releasing Ambrose's tenant farmers from the unkind rule that had been the Kensington legacy.

With so much acreage now belonging to Courtland Grace, Fletcher was rarely to be seen. He and Tykie rode the land daily, Fletcher planning the planting with painstaking care and overseeing the tenant farms in a manner that quickly endeared him to the men who worked the fertile land. Though he still suffered from occasional bouts of dizziness, he had filled out and the sun had bronzed his skin so that Athena, studying him discreetly from afar, could scarcely believe he had come so close to dying earlier that spring.

With summer lying ripe upon the hillsides, the pens filled with sheep, each dairy cow with a healthy calf at her side, a lazy contentment had fallen over Courtland Grace. Athena found the warm, desultory days a balm for her ravaged spirit. Even the news concerning the war was unthreatening; at the moment Major General Wolfe and his army were camped at the Île d'Orléans below Quebec in a standoff with the French that promised little, if any, bloodshed. Six companies of Rangers were currently with him, and Athena couldn't help believing that if the twins were there they were in no immediate danger.

As for Lochiel and his Highlanders—here the peace that was beginning to reclaim her abruptly shattered. Why could she never think of Lochiel in the same, detached manner she thought of Stephen? Why did a band of pain always wrap itself about her heart and betray itself in the shadow that darkened her eyes? Despite the length of time, she could not forget his cruelty on the day of Stephen's burial.

"Master Fletcher be returnin'," Tykie observed, his deep voice startling Athena from her thoughts.

Lifting her head, she brightened seeing the single horse bearing down the winding lane toward the house. Suddenly the smile died from her lips and was replaced by a puzzled frown. "How odd! Fletcher left this morning on Sweetbriar. Does that look like a bay to you, Tykie?"

Tykie pushed the hair from his eyes and squinted into the sun. "Nay," he said slowly. " 'Tis a chestnut, an' no mare judgin' frae the build o' him."

Pushing herself away from the gate, Athena held her breath, her slim body stiff with dread. Too often in wartime bad news traveled via a solitary rider, and she knew that the one heading toward them was not her brother Fletcher, despite the fact that he was too far away still to be recognized.

As Athena and Tykie watched, the chestnut disappeared behind a bend in the drive, only to reemerge at a canter from beneath the towering oaks. Drawing to a halt in the stableyard, the rider swept off his tricorn and lifted his head to survey the silent house before him. Seeing the golden glint of his unruly locks in the sunshine, a disbelieving cry burst from Athena.

" 'Tis Colm! Oh, Tykie, 'tis Colm!"

"God hae mercy," the big Highlander breathed, "ye be right, lass!"

Athena was already running across the grass, calling her brother's name, her skirts flying about her ankles. Dismounting and letting the reins trail to the ground, the tall young man in the faded buckskins began to run as well, his arms outstretched. Seconds later Athena had fallen into his embrace, weeping and laughing and depositing kisses on every inch of his unshaven face.

"God, Athena," she heard him breathe into her hair. " 'Tis good to be home!"

"You're not hurt, are you?" she inquired anxiously, clinging to him with all her might.

He laughed, his clear blue eyes so like hers with their thick fringe of gold-tipped lashes. "Me? I've the devil's own luck, don't you remember? I've been reassigned, that's all."

He gazed down into her face, noticing the womanly fullness of her smiling mouth, the enchanting sparkle in her eyes, and brought up a trembling hand to cup her square Courtland chin. "You've grown too bonnie for your own good," he observed. "Jemmy told me as much, but I wouldn't believe him. Not our awkward, long-legged baby sister, I said!"

"You've seen him recently?" Athena breathed. "Where is he?"

Colm's brow wrinkled. "We haven't served together for months. Last I heard he was on his way to Canada."

"And you?" she asked anxiously. "You've been reassigned? Where—"

A joyful braying rent the air, and Athena had just enough time to step out of the way before a galloping Tykie had swept Colm into his arms. Despite the youth's lanky height, he was all but lost in the Highlander's embrace. Athena watched with tears in her eyes as they clapped each other on the back. After a moment, however, she began to tug impatiently on her brother's arm.

"Come inside! You need rest and something to eat. I'm certain Prue's taken the bread out of the oven by now. How thin you've grown!" she observed, studying the lean frame in the faded buckskin breeches.

"Stop fretting like a mother hen," Colm teased. "I'm fitter than I've ever been in my life, Major Rogers has seen to that. And you, Thena, have no cause to scold. Look at you, have you been rolling in the mud?"

"I've been trying to break Ballycor's unruly son to the saddle." She laughed and pirouetted before him, russet skirts billowing about her slim ankles. "This is how he has thanked me for my patience."

Colm groaned. "Don't tell me you still have that terrifying white beast?"

Athena nodded.

"I understand most of the horses in the area were confiscated by the military. Ballycor would have made a fine addition to some pompous colonel's stables. How did he happen to escape such a fate?"

Athena shrugged. "I suppose his temperament was too wild." She didn't want to explain to him how Lochiel had spared her beloved stallion for her.

"I spent the night in West York," Colm added as the three of them started back for the house. His expression was troubled as he gazed at his sister's profile. "From what I've been told, you've suffered quite a bit since Jemmy saw you last."

Athena smiled at him brightly. " 'Tis in the past now, Colm. Nothing that happened has the power to hurt me anymore." She wondered if her voice sounded as unconvincing to him as it did to her. "You knew Fletcher had been shot?" she added hesitantly.

Colm scowled. "Aye. The letter you wrote informing me of the accident didn't reach me until barely a month ago. Luckily I received your second letter, assuring me he was recovering well, at the same time. I wanted to come home right away, but I just couldn't get leave. At least I was spared the agony of not knowing whether he'd recovered or not."

Athena slipped her hand into his. "He's doing ever so much better," she informed him happily. "Just wait and see."

The reunion between the two Courtland brothers took place an hour later, when Fletcher returned from the fields to find Colm bathed, freshly attired, and reclining like a pampered pasha on the terrace while Athena, Prudence, and Mercy plied him with platters of tempting morsels.

It was an emotional moment, both young men keenly aware of how fortunate they had been thus far in escaping death, Fletcher on the battlefield of Louisbourg and Colm during his numerous scouting trips into enemy territory as a Ranger. There followed a lengthy conversation in which Colm told them of his whereabouts during the past winter and brought the encouraging news that the colonial armies had finally been moved into position for the assault on Montcalm's troops.

"We've wasted the entire spring waiting for Amherst to make up his mind where to send us," Colm added with a shake of his head. " 'Tis apt, the nickname they have for him in the ranks: the Cautious Commander."

Fletcher nodded soberly. " 'Tis said he'd rather take a year to decide something than take a risk, and I'm not surprised that so little has been accomplished since I gave up my command."

"You can rest assured that things will be moving quickly now," Colm added with a gleam in his eye. "Eleven thousand Provincial and Regular troops have assembled at Lake George, and rumor has it that Chevalier de Bourlamaque is going to withdraw from Fort Ticonderoga the moment Amherst's men attack. 'Tis said he no longer holds faith in a French victory."

"Which will leave only Crown Point standing in the way of an open southern route into Canada." Fletcher had caught his brother's enthusiasm. "Once Amherst's men join Wolfe's on the banks of the St. Lawrence, the assault on Quebec can begin."

"I've a feeling that's where Jem is now." Colm's expression was troubled suddenly, thinking of his twin brother, who, more likely than not, was among the six companies of Rangers that had joined Wolfe in early June for the standoff at the Île d'Orléans.

"I've no fear of defeat in that quarter," he added confidently, mostly for the benefit of Athena, who sat quietly beside him, her face betraying nothing, although he saw her slim hands clench in her lap. "Twenty-two frigates and ships of the line arrived from England several weeks ago to take their place in the St. Lawrence."

"Then the city's been blockaded?" Fletcher asked.

"Aye. They've put the fleet under the command of Vice-Admiral Charles Saunders. I've heard naught but good about him, and with Quebec besieged from both land and water they're bound to surrender soon enough."

"If only Amherst will stop wetnursing his troops and give the command to march," Fletcher remarked dourly. The general had delayed enough, he knew, aware of how easily morale could slip among troops that had been idle too long.

"I believe I'll send Mercy inside for another pot of tea," Athena said suddenly, coming to her feet. She wasn't sure she wanted to hear any more. Colm and Fletcher made everything sound so easy, as though the colonial army need only join forces with Wolfe's waiting men in order to intimidate Montcalm into surrendering.

Surely they must be aware that the French hadn't been sitting idle during the long months of hesitation and indecision on General Amherst's part! For all any of them knew, Quebec might be so well fortified by now that the troops marching north to attack it were heading to their deaths.

"Maybe he isn't there," she whispered aloud, lifting her skirts to hurry inside. "Maybe they've sent him elsewhere—to Crown Point or even Lake George."

But it was not her brother Jeremy she was thinking of.

Colm remained with them for two further days, accompanying Fletcher on tours of the tenant farms and trying his best to recapture the feeling of peace that being at Courtland Grace had always meant for him. Two days proved scant enough time for a war-weary young man on his way to still another battle, yet Athena and Fletcher strove tirelessly to make his stay a pleasant one.

They rode together in the mornings when the sun had barely reached the mountaintops, returning through the rising summer heat to a lavish breakfast prepared by the fussing Prudence. Later Tykie joined them for supper, a long-standing custom that Aunt Amelia had forbidden, and the big house once again rang with laughter. Yet it proved a pitifully short respite, all of them painfully aware of Jeremy's absence and the fact that Colm, too, would presently be gone.

Leavetaking was hard on all of them. Assembling on the front steps on the morning of Colm's departure, Athena, Fletcher, and their loyal staff found it difficult to meet each other's eyes. Only Tykie seemed in a reasonably cheerful frame of mind, for he had insisted on accompanying his young master to town, where Colm was to rejoin his company of Rangers.

While Hale held his horse, Colm shook hands with his older brother, then wordlessly embraced him. Prudence and Mercy, both sniffling tearfully, were given resounding kisses intended to make them laugh, although Mercy only cried harder in response while the softhearted cook turned away to noisily blow her nose.

"We'll both be home before you know it, Prudie," Colm assured her. "And when we are, Jem and I will keep you so busy in the kitchen you'll curse the day we returned."

"I'd never do such a thing, Master Colm!" Prudence protested. "Why, 'tis what I be here for, to cook for you an' young Jem!" To prove her point she thrust a bulging satchel into his arms which contained, she assured him, sufficient food to see him through the long march ahead.

Tucking the heavy bundle into his saddlebag, Colm was tempted to believe that Prudence's rations might well last him until the end of the war. The thought made him grin, yet his expression sobered as he turned to Athena, who was standing, white-faced, at Fletcher's side, her eyes downcast, the long lashes curling against her cheeks.

No one who knew her well could fail to mistake the sorrow that lingered in her eyes despite the effort she made to hide it. Holding her in a fiercely loving embrace, Colm exchanged a hard look with Fletcher above her golden head, and in it lay the unspoken promise that he and Jeremy would return unharmed. Athena had suffered enough and didn't deserve the added heartache of losing her brothers.

"You keep that ill-tempered beast of yours fit while I'm gone," he told her, referring to Ballycor. "Trey Warwick promised to bet on him for me. Don't you dare let him lose his first race."

Athena smiled up at him through her tears. "I won't."

Swinging himself into the saddle, Colm looked down at her as she stood wiping her nose on Fletcher's impossibly large handkerchief. A mischievous light gleamed in his eyes. "And promise me you'll take no more husbands—at least not until Jem and I return."

The hint of a smile curved Athena's lips. "Next time I promise to wait long enough until you've had the chance to render judgment," she vowed.

Satisfied, he bent to kiss her fingertips. "Damned generous of you, my dear. Fletcher?"

Acknowledging his brother's farewell with a nod of his head, Fletcher Courtland tightened his arm reassuringly about Athena's shoulders. They were silent as they watched him ride away, the sunlight glinting on his golden hair.

I mustn't cry for him, Athena was thinking to herself, biting her lips to keep the threatening tears at bay. She hadn't wept when Fletcher had come so close to dying, nor when Stephen had fallen bleeding at her feet, nor even when Lochiel had shattered her heart into so many thousands of pieces. To weep now would mean to reopen the wounds that time was slowly beginning to heal.

The twins were Rangers now, Athena reminded herself, skilled at stealth attacks and able to melt away into the forest like Indians. She needn't fear that a stray bullet would find them.

Yet what of the British regiments? A sudden fear clutched at her heart, recalling Jeremy's scorn when he had described for her the manner in which they marched upon their enemies in full-dress parade, regimental flags flapping jauntily in the breeze, bugles blaring and drums resounding.

It had been quite simple for the French to plow down their scarlet-coated lines, the rigidly marching columns of soldiers affording easy targets.

Surely the British commanders had learned enough from those brutal defeats to train their men to attack like the French and Indians did: from behind trees, embankments, any adequate shelter? European warfare, fought with army facing army on a wide open plain, could not be waged against the scalping Indians in the thick of New England forests. Surely the tragic slaughters of the past had taught them that?

Looking down into his sister's face, Fletcher was startled by the haunting fear in her eyes. His hand tightened about her shoulder, the pressure rousing her from her thoughts. She was very pale when she turned to look up at him.

"You needn't be afraid, love. The twins have always been able to take care of themselves."

She nodded and tried to smile, but the effort was too much. Hot tears stung her eyes and she looked away, ashamed to admit even to herself that it was not the twins she feared for.

Lochiel Blackmoor's face was etched with weariness, yet the flash of his white teeth against his bronzed skin held a hint of devilment. Guiding Glenrobbie with his knees, he negotiated his way through the lines of men, the din of musketry and the wailing of the pipes resounding in his ears. Smoke hung thick in the air, obscuring the setting sun, and when Sergeant-Major Andrew Durning appeared at his side, his face was grimy with it.

"That's the end o't, lad! The Chevalier be gone an' Carillon be ours!"

Lochiel reached down to grip the exhausted sergeant's shoulder. "How many did we lose?"

The sergeant's grin widened. "Casualties be few frae wha' I saw comin' through the lines. Bourlamaque turned tail an' ran, the cursed coward!"

Lochiel could feel the tension drain out of him, relief buoying his spirits so that his exhaustion was suddenly gone. Since early morning Amherst's troops, among them the Seventh Highland Company, had surrounded and bombarded Fort Ticonderoga with unrelenting musket fire and artillery cannonades. The Chevalier de Bourlamaque, a man of apparently faint determination, had answered the attack with feeble reprise and, as the sun began to set over the mountaintops, had blown up the fort and abandoned it to the surrounding British.

" 'Tis a mere fifteen miles tae Crown Point," Sergeant-Major Durning added as Lochiel swung himself down from the saddle. "We could be marchin' within the hour an'—"

Lochiel's deep-throated laughter rang out amid the continued popping of stray musket fire. " 'Twill be dark by then, Andy, and the men are exhausted. Crown Point can wait until morning. Mayhap," he added thoughtfully, "news of Bourlamaque's desertion will have reached their ears by then and we'll find Crown Point abandoned as well."

Apparently General Amherst seemed to share Lochiel's sentiments, for after a brief conference with his officers it was agreed that camp would be made in the ruined fort and that the march on Crown Point would begin at dawn the following morning. Though he was bone-weary, Lochiel found sleep that night as elusive as the stars twinkling overhead. Lying on his bedroll with his arms propped beneath his head, he listened to the hooting of an owl in a nearby tree, its presence reassuring him better than any sentry ever could that there were no renegade Indians or Frenchmen roving about the forest.

The night air was cool and smelled of rich, damp earth, reminding him, to his annoyance, of the autumn gardens of Courtland Grace and the first time he had made love to Athena Courtland. The tension that was beginning to ebb away from his body was suddenly back, and he cursed himself for letting his thoughts wander where they would.

She was the past now, a memory that would fade in time until the raw pain of imagining her exquisitely lovely face faded into an indistinct vision of cool blue eyes and a haughtily upturned nose. She had deserved that final, brutal treatment at his hands, yet Lochiel, thinking on it now, found no satisfaction in what he had done. Instead he became aware of an ache within him, as lonely and unfulfilled as the desolate sighing of the wind in the pine boughs overhead.

His temper flared. Damn her! Like all Highland soldiers he had long ago learned to find rest in any sort of weather, to clear his mind so that sleep could claim him the moment he rolled himself up on the ground in his plaid. Yet exhausted though he might be, with an attack on Crown Point looming beyond the dawn, he found he could not shake the image of Athena's slim white body from his mind. Not until the first graying fingers of light stole tentatively across the eastern sky did sleep finally claim him, but by then it was too late, and the drums of reveille brought him cursing from his bed, his head throbbing and his mood foul.

The march to Crown Point went exactly as Athena had feared, with the regiments high-stepping in impossibly straight columns behind the drums and bugles, their banners snapping in the stiff breeze. The procession was nearly a mile long, threading over the valley floor in bright scarlet and tartan plaid, accoutrements gleaming in the rays of the rising sun. Three companies of Rangers had joined them during the night, bringing the number of Provincial troops to well over a thousand. Morale was high and the threat of ambush unthought of, for down to a man they all believed they would find the fort deserted.

Lochiel was riding in the lead, although the unruly mare he had mounted when Glenrobbie had cast a shoe at the onset of the march afforded him naught but endless irritation. In addition, Sergeant-Major Durning's tireless prattle set his teeth on edge, yet his terse requests for silence did not daunt the grizzled officer in the least.

"When Crown Point falls into British hands, the Frenchies'll hae no course than tae flee into Acadia," Andy observed. "And once our lads join Wolfe's on the shores of the St. Lawrence, 'twill be the end o'bloody Montcalm!"

"Your optimism may be misplaced," Lochiel warned darkly. "We'll have a real fight on our hands if the French haven't abandoned the fort."

Andy gestured behind him at the noisy, awe-inspiring spectacle of an army on the move. "They'll take tae the hills once they see wha's comin' for 'em," he predicted with a laugh.

Lochiel made no reply, for his mare had chosen that moment to shy violently at a covey of quail that exploded from the tall grass along the roadway. He managed to keep her from bolting only by jerking cruelly on the bit and guiding her into a tight, prancing circle with the pressure of his knees.

"I always kenned ye had a special touch wi' the lassies." Andy chuckled admiringly once the nervous animal was again under control.

Lochiel's eyes were as hard as flint as he glanced at his talkative companion. Andy had seen that warning look often enough, and he sobered instantly, thinking to himself that Major Blackmoor was once again in a fine fettle and God alone knew what had happened this time to cause it.

Crown Point, from the look of things, had indeed been abandoned. By the time the lead riders caught their first glimpse of the imposing stone and clay fortification, the sun was standing clear of the emerald mountain peaks. There were no tents erected on the level field before the fort itself, nor smoke rising from behind the thick timber walls. The dozen Rangers who had been sent ahead to scout returned with the news that it appeared to be deserted. The news spread like wildfire through the ranks, sending a deafening cheer into the morning air. With the pipes of the Seventh Company and the newly assembled Black Watch skirling madly, the command to march into the fort was given.

Afterward Lochiel could never remember from what direction the unexpected musketry fire came. It was doubtful that anyone still remained in the fort, and indeed it was determined later that a handful of renegade Iroquois, perhaps disillusioned by the French withdrawal, had lingered in the area long enough to try to take a few scalps. Though daunted by the mile-long columns of soldiers marching toward them, they had remained long enough to fire into the tight ranks of scarlet- and blue-coated uniforms before escaping into the hills.

The first crackling gunshots coming from the trees on the left side of the roadway caused the mare Lochiel was riding to rear in terror. It was only his expertise at handling horses that kept her from turning and bolting and perhaps trampling the men behind her in her panic-stricken flight. The second volley of shots was aimed more carefully, and Lochiel ducked instinctively, hearing a whining lead ball pass inches from his head. His mare was not as fortunate, and she squealed as another caught her in the chest, ripping through her ribcage and killing her instantly.

Lochiel was hurled into the air as the animal fell, cracking his head with a glancing blow on a pile of granite boulders that littered the roadside ditch. He could hear his collarbone snap upon impact, and his last thought as the swirling darkness claimed him was relief that he hadn't been riding Glenrobbie.

"Take him easy, lads! What kind of litter bearers are you? Do you want to dump him on the ground?"

The angry words and the agonizing jolting of his broken shoulder roused Lochiel from the black void into which he had fallen. Gradually he became aware of the fact that he was lying on a swaying canvas stretcher, every movement sending white-hot waves of pain through him. He knew that he couldn't have been unconscious very long, for the sun that blinded him when he opened his eyes had barely risen beyond the treetops.

"Set him down over there, corporal," the same authoritative voice instructed. "There's a few worse off than he is, and we'll see to them first."

Lochiel clenched his teeth as the stretcher was lowered to the ground. He had had broken bones before, but the wrenching pain every movement brought told him that this was a particularly messy break and he dreaded its setting at the hands of an indifferent company doctor.

Where was Andy? he wondered through the searing heat that lashed him. Andy was the only man he knew who could set a bone so that it healed without crippling. Furthermore Andy would take the time to administer a healthy swallow of Scotch whiskey to dull the pain, then probe with gentle, patient fingers until he heard the bone slide back into place.

With an effort Lochiel forced open his eyes. A face he did not recognize swam before him and he tried to muster sufficient strength to whisper Andy's name.

"So you're awake, Major Blackmoor," an unfamiliar voice said with a trace of sympathy. It was obvious from the wounded man's drawn expression that the pain was very bad. "We'll have that shoulder set in no time."

But Lochiel wasn't listening. His gaze had moved beyond the strange man's shoulder to another face that was bending close, noticing with disbelief the square chin and the dark blue eyes framed by unruly gold curls that reflected the radiance of the rising sun.

"Athena!" he whispered, and there was something in his voice that went beyond the tearing, white-hot pain, bringing the blue eyes closer, the tawny brows above them cocked in astonished inquiry.

"What d'you make o' that, eh, Colm?" the man bending over the prostrate form asked with a laugh. "Major Blackmoor here thinks you're a girl!"

Colm Courtland gave a startled exclamation at the mention of Lochiel's name. Pushing the corporal aside, he studied the white face before him, noting how taut the skin was drawn over the chiseled cheekbones, how the lean body was beginning to tremble with the onset of fever. The Highlander's eyes were open, and for a brief moment their glances met and held. Slowly, recognition dawned in the flint-gray depths, Lochiel's clouded thoughts racing back to Fort Shuyler and the taunting young Ranger he had confronted there. There was no doubt in his mind that this man was the same one who had laughingly informed him that both he and his twin brother were Athena Courtland's lovers.

"Damn y-you!" he ground out, blinding hatred consuming him. Before the startled Colm could react, a surprisingly strong hand had him about the throat, squeezing relentlessly, and it took the effort of both himself and the Provincial corporal to break that deadly hold.

"The man's obviously crazed with pain!" the corporal panted as Lochiel's body finally went limp and sank back to the ground. "Either that or he thinks you're someone else. What was that name he mentioned? Athena? Do you know anyone named Athena?"

Coughing and massaging his aching throat, Colm stared thoughtfully into the face of the unconscious man before him. "I might," he allowed softly, but his expression was shuttered and he offered no explanation to his questioning companion.

Twenty-two

"Mrs. Kensington?"

Startled, Athena lifted her head, bright golden curls tumbling from beneath her wide-brimmed bonnet. "Oh, Nate, you gave me such a fright!" she exclaimed, scrambling to her feet and hastily wiping her hands on her skirts.

The young man with the pleasant features and shy brown eyes blushed at her words. "Mrs. Goodson told me you were in the garden. She said I should come round to see you." His tone clearly indicated that he had expected to find her at some ladylike pursuit such as snipping roses, not pulling weeds on her hands and knees.

There was a smudge of dirt on Athena's cheek, and the hem of her flounced muslin dress was streaked with grass stains, yet to young Nate Belker she was still the most beautiful creature he had ever seen. Despite the fact that he had roughhoused with both Athena and the twins when they had been children, and his father, the village blacksmith, had come to Courtland Grace to shoe Master Foster's horses, Nate had always felt awkward and tongue-tied in her presence. Even as a child she had captivated him, and as she grew older and ever lovelier, he had come to believe that he was scarcely worthy of speaking to her at all.

"What is it, Nate?" Athena asked, her eyes dancing as she became aware of his embarrassed silence. Poor Nate never quite knew how to treat her now that they had outgrown their familiar childhood friendship. She had always wondered whether he harbored some romantic yearning for her despite the fact that everyone in all West York knew how dearly he would love to win Mercy Goodson's hand.

Nate colored darkly at her question. How could he explain to her that she didn't look at all like the widow he had expected? Dressed in a pale peach frock with creamy lace at the scooped neckline and three-quarter-length sleeves, a slouch-brim bonnet covering her fair curls, Athena reminded him of a rare and beautiful flower, too young and enchanting to have wed a man and lost him.

"I imagine you've come to see for yourself what a shocking creature I am by refusing to wear black in memory of my husband," Athena remarked, pulling her bonnet from her head and shaking her long hair free. Nate stood enraptured by the sight of the streaming gold banner that cascaded to her hips, and his silence caused Athena to burst into laughter.

"Well, have you?" she prodded. "Or is it Mercy you've come to see?" She slanted him an arch look, aware that Mercy, slowly outgrowing her girlhood infatuation for Jeremy, had begun exchanging coy glances with the blacksmith's son at Sabbath worship last week.

"Oh no, Mrs. Kensington!" Nate burst out, shocked that she would think him so forward. " 'Tis you I've come to see. I've a letter for you that Mr. Benjamin brought with him from Schenectady. 'Tis from your brother Malcolm."

Athena's smile faded. "From Colm?"

Nate nodded and dug into the pocket of his homespun breeches. Handing her a wrinkled piece of parchment, he took no offense at her distracted thanks. Tipping his cap in deference, he started toward the garden gate, where her soft voice unexpectedly stopped him.

"Why don't you go inside and let Prudence get you something to drink? 'Tis hot today and the kitchen is cool."

Nate could scarcely hide his grin of pleasure. "Thank you, Mrs. Kensington, I'd like that very much!"

Athena watched him hurry to the small door that led from the herb garden into the kitchen and couldn't help smiling, knowing he was eagerly hoping for a glimpse of his beloved Mercy. Poor, shy Nate! If only he'd work up enough courage to ask for her hand or at the very least give her some sort of indication of how he felt about her.

"You're just the sort of person to give others advice about love, aren't you?" she asked herself derisively, her mood suddenly bitter. Settling herself amid sweeping skirts on the garden wall, she unfolded the letter with fingers that were suddenly unsure.

Colm had promised to let her know where his company was being reassigned, and Athena scanned the scribbled missive with anxious eyes. Crown Point! Her heart grew numb. Surely he wasn't going to take part in General Amherst's attack on the impregnable French fortification? Her eyes flew to the date at the top of the page to find that the letter was over three days old. Anything might have happened in the meantime!

Swallowing nervously, Athena read on, and without warning a name leaped out at her, making her forget all else. Lochiel Blackmoor! Her breath caught in her throat, and she clutched the letter tightly, hastily perusing Colm's maddeningly brief description of his encounter with the Highland officer.

"You can imagine my surprise," Colm had written, "when I came face to face with the very man who caused you so much trouble, Thena! Furthermore, I realized when I saw him that I'd met him once before; at Fort Shuyler last spring, where he mistook me for Jem. I'd dearly like to know what my brother did to deserve the man's enmity, for the major, suffering a broken shoulder and delirious with fever when I saw him last, deliberately tried to throttle me when Corporal Hastings and I carried him into the fort on a stretcher. He's not the sort of fellow I'd care to anger, and I vow it took the two of us just to pull him off me. 'Tis just like Jeremy to make enemies like that and leave me to bear the brunt of their vengeance!"

There followed a brief itinerary of the upcoming march on Quebec, yet the letter had already slipped unnoticed from Athena's trembling fingers. Lochiel was ill! A broken shoulder, Colm had said, complicated by a fever. Her face was suddenly very still, as if all the animation within her had fled, and she shivered recalling what damage a fever could do.

Three days had passed since Colm had delivered his letter into Parker Benjamin's hands. Three days, perhaps more, in which the raging heat had waged relentless war on Lochiel's injured body. Athena's slim hands clenched, recalling Fletcher's description of the negligent care he had received from an often drunk army physician and how he had jokingly added that he had been fortunate enough to have the services of a doctor at all. Had Lochiel been placed in a similar position? Or worse, was he being looked after by someone without the least bit of medical knowledge?

"Why should I care?" Athena asked herself, pacing restlessly to and fro amid the riotous summer flowers. Her lovely brow was puckered in a frown, and her eyes blazed with bad temper. Lochiel Blackmoor meant nothing to her! Why should she care that he was ill? Surely he was strong enough to survive a broken collarbone!

"I hope 'twill teach the arrogant sod a lesson in humility!" She kicked angrily at a pebble in her path, not caring that her soft kid slippers, already dirty from the weeding she had done earlier, were not meant to withstand such treatment.

In the next moment her mood had vacillated, and she found herself trembling despite the heat of the summer sun, convinced that Lochiel had been left to waste away by his fellow officers, who had neither the time nor the inclination to cater to their wounded. Doubtless they had left him in the abandoned fort with no one to look after him or carried him as far as the next settlement, where he had been entrusted to the care of some ignorant farmer to whom it didn't matter one way or the other if he lived or died.

"What utter nonsense, Athena!" she muttered to herself. And if such were indeed Lochiel Blackmoor's fate, she ought to be glad. 'Twas the least the bloody cad deserved.

She wasn't even aware of the fact that she was crying until she felt hot tears splash onto her hand. Suddenly the anger within her was gone, replaced by a wrenching ache that she could no longer deny, as the depth of her love for Lochiel Blackmoor. And then she was running toward the stables, stumbling over her skirts and feeling the hot, telltale tears continue to scald her cheeks.

"Tykie!" she cried, aware that there wasn't another moment to lose. "Tykie!"

Yet in the end Athena went without him. Convinced that neither he nor Fletcher would permit her to ride pell-mell into what might very well be an active confrontation with the French, she told no one of her plans. Leaving a brief letter of explanation in Fletcher's study, she saddled Ballycor and galloped off amid a cloud of dust, her hair tucked once again beneath the battered cap, her slim body clad in buckskin.

The daylight was nearly spent by the time she rode into view of the abandoned fort. Crown Point lay amid the rolling hills west of Lake Champlain, its awesome timber walls facing the swift-moving river. In the long twilight of summer the band of water shone like silver, reflecting the feathery cirrus clouds that were drawn across the sky. A warm wind blew through the valley, bringing with it the fresh scent of pine, while in the tall grass crickets chirped a wistful melody. Far away across the fields a herdsman with a torch rounded up his cattle for the night, the tranquillity of the coming evening broken only by the intermittent barking of his dogs and the lowing of the wayward beasts.

To Athena, drawing the lathering Ballycor to a halt on the rocky ridge of the opposite hillside, the coming of night brought no sense of peace. She had ridden the stallion far too hard, yet for once her thoughts were not on his welfare. She was staring down at the fort with narrowed eyes, wondering if the smoke that was curling above the treetops came from French fires or English. Too late she realized what her haste had cost her. If she had taken time to stop along the way to ask questions of the settlers, she might have learned whether Crown Point had fallen to Amherst's troops or not.

"Impetuous as always, aren't you?" she asked herself with a self-deprecatory shake of her head.

In the end she had no choice but to ride down to the fort, her throat tight, one trembling hand resting on the butt of the pistol tucked into her belt. No one, not even the French, she kept telling herself with forced bravado, would dare shoot down a solitary rider—would they?

It was growing darker now, and a chill wind had sprung up from the far side of the river. Athena shivered in her thin jacket, her heart hammering faster the closer Ballycor came to the enormous timbered ramifications. Her nervousness must have communicated itself to the stallion, for he began to snort and toss his head, his behavior increasing Athena's uneasiness. The forest around her was very still, and as the daylight waned she found herself searching the shadowed thickets with anxious eyes, imagining that each of them sheltered a crouching Indian warrior with a tomahawk at the ready.

The front gate of the fort was closed, and Athena, drawing to a halt beneath it, lifted her head to scan the walkways far above for signs of life. If the fort were still occupied, wouldn't the guards up there have challenged her by now? Surely it must be abandoned, yet how to explain the smoke she had seen rising through the trees?

"You, there! What do you think you're doing?"

Alarmed, Athena whipped her head around, her eyes straining to find the origin of the voice in the gathering darkness behind her. Her hand tightened about Ballycor's reins, the big stallion prancing nervously as he sensed his mistress's fear.

"Haven't you got ears, lad? I asked what you're doing here."

Athena's wildly pounding pulses began to slow as she realized that the voice which had addressed her did not sound as though it belonged to a Frenchman. "I'm sorry, but I dislike speaking to someone I cannot see," she called out boldly, deciding that a show of courage might stand her in better stead than quivering cowardice.

"Cocky little gent, ain't you?" There was a rustling in the bushes off to the left, and Athena held her breath as the shadow of a tall man loomed onto the roadway. When he came closer, she saw that he was wearing leggings and a much-mended flannel shirt. Several snares were thrown over his shoulder, and he carried a musket in the crook of one arm. A long black beard and shaggy hair attested to the fact that he rarely made use of comb and razor, and Athena's breath passed through her lips in a long, relieved sigh.

He was nothing more than a fur trader, a man who made his living trapping in the vast wilderness of northern New England and the great Northwest Territory for the rich plunder of beaver, silver fox, marten, and raccoon. She had known his kind since childhood, and though trappers as a rule were not the most scrupulous of men, Athena had never had reason to fear them. Like the Indians, they were governed by laws of their own, and as long as one understood their ways there was little reason to feel threatened.

"I'm looking for my brother," Athena told him when he came to a halt before her, long legs straddling the road, his piercing eyes regarding her solemnly from beneath bushy brows. She knew better than to reveal her sex to him, yet knew also that only a direct approach would yield her the information she so desperately sought.

"He's with the Rangers, and word has it he was injured when Carillon and Crown Point fell. Do you know if General Amherst's troops are still there?" She gestured at the imposing structure before her.

"They been gone three, maybe four days now," he told her slowly, speaking in the unhurried manner of a man unaccustomed to conversation. "Carillon, Ticonderoga, whatever you want to call it, fell without much of a fight, and Crown Point here was abandoned when the army arrived."

"But the fires—I saw smoke—"

The bristling beard twitched, and Athena realized he was smiling. "That be my dinner roastin'. Will you join me, lad? It's a haunch of venison I got sizzlin' on a slow fire."

"Thank you, but I'd like to head on before it gets much darker." She hesitated. "You say the fort was abandoned by the French? How then do you account for the wounded? Was there some sort of skirmish or . . . or an ambush?" She swallowed hard at the thought. "My brother—"

He hitched his snares to the other shoulder and pointed east with a blunt forefinger. "There was a few redskins lurkin' in them trees over there when Amherst's men moved in. Reckon they was thirstin' for blood because they took a few potshots at the lobsterbacks before tailin' it into the hills. I heard tell a few of the soldiers got killed."

Athena's small white teeth clamped down hard on her lower lip. "And the wounded? Where were they taken? I assume they're not in the fort any longer."

He jerked his thumb toward the road behind him. "They was carried down to Harryton. It's a little settlement just over that mountain ridge."

Suddenly impatient to be gone, Athena thanked him gravely and dug her heels into Ballycor's sides. The big animal sped away, his long-legged stride eating up the road beneath him. Though it was too dark to see, Athena urged him on as fast as she dared, her earlier fear of the silent forest forgotten. This time it was a different fear that drove her relentlessly, chilling her more thoroughly than the cool air that streamed into the valley with the coming of the night.

Harryton was a settlement of no more than half a dozen farms, and Athena might have missed it altogether if it hadn't been for the flickering campfires that were visible through the trees. Drawing Ballycor to a halt at the edge of an unplanted field, Athena searched the darkness until she finally spotted the familiar gray canvas tents of the British army. She counted half a dozen in the dim moonlight and wondered how many soldiers were in bivouac there. Was Lochiel among them, or—and here her heart gave a frightened leap—was he one of the dead the trapper had spoken of?

Urging Ballycor forward with the pressure of her knees, Athena rode boldly into camp. Drawing to a halt in the circle of light from the nearest fire, she glared defiantly down at the sentry who hurried to confront her.

"You've got no business here, lad," he informed her before she could speak, his youthful face filled with mistrust as he stared up at her. "Military camps be off-limits to civilians."

Athena lifted her chin, thinking to herself that she'd be damned if a mere foot soldier was going to prevent her from finding Lochiel. Though he wore pipe-clayed breeches and the familiar blue coat of the British army, she had no idea to which regiment he belonged.

"I can assure you," she informed him haughtily, "that I do have business here, and 'tis far more legitimate than you may think."

He hesitated, momentarily put out by the well-bred voice and flashing blue eyes, and Athena pressed her advantage by urging Ballycor forward. Taking this as an act of aggression, the sentry recovered quickly and sprang into the big stallion's path, musket held before him to bar the way. Disconcerted, Ballycor snorted and tossed his head, and Athena had no choice but to rein him in.

"Look here, my good fellow," she began furiously, hand on her slim hip, "I don't believe you realize—"

"What the devil's going on here, McMillan?"

Another soldier had appeared out of the darkness, a tall young man with unruly blond curls who carried with him a half-eaten ration of venison on a battered tin plate. "Can't a fellow enjoy a meal without—"

"Colm!" Athena cried, her voice hoarse with disbelief, "oh, Colm, it's me!"

The Ranger's head whipped around at her words, his eyes widening as he took in the imposing white stallion and the slim young lad who rode him. "God's blood!" he ground out, recognizing the familiar features beneath the brim of the leather cap. A torrent of disbelieving words burst from him. "What in God's name are you doing here? How did you know where to find me? And what the devil is it you're wearing? You look—no, wait, don't say a word," he cautioned, catching himself in time.

Striding forward, he pulled her none too gently from the saddle, effectively muzzling her with the palm of his hand in the event she chose to make some impulsive remark and thereby give herself away.

"McMillan," he ordered without turning around, "take my . . . my brother's horse and see that it's properly fed and watered."

The sentry's eyes bulged. "Your brother, sir?"

"Aye, my brother," Colm repeated authoritatively. "Come on, lad," he added, pulling Athena bodily away.

"Since when does a British soldier address a Ranger as 'sir'?" was the first thing Athena asked when Colm finally released her in the darkness behind one of the tents.

"Since General Amherst made me a captain. I volunteered to quarter his wounded, you see, and I imagine he mistook my compassion for bravery and decided—'Od's wounds!" he interrupted himself furiously. "Stop trying to change the subject, Thena! What in God's name are you doing here?"

He was startled to see tears well in her eyes. "Oh, Colm, 'tis because of your letter!" She swallowed hard, aware that there could be no more pretense, not for Colm and not for her. "Is—is Lochiel still here?"

"Lochiel Blackmoor?" Colm inquired impatiently. "Aye, and faring none too well, but what—"

"Please," Athena whispered, "I want to see him."

Startled, Colm stared down into her face, and what he saw in the dim light brought an astonished expression to his own features. "Come," he said tersely, taking her arm in a tight grip.

The tent into which he led her was dark, and only the flickering light from a nearby fire illuminated the still form lying on the single cot within. Tears blurred Athena's vision as she bent over Lochiel, her heart aching with possessive love. Kneeling beside the cot, she touched his hot forehead with a gentle hand and stroked the dark, unruly hair that fell across his brow.

"Isn't there anything you can do for the fever?" she asked, glancing up at Colm with hopeless eyes.

"We've tried everything," Colm informed her harshly. " 'Twill simply have to run its own course." He fell silent, studying her thoughtfully. "Athena," he asked abruptly, "are you in love with him?"

She nodded and looked away, tears sliding, unnoticed, down her cheeks. Lochiel stirred and groaned at that moment, and Athena leaned close, anxiously studying the thin, beloved face before her.

With obvious effort Lochiel forced open his heavy lids. Everything seemed to swim before him, and for a moment he believed that he was looking into the misty face of the child whose miniature Fletcher Courtland had carried in his locket, the beautiful, golden-haired child who had given him an oat cake on the long march south from Glenfinnan with Bonnie Prince Charlie. No, that was wrong, he reminded himself, aware of his own confusion. The portrait in the locket had been of Athena, not that little girl, and it was almost as if she were here with him now, her slim, cool hands soothing his fevered brow. Yet how could that be when he knew her to be miles away at Kensington Manor?

He groaned again and was astonished when the beautiful face bent closer instead of disappearing. "Lochiel?"

He stared at her disbelievingly. "Athena?" His voice, hoarse and nearly inaudible, grated in his ears. "Are you really h-here?"

"Hush, my love," he heard her say. "Don't speak. You must save your strength."

"But—"

"Lochiel, please be still," Athena begged, frightened by the gauntness of his features and the deep lines that were etched beneath his eyes and about his mouth. "I've come to help you, but you mustn't waste your strength by trying to speak."

For a moment he was silent, then his lips curved into a crooked smile. "I must be d-daft to obey orders from a chit like you."

Athena felt certain her heart would break with love for him, and she reached for his hand, her slim fingers sliding about his. Hope stirred within her when he squeezed them reassuringly.

Colm had been watching them keenly and did not miss the swiftness with which Lochiel Blackmoor's haggard features relaxed. He felt stunned by the love he saw on his sister's face for this arrogant man, whose skill at soldiering and whose courage on the battlefield were all but legendary within the Highland regiments. For the first time in his life he felt awkward in her presence.

"Athena, you're cold," he observed at last, aware that she was shivering. "Come with me out to the fire. There's soup and hot tea."

She shook her head, as he had expected her to, and he left her without another word, knowing it would be impossible to persuade her to leave. His expression was grim as he strode out into the darkness. Major Blackmoor's shoulder was mending, yet the fever that was sapping him of his strength refused to break. 'Twas obvious that his time was rapidly running out, and God help poor Athena were he not to survive.

Athena would have scoffed at her brother's sentiments had she known of them. Lochiel was not going to die, not if she could help it! Mustering every bit of her determination, she rolled up the sleeves of her jacket and went to work. She knew that in order for the fever to break she must cool the raging heat within him, and this she did with cold compresses, wetting them continuously and patiently bathing his body, which was racked by spasms, and his fevered brow.

"This is insanity, Thena!" Colm protested when he came inside hours later to find his sister slumped wearily beside the cot. "Don't you think we tried all that? I'm inclined to believe 'tis no ordinary fever but a recurring ague he contracted during some foreign campaign. The best thing for you to do is get some sleep and let the fever run its course."

But Athena merely pursed her lips and stubbornly shook her head. As the hours ticked by, however, she began to realize that perhaps Colm might be right. Lochiel did not respond at all to her gentle ministrations, and his shallow breathing rasped loudly in the silence of the night, yet she would not admit to herself that her care was for naught.

" 'Tis simply too cold in here," she reasoned aloud, for the damp night air had insinuated itself on icy fingers inside the tent, and she herself was shivering despite the heavy jacket wrapped about her shoulders.

How best to keep Lochiel warm? She had begged as many extra blankets from Colm as she could, and there was nothing more she could do for him. Except, she realized as a sudden idea struck her, warm him with the heat of her own body. Her spirits rose for the first time that night, recalling how Tykie had held her firmly beneath the single blanket they had shared on the journey to Fort Shuyler when she had shivered in the cold mountain air.

"I may not be able to keep you as warm as Tykie could," Athena whispered, pulling off her jacket and boots and easing herself in beside him, "but 'tis the best I can do."

She tried not to let her fears overwhelm her as she slipped her arms about him, resting her cheek against his hair and pressing her body to the length of his. She could feel the heat of his fever burn her wherever they touched, but she merely held him close and breathed in the familiar, beloved scent of him.

The night was still and very dark, the moon having set long ago, and Athena lay quietly, listening to the sound of Lochiel's breathing. The fierce, aching love that had overwhelmed her earlier tugged at her heart, and she tightened her arms about him and buried her face in the comforting strength of his shoulder. For the first time since Stephen's death a feeling of peace came over her, easing the ravages of her soul, and when her lids at last began to grow heavy, she closed her eyes and slept.

She awoke only once that night, coming out of a deep sleep to find Lochiel breathing evenly beside her, one arm thrown lightly across her breast. His forehead was cool to the touch, and Athena, aware that the terrible fever had broken at last, snuggled closer against him and drifted back to sleep.

"Tell me truly, Athena, do you usually take to a man's bed without waiting for an invitation?"

Athena's eyes flew open at the sound of the mocking voice above her, and she stared in confusion into Lochiel Blackmoor's amused gray eyes.

He was standing above her dressed in his uniform, his arm in a crude sling, his hair neatly combed, and his jaw clean shaven. Though there was a gauntness to his face and shadows beneath his eyes, he did not look at all to her disbelieving gaze like a man who had been suffering in the throes of a fever the night before.

"What—what are you doing out of bed?" she demanded, pushing the hair from her eyes and glaring up at him in angry bewilderment.

"I found myself too sorely tempted by the unexpected presence of a bed partner when I awoke," he said obligingly. "I thought I was dreaming the night before, and you can imagine my delight when I awoke to find you very real and warm beside me."

Athena scrambled to her feet and hastily rebuttoned her shirt. Lochiel's seemingly miraculous recovery had unnerved her, and she wasn't exactly sure what to say to this smiling man, whose teasing was as unexpected as his appearance before her.

"You were so ill last night," she said uncertainly, struggling to hide the fierce joy that was beginning to throb within her. "Are you really feeling strong enough to rise?"

He grinned at her disarmingly. "Aside from the pain this cursed shoulder gives me, I feel very well, thank you. As for my illness, 'tis naught but a fever I contracted years ago in the damp hold of a ship and which recurs from time to time in conjunction with some other injury—a broken collarbone, for example."

He was staring down at her like a man starved, finding her disheveled beauty more distracting than anything he had ever known. He could scarcely believe that she had come to him when he needed her, and for the first time he dared ask himself why, for surely she would not have done so had her feelings toward him been indifferent ones.

"You must be hungry," Athena said awkwardly. "Shall I get you something to eat?" Inwardly her heart was beating very fast, and she felt breathless as she looked up into his face, scarcely daring to hope that the tenderness in his eyes was for her alone.

He reached out and took a silky curl between his fingers, stroking it with his thumb while his gaze moved to her parted lips. "Why did you come, Athena?" he asked softly.

She could no longer deny the fierce love that swept through her at his nearness, his touch causing her spirit to soar. "Oh, Lochiel," she breathed, her eyes shining, "I—"

"God's blood, I can't believe you cured him, Thena!"

The gentle hand released her abruptly, and Athena stared in confusion from Lochiel's tight-lipped countenance to her brother Colm, who stood regarding them in astonishment from the opening of the tent. A long moment of silence followed before Lochiel finally spoke.

"I believe I'm beginning to understand," he said slowly. " 'Twasn't me you came to see, 'twas your Ranger captain. Am I right, Athena?"

"I didn't even know Colm was here," she said honestly, though her voice shook as she tried to understand why Lochiel had once again erected a wall between them. " 'Twas your injury that brought me here. I—I wanted to help you."

Lochiel ignored this whispered confession. God, what a fool he'd been to imagine for a moment that he had truly won Athena's love! Once he had ached merely to possess her, and despite the fact that he was aware of the existence of her other lovers, he had overlooked them and taken from her what pleasure he could. Now he knew that he wanted so much more from her, that possessing her body was not enough. He wanted to win her heart, to share her every thought and dream, to know that her strong, abiding love was his alone. But apparently that was not to be, for once again he had been mistaken in thinking Athena cared for him, her presence here putting an end forever to the illusions he had believed might be real.

"I imagine you were quite surprised to find him here," he grated, indicating Colm with a curt gesture.

"Of course I was," Athena agreed, brow puckered in bewilderment. "I love my brother very much, but he isn't the reason I—" Her words ended in a startled gasp as Lochiel's hand fell without warning on her shoulder, spinning her around so that she was staring up into his white face.

"What did you say?" he rasped.

She swallowed hard. "I said I was surprised to find my b-brother here."

The pulse in Lochiel's throat was beating wildly and he seized her by the arms, his grip painfully strong for a man who had been so ill the night before. "Athena, don't tell me—"

"What the devil are you doing?" Colm demanded. His expression was dangerous as he jerked Athena from Lochiel's grasp, unmindful of the other man's wounded shoulder. "If you abuse her, major, you'll find yourself answering to me!"

Grimacing in pain, Lochiel let her go. His breathing was harsh as he gazed from one face to the other, cursing himself for never having noticed the resemblance between them before. God's blood, was it possible—could he really have been so blind?

"He's not the one who came to Courtland Grace to see you last October," he observed at last, still unable to admit to himself the extent of his mistake.

"That was my brother Jeremy," Athena explained, unnerved by the expression on his face. "Colm and Jeremy are twins." She gazed at him in bewilderment. "Didn't you know?"

"No," Lochiel said softly. "I didn't."

What the devil was going on between them? a puzzled Colm was asking himself. It was clear from the Highlander's suddenly haggard appearance that he was not as well as he would have them think. And what did it matter that he hadn't known Athena's brothers were twins? Her sudden intake of breath made it obvious that Athena seemed to understand very well.

"Oh, Lochiel," she whispered, her voice quivering with fathomless pain, "surely you didn't think that I—that they—"

She turned her back on him, struggling with the magnitude of her discovery. No wonder he had always withdrawn from her whenever they had been so close to putting an end to the damning pretense between them! He had mistaken Colm and Jeremy for her lovers! She understood now the cruel remarks he had made concerning her behavior and it galled her that he could believe her capable of such a thing.

"You should have asked me!" she burst out, eyes brimming with accusing tears. "You should have trusted me to explain about Jeremy and Colm and about Stephen, too! I imagine you thought me in love with him when in truth . . ." she choked on the bitter words, "in truth I only agreed to marry him because you'd made it plain that you didn't want me!"

There was stunned silence when she finished speaking and it was Lochiel who finally broke it. "I saw you weep over his body that night, Athena. Surely you aren't going to convince me that your grief wasn't genuine!"

"Of course I grieved for Stephen!" Athena cried. "And I'll have his death forever on my conscience, but that doesn't mean I loved him!"

Stunned by the truth he could no longer deny, Lochiel stared down into her anguished eyes. "My God, Athena," he whispered roughly, only now beginning to understand what his arrogance and jealousy had cost them, "I never knew—"

"No, you didn't," she interrupted bitterly, "and you might have asked me instead of assuming that I had the morals of the lowest scullery maid!"

"God, Athena, I didn't honestly believe—" He broke off, aware that words could never still her pain even though he saw now that he had never truly thought of her that way. His jealousy had corrupted him, caused him to lash out at her unfairly and ruin forever that which lay nearest his heart.

"I hate you, Lochiel Blackmoor," Athena said in a whisper, her heart aching for the dreams lying shattered at her feet. "If you had only asked me instead of assuming that I—that I—dear God, couldn't you have realized that night that you were the first? The very first?"

"Athena—"

"The first and ONLY man, Lochiel," she finished bitterly. "Even Stephen never—" She found her voice failing her and wished she could rage at him, fling his terrible accusations back in his face, but instead she felt numb and so terribly, terribly tired.

"I hate you, Lochiel," she repeated, though this time the words were infinitely weary. "I hope I never see you again."

Without another glance in his direction she vanished into the harsh light of the coming dawn while Colm, shocked by what he had just witnessed between them, quickly followed. Lochiel, knowing it would be futile to go after them, collapsed wearily onto his cot and with his face in his hands, bowed his dark head in defeat.

Twenty-three

Under the protection of fifteen thousand French troops and an awesome array of mounted cannons, the city of Quebec was easily able to withstand a three-month siege waged by Brigadier General James Wolfe and his weary army. As summer waned, the British found their batteries exhausted, and with desertion and illness rampant among his men, General Wolfe was forced to admit that perhaps Quebec was, as the French had boasted, all but impregnable.

It was at this point, with morale at a new low, that a handful of Rangers, among them Jeremy Courtland, made a courageous foray into the city itself to discover where, if any, its weaknesses might lie. Though only two of the scouts returned alive, they brought with them the startling news of the discovery of a little-known footpath leading up the otherwise unscalable cliffs known as the Plains of Abraham upon which Quebec had been built.

That evening, the twelfth of September 1759, General Wolfe gave the order to launch a half-dozen British flatboats, and the tide quickly carried them past the French batteries to land at the Anse du Foulon. Here the small French patrol at the bottom of the cliffs was quickly overpowered, and by dawn over five thousand British Regulars had scaled the Plains of Abraham and were waiting for Wolfe's order to storm the city.

The Marquis de Montcalm, having expected the attack to come from Beauport to the east of Quebec, where Wolfe had been concentrating his firepower in the past, was taken completely by surprise by an assault from the west. Troops were hastily assembled to meet the unexpected enemy, but by then it was too late, for the British wasted no time in taking one of the largest of the French battery posts, and in doing so opened the St. Lawrence River so that the waiting English warships could sail into range of the city itself.

Unable to withstand the strength of the British assault, the French troops fell back in disorder. The Marquis de Montcalm, who had been shot in the chest, ordered himself propped on his horse by two of his soldiers so that none of his men would suspect their leader of having been mortally wounded. His courage was to prove futile, however, for he died a short time later, and within fifteen minutes of the announcement of his death Quebec fell, and with it went the hopes of the French empire in America.

In West York, as elsewhere in the colonies, the ensuing British victory was joyously received. At Courtland Grace there was even more cause to celebrate, for the fall of Quebec brought with it not only the end of the war but the safe return of the Courtland twins—and an unexpected wedding.

It was on a cool, overcast morning not long after the war's dramatic end that the bell in West York's churchtower began to peal a joyous summons to the townfolk who had been invited to attend. The wedding itself was to take place in the spacious drawing room of Courtland Grace, and Prue Goodson, hearing the distant chiming of the bells, threw up her hands in despair as she slid an enormous dish of baked ham into the oven to keep warm.

"The guests'll be comin' any minute and we're simply not ready!" she wailed, hastily wiping her hands on her apron and reaching for a spoon. "There be nowhere near enough for them to eat!"

Mercy was forced to laugh at this, for she and Wills had spent the last half-hour arranging countless dishes on the buffet table that had been set up in the dining room. Fletcher had insisted on a grand supper and dancing to follow the ceremony, and Prudence had outdone herself with the meal, working feverishly all week so that everything would be ready in advance.

The sideboards groaned with tempting offerings, among them three wild geese stuffed with apples and roasted to a crisp, juicy brown, and a side of venison that had been spitted for days over a slow-cooking fire. Pumpkin and squash, sweetened with molasses, were to complement the glazed ham, while smoked fish had been set out in honor of the bride, who claimed it was one of her favorite dishes. Freshly baked pies brimming with apples, quinces, and cherries steamed beneath their linen wrappings, and baskets of oranges, tamarinds, and sweets had been placed nearby. Wills had seen to it that beer, cider brandy, and rum were brought up from the cellar and that Madeira and claret were made available to guests who might thirst for more refined libations. In honor of the occasion the faithful servants had changed into their finest clothes, and only Prudence, a dab of flour on her reddened cheek, still wore her homespun work dress.

"There'll be enough for everyone," Mercy assured her mother, gently prying the spoon out of her hand. "Why don't you get ready while I see if Reverend Axminster has everything he needs for the ceremony?"

"You'd better see to Miss Athena first," Prudence suggested firmly.

" 'Twill be dreamin' out the window she'll be and payin' no mind to the time. Master Fletcher'll have that child's hide if she's late for Jemmy's wedding!"

"I'll see to her," Mercy promised, knowing Prudence was right. Miss Athena had taken to gazing moodily out the window for hours on end these past few months, and sometimes Mercy couldn't help feeling that her mistress had become a total stranger. 'Twas obvious that she was unhappy about something, though she did her best to hide it from everyone.

Mercy sighed as she ascended the stairs to Miss Athena's room. So much had changed since Mistress Bower's death, and despite the fact that the twins were home and Master Jeremy was due to marry the sweetest girl a man could wish for, Mercy felt the loss of those happy former days like a physical ache and suspected that everyone else at Courtland Grace did too.

To her surprise she found Athena standing, fully dressed, before the pier glass, a brush in her hand and a cheerful expression on her lovely face.

"I imagine you expected to find me in corset and stockings," she said with a mischievous smile. "Never fear, Mercy, I wouldn't dream of being late for Jeremy's wedding."

"Who helped you dress, miss?" Mercy asked curiously, aware that her mistress could not have handled the numerous petticoats and heavy satin skirts alone.

"Anne Marie," Athena replied, referring to the young Canadian girl who was shortly to become Jeremy's bride. Though all of them had been astonished when Jeremy had returned from Quebec with the shy, brown-eyed girl, they had quickly welcomed her into their hearts upon hearing how she had saved Jeremy and his companion from being captured by the French.

Six Rangers had slipped into the occupied city of Quebec on a scouting mission for General Wolfe on the night of the fateful British attack, and only Jeremy and his friend had managed to escape. With a French patrol hot on their heels, they had fled through the streets and had been rescued by Anne Marie Bretogne, who had taken pity on them and hidden them away in the interior of her carriage. Trembling with fright, the dark-haired girl had bravely ordered her coachman to drive the two young men to the outskirts of the city, thus enabling them to alert General Wolfe to the existence of the footpath that led to the summit of the Plains of Abraham.

"My parents were French, yet they sympathized with the English cause," Anne Marie had explained in her soft voice on the night of her arrival at Courtland Grace. "Though it was never proved, they were killed by radical French patriots, among them a high-ranking officer in Montcalm's army."

"Surely you don't believe that!" Athena had protested in horror.

The French girl nodded solemnly. "A fire swept through our house one night, killing both of them in their beds. I was away visiting relatives at the time, yet friends have told me that it was raining very heavily that night. 'Twould be hard for a fire to start under such circumstances without human help, *non?"*

"And for their sake you gave shelter to Jeremy and his companion?" Colm asked soberly.

Anne Marie colored at his words and cast a shy glance at his twin, who sat beside her on the sofa. *"Oui* and *non.* I wanted to help, especially when I saw them running from the gendarmes, but not alone for my parents' sake." Her blush deepened and she dropped her eyes to her lap. "He seemed so terribly in need of help and looked so kind that I—I—"

"What Marie means," Jeremy said with a fond laugh, taking her small hand in his as she fell silent and cast a helpless glance in his direction, "is that she was so taken with my good looks and charm that she fell in love with me the moment she saw me. There was never any doubt in her mind that she'd risk life and limb to save me."

They had all laughed at this, yet all of them were aware, too, of how much Anne Marie had sacrificed for him. There was no question that she adored him and that Jeremy loved her fiercely in return. Thinking back on the night of their arrival, Athena remembered the lump that had risen to her throat when she had noticed for the first time how very much in love they were. How her heart ached to share their happiness, and how cruelly she continued to long for Lochiel!

"Ooh, I'll never get my hair fixed in time!" Athena cried in sudden vexation, hurling the brush onto her bed. She didn't want to think about Lochiel nor admit to herself how certain she was growing as the days went by that he hadn't survived the terrible slaughter at Quebec.

"Here, let me help, miss," Mercy said soothingly, aware of the sudden change in her mistress's mood.

Athena stood silently before the pier glass while Mercy patiently combed through the unruly blond curls. Was it true that Lochiel was dead? According to Colm several Highland regiments had taken part in the final assault on Quebec, and despite the British victory there had been a heavy toll of casualties, General Wolfe among them.

"Are you wondering about Lochiel?" he asked her softly on the night of his return when she had come to his room and stood silently in the doorway, the unasked question trembling on her lips.

He had sighed when she nodded and turned restlessly to the window, his heart aching for her pain. "I'm sorry, Thena, I've no idea what happened to him. The Seventh Highland Company was there at the Anse du Foulon when the order to attack was given, but afterward I was never able to discover how many of their men they'd lost. I assure you I did my best to find out, but with the confusion and Jeremy's return with Anne Marie—"

"I understand," Athena had said and had quietly withdrawn. She had never mentioned Lochiel's name again and was thankful that Colm hadn't either.

"There, miss, 'tis perfect!"

Mercy's voice brought Athena from her thoughts with a start. Surveying herself in the glass, she saw that her hair had been tamed by Mercy's skillful hands, the thick curls neatly plaited and pulled gently from her brow so that the golden loops fell to her shoulders. Wayward tendrils escaped to curl against her temples, the effect pleasing even to her own critical eye.

"I don't think anyone save Miss Bretogne will look more beautiful than you today, miss," Mercy sighed dreamily.

"Oh, go on, you'll turn my head with such talk," Athena scoffed, yet a smile lurked in her dark blue eyes. The gown she was wearing was of pale yellow satin, the wide skirts divided into panels and caught up with loops of bright blue ribbon to reveal the cerulean petticoats underneath. The lace-trimmed bodice was embroidered with tiny blue cornflowers, and to complement the subtle array of colors Athena had fastened a delicate chain of teardrop-shaped aquamarines about her white throat.

"May I come in, Athena?" came a softly accented voice from the door.

Both Athena and Mercy clapped their hands in delight as Anne Marie stepped shyly inside. Though she had refused to dress elaborately for her wedding, the dark-haired Canadian girl was breathtaking indeed in the simple gown of white watered silk that the local seamstress had hastily sewn for her. Her petticoats rustled softly as she turned obligingly at Athena's request, and her large brown eyes anxiously studied the other girl's face.

"Do you think Jeremy will like it?" she asked hesitantly.

"Of course he will," Athena responded, hugging her impulsively. "Mercy, where are my mother's things?" she added over her shoulder.

"Here, Miss Athena."

Anne Marie gasped as she opened the box that was placed in her hands. "I can't possibly wear this!" she exclaimed, holding aloft a gossamer veil embroidered with delicate lace flowers and shimmering with hundreds of tiny seed pearls.

"Of course you can," Athena said firmly. "There's a handkerchief, too, and a pair of gloves that I know will fit. My mother wore them when she married my father, and I'm certain she would have been delighted to give them to you today."

There were tears in Anne Marie Bretogne's eyes as Athena and Mercy affixed the flowing white veil to her glossy brown hair. She had left Quebec a fugitive with naught but the clothes on her back, breathless with the certainty that the man she had saved from capture was the one man she would love the rest of her life. She hadn't expected Jeremy Courtland to be so wealthy or to possess a family whose warmth toward her had replaced forever the aching void left by the death of her parents two years ago.

"You have all been so kind to me," she said tearfully, throwing her arms about Athena. "When I came here with Jeremy I never dreamed—I never knew—"

"Stop crying," Athena protested with a tender laugh, surprised at the rush of fondness she felt for this shy young girl and understanding for the first time why Jeremy had been unable to leave Quebec without her. "You don't want to have red eyes for the ceremony, do you?"

"Mon dieu, non!" Anne Marie protested, and made them all laugh by vehemently blowing her nose in Fiona's embroidered silk handkerchief.

Anne Marie and Jeremy had requested a simple wedding, yet the number of guests invited filled all four rows of the chairs Wills had set up in the elegant drawing room. Leda Kensington and her daughters were present that afternoon, as was Katrine de Vries and her parents, Katrine having graciously agreed to play the pianoforte during the ceremony.

Athena was hard put to hide her amusement at the worshipful glances the Dutch girl kept casting at Colm and Fletcher, for both her brothers looked extremely handsome in their dark suits and satin hose. Fletcher, who usually cared little for the clothes he wore, had spared nothing on his appearance after Anne Marie had shyly asked him if he would do her the honor of giving her away. Colm was just as pleased to act as Jeremy's best man, while Tykie had beamed proudly when he was called upon to assist Wills as an usher.

Athena had to bite her lip to keep from laughing when she came down the aisle as Anne Marie's bridesmaid and caught sight of Tykie for the first time that day. What an impressive spectacle he made in tight-fitting brocade breeches and silver hose that revealed his tree-trunk-thick calves, his stock so tightly knotted that his bearded cheeks were suffused with color.

Yet as the ceremony began and Reverend Axminster intoned the sacred words in his somber voice, Athena's amusement fled. She found herself having to swallow hard as she watched Jeremy, his expression infinitely tender, slip a glittering gold band onto Anne Marie's slim finger. Hearing them repeat the words that made them man and wife, Athena held her bouquet in white-knuckled hands, her heart so full with unexpected pain that she had to turn away. It was as if Reverend Axminster's invocation of love spoke directly to her soul, and she ached for Lochiel as never before, the words forcing her to come face to face with the realization that there could never be a life for her without him.

As soon as the ceremony was over she fled the room, unable to bear the smiling faces around her any longer. While everyone else rushed forward to congratulate the bride and groom, Athena pushed her way woodenly through the throng, tears running freely down her face as she reached the front door and ran out into the glaring autumn sunshine. Throwing herself face down in the cool grass, she wept as if her heart were broken, her slim body racked with sobs as she gave vent to the grief she had borne in silence for so many months.

" 'Tisn't fair!" she choked convulsively, pressing her face into the fragrant earth. Why had she fallen in love with a man like Lochiel Blackmoor, whose unyielding pride had ruined everything that had existed between them? Why had she given her heart to a man who might well be lying dead on the battlefield of Quebec?

"If only I'd told him how much I love him," she whispered bitterly to herself. "I should never have gotten angry over something as silly as being accused of having twin lovers! How could Lochiel have known that Colm and Jeremy were my brothers?"

Taking a deep breath, she sat up and wiped the tears from her face. It was time to return to the house, yet Athena was ashamed of her swollen eyes and dusty gown, which she knew she'd never be able to hide from those assembled inside.

" 'Tis just like you to throw a pall over a happy occasion like Jemmy's wedding," she berated herself. Rising wearily to her feet, she crossed the lawn to the stables and washed her face under the cold, bracing water that spilled from the pump. The thought of returning to the house was unbearable, yet Athena knew it wouldn't be fair to Jeremy and his bride if she lingered outside any longer. She would simply have to learn to live with her pain and hope that someday—

"Athena!"

She turned guiltily toward the house. Had her absence already been noticed? Puzzled, she saw that the drive between the front door and the stables was empty. Had she merely imagined someone calling her name?

"Athena!"

She whirled about, and her breath came in a gasp as she saw Glenrobbie burst into view around the far corner of the barn. Reining the gelding in so hard that the big animal reared, Lochiel Blackmoor stared down at her, his face pale.

"They told me in town about the wedding," he ground out savagely. "My God, Athena, tell me I'm not too late!"

She twisted her hands together, her throat so tight that she could scarcely speak. "T-too late?" she whispered.

"Aye, too late!" he roared, tossing down the reins and dismounting. "Who is it you've married this time? I swear before God he'll not keep you, Athena!"

"I haven't married anyone," she said, her heart skipping a beat, scarcely daring to hope that his anger hid something that ran deeper than hate. " 'Tis my brother Jeremy who's taken a wife."

Lochiel came to a halt before her, a startled look on his hawkish features. "Your brother?" he repeated. "One of the twins?"

Athena nodded.

Lochiel grew still at her words, and when Athena dared to steal a glance at him, she saw that the terrible anger in his expression had faded and that a crooked smile was beginning to tug at the corners of his mouth.

"Then you're not married, Miss Courtland?" he inquired softly.

She held her breath as she shook her head.

The silver eyes came closer. "Are you saying that I nearly drove my horse into the ground trying to get here before you married the wrong man a second time when in truth you weren't about to marry anyone?"

She nodded wordlessly, her heart hammering against her ribs.

"Was it wrong to hope all these months that you were thinking about me and perhaps missing me, too, even if it was just a wee bit?"

"I-I might have," Athena allowed in confusion. "Oh, Lochiel," she burst out in the next breath, "don't make fun of me, please! I can't bear it!"

She had only a brief glimpse of the fierce tenderness that sprang into his eyes before he swept her off her feet and into his arms. She could feel the drumming of his heart against her cheek before he tilted back her head and his lips captured hers in a kiss that shattered her numbness and sent her heart soaring in joyous flight.

"What a fool I've been, Athena," he murmured against her mouth, pressing her to the lean length of his body. "I chose to believe the worst about you merely because I couldn't admit to myself how hopelessly you had ensnared me in your bewitching web. I acted like a madman because I could not tolerate the thought of you loving someone else, allowing someone else to hold you in his arms and receive your sweet kisses."

Athena felt tears brimming in her eyes, scarcely daring to believe the caressing words that fell from Lochiel's lips. Could this be the same man who had so cruelly hurt her in the past? Never had she seen those silver eyes so tender as he stared like a man possessed into her upturned face.

"When Stephen died and you wept over his fallen body I mistook your grief for love," he continued hoarsely. "I might have been able to win your hand away from the Rangers I believed were your lovers, but how could I compete with the memory of a ghost? How cruelly I treated you afterward," he added, his deep voice dropping to a despairing whisper at the memory. "I never thought to see you again, and then you came to me when I was ill and needed you. When I awoke that morning to find you beside me, it gave me cause to hope all over again that perhaps you loved me, if even a little."

"And then you saw Colm," Athena remembered, "and you thought it was him I'd come to see, not you."

Lochiel nodded, his expression filled with self-loathing. "I was an unspeakable cad and a fool. Rather than putting my trust in you, I chose to make the same mistake all over again. Why? Because I was half crazed with love for you and too cowardly to risk once again the pain you caused me with your supposed betrayals. But now I know the truth," he added huskily, staring down at her with eyes that burned like flames, "and throughout the long campaign in Canada I dreamed of nothing save you, Athena. I prayed that I would return from Quebec alive so that I could beg your forgiveness. I came as soon as I could get away. You can imagine how I felt upon learning that a wedding was to take place at Courtland Grace this very afternoon."

He released her abruptly, and some of the agony he had suffered showed in his drawn expression. "I knew I'd not be able to bear it if I lost you again."

"I wasn't the one getting married," Athena reminded him softly.

"I know that now, yet I wonder if I wasn't a fool to come here after all," Lochiel admitted, voicing the doubts that had haunted him since leaving Quebec. "The war is over, Athena, and you can finally live in peace with your family around you. What right do I have to selfishly ask you to give up everything you hold dear in order to build a life with me in a harsh country you know naught about?"

He had turned away from her as he spoke, and Athena stared at his broad back in disbelief, certain that if she so much as made a move toward him the enchanted spell that surrounded her would break. She didn't want to find that all of this had been a dream; that Lochiel hadn't held her in his arms and kissed her, that he hadn't told her he loved her and wasn't asking her now to give up everything she owned in order to become his wife.

A smile touched the corners of her mouth and lit up the sapphire depths of her eyes. Moving toward him, she wound her arms about his waist and rested her cheek against his back.

"Surely you must realize by now, Major Blackmoor," she said softly, "that I would find life here at Courtland Grace cursed dull without the constant threat of attacking Frenchmen hanging over my head. The thought of building a new life in the wilds of the Scottish Highlands intrigues me. Couldn't you tell me more?"

Lochiel could scarcely believe her saucy words, and there was an expression of wonder on his hawkish features as he disengaged himself from her arms and turned around. "It won't be easy," he warned her. "You've no idea how primitive the Highlands can be, especially in winter."

"Oh, but you're mistaken, sir," Athena informed him primly, laughter lurking in her eyes. "Not only have I been to school in Edinburgh, but I fell in love with the Highlands when my mother and I visited them years ago. We even saw Bonnie Prince Charlie and his clans marching through the village of Aberstrath on their way south from Glenfinnan. My mother's aunt lived there, you see."

She was startled when Lochiel took her suddenly by the arms, pulling her to him so that her face was only inches from his. "How old were you then?" he demanded hoarsely.

"Five or six." Her brow furrowed. This was not at all how she had expected him to react! Before she could speak, however, he threw back his head and gave a hearty shout of laughter.

"And you, wee minx that you were," he said when he could speak, "couldn't help flirting with the soldiers, giving them oat cakes you claimed to have baked yourself."

"I only had one," Athena blurted defensively, "and I gave it to the laddie I thought the bonniest of all. Oh—!" she broke off with a gasp, her eyes wide as she stared into his smiling countenance. "How did you know of that? I never told you, and you—you couldn't have been there!" Her voice dropped to a disbelieving whisper. "Could you?"

"Aye, Athena," he said softly. "I've never forgotten that day or the beautiful child who grinned at me so saucily. 'Twould seem our fate was sealed from that day forward, though neither of us knew it at the time."

"Then surely you have no reason to doubt that I'll willingly return with you despite the hardships you claim we'll face." Athena was very solemn now, and her voice shook slightly with the depth of her emotions. "How can there be hardships when the two of us will be together?"

A look of fierce tenderness crossed Lochiel's rugged features, easing the lines of suffering that the long years of war had etched into his youthful face. "Ah, my love," he whispered, "was there ever another like you?"

Tightening his hold about the slim young woman he held in his arms, Lochiel molded her to him, kissing her until her senses reeled and there was nothing left in all of creation save Lochiel and the gentle strength of the arms that held her.

Quite unexpectedly he lifted his lips from hers and laughed, his silver eyes glinting. "Didn't you tell me your brother got married this afternoon?" he asked.

Athena stared at him in bewilderment. How could he be thinking of something like that while kissing her?

"Are the guests still here?" Lochiel prompted as she remained silent.

"Yes, but—"

"And the minister?"

She nodded and gave a breathless gasp as Lochiel swung her into the air, her skirts belling about her. "Then why should we wait? Surely your brother won't object to making his wedding day ours?"

"You can't be serious!" Athena protested.

He laughed again and kissed her deeply. "Oh aye, I am. 'Tis the perfect opportunity, what with the guests already invited and the minister here."

"Oh, Lochiel, I'm not at all certain—"

He set her gently onto the ground but kept his arms firmly about her waist. "Consider, too, my love," he added, nuzzling her ear, "that if we get married now, we'll be able to celebrate our wedding night tonight."

Athena shivered as his lips moved from her ear to her throat, desire kindling her blood as he fitted her against the hard length of his body. "Faith, 'tis difficult to argue with such reasoning, sir," she murmured breathlessly.

"Then you agree?" he demanded, smiling expectantly into her heavy-lidded eyes.

She didn't have the chance to answer, for he had seized her hand, and then they were running together across the sun-drenched lawn, laughing like children as they burst through the door and into the waiting warmth of the house.

Epilogue

On a warm summer evening in late August, Lochiel Blackmoor and his wife, Athena, strolled to the edge of their garden to watch the sunset, the dogs racing joyously ahead of them. Heat lightning played across the surrounding hills, illuminating the heather-covered slopes in ever-changing primal colors. The sun hovered like an enormous crimson orb beneath a golden bank of clouds while the first evening stars twinkled high in the darkening sky.

Seating herself in the soft grass, Athena sighed contentedly as she leaned her head against her husband's chest, his strong arms wrapping themselves securely about her. The breeze tugged at her hair, blowing a few wayward strands against Lochiel's shoulder, and he lowered his head to breathe deeply of their sweet fragrance.

" 'Tis a beautiful night," he murmured, though he was not looking at the scenery. The dying rays of the sun burnished the surface of the lake in the valley below and reflected with blinding brilliance the mullioned windowpanes in the cozy stone manor house known as Tor Blackmoor where Lochiel and Athena made their home. Yet Lochiel saw none of these things. He was looking down at the delicate profile of his wife's face, his heart filled with the contentment that always came over him whenever he held her in his arms. Bending his head, he allowed his lips to travel over the silken skin at her temple, but Athena struggled, giggling, from his grasp.

"Is that you all ever think about?" she teased. "I thought we'd come to watch the sunset."

"You should know me well enough by now," Lochiel replied, "to realize that I have no interest whatsoever in viewing nature when you are beside me. 'Twas merely a pretext to get you off somewhere where no one could bother us."

"We're alone at Tor Blackmoor tonight," Athena reminded him pertly. "Tykie's gone down to the village, and Colm was invited to the Gillians' for supper."

Lochiel groaned aloud at the thought of Tykie running rampant through the countryside. "I'm waiting for a catastrophe to happen with your miserable Tykie courting every widow in this glen," he growled. "There'll be hell to pay when each of them inevitably finds out about the others."

Athena was forced to laugh at his dire prediction. Since accompanying them to Scotland last year, Tykie had taken an extremely healthy interest in the local ladies, and she and Colm had already placed their wagers as to which charming widow would ensnare him before the weather turned cold.

"As for your brother Colm," Lochiel continued severely, " 'tis time he married that Gillian lass and set up a household of his own."

Athena ran her finger down the length of his lean cheek in a tender caress. "You know perfectly well that Colm and Moira intend to wed as soon as their house is finished. He told me this morning that it lacks only the roof and that the furnishings should be arriving from Inverness any day now."

Lochiel captured her slim hand in his and kissed the tips of her fingers, pleased with the news. Both he and Athena had been delighted when Colm had asked if he might accompany them to Scotland. Neither of them had expected him to fall so completely under the spell of the mist-shrouded Highlands or in love with gray-eyed Moira Gillian, who lived with her parents in one of Lochiel's tenant crofts. Lochiel had given his brother-in-law several acres of land on the opposite shore of the lake from Tor Blackmoor, and here Colm had begun to build a house for himself and his bride.

Though Lochiel was fond of Colm, he chafed impatiently for the time when he and Athena would find themselves alone in the beautiful house they had built atop the ruins of the original Tor, which had been razed by Cumberland's troops fifteen years ago. How much had changed in the past year alone, Lochiel reflected, drawing his wife down into the fragrant grass and resting his cheek against her glossy hair. They had been married on the same day as Jeremy and Anne Marie, and he felt certain that their scandalous behavior was still a matter of avid discussion among West York's inhabitants.

Jeremy and his wife were now living in Kensington Manor, which Leda Kensington had sold to the Courtlands for a moderate sum before packing her daughters off to the more favorable husband-hunting grounds of Albany. Jeremy had remodeled the ostentatious interior of the house to reflect the simpler tastes of himself and his wife. While removing the heavy oak bookshelves in Ambrose's former study, he had uncovered a leather satchel containing the proxy papers that Amelia Bower had signed under duress and a lengthy will, which, upon being read, had changed the course of their lives forever.

Lochiel shook his head as he recalled how astonished all of them had been to discover that Fiona Courtland's aunt, a woman of some ninety years, had died earlier that spring, leaving the sum of her worldly goods to her grandniece Athena. Along with a generous stipend—enough, in fact, to rebuild Tor Blackmoor to its former splendor—Athena had inherited the farm in Aberstrath where she and her mother had first seen Bonnie Prince Charlie's troops marching to war. In addition, she had also received an impressive townhouse in Edinburgh, where both Athena and Lochiel intended to withdraw every year to escape the harsh Highland winters.

"Small wonder Stephen was so eager to marry you!" Fletcher had remarked when the contents of the will had been made known. "You'd become an overnight heiress, Athena, and didn't even know it."

"Stephen must have found out about the will from Aunt Amelia," Jeremy added thoughtfully, "and doubtless threatened her not to disclose its contents to anyone until after you'd returned home from Fort Shuyler."

"And in the meantime, knowing his father was so heavily in debt, he forced Aunt Amelia to sign the proxy papers," Athena agreed. "That way he could be sure of getting his hands on my inheritance." Bitterness overwhelmed her at the thought of how trustingly she had accepted her marriage to him.

" 'Tis over now, my love," Lochiel had told her softly, as always able to read her every thought. "I'll write your great-aunt's solicitor at once and see to it that your inheritance is ready to be claimed by the time we arrive in Edinburgh."

She had slipped her slim arms about his neck and kissed him sweetly, her blue eyes shining. "And you said rebuilding Tor Blackmoor would be a project fraught with hardships," she teased.

"I should have realized that my luck would never fail me as long as I have my golden witch by my side," Lochiel had replied, and the look in his silver eyes had caused her throat to constrict with love.

Aye, Lochiel thought to himself, the glorious sunset forgotten as he gazed down at his wife's sweet profile, his fortune had truly changed for the better now that he had claimed this most priceless treasure for his own.

"You're very quiet," Athena observed, turning her head, which lay on Lochiel's shoulder, to peer intently into his face. In the gathering darkness she saw that he was smiling, his handsome features lit with contentment.

"What are you thinking of?" she asked, intrigued. "Colm's wedding?"

Lochiel shook his head.

"Fletcher's?"

Just this morning a letter had arrived from Mercy, now happily married to her beloved Nate, informing them that Fletcher's interest had been more than aroused by the visit of Katrine de Vries's charming young cousin. Though Mikka de Vries was scheduled to return to Holland at summer's end, Mercy had been optimistic enough to predict that she would never go back—if Fletcher would only summon up sufficient courage to ask for her hand. Neither Athena nor Lochiel, in discussing that likelihood, had doubted that he would disappoint them.

"I'm not thinking about any of your brothers or their cursed weddings," Lochiel growled into her ear. Laying her gently back into the grass, he bent over her, his hand sliding along the curve of her hip to her belly, which was already beginning to round with the child they were expecting some time that winter.

"I was thinking," he told her wickedly, "that soon you'll grow too fat to be made love to and that I'd better avail myself of your infinite charms while I still have the chance."

Athena felt the kindling heat in her blood, his seeking hands filling her with a need that never failed to match his own. " 'Twould be wisest," she agreed, yet he cut off her breathless words with his lips on hers, his passionate kiss stirring her as though it were the very first time.

His hands played a familiar rhythm over her body, unlacing her bodice, drawing the stockings from her thighs, whispering words that spoke of his love until she lay naked in the moonlight beneath him. Trailing his fingers across her smooth white thigh, Lochiel gazed down at her with something akin to wonder on his passion-darkened face. He knew every tempting curve, every lovely line of her body so intimately, and yet he never failed to marvel at its perfection.

"Ah, my love," he whispered, echoing words he had once only dreamed of speaking on a long-ago autumn night, "you've found your way into my soul and I'm afraid I'll never be able to get you out."

The blue eyes lifted to his, held him prisoner with their sultry need as her lips curved and she asked softly, "Why should you ever want to?"

He laughed, his heart constricting with tenderness, and lowered his head to caress the rosy nipples of her breasts. Athena moaned at this sweet assault upon her senses. Her flattened palms moved languorously over the muscles of his back and she pulled him against her, her hips rising to meet him, impudently demanding the pleasure of his love. Their naked bodies came together, smooth flesh shivering, and Athena sighed as Lochiel filled her, becoming part of her most intimate self.

Q05

They were both lost in the splendor of the moment, their passions burning as they swayed together beneath the rising moon, all else forgotten in the ecstasy of their joining; Lochiel, the tender yet fiery lover whose touch was fulfillment itself and Athena, the one woman whose love could ever content him.